Doctor Love

GAEL GREENE

 ST. MARTIN'S
MAREK

NEW YORK

Library of Congress Cataloging in Publication Data

Greene, Gael.
Doctor Love.

"A St. Martin's/Marek book."
I. Title.
PS3557.R3797D6   813'.54   81-21553
ISBN 0-312-21486-3   AACR2

Design by Kingsley Parker

10 9 8 7 6 5 4 3 2 1

First Edition

For Saralee with love

Doctor Love

*T*he smallest movement woke her every time. Damn it. Barney tried for a moment to recapture the teasing image of his interrupted dream. But Debra's questing knee chased the images away. I can't even groan in my sleep, thought Barney. Can't turn over, certainly can't get up and take a leak without knowing she will start, stretch, sigh, moan, cry out . . . and, from the dimmest blurred instinct that moved her hand long before her brain came fully awake, reach out for me.

"What have we here?" cooed Debra, coming alert with instant possessiveness.

"We" indeed. Barney's pretty, freckled, myopic explorer, Debra. What have *we* indeed, insatiable wanton. What did she expect to find between his legs? A piano? In her sleep now she went down on him, waking with him in her mouth. Barney was thinking about the clock radio set to activate in minutes. And the hospital-board meeting this morning. He would have very little time to touch base with his staff in the Emergency Room. And there was the laundry to drop off on Columbus Avenue. No one warns you about the dumb details of divorce. Oh well, hell. It felt good. Barney gave in to it. How could a dirty aging young man resist? For a moment he was distracted by Debra's artistry.

God, she could suck cock. For a woman born hating the morning she certainly had vast inner resources for sucking cock. He watched her turning herself on, still in a semisomnolent state, rubbing her pussy on his knee as she made love to him. No disgusting slurping sounds, just pressure and touch. Exquisite interruptions, little teasing licks. Then a sudden capture. Barney could feel the back of her throat. He shuddered. Barney heard her crying, heard his moan, felt himself close to coming but decided to hold back. He lifted her off his cock. Threw her onto the bed, pushing her knees back to her shoulders, opening that cunt already wet, always wet, that wonderful slippery welcome, changing the angle slightly.

Debra gasped. "Yes. Barney. Do that Barney." Her fist in her mouth did not really muffle the scream.

I must be hurting her, Barney thought. I know I'm hurting her. God damn she's noisy. It can't really be seriously painful. She loves it fast and deep. What's wrong with me this morning? I can't catch my breath. Barney's arm cramped. The pain shot through his chest, breaking the rhythm.

"Barney. Fuck. Fuck me. Oh God, Barney. Do it." Debra was crying. Her head beating the pillow.

Barney was not always sure when she came. Getting there for Debra was sometimes such a production number. She let it build, hung on the edge, fell back, let it build again. Loving that ride. So even when he knew for sure, he would let her come two or three times before he let himself go. Damn it. What was wrong with him? He felt cold and sweaty. Terrible heartburn. Got to be heartburn. Must have had too much coffee last night. He held himself still, stiff against her, letting her ride his cock. Close to coming. A cramp in his side. He ignored it, thrusting deep again and again. Debra sobbed. Shooting it into her as she came, Barney couldn't catch his breath. Jesus. He was gasping like a beached fish. He lay there willing his blood pressure to fall back to normal.

Debra, of course, was oblivious. She lay curled on her

side, far away as if he had ceased to exist, her knees up, body flushed, hugging herself, contracting . . . collecting herself, he imagined. Barney tried to sit up, found himself locked in a vise. He rolled away, clammy . . . furious. Only a hypochondriac would let a simple muscle spasm escalate into something for intensive care. Joe Namath lived with pain worse than this every day of his life, thought Barney. "Shit."

Debra started. "Barney, what is it?"

"Nothing. Nothing at all." Barney heard the snap in his voice. "I'm not myself this morning, sweetheart," he said, more softly, hugging her close. Barney didn't like the thought creeping into his head. When was the last time he had failed to order an EKG for a patient panting like this, with pain like this? He tried to cancel the thought. Barney Kincaid never gets thrown like this. He had the blood pressure of a teenager. When was that last stress test? Less than six months ago. Normal for a well-preserved man of forty-two with no vices at all. Sex not a vice, he'd always reassured himself. More than a hobby, yes, but less than a crippling obsession. And if you believed in the value of aerobic exercise, what could be healthier, Barney could argue, than spirited fucking? "I didn't drink that much coffee last night, did I, sweetheart?" Barney found his pulse. Not counting. Afraid to count. "Three ounces of espresso, if that."

"And then the stingers and an Irish coffee after, darling," Debra reminded. "That will do it." She stroked his arm as if concerned, but Barney thought he detected a little smirk of superiority. Debra drank nothing but wine, red wine only, specifically Bordeaux, apologizing in a way that made you feel like a piker if you offered her a Beaujolais. If someone was naive enough to protest, "What . . . red wine with fish?" she would smile tolerantly as one might indulge a retarded child. Barney was such a snob himself, how could he condemn her? Debra snuggled against him delicately, arranging her sticky little twat on his outstretched hand. He felt a wave of annoyance. She loved it when he played with her pussy after fucking. Loved it when he made her come a dozen times before breakfast. She never said no. Never once in all the months that he'd known her had she pleaded a headache. Never once been "too tired" or "not in the mood." ("I spent the last three years of my marriage longing, begging . . . wasting away for sex," she told him. "Now I'm thirty-eight years old and I'm not going ever to say no again.") Well, yes, she might cry out, "No . . . no more." But it was a game, a submission game. She never meant it. Just loved to be forced once in a while. One of these days, thought Barney, he ought to tie her up and do it till she screamed for mercy so he would know just once the hungry bitch had actually had enough. If that were possible. Could take days. Weeks. What appetites they have. Women weren't always that way. In the old days you used to have to talk them into it. Trick them. A woman had to be seduced. Women. What do they want? "They eat green salad and drink human blood." That was Marvin's favorite line from *Herzog*. Marvin who jumped out a seventh-story window. Marvin who had lived those last years surrounded by mouldering memorabilia of his childhood as a wunderkind, Marvin's mess. His death the ultimate mess. Barney's best friend, Marvin. Marvin, a serious man. Dead now nearly . . . how long? Five years, six. Time moved too quickly. Barney tested his arm. The cramp had subsided. The burning was gone. The pounding let up. He gathered his strength and managed a fair imitation of his usual morning leap from bed, running a hand through damp curls, as he caught himself in the mirror.

"What a sight, Barney. Sure you're all right?"

Barney felt her watching his progress as he sidestepped to avoid the scattered underwear. A tangle of lace and elastic. A wisp of red satin. Lewd little panties. Something a stripper would wear. He smiled. Debra was an adolescent's dream of a sex goddess. How he had loved her last summer, crazed by her lust . . . her hunger, her response. "Let's make love as if there were an ambulance waiting," she quoted Swinburne. Reaching beyond the stars. Dying. A thousand deaths. Blissed on excess. Whipping the beast in Barney to the brink of depravity. He sighed. That kind of intensity couldn't last. His love for Lindsay, sane and cerebral . . . that would survive. He would have them both, Debra and Lindsay. Together if you could eliminate their flaws, you'd have the perfect woman. Why did they always have such unforgivable flaws?

"That's your safety valve," Lindsay had suggested, fresh from a session with her therapist. "First you invest a woman with exaggerated virtues, then you retreat as you discover the flaws." That could be true, Barney conceded. He tucked the comforter over Debra's shoulders, touched by her pink-and-blonde innocence in sleep. "I'll wake you when I'm through in the bathroom, darling."

Ambulance lights were flashing. Barney raced into the Emergency Room behind a blur of cops and technicians. The second of two bloody loads, Nurse Mallory said. That was clear at once. There was a kid with a flap of skin sliced back, the skull exposed like a cracked egg. The paramedic had already got an IV going. Right pupil widely dilated. Blood all over the floor, all over Nurse Mallory's shoes.

"I sent a sample for cross-matching," Mallory said. "Look at the blood pressure."

Crazy how strong it was.

In the next cubicle, Kala Djarta was intubating a little boy. The child was unconscious. That meant Djarta would have less trouble getting the tube in. Djarta was on tryout. For every strength she had a weakness. But she learned fast. Probably Barney would keep her on as a junior partner. They would need more trained Emergency Medicine people if they got the New Grace Hospital Emergency Room contract. Somebody was screaming. A little old lady shuffled toward Barney, grabbed his arm. "I'm waiting already so long, doctor," she said. "It's the pollution. I've got it."

Barney gently pulled his arm away. "Later, my dear," he said. "We'll get to you soon." There was a young man with all the skin on his legs gone. He'd been thrown from a motorcycle. Barney waded in. It was a chaos he thrived on. People screaming for attention. "Later." He patted the red-eyed young woman with a howling infant in her arms. Mallory, his brilliant triage nurse, was a monument of calm, cutting through the crap and hysteria, keeping the petty wounds and barbarian relatives at bay, shooting the bodies through in unerring order of priority. Barney's happiest moments came on mornings like this, when everything he knew was tested. When he raced into the ER needing to take a leak and realized ten hours later he'd not yet found a moment to pee. When all the jagged wounds were neatly sutured and all the erratic hearts shocked and reined into dutiful rhythm, all the chronic complainers soothed and reassured. He would ride the craziness in a kind of high, intoxicated by a sense of his own power. Methodical. Calm. Never raising his voice. A small half smile on his lips. A special gentle intimacy for children. Good-natured firmness with querulous old women. A special skill in communicating with teenage drug abusers. Confidence in his speed and ability. Feeding facts into his brain. Memory shooting him answers in strange and wondrous flashes. Sensing a kind of bell inside his head alerting him to danger. Fueling a fine sense of control. Dr. Barney Kincaid wrestling against time and fate. A power trip, perhaps. Something he could only confess to himself.

Bodies were two deep in the corridors even after the crush of accident victims had been wheeled away to surgery and trauma wards. Of course, Barney wanted certain cases left out in the corridors where everyone could keep an eye on them. Damn unseasonal carnage. Weekday winter mornings were mostly uneventful. This morning's ER gore looked like a summer Saturday night on a full moon when the crazies run amok. There was even a gunshot of the foot lying stabilized, waiting his turn. By noon, the load was normal again, and he snuck off for an hour to organize his evidence against Emile Gunderson.

A rather classic hospital foul-up had delivered the case against Dr. Gunderson to Barney totally by accident. All deaths had to be reviewed by a member of the Intensive-Care Unit Mortality Committee. This case of Gunderson's had been reviewed by Riverton, a surgeon. Riverton had questioned Gunderson's procedure. Gunderson had blamed a nurse, insisted she misinterpreted instructions. That was the end of it. The case had been closed and then, somehow, misfiling, sloppy housekeeping, who knows, had been slipped into a batch of charts assigned to Barney for review. Exasperated to find Riverton's signature after plowing through pages of staff chicken scratchings and Gunderson's eccentric script. Barney was about to toss it away when something, an extrasensory click, an alert in his brain signaled, catching his hand. The case sounded familiar. Digging in the files he found four other patients—each of them dead of the same "misunderstanding." When he had first brought his accusation to the ICU Mortality Committee, they were incredulous. "If you want to investigate, go ahead," rheumenologist Ben Weegan said with obvious distaste, the old fart. "I promise you it's a waste of time— Gunderson may not be brilliant, but he's a reasonably competent man."

"With a lot of friends," added the cardiologist Greenstein.

"*E*veryone's gone to lunch, Dr. Kincaid," said Mallory. "And we have a little boy with a bad laceration. Needs some fancy needlework." The kid

Barney was sewing was silent, anesthetized from the ear down. The mother was sobbing and hiccupping. Barney admired his stitches, precise and beautiful. Incredible how many kids came out of medical school equipped to stitch an elephant but not a cheek. The subcuticular stitches were what counted.

"Hey Doc."

He was black, wearing an embroidered yamulka and surgery-scrub green. He blathered at Barney in a language vaguely related to English.

"Nurse," Barney shouted. "Get this man whatever he wants. And get him out of here." Barney felt his hand tremble.

"He doesn't know what he wants," snapped Nurse Coburn, cranky as always, a crankiness tolerated because of her awesome energy and brilliance.

"They send me down in dis place for a knee sport."

"What kind of a knee? What kind of a support?" Gilles Coburn was exasperated. "Go back and find out."

Barney scrawled his signature on a chart, releasing the cheek trauma, feeling hot and strangely shaky. He studied the board for a likely candidate to polish off without labwork, thinking what he needed was something to jolt the blood sugar. A milkshake, maybe. He looked around for an aide.

"Hey. Hey, you finks, don't hang up." Mallory slammed down the phone. "You know that old man out there, Mr. No-Name. I've called every nursing home in our zone, Dr. Kincaid. And nobody wants to claim El Dumpo. We've got to have his chart. How can I find his chart without a name."

"Did you look for laundry marks?" asked Coburn.

"First thing. And tattoos. Boy, it's the same old story. Two sneaky bozos carted that poor old man here from some nursing home and ran off before I could stop them. They even cut out the labels. Folks must think this is a boneyard."

Barney grinned. Mallory would flush out the culprits. She and Coburn were the real strength of Barney Kincaid's emergency service. If he and Turner got the contract to run

New Grace Hospital's ER, he would have to clone them both. Coburn, with her secret rage and passion for perfection. Mallory, so cool and deep. Nurse Fudgesicle, that's how he thought of her. Barney didn't approve of playing around on his own hospital turf. That didn't mean he didn't do it. He hated himself, but what could a healthy, red-blooded lover of woman do? Still, for some reason the Fudgesicle was untouchable. Taunting him with her majestic indifference . . . her iron dignity the real barrier.

"What about the fireman in Three-A? Smoke inhalation?" Barney asked, not really wanting to move from his chair. "Did someone send out for that milkshake?"

"Glass in the knee," replied Mallory.

"Bleeding?"

"A little."

Lifting himself from the chair, Barney felt like he was carrying a baby elephant on his back. Through the drawn curtain of the next cubicle, Barney could hear his partner, Henderson Turner, practicing law: ordering X-rays and lab tests some old lady probably didn't need because nobody was going to accuse Goodman Memorial of malpractice this year.

The fireman groaned. "Jesus, Doc, what are you doing in there?"

"Hurts, huh."

"Don't look," Mallory instructed. "It won't hurt if you don't look." She patted the fireman's thigh.

"Hey, Hen—what the hell's going on?" Barney could see blood hitting the curtain in the next cubicle. "Mallory, hold this knee." He ran.

"I don't know, Barney," Henderson whispered. "All of a sudden I'm standing in a pool of blood." The old woman coughed, sending another shower of blood down Henderson's coat. Hen raced away. Poor bastard. He was a brilliant diagnostician. But in a crisis he couldn't speak. The verbal apparatus stuttered and shut down. Couldn't even ask for a piece of equipment. Had to run off and get it if one of the mind-reading nurses—smarter than any doctor by far—wasn't hovering at his elbow. Fortunately, even the aides and orderlies had learned to read Henderson Turner's mind. An aide materialized with an IV kit. Barney pulled the tourniquet on the old woman's arm tight. Poor old alcoholic. Her veins were like linoleum. A sharp pain shot across Barney's chest and ran down his arm. He dropped the old lady, caught her just before she hit the floor, sure now that he was having a heart attack. He tried to cry out.

"Christ Barney. What are you doing to my old lady?" Hen tugged the woman away from Barney's rigid hug. He propped her against the wall. "Where does it hurt, Barney?" He tore at Barney's collar, fingers on Barney's pulse.

"You know damn well where it hurts, Hen. Exactly where it's supposed to . . ."

Hen was struggling to speak. "Describe . . . describe . . ."

"Like a truck on my chest, damn it. Mallory," Barney yelled. He was terrified, furious . . . the fury blotted away only by the pain. This couldn't be happening. It was like a nightmare in excruciating slow motion. A preposterous mistake.

The Fudgesicle pushed the curtains aside. She started to laugh.

"Hit the cardiac alert," said Barney. "Oh God damn. I'm only forty-two years old." Even as he spoke he waited to wake up from the dream.

"Don't worry, Barney," said Hen. "Only the good die young."

"Why is this woman on the floor?" Mallory scolded, leaning over the patient sprawled on the floor.

Barney caught a flash of lace on a long, slender thigh. Incredible, he thought, in the middle of an infarct a man can still appreciate thighs. Hen was hooking up the electrodes. "I'm not sure I want to get sick in this hospital, Hen. Who can I trust? Who haven't I insulted?"

Doctors, nurses, students, aides. Good God, it felt like an army had descended. They were using up too much of his precious oxygen, damn it. Hon was tugging on Barney's sleeve.

"Barney, eventually I've got to call a cardiologist."

"Not Greenstein. He'll laugh while I die."

"Foley is on today."

"Foley. I trust Foley. Do you trust Foley?"

"As long as it's your heart, Barney, and not mine."

"Stop clowning you two," snapped Mallory, tearing off tape.

"Remember I died laughing," said Barney, thinking for the first time that he could actually die. "What does it say, Hen? Bad, huh?" Henderson handed the EKG tape to Dr. Djarta. She studied it, frowned and handed it to Mallory's outstretched hand. The three of them stood stonily studying it. Mike Steffans sauntered in, a few minutes early for the afternoon shift.

"What is this?" Steffans asked. "A civil defense exercise?"

"There's nothing there, Barney. Foley should take a look. But I'm telling you, nothing. No ST elevation." Hen handed Barney the coil of paper. "Any shortness of breath? Pain now?"

"What about this little jiggle?" Mallory asked.

"Since when is Mallory the cardiologist on this case? You creeps." Barney's hand was shaking. He felt drained and frail waiting for the next onslaught of pain. Barney held the strip three feet from his nose.

"Nurse Mallory. You can give Dr. Kincaid back his glasses," Henderson commanded. "Maybe it's pericarditis. Or angina."

"Oh God." Barney started. The old lady was gone. Had she crept away? "Your patient, Hen. We forgot all about her. Tell me one of those orderlies didn't just sweep her up."

Mallory pushed him down again. "Djarta is working on her next door. She's fine." Mallory took Barney's hand. It was not a pulse-focused gesture. She looked right into his eyes, seeing him . . . Mallory, who always looked at the air to the left of his face. "If you're not going to die in the next twenty minutes, I'll get back to work." Barney felt the tears come. She squeezed his hand and left. Immediately Barney felt better. He knew Mallory would not leave unless he was definitely out of danger . . . or dead. Dead. A myocardial infarct at forty-two. He might as well be dead. Barney groaned. They were keeping it from him.

"Oh shit Hen. I should have known midlife crisis would get me. First the eyes go. Your arm isn't long enough to hold the menu. Then you find it tough to get it up twice in one night. Then the knees go and the memory—"

"Twice in one night. At forty-two." Henderson shook his head. "Tell me you're exaggerating. This is a man with five children under twelve talking. I'm lucky to find the energy twice a week."

"Forget I mentioned it," Barney said. "Divorce is like a second adolescence." Barney groaned again. Clearly the glorious Indian summer of his second adolescence was finally over. If I live, God, he negotiated silently, I'll give up kinkiness forever. Even so, he knew it was a rash promise. Even saints have their secrets. He'd read some gossip somewhere about Marilyn Monroe and Dr. Schweitzer. Are you there, God? He visualized an old man with a white beard. "What makes you so sure God is a man?" Debra liked to taunt. He tried to imagine God as a woman. She looked like Betty Friedan.

Foley was there, his skin cool and dry. Barney had a feeling he was going to survive.

"Nobody cares. Nobody ever says, 'Willie Mae, what for y'all bin so pendable.'" Willie Mae grinned at Barney as she drew the curtains open. "Too bad you can't get up to see the storm, Doc," she said. She wiggled her fat round ass. Willie Mae had turned into a collection of bulges when he wasn't looking. Barney remembered the cute black teenager Willie Mae fresh out of reform school when she first came to work for Goodman Memorial. Hell, was it eight years ago? Everyone was getting old overnight. Brigitte Bardot. Elvis Presley, dead at forty-two.

Barney felt like a feeble old man in the soft blue nightshirt his father had brought to the hospital last night. "Don't get scared," Barney said as his father tried to conceal shock and fear. "I'm just hooked up to a heart monitor so the nurses out there have something to watch if there's nothing good on the late late show. It's definitely not a heart attack, Dad." His father's eyes were brimming. "I swear. My doctor, Adam Foley, swears there is no heart damage. Probably won't be any. It's something called pericarditis. A virus attacks the heart lining. You rest a little and take cortisone and that's it. Honest, Dad." Barney started to cry himself. He was relieved to find himself believing that everything Foley said was true. There had been no infarct. In his anxiety, Barney had probably exaggerated the pain. Mama was downstairs hysterical, said Dad. She'd taken a Valium and then another and was begging to come up. Barney dispatched Foley to calm her down. "Tell her I'm sleeping," he said. "Let her look at me, if she insists. But I'm not strong enough for my mother in full anguish."

"It's a bleezard out there," observed Willie Mae. "Half the trains is out. The buses come iffen they feel like it. But Willie Mae is here." Her skin was blue-black against the shiny white stuff of her uniform, the pants straining across her big heart-shaped ass. Once Barney had caught her rubbing against the coffee machine in the canteen. Masturbation? Conscious, unconscious . . . he couldn't tell. The sweet lewdness of her laugh had gone right to his dick. But then his beeper had gone off and he was racing off to the Emergency Room, that particular lewdness resolved. Thank God.

"Twelve inches of snow, Doc," Willie set his breakfast on the bed table. "I'm crankin' you up a little," she said. "Half the mornin' shift callin' in sick or defeated. Poor Willie Mae.

I'm in the soup today." She stuck out her lower lip, a satiny mauve curl of flesh. "Don't eat that crap, Doc. I'll get you a Danish from the machine, iffen you like."

"Oatmeal is probably good for me," said Barney, seeing all too clearly how the entire hospital experience was designed to make you feel like a child again. There was a menu for the day beside the tray. He was to check off his choice. Nauseated from the smell of the oatmeal, there was no way he could contemplate facing lunch.

"Nothing in this hospital is good for you, Doc. Everyone knows that." Willie Mae was chattering away. "The trick is to cure yourself fastest fore they get you one way or the nother."

Barney felt hot and clammy again, his precious privacy invaded by the tubes and sensors of the monitors. He lay there listening to his heart. It seemed revved up, unfamiliar, not really his own. Was Foley being excessively cautious or was he waiting to see if Barney's heart had more nasty tricks on tap? Even when it was clear the pain had subsided, he refused to let Barney go home. He wanted three or four days of strict bed rest, and tests, he said. Barney was so tired by then, and frightened, he surrendered, feeling feverish and weak again the minute he gave in. Barney was furious he hadn't asked more questions. He'd been so relieved by the diagnosis—pericarditis, an inflammation of the heart sac, so far with no residual damage to his heart—he had hesitated to voice all his doubts. No point in hearing assorted fears confirmed . . . yet. If he kept quiet, his heart might continue to do its spunky best.

Barney had chosen medicine as his life work so he would never be this vulnerable. As a doctor he would always know the odds and the alternatives, make informed medical judgments, protect his family. Uncle Ernie had died at forty-six of an infarct. Mama supposedly had a slight heart murmur. Barney had never been able to detect it himself, but she'd been warned as a teenager and been coddled because of it all her life, so he was loath to take that illusion away. Failing hearts were definitely a family tradition. Even

by marriage. Reeney's brother had his massive attack at
forty-eight. Reeney would be furious if Barney died just
now, the divorce in limbo. She never stopped complaining
how tough it was surviving on forty thousand a year—the
outrageous allowance agreed on in their separation pact.
Barney relished the thought of Reeney with her paste-on
nails and eyelashes, her forty-dollar-a-week health-club
habit, her indoor tennis at thirty-five dollars an hour, and
the little twenty-five-dollar omelet lunches at La Goulue, on
widow's benefits. Barney was swept up for a moment with
the thought of dying as the best revenge. Then he remembered—new will or old will, Reeney would get everything
unless she remarried. What there was. Not that much. The
house on the dunes in Amagansett. The land they had
bought in Key West in a fit of hopefulness six years ago,
when it would have been clear to anyone less stubborn than
Barney that the marriage was in extremis. The duplex on
East Ninety-third Street. Lots of insurance. Everything else
she'd already laid hysterical claim to. Barney could see
Reeney in Bendel's shopping for something in black, something suitable for a funeral but not too somber for dancing
at Le Club after, you know. Would she be outrageous
enough to do a black veil number? He envisioned a ravaged
hysteric, hair scraggly, face streaked and swollen with tears,
giant shades, too bereaved to think about appearances. That
would be Debra. Reeney would go for tasteful sadness,
Debra for high drama, passion unrepressed. Till Lindsay
walked in, ah, yes—that would test Reeney's veneer of class.
Lindsay, so gentle and composed. Eyes still red, of course,
cheeks pale, hair squeaky-clean, brushed neat with a plain
barrette. No black for Lindsay. That would be too phony,
self-conscious. She would wear beige or gray, uncalculatedly
uncalculated. Oh God. Debra and Lindsay in the same room.
Barney got hot and clammy again. Debra would recognize
Lindsay at once. But Lindsay, after the first shock of
discovering Barney's shattering infidelity, preferred to pretend Debra did not exist. Debra's voice on the six o'clock
news, even a promo for Channel 3's *City Edition,* was enough

to give Lindsay red blotches. He'd sworn to her months ago
that he would give up Debra forever. Forever lasted exactly
two months. Debra, it seems, would never give up. What do
you say to a naked lady? thought Barney. For Barney, saying
no was never easy.

What a shame, thought Barney, that a man couldn't
hang around for his own funeral. Of course, if Elisabeth
Kübler-Ross and the death-is-but-a-passing guys were right,
maybe he could hover about for the festivities. He imagined
himself floating over his own body—how tanned and healthy
and young he looked in that massive mahogany box. Or
would Reeney choose something contemporary—burled
walnut, maybe, or bird's-eye maple?

He debated calling for a bedpan but he wasn't quite
ready to get intimate with the icy steel.

*T*here was quite a crowd
gathered for the memorial services. "Well, kid, didn't I warn
you all that whacking off would stunt your growth and grow
hair on your hands." It was Garland, Margaret's boyfriend,
who mowed the lawn in those flush days after the war, when
Dad's shoe store grew into a modest, thriving empire and
they moved briefly to Woodmere, taking Margaret, the live-
in maid. And there was Margaret, comforting his sobbing
mother. Margaret in her old blue chenille bathrobe, knotted
tight around her waist, her face sticky with cream—just as he
remembered her. That smell—almonds and vanilla and that
other smell, her woman smell, blurred by her perfume,
Jungle Gardenia.

Had there ever been a hornier twelve-year-old? It was a
miracle he didn't fall ill from dehydration with all that
masturbation. He was the lovesick slave of the sunny golden
goddess in his nudist magazines. "My Diana," he called her.

Alone in his room Barney would whisper to her glossy image
and imagine her crawling into his bed, teaching him to make
love. "Touch me here," she would say. "Hold me. Put your
tongue in my ear." She would kiss his fingers and tell him to
be gentle. "You have such a wonderful cock, so big for a
young boy," she would say. The fantasy with his golden
nudist was so vivid. More real in a way than the strange,
harrowing moments with Margaret. How free and loving
she was defending him from neighborhod bullies, from
smothering household directives. But how distant she pretended to be letting the twelve-year-old Barney touch her
breasts, her face never registering anything, no response,
pretending it wasn't really happening. He wondered if she
liked it or simply suffered his touch. What a struggle it was.
Each time he had to start from the beginning as if it had
never happened before. Get her to let him look at them. To
touch them clothed. To touch them bare. Oh God, the thrill
. . . Thirty years later he could still invoke the shivers of
ecstasy. Oh, there were so many rules. Why were there so
many rules? Getting there was slow, the excitement excruciating. Barney walked around all afternoon with a hard-
on, whispering to the latest photo of the Goddess Diana,
shooting off with Margaret's smell of almond and vanilla
haunting him. Would she let him touch her nipple? He
wanted to kiss her breasts. No kissing, she said. And she
wouldn't touch Barney, nor could he touch her down there.
He would beg. She was steel. Bitch, wouldn't give an inch.
"Pretty please, Margaret Pretty please." Barney was on his
knees beside the big old chair where she did her sewing,
begging, pretending to be a dog. "Please, Margaret. It's just
your little puppy. Puppies like to lick."

She would tug at her robe, pulling it up a little so she
could slip it off the shoulders without loosening the barrier
at her waist. She would stretch and yawn, her face shiny
from the night cream . . . the room full of vanilla and
almonds. Barney's swollen penis would make a tent in his
pajamas. Sometimes he would try to push between her legs.
"Barney," she would scold, kicking him away. The rule was

he must come sideways or from behind, bending over the chair to press his cheek against her shoulder. Once he even slipped on a goddamned bedroom slipper. She sure didn't make anything easy for him. But from behind he could hump the chair, imagining her bottom pressed against the cushion. The chair was stained from his uncontrollable comes.

That one night she was stretched across the bed sewing glittery things on a scarf. "Is this what you're looking for?" Margaret was pale, thin, with deep purple circles around her eyes like the people in the concentration camps in *Life* magazine. She seemed old to him then, but she couldn't have been more than twenty. She made high round circles on her cheekbones with dye from a metal rouge box on the vanity Mama had made for her from an old desk painted white, with a striped skirt tacked on and a big mirror. Margaret's room was small but it was the best room in the house for Barney because the tree in the garden out back grew in through her window. In summer he could touch the leaves, soft and green-smelling, not as soft though as Margaret's skin. "Is this your idea of a sweetheart?" She flipped his nudist magazine till it fell open to that incredible photograph of Barney's true love, the Goddess Diana, now Miss Nudist America. He had dozens of pictures of her squirreled away, but this was the best: Diana, sun-dappled, one perfect breast framed by her archer's bow.

"You shouldn't be sneaking around in my room," said Barney, really hurt, violated by her betrayal.

"Nobody ever said you should come into my room either," she said.

"Well, you shouldn't be digging in drawers and things." He wondered if she'd found his copy of *As One Girl to Another,* stolen from Cousin Heidi's bedroom in the flat upstairs, and the unused Trojan.

Margaret ignored him. He snatched the magazine away and sat beside her on the bed. Her bathrobe had fallen away from her thigh. Barney stretched out beside her. "Touch me, Margaret. Just touch it." She yawned and went on sewing. "Please, Margaret." Barney rubbed himself against her. She pretended nothing was happening. "Margaret." Barney was rubbing and bumping and breathing hard, going to come, so close. Impossible for her to sew now. He couldn't believe she was letting it happen. He grabbed her from behind, his hand just lightly resting where her thing ought to be. She turned around and looked at him with a wicked little smile. "Who invited you to lie on this bed?" She pulled the robe tight. "Damn. I broke the thread." She got up.

"Want something from downstairs?" she asked. He lay facing the wall, curled into a miserable bundle. "Oreos and milk?" He didn't answer. She left him alone on her bed.

"It's desolation here." Mama affected a slightly British accent on the phone, and a shrillness veering this morning toward hysteria. "A real civil disaster, Barney. Eleven inches of snow. Your daddy won't let me go out the front door. And God forbid he should slip and break his arm again, that's all we need. I'm sick not seeing you. I keep thinking they might be lying to me. What does your doctor say, darling? I was speaking to Lilly Mellin, you remember Lilly, with the son in the basketball scandal? He had pericarditis . . . there was some kind of permanent damage. You are not going to have that kind of damage, please Barney, make the doctor promise."

Crazy, how even at forty-two Barney still got that sick ache in his throat when she called, close to throwing up. He used to just throw up. Then for a while he took antinausea medicine. The medicine was worse than throwing up.

"Oh Mama, everything is fine. I'm normal. My EKG is perfect. Not a twinge or anything. . . . I'm just staying here overnight because Foley is a tyrant and doesn't trust me to

rest at home." Lying. Barney's hand went numb just to
punish him for lying. The truth was Barney hated sick
people. Complaining sick people not sick enough to com-
plain were the worst. One might ask why a man who hates
sick people happened to become a doctor. A staff psychol-
ogist once asked Barney that question and he and Barney
agreed the answer was not reassuring. Anyway, that's why
Barney was not an internist or a neurologist or a surgeon or
a pediatrician. As a doctor of emergency medicine he would
treat the emergency, not the person, he'd thought. In fact,
he'd come to enjoy relating, winning the trust of almost
anyone. These were pleasant fleeting involvements but
nothing long range that could develop into psychological
dependency. "Half my practice is really psychotherapy," an
Ob-Gyn man had confided to Barney. That would drive
Barney up the wall. He had developed extraordinary skills.
He wanted to use them. Triage was a skill. Recognizing the
priority of need when everyone is howling for attention.
Saving the dying whenever possible. Resurrecting the dead.
Sometimes. If they emerged vegetables, that was unfortunate. Someone else would deal with that. Someone upstairs
would struggle with the issues of heroic life-sustaining
efforts versus pulling the plug. In ER the first task was to
revive the patient. No one dared waste precious seconds
debating whether the patient was still salvageable. From the
ER, menopausal women and iffy pregnancies and wasting
neuropathologies got shipped upstairs to the full-time sav-
iors, the guys with the patience and guts to tend the
chronically ill and the hypochondriacs. Barney admired that
kind of mind, but boy he sure didn't have it.

Barney's mother was not fragile at all. She played that
role to please Dad. Maybe even to control him.

"I feel so helpless, darling," Mama was saying, "not
being able to get there. The streets are a mess. If only you
were at New York Hospital. Then," she laughed, "I could
hire a little boy with a sled to pull me there."

New York Hospital. She would never forgive him for
being in Riverdale at Goodman Memorial when he could

have been embalmed in the status chic of New York Hospital
if only he'd sold out his dream fifteen years ago. Barney
decided not to revive that dreary argument. He threw her a
kiss and thanked God for the blizzard and the vagaries of
snowplow operations in Riverdale. He'd have to persuade
Foley to let him out of here fast before major visitation
rituals shattered the serenity. Given a little encouragement,
his mother could turn visiting hours into a grander display
of ostentation than a five-star bar mitzvah.

*T*he snow drifted against the
glass pavilion but inside it was warm, too warm. Barney
loved the sound of the calliope, loved rising into the air and
then dropping. He was happy till he realized he was riding
the merry-go-round in pajamas, torn pajamas, shabby cutoffs. Why was it so warm? And wasn't it strange . . . the
horse's mane felt like real hair, thick, silken masses of dark
chestnut hair. The horse he realized suddenly was a mer-
maid. He felt her body between his legs, felt his penis
growing hard. He woke up. The Fudgesicle was tugging at
the sheet. He'd dozed off in the icy winter sunlight.

"What's the matter with the students on this floor,"
Mallory muttered. "Don't they teach them how to make beds
anymore? You're hot," she said. "It says they took your
temperature forty-five minutes ago and it was ninety-eight
point two. I find that hard to believe." She stabbed a
thermometer under his tongue.

"It was just a hot dream, nurshh—" said Barney.

"Don't talk." She was holding his arm by the wrist
disapprovingly as if it were a rotting salami. No tender
loving care from the Fudgesicle. Barney closed his eyes and
became aware of her cool fingertips. He lay there willing his
pulse to slow down . . . counting the throbs against her

fingers, feeling all the weight of his big fat angry enlarged heart in its swollen pericardial sac. It was a bore sharing awareness with a sick heart. A hospital was certainly not a wholesome environment for a man with his galloping hypochondria.

"Dr. Foley says you're in remarkable shape," Nurse Mallory allowed, grudgingly, Barney thought. "You're going to live, Dr. Kincaid," she said, "if our nurses don't find a way to kill you. Perhaps we should arrange for you to have a private special."

"You," said Barney, grabbing her wrist. "Just checking your pulse."

She pulled her arm away. "Dr. Kincaid. Pericarditis is not a joke."

"But you just promised I'm going to live," said Barney. "I was hoping maybe you were ready to live too." He realized he could be delirious, trying to melt the Fudgesicle.

"I have a good life, doctor," she said. "A fine life. You know nothing about my life."

That was true. Anne Mallory was reserved, awesomely private. She did not kid around. She did not fool around. She did not gossip or hang around after hours. He believed she was married to a medical student . . . helping to finance her husband's less-than-brilliant passage through some less-than-first-rate med school somewhere out West. She read in the cafeteria. Maybe she took classes. He was not sure he'd ever actually seen her smile.

"I must say you never encouraged small talk," said Barney. "But I'm grateful for your visit now."

"It's my lunch break," she said, gesturing toward a container of yoghurt she'd set on his tray-table. "I've been wanting to speak to you. There's something I've been thinking about—oh, for God's sake." She leaped into the air and did a sort of tango.

Barney felt his heart lurch.

"It was just a cockroach," she said, grabbing his wrist again. "I killed it. Calm down please. Be calm." She put her stethoscope to his heart.

There was a knock at the door.

"Barney." Debra stood in the doorway. So blonde. Barney always forgot how blonde she was.

"I'm going," said Mallory and she was gone in a screech of rubber, yoghurt and all.

Debra stood there. Her face flushed—looking like Julie Christie in *Doctor Zhivago* in her wild tawny fox hat—her matted red-fox halo. He remembered suddenly how much he had loved her last summer and his heart ached. He felt giddy with pleasure to see her. Healthier already though foolish lying there taped to his sensors. "How did you get here?" he asked. "Everyone says the city is paralyzed."

"Not even blizzards can stop your determined consumer affairs reporter, darling," she said, mugging, quite pleased with herself. "Neither rain nor sleet . . . Actually I took the subway as far as it went. And then I hitched a ride. Luckily it was a Volkswagen that picked me up because believe me, darling, nothing else is making it up that hill you have outside." She peeled off a sodden scarf, shook the bedraggled fur, struggled out of her long black reefer, ran fingers through her hair, and turned to Barney. Measuring his welcome. They'd gone through too many bad times lately, the reality of the autumn betraying the summer's seeming promise, his vow to Lindsay limiting the hours free for Debra. He sensed her wariness now. Wanting to know if he was angry or touched that she'd burst in. Was he sick . . . contagious? How serious? How long before he could have sex? Barney would just bet that's what she would like to know, the insatiable sex fiend. He grinned to himself. He was exhilarated to think she'd got here. He loved women who know how without being told. He could imagine her kneeing a mugger or taming a lion . . . killing for a story. In her work she was fearless. As a woman, though, she was a pushover. Anything Barney wanted she would give him. Why did that annoy him?

Debra kissed the corner of his mouth, rosy cheeks cold against his flushed dry skin. He turned toward her, letting her make love to his mouth, touched her breast in the bright-blue sweater. She caught her breath, shook her head as if to brake the sexual tide, and got down to medical business, sitting carefully on the edge of the bed, taking his hand. What did the doctor say? What did it feel like? What was the treatment? The prognosis? Any side effects? Debra, Barney had discovered long ago, was a medical groupie. As a child she had wanted to be a doctor. Her father had wanted to be a doctor, too. Neither of them made it. The Depression put him into the furniture business in Poughkeepsie. Failing chemistry and a too-early-budding libido diverted her. Once Debra had persuaded Barney to let her put on a doctor's coat and hang out in the ER. She wanted to know everything as a charm against sickness. "I feel so safe having a doctor in my life," she once told him. "I feel like you're keeping an eye on my insides. No cells are going to go crazy and misbehave with you watching." In bed she loved to play doctor. Loved to have Barney examine her twat—"it's feverish, doctor"—to palpate her breasts and probe her ass and all the parts of her pussy as if he were an earnest and disinterested physician who ultimately, of course, could no longer contain his simmering heat.

"Well, but of course I would get here somehow, Barney. It's terrible to be sick. But it's wonderful, too. Everyone makes a big fuss and you get flowers and toys."

"I'm afraid I could love it too much," said Barney. "If I just let go I could give in to it. Sick people are such babies."

"Silly. A man of your legendary discipline. Come on, darling, let everyone baby you. See, I brought you goodies." There was a giant apple too perfect to eat and the current issue of *Penthouse*.

How could you give up a woman who indulged your childishness? thought Barney. "Come, darling, we'll look at the pictures together."

Debra stretched out beside him, careful not to get tangled in his hookup lines, snuggling close: "Which one do you like, Barney? Do you like her, Kitty? 'Kitty likes older men,' it says. Are those the kind of tits you like? What's a good pussy?"

"That's a good pussy. It's like a flower. That one's not as nice."

"Yeeck."

"I like Kiki," said Barney. Kiki was blonde and small but very bosomy, freckled, a lot like Debra, the same nose. Debra was pleased. Barney could tell from the way she licked the canary feathers from her lips. Barney read aloud: "Kiki likes to play in tents with her boots on."

Debra kissed the inside of his palm, sucked his thumb, ran her tongue between his fingers. "Oh, look who's here," she said as his cock began to get hard, a precise little bump under the sheet. Debra put her hand there. "Are we allowed—"

"Well, my doctor hasn't specifically forbidden—"

She pulled the sheet aside and slid down to his cock, circled the tip with her tongue, licked it all over. Barney heard the monitor alarm go off, the footsteps racing down the hall.

"God damn." He struggled with the covers. "The monitor."

Debra came up flushed and puzzled just as the stampeding horde burst through the door. She sat there with her mouth open, chin sticky, terrified as a nurse began to pound on Barney's chest.

"Wait," cried Barney.

Foley came into the room, spied the *Penthouse* and Barney calm and contained in the middle of agitated staff. "Enough," he cried. "Perhaps you'll all step outside," he said. "Do I recognize Miss Teiger."

"Debra," said Barney. "My heart must be pounding. I think we've done a lot for my reputation in one afternoon. Go home, darling. Isn't she a wonder, Foley, getting here through the blizzard?"

Debra pouted. "I'll come tomorrow," she said. "I'll come every day," she promised.

"I'm not going to be here that long," said Barney. "And tomorrow my mother will come with Reeney and Candy."

Debra snatched up her coat and whirled the scarf with a

flourish as if it were a cape and she were Dracula and would gladly eat the competition alive. "Yes, of course, the traffic problem. How shall you schedule the women who adore you so we don't collide in the corridor?"

"Come the day after, sweetheart. If I'm still here," said Barney. "Come when I'm off the monitor and . . . you . . . know . . . what . . ."

She smiled a little and left, eyeing the flat of the bed between his legs as if her unfinished business were a personal challenge. What a nut. After Foley had chewed him out and left, Barney lay there remembering again how insanely he had loved her. Insane was precisely the word. He had been out of his mind. It seemed like months. Several weeks, literally out of his mind. Careening. Out of control. Even today, several months safely retreated back into sanity, Barney could at will recapture the sense memories of madness. The heat of that summer. The intense exhilaration of falling wildly in love. Why was that always the best part of the relationship? Falling wildly in love. It was wonderful. And terrifying. Barney, responsible father, devoted son, dedicated doctor, had lost all control. Nothing mattered, not the hospital nor Candy, still very bruised and confused by his breakup with Reeney, not even Lindsay, the woman he was sure that he loved and planned one day to marry. Nothing mattered but Debra. The sun on her skin. Fog misting the air as they walked in and out of the surf's tongue. Licking salt from her knees. Walking around with an almost constant erection. The intensity of his lust, the intensity of her hunger. Falling in love. How many times had he fallen in love? Never like this. They couldn't keep their hands off each other. She had seemed so powerful then, regal, confident, a goddess. He could not have imagined that a woman so uninhibited and sensual existed. A beautiful sky could make her feel faint. The light coming through wild flowers moved her to tears. She was mesmerized by tastes and smells—chocolate, fresh-cut grass, wood burning, the sea, his mouth, sweat, the sheets, her taste, his. And sexual. In his most feverish fantasies he had not invented any woman so awesomely sexual. Open. She was open to anything, everything. She was always ready for sex, hot. Hotter than he. Raw from too much, still hungry for more. She could come in any position. "Clitoral must be a mistake," he said. "I wasn't anywhere near your clitoris that time," he said.

"Oh, you must have rubbed against it somehow," she protested. "I feel it on fire."

Barney let the notion ride. He was not about to deny the theory of clitoral orgasm and possibly undermine the super-structure of the feminist movement. He was becoming a fervent feminist himself. Besides, Debra could have an orgasm from touching, from kissing, from a finger on her nipple, from squeezing a muscle as he whispered to her over the phone. Lying next to her on the beach at Flying Point: she untied her bikini bottom and opened her thighs to the sun. "The sun is kissing me, Barney," she cried. He felt himself growing hard inside his swimsuit. Not wanting to sleep. Watching her constantly. Coming, a great shattering explosion, getting hard again, feeling his cock bigger than a baseball bat. Feeling like a teenager. Driving Debra to ecstasy and tears, to madness and giggles. Her little-girl voice teasing, her dusky earth-mother voice commanding him to serve her. He would watch her gathering the fragments of her consciousness in the filtered light of her blue bedroom, the sheer white curtains blowing on a late July afternoon— the field grass buzzing, the bay streaked with mauve behind. And he would have a sudden vision of Lindsay, wounded, crawling across the sand, Lindsay betrayed, Lindsay he'd promised to love. Love. Whatever the hell that was worth.

Of course, the intensity could not last. He could hardly breathe. He hired a moonlighting friend to take his shift one night so he could hurry to her. He dumped his daughter, Candy, at his folks' without warning, without explanation. He filed charts without reading them. He made feeble excuses to Lindsay. Finally one night he made love to Lindsay and she lay there weeping, somehow knowing. He skipped out on a board meeting and took a seaplane for a last night with Debra in the cottage on the bay before fall. It was wonderful. Of course, Barney could not simply let himself fall apart like that.

"You made it stop," Debra often accused him.

"Yes. I thought I'd just give it a little time and space, let it cool."

"Exactly. You turned it off. You threw it away," she said. "It was so wonderful. Why couldn't you just go with it? Let it be whatever it could be?"

There was no way to explain it to Debra. Sometimes it seemed they didn't speak the same language. He knew very well she was ready to move in, to commit herself totally, the first week. One month out of her marriage she was ready to love, risk everything. He had to weigh his commitment to Lindsay. What did she expect? He had to get his head straight after a long and terrible marriage. A man had to face responsibilities. A man cannot take off, hurtle into the stratosphere that way. Women can do it because many of them have nothing more important. Love, it seemed, was their first priority. Debra was a love junky. She was drifting through life with no responsibilities, no children, no dependent parents, only a vague sense of duty to the consumer, perhaps to her career. Barney had a complexity of responsibilities: Candy, parents, in-laws, the corporation, Keogh plans, private schools, college tuition. Perhaps it would be pleasant to disappear, drop out. Be a farmer or a carpenter. Barney actually enjoyed working with wood and tools. But he'd never understood how men—professional men brought up in the Fifties—could walk away from responsibility so casually. He'd need a prefrontal lobotomy to handle the guilt.

It *is* possible to love two women. That fall Barney had realized he loved two women. Neither of them took the news well. What did they want from him? Why did they try to force him to choose? Would it be better not to love at all? Just keep collecting bodies and moving on, like some guys he knew with five or six steady sleep-ins, always on the prowl to connect with something new. It wasn't easy loving two women at once. When Lindsay found out about Debra she was devastated. When Debra realized there was a Lindsay he did not intend to give up, she went into hysteria. They both acted as if dividing himself was a lark for Barney, never sensing how painful it was for him knowingly to cause pain. Why should Barney give up either one? He'd just escaped from a stultifying marriage and he was only forty-two. He had married too early. His extramarital life had been constricted and tame. He deserved more time to be single and as adolescent as he needed to be.

With all his conscious, controllable intellect, Barney longed to find everything he wanted in one woman. He was coming to believe no such woman existed. Marvin, some months before making his final highly persuasive comment on the inability of man to tolerate frustration by leaping out the window, had claimed to have found a measure of happiness. "To seek perfection is just a way to hold on to those cozy little pangs of deprivation," Marvin observed. "I have learned to accept that Nancy hasn't got legs like Cyd Charisse and she doesn't care about jazz but she is my woman—poop belly, unwaxed floors and all. You know. I love her sweetness, her vulnerability, her illusions, her hysterics, even her temper." Marvin. Poor dead Marvin. Why go to the boneyard for wisdom? Marvin tended to be dramatic. He exaggerated and made threats. A thousand times Barney had berated himself for ignoring Marvin there at the end. But how could he have guessed? He'd seemed a little manic. Nothing unusual. No one told Barney Marvin was on speed. "I'm at the Gem," said Marvin that day on the phone. A typical call except maybe his voice was shakier than usual. "Come down for an egg cream and maybe I won't kill myself," he said.

"Come on Marvin," Barney had said. "You know I can't just walk out of the Emergency Room. I'll get back to you later." He forgot to call but it didn't really matter. That afternoon they were already scraping Marvin off the concrete.

"Aren't you hungry?" the nurse asked as she stuck a

thermometer in his mouth. He was glad he had an excuse
not to answer. In a half doze he heard her leave with the
lunch tray.

As the dignified widow, Reen-
ey never looked better. Barney was often astonished to see
that Reeney was so striking. In flashback of those last
tortuous months together he saw only her face contorted in
anger, the mouth curled in accusation, the eyes red and
swollen. But Reeney was beautiful, standing there in the
family room of the mortuary behind Barney's coffin. She
was wearing her hair brushed back, full and shining with her
diamond ear studs. Was that really proper? Diamonds at a
funeral. Reeney, Barney supposed, would go by Emily Post.
She loved to entertain. She would do the funeral very *House
and Garden,* he imagined. Oh yes, there were crudités in a
wicker basket and waiters passing pastry puffs of God knows
what. Barney wondered who was catering this goddamned
event and who the hell was paying for it—smoked salmon,
crabmeat, even caviar, the ostentatious bitch. Would she con
his executor into footing the bill? As the widow—almost ex-
wife, saved from divorce by Barney's sudden demise—she
would be expected to mourn mildly, but nobody would be
offended if she wasn't ranting and raving. Well, she could be
a little less cheerful, the phony cunt. What would Candy
think? Barney wondered about flowers. Barney loved
flowers. But Reeney would loathe a hodgepodge of flowers
that didn't fit into her color scheme. "In lieu of flowers the
family of the deceased would appreciate contributions to the
Home for Fallen Cheerleaders." Barney grinned. Reeney
could hardly be expected to demonstrate such generous
whimsy. She'd go for something noncontroversial. The
American Boy Scouts. Or something uppercrust and trendy.

Like hemophilia. As for a clergyman . . . Barney looked around. She knew damn well he'd want something nonsectarian. But there'd be a struggle between Mama and Reeney. A rabbi versus some power of Ethical Culture. "He can go to bed with the goyim but he isn't going to be dead with the goyim," Mama was explaining to Aunt Cristal.

Aunt Cristal was truly a phenomenon. She was ripe as . . . ever, a luscious ageless beauty with ivory skin and blazing brown eyes. Hard to believe she was sixty. He remembered her flushed and giggling, locked in an exaggerated tango with Uncle Ira. Today in tight black satin she was just a little rounder, perhaps a little smaller than the Aunt Cristal Barney had made love to more than twenty years ago. Home from junior year at Harvard, the big shot, gabby pseudointellectual sloshed on Moscow Mules on the porch of their bungalow at Cass Lake. Eating her on the glider. He remembered the creak, trying to fuck her on the porch glider, finally pulling her and the pillows to the floor, toppling the pitcher, her passionate response, her giggle. Barney wondered whatever happened to ginger beer. Nobody drank ginger beer anymore.

Barney realized suddenly that he was no longer hovering overhead. He was standing not two feet away from Aunt Cristal and everyone was oblivious. Was he dead? This fantasy had begun as an exercise in being alive at his own funeral. Had he somehow died? He tried to pinch Aunt Cristal's rump, but her girdle was like armor. Cristal wiggled her ass. Had she felt his pinch? Or simply wiggled. Cristal was a wiggler. Barney looked through the curtains at his coffin. Closed, of course. Dignity in death. Lindsay sat flanked by her two daughters, Emily and Fawn, an island of contained sadness in an ocean of emotional lava. She looked aloof, but Barney knew it was simply shyness and perhaps shock at all this ethnic hysteria. The kissing The sobbing. The black humor. The business and social asides. The wheeling-dealing. As much as Lindsay might enthuse about *that* wonderful lack of inhibition, *that* vitality. Emphasis on *that*. "Hebrew," she used to say.

"You can say Jewish, Lindsay," Barney assured her. "Your tongue won't turn to corned beef."

Barney was pleased and astonished. They were all there. All the women who had passed through his life. Debra, sobbing behind wraparound sunglasses. Barbara Bloome from high school days, when they'd petted and necked and humped to near death. Caroline, the sex-crazed Bronx housewife who'd waited for him in motels twirling tassels or naked in thigh-high boots.

"He was such a spiritual boy," said Amy. Oh God, now Barney knew he was dead, and yet here she was in her little white cotton gloves. "We spent hours in that little country cemetery. He would read his poems aloud. We drank a lot to keep from freezing . . . necking out there in January. The drunker he got the more he sounded like Dylan Thomas."

Reeney snorted. "The voice was Thomas, my dear," she said. "The sentiments, as I recall, were pure Hallmark." Reeney was a Bennington snob with a real disdain for Wellesley girls.

"Why do men fall in love with angels and marry bitches?" said Jill, naughty Jill Massacio, who succumbed to Barney's letter sweater and did dirty things in the high school physics lab.

"This is ridiculous," said Reeney. "This is a funeral, not a consciousness-raising session for a congress of home wreckers. Who are all these women, Barney?" Reeney hissed. "And don't try to tell me it's the Nursing Association of Goodman Memorial, kiddo, because this is old Reeney and you never fooled me."

There were three women weeping—slim, blonde, stylishly dressed. Who could they be? Barney thought one of them might be Lauren Hutton. He'd hungered for Lauren but that was one fantasy he'd never brought off. He backed away, spying Iris and Ellen Sue, Lilyanne's seductive twins—grown up now, but he'd recognize them anywhere. Iris sat next to Lindsay. Barney shuddered. What would Iris say? At thirteen the twins had been sexual psychopaths. It was not Barney's fault. Audrey had come in surgical green. In profile he'd thought for a moment she was Beth, the little Irish girl who flunked out of med school that freshman year. Beth Killarney—alphabetical order had thrown them together. He'd not seen Audrey since before Candy was born. Her silent rage at the end was more terrifying than hysteria. How wonderful that she'd forgiven him and come to his funeral. He had left Reeney for Audrey and he would never have gone home again except for a virus the malevolent fates dispatched, and somehow he'd found himself in bed with Reeney. Oh Barney. Spineless wretch. Couldn't even resist his own wife. Why had he let that happen? So many years thrown away. So many years with the wrong woman.

Barney smelled grass. He turned. He laughed. Ellen Sue, one of Lilyanne's twins, was trading a joint with Reeney's Ethical Culture reader. "Mom used to let him baby-sit with us," Ellen Sue was saying. "Boy, did he do a mean twist. And the hula hoop. And most of the time he got away with maybe two or three hours of sleep. He ate bananas for breakfast."

Barney grinned at the memory. He could go thirty-six hours without sleep and often did in the early days of his residency, moonlighting nights, popping Dexedrine in the first gratifying discovery of the Emergency Room. Reeney had gone upstate to her folks' house on the lake for the summer. And when he wasn't working, three nights on, one night off, he was making love to Lilyanne. That crazy summer. He could still feel the heat like another presence in the room. That was before air conditioning. They made love with New York soot blowing in the window till the bed was soaked with their sweat and they lay there blowing to dry each other.

The dignified widow was fast losing dignity, Barney observed, as Reeney stormed to his mother's side. "So, Mother Kincaid, this is quite a convocation your son has assembled here. Do you know how much money I could have gotten from a sympathetic judge with evidence like this. The taste of the man. Cheerleaders. Playboy bunnies. All these tarts. What did they see in him?"

"You're imagining, Reeney," Mama soothed. "A few cheerleaders he couldn't resist. But I'm sure these are patients and friends from school."

Barney was looking for Lilyanne. She'd been blind with rage when she found out he was fooling around with her twins. Certainly never believed two barely pubescent thirteen-year-olds had attacked him. Of course thirteen-year-olds flirt but . . . how dare he suggest it was virtually rape? Barney moaned at the memory of her anger, his loss. No, Lilyanne would not come to his funeral.

In fact, none of them would be there, not Audrey or Barbara or Caroline, certainly not Lilyanne's twins—would they even remember his name? And Amy—the only one who'd made him ache with love—was dead. None of them would come, except Lindsay of course, and Debra. Reeney because Emily Post required it. Who knew what had become of his defender–sexual tormenter, Margaret, and her blue chenille bathrobe. She'd left so suddenly, without even saying goodbye after the doctor had found a calcified spot on Barney's lung and Mama discovered Margaret's brother had TB. He'd lost touch with all the women who'd meant something to him. Astonishing to think how easily he had severed all ties from the women who had shared his moments of animal madness and frantic longings. He had loved Amy . . . if the definition of love was willingness to make a lifetime commitment. Well, Amy wasn't ready for him. He remembered the ending in a blur of pain. He had not gone to her funeral because there was no reason to revive those old feelings. For a time he dreamed of Amy, nightmares of her dying, himself at the wheel of the car that killed her, himself confused and helpless in a Georgetown emergency room trying to convince a row of gorillas in football uniforms that he was, yes, he was, a doctor. But Audrey. "I can never say goodbye to you," he'd told Audrey, saying goodbye four times, returning in tears every time, then a fifth goodbye and that, pitiful coward, was it.

Perhaps they would read about his death on the obituary page of the *New York Times*. Barney was assuming the *Times* would notice his demise. What if his obit got bumped for a major television comedian, a Broadway bit player and some nobody related to the Sulzbergers. What if somebody really historical died the same day and took up all the space? Would he be relegated to a paid death notice? The ultimate ignominy. Would the *Times* be impressed that Barney Kincaid was the first man to be certified in the new specialty of emergency medicine? Would the *Times* care that he had organized the metropolitan burn emergency system and written brilliant iconoclastic letters to the *New England Journal of Medicine?* Some of his greatest triumphs were doomed to go uncelebrated, he knew. Like weaning a militant feminist from her two-speed vibrator. And getting a very prominent anthropologist to let him eat her under a table in the Widener Library. Those were the moments that ought to be memorialized. He'd be lucky to get three paragraphs.

Dr. Barney Kincaid, Goodman Physician, 42, Was First Doctor Certified in Emergency Medicine

Dr. Barney Kincaid, director of Emergency Facilities at Goodman Memorial Hospital in Riverdale, died of a massive heart attack today at the age of 42.

Dr. Kincaid, who was also an associate professor of emergency medicine at the Alfred Schweitzer College of Medicine, organized Burn-Alert, the metropolitan emergency burn system that designates burn centers with helicopter landing pads. His essays on fish-hook extraction and triage appeared in the *New England Journal of Medicine*.

> He is survived by his wife,
> the former Renee Frankel, a
> daughter, Candace, and his par-
> ents, Joseph and Ruth Kincaid.

Not very impressive. Barney felt cheated. He had meant to do so much. For five years he had talked about finishing the novel started senior year at Harvard. Eleanor Millstein, the literary agent, had said his poems were good enough to be collected in a book. Of course, once she realized she was not moving into his new bachelor apartment, Eleanor had a small hysterical fit, jammed his new IBM Selectric with her shoe, and fled—a full set of Xerox copies and two original poems still in her possession. If he recovered, he'd have to find the courage to phone and get his poems back. There was the textbook he had been gathering material for . . . two file cabinets crammed, only the introduction actually committed to a first draft. He'd promised Candy they would visit Paris together on her thirteenth birthday. And lately he'd begun thinking about hang gliding and riding the white water out West and how he'd never been to Bryce Canyon or seen the Tetons.

Barney knew in some atavistic Talmudic corner of his now totally reformable brain that the Great God of Irony would not let him die because he was just barely living . . . not worth the tragedy of an early death. And dead he'd be lucky to rate even three businesslike paragraphs in the *Times* below the author of a book on macramé, possibly above the doorman of Jacqueline Onassis's apartment building. He'd once refused to pay a bill for having the *Times* delivered to Amagansett because the paper had arrived soaking wet five mornings in a row. Would the *Times* hold that sort of delinquency against a dead man?

Dr. Barney Kincaid
Emergency Physician
Sex Athlete Dies Mid-Stroke

Dr. Barney Kincaid, Emergency Department chief of Goodman Memorial Hospital in Riverdale, died this morning in the searing passion of a small orgy.

Police arrived in response to an anonymous call to 911 and found Dr. Kincaid, who was also an associate professor of emergency medicine at the Alfred Schweitzer School of Medicine, on the floor of a mirrored room carpeted with mattresses, his body draped with a black lace, maribou-edged peignoir.

Dr. Kincaid had been warned by his colleague cardiologist to abstain from strenuous sexual exercise after a severe angina attack earlier in the week. Debra Teiger, consumer affairs reporter for Channel 3, was giving Dr. Kincaid cardiovascular resuscitation when an emergency ambulance team of paramedics trained by Dr. Kincaid himself arrived and took over the futile effort to revive him.

A small crowd of women in black gathered at the Emergency Room and wept at the news of his death. Marcia Wisemann, founder of the militant feminist group, Shriek, said she would start a campaign to raise funds for a memorial to Dr. Kincaid. "It could be simply an ionic column," she said. "Or even a tree. Those of us who know will get it."

The doctor's literary agent, Eleanor Millstein of E.M. Eye, said a collection of his poems, financed by the Fallen Cheer-leaders Collective, would be published in late spring.

Harvard University, where Dr. Kincaid earned his Bachelor of Science degree, said a group of anonymous Radcliffe alumnae had set up a memorial fund in Dr. Kincaid's name to finance his daughter's Harvard education, with the surplus going toward scholarships for disenchanted massage-parlor hostesses.

"You promise not to get the wrong idea if I come in for a chat?" It was Dylan Tarnapol, Goodman Memorial's young rabbi on call, painfully, self-consciously, hip, so laid back he perpetually looked about to fall over. Barney groaned. "Then it's true," he said. "I am terminal."

"Bullshit, Kincaid," said Tarnapol. "You should have been an actor, my friend. I hear they've voted you an Oscar for your performance as a dying man on the Emergency Room floor. So, what have you got? Tennis elbow? Wait . . . I got it . . . Casanova's knee. Hee hee." Tarnapol lit up a joint. "Great little pain killer," he observed, "cannabis."

"But I'm the one in pain," said Barney with a grin, marveling at the young man's cool. There was just no way possible Barney would have dared bring dope near Good-man Memorial.

"My pain is psychic," said Tarnapol. He'd been named by his folks, nomad Bohemian hippies before hippie time, after the poet. Late one night after harrowing hours trying to wrest lives from some terrible Saturday night carnage, he and Barney had collapsed on a sofa in the deserted waiting room, too tired to go home, Tarnapol slightly stoned as usual. In a kind of meandering dialogue—puns, conundrums, and mutual confessional—they discovered each had chosen a profession in hopes of putting a hex on death.

"Kincaid," Tarnapol had said that night. "Very solid name. Distinguished. I like it. You make it up?"

Barney bristled as he always did when someone touched that nerve end. "I'm Jewish," he said. "I'm not trying to hide—" Then hearing the bristle in his voice, he paused. "Well, I'm more Jewish than Pat Nixon but, hmm, not nearly as Jewish as . . . Buddy Hackett. My father decided he'd had too many school yard fights over the name Cohen."

"In Brooklyn?" marveled Tarnapol.

"He grew up in a little town called Lake Hill, north of Woodstock. My folks moved to Brooklyn just before I was born." Joseph Kincaid's legalized move to escape in the melting pot had never been discussed or explained. Barney had grown up speculating about it silently, as if it were an unspeakable family scandal. As far as he could see, his family was as mildly Jewish as most anyone else—observing the high holy days, celebrating Christmas as if it were a national holiday, giving money to the United Jewish Appeal, deciding suddenly and without consulting the reluctant incipient agnostic that Barney would be bar mitzvahed after all. Barney had figured out what sex was all about by himself and all on his own at about the same time he'd evolved a position on religion. He'd grown up in Jewish neighborhoods, Brooklyn and then Woodmere. He looked Jewish in a rather all-American way—blue eyes, strawberry-blond curls darkening a bit now and perhaps just a bit springier than need be, nose straight enough but wide, something between peasant and Pinocchio. Maybe if that family name had been Einstein or Chagall or Rothschild, but Cohen . . .

the cliché. Maybe Dad was right. Barney had never felt secure about it. But he was a snob himself. Kincaid was a brilliant choice. It symbolized everything American, New England, Wasp, Barney's own Great American assimilation dream. He was Barney for his father's father, dead six months before Barney was born. A mythic character, according to Catskill legend, a saint to everyone who knew him, everyone except his wife, Grandma Rose—an extraordinary woman with no sense of humor. And where should she find time for humor, with five daughters and four sons to raise all on her own in a country boarding house while Grandpa Barney made dolls. Dad's papa was a poet, a philosopher, a rabbi's son, a pillar of the poker table. He carved beautiful dolls and gave them away. Once in a while he earned a few dollars teaching Hebrew to a bar mitzvah candidate. Sometimes he worked in the fields. Rarely. He never learned English. He loved to dance. He tended the garden behind the peeling yellow clapboard, producing bushels of tomatoes and grapes he made into wine. Whatever he grew, she criticized. It was too sour, too big, too much, already rotten. The boarders adored his father, Dad remembered, and they whispered rudely about Rose for the way she pinched pennies and punished the slow payers with chicken wings and backs while her favorites got the white meat.

There was one home movie of Grandpa that Barney loved. At a wedding party surrounded by his grown-up kids, their wives and girlfriends in the draped, long-waisted dresses of the Thirties. Dancing with Barney's cousin Heidi, then five, Dutch-boy bob flying. He has Heidi standing on his shoes and he is doing a flashy tango. And then he is alone. Playing to the camera. Imitating Charlie Chaplin, dancing, leaping into the air, wiggling his fingers and wagging his knees in a baggy, comical, spirited Charleston.

Barney would have loved to be that free and uninhibited. With grass, not as a habitual thing but with women mostly, a slim and powerful joint appearing suddenly lit, passed without question, he felt looser, lighter. In bed, when everything worked, he felt that grace too. In the hospital, of course, he moved with the assurance of a champion. But on the street, and always socially, he felt the weight of constriction, unease. Neither Dad nor Barney was the least like Grandpa. The Americanization of Poland's exiled Jews produced some very uptight hybrids. Look at Tarnapol. His folks almost disowned him when he decided to become a rabbi, a slap in the face to their flamboyant atheism.

"I'm glad to see you looking like a man with a future," Tarnapol was saying. "Which leads me to a sensitive subject." Tarnapol looked at Barney as if he were searching for the gentlest way to deliver bad news, his stub of a nose twitching above the pencil moustache that was supposed to make him look older but simply made him look Puerto Rican. Barney could feel the tension. "It's about Emile Gunderson," he said, looking away.

Barney felt himself bristling. On his deathbed, Gunderson and his cowardly claque would pursue him. "Not you too, Tarnapol. What about Gunderson? What do you have to do with Gunderson?"

Tarnapol cracked his knuckles. "Well, it seems the man's been here for twenty years and he has a big practice and a lot of the privates are his buddies. The whole mishpocheh is getting nervous, wondering why you're after Gunderson."

Barney groaned. He had not foreseen provoking a cabal of cowards by exposing what he suspected was a real scandal. "Gunderson is Jewish, Tarnapol. Is that what you're saying?"

Tarnapol shrugged. "These days, who isn't?"

"Gunderson," Barney marveled. "Where did he come up with a name like Gunderson?"

"It's no more preposterous than Kincaid, my friend," said Tarnapol. "And he came by it honorably. His mother married a Gunderson. Anyway, how the man votes in heaven is not the point. The word is you have some personal grudge."

Barney's blood was pounding. "That's a lie," he said. "I

never even thought about Gunderson till I discovered his little hobby of popping patients off to the morgue prematurely. I don't have all the details yet but I'm collecting them. That's it. Tarnapol, you don't know me that well. I assure you I would pursue this inquiry if Gunderson was my brother. I just happen to be one of those old-fashioned dreamers who cares about good medicine. I didn't realize what an exclusive fraternity I belong to." Barney took a deep breath, pressing his hand against his heart to assure his body everything was fine. The monitor must be going crazy. Where were those nurses? Were they on Gunderson's side too . . . willing to let him die?

Tarnapol patted his shoulder. "Hey, Barney, calm down. Is your pulse okay? Shall I call someone? Oh God, I'm hopeless. I shouldn't be assigned to a hospital. I have no grace. Timing. It's my timing. Are you all right?" He smoothed the covers, a frightened Puerto Rican Jewish rabbi. "If I'd been born ten years later I would have been a good rock singer. I have a pretty good voice, Barney. Are you okay?"

Tarnapol looked so genuinely disturbed, Barney had to laugh.

"Maybe you should tell Gunderson's buddies I'm under the weather and I seem to have lost interest in his case."

"That's a good idea," Tarnapol agreed. "Actually I think what I stopped by for was to remind you about the hospital's celebrity auction fund raiser. I was reading in Liz Smith's column you've been dating that consumer affairs reporter, Debra Teiger. Maybe she could donate something, I don't know. An item. A service. I don't know. Just a thought."

"Everyone reads Liz Smith," Barney marveled. "Gossip is the new gospel."

"Since fund raising is the main thrust of religious endeavors these days, an enlightened pastor reads Liz Smith. The rich and the famous are easy marks," Tarnapol observed. "Their guilt is fresh and unjaded."

"Consumerism isn't your most glamourous field,"

Barney warned. "But I'll ask her to come up with something. A wrecked Pinto maybe." He smiled to himself. An hour of Debra's untelevised talent would be worth a tidy sum.

*B*arney woke up next day exhausted from the rigors of hospital routine, cranky from a harrowing morning, being awakened at seven A.M. by an unrepentently cheerful aide and ordered to "wash yourself." Sleep had eluded him from that moment on. Lukewarm tea, toasted Wonder Bread and a purple ooze claiming to be grape jam did not improve his spirits. Grudgingly he had agreed to let a student nurse massage his feet. The clumsy cretin had dropped the phone on his left instep—on the most fragile, irreparable metatarsals. They were waiting for Dr. Foley to take him off the monitor so they could send him down to X-ray and assess the devastation. Foley breezed in, cheerful and optimistic, to liberate him from the monitor just as his family surged into the room. Mama paranoid, anxious, forcedly cheerful. Candy adorable. Reeney strangely shy. Dad, as always, unreadable.

"He looks better in your nightshirt than you do, Joseph. Barney you've got such bony knees." Mama had swooped into the room ahead of everyone, unloaded her shopping bag—bananas, of course, unblemished bananas, bags of prunes and dried apricots, and a sour-cream coffee cake. "My neighbor, so sick she can scarcely drag herself from bed, insists for Barney she must make her sour-cream cake. Oh my baby, let me look at you." She felt his brow, caressed his cheek . . . looked deep into his eyes.

"I have my stethoscope here, Mama," said Barney. "You can listen."

Dad, settled in the corner, beamed. "She's been on the

phone for two days doing research on pericarditis," he said. "I bet she knows more by now than your doctor."

"Barney if you aren't eating that Jell-O, Candy should eat it," said Mama. "Hopefully, you won't be too long on the cortisone," said Mama. "Look how skinny Candy is . . . like a broom. Candy, eat Daddy's Jell-O."

"Mother."

You would know—you could stake the family fortune on it—by the tone of Reeney's voice that the mother in question was not hers.

"Mother. We don't nag Candy about eating. It's counterproductive. Candy is slim. Slim is fine."

"We didn't believe in malnutrition in my day. But what did we know . . . brains had not yet been invented," Mama sighed. She fluttered about nervously, still in her coat, wiping every surface in sight with damp Kleenex. Barney was surprised to feel that sudden surge of adolescent guilt as she picked up Debra's copy of *Penthouse* and quickly hid it between a *Newsweek* and a few medical journals. She glared at Barney. Bad boys never grow up, thought Barney.

"Why don't you take your coat off and sit for a minute, Mother," said Reeney. "You're making Barney nervous."

Barney looked at her, touched. He'd tried to treat Reeney like a stranger, but she was a woman who knew him well. He wondered if she secretly wished they were still together. Had there been something good, something meaningful in those years of sham and sniping that kept her hanging on to a moribund marriage?

There was no way this woman, his wife, would ever fully know him, Barney thought. He longed to be able to tell her the history of Barney the lover, the sexual athlete and erotic alchemist. For years he and Reeney had almost no sex at all. Occasionally they fucked in anger, both of them excited by almost euphoric rage. And once in a while each was able to respond to the other's unstated need, a coil of tension or anxiety where sex is a more effective therapy than counting sheep or a sleeping pill. Reeney would press her hand against his side or the length of her leg against the length of his, a signal he recognized at once. Barney had felt obligated to kiss her. Never on the lips anymore. That was too intimate. Her lips had become forbidding. He could not lie to her lips and the truth about the two of them was too disturbing to examine. He would kiss her shoulder and her breasts. Her breasts were heavy and hurt at unpredictable times in her menstrual cycle. Years ago that had intrigued him. Now it was simply a fact. She slept with one arm tucked under her to keep her own weight from crushing them.

Reeney was now very brisk, very matter of fact, her kiss cool, almost clinical, her questions rather informed for a Jewish American Princess who'd never shown any interest in anything but buying out Bendel's and the social-climbing potential of selective philanthropy. She'd brought Barney a book, the new Uhnak, a best-seller, easy to read, no kick in the ass there. She acted as if their last encounter had never occurred.

Early, not long after the separation, lonely in his unfurnished apartment, panicked one night because he just couldn't get it up with an incredibly beautiful Swedish woman, stoned and scared, he had walked into the house on East Ninety-third Street at two A.M.

"I could have shot you as an intruder if I'd had a gun," Reeney had gasped, her heart still pounding with fear.

"Intruders don't have house keys," he said.

"I can't believe the court will let you keep house keys," she cried. "How dare you just walk in. At this hour. At any hour. What makes you think I'm alone?"

"You better be alone," he growled. "I won't have you fucking around with cabana boys in the same house with my child." He backed her against the wall.

"Don't shove me around," she shrilled.

"That was hardly a shove," he whispered, trying to quiet her down. "When I shove, you'll know it." He felt her breasts against him, like a soft, sweet-smelling pillow, her perfume, Bal à Versailles, surely the most expensive perfume in the world, he knew damn well, having put out for gallons of it.

She used it by the tubful. He heard that funny little intake of breath. Reeney getting hot. He didn't know if she was still fucking around, wasn't sure how much sex she got, couldn't remember the last time he'd felt hot specifically for Reeney, the last time they'd fucked in response to a sexy moment or in a rush of anger that filled him with heat wanting to fuck her in the mouth till she choked.

Now he pushed her down to her knees. She struggled to get away. "Is it rape now, you jerk?" He rubbed his cock against her gritted teeth. "Not here, Barney," she said. He pulled her up and shoved her toward the bedroom. She was laughing. "When I think of how many times I wished you would . . . anything. What a joke."

"This isn't a joke," he said, twisting her hair till she knelt on the floor.

She was shaking. "I love it, Barney," she said. "I love seeing the real you. Hurt me. Go ahead, you animal." He twisted her head till she was face down on the floor, fucking her from behind, feeling her tense, feeling her come . . . waiting for another come, then not waiting anymore.

She pushed him off her, crying, "You fucking hypocrite. You creep. Playing around all those years. Fucking everything in skirts. How dare you leave me for one little meaningless roll in the hay. One little fuck that I goddamn well needed. I was entitled. Right? Say it."

Barney slipped on his jacket, tucked the tie in the pocket. "Yes. You were entitled." He felt stupid, sorry for her, felt a tiny stab of sympathy.

She smiled. "That was easily the best fuck I've had in two days," she said. She laughed at his involuntary flinch.

Barney fled. It would be a long desperate moment before he would ever go near her again, he vowed.

Was Barney a good lover? If you asked Reeney, Barney imagined she would shrug, smile that superior, deprecating smile. Reeney had no idea. Barney had mused idly about sending her a letter.

Dear Mrs. Kincaid:

In the spirit of enlightened sisterhood, I write to you with this information. Your husband is a mythic lover—sensitive, inventive, wild, intuitive, inexhaustible. How could you ever let him go?

Multiple orgasmically yours. . . ???

Should he sign it "anonymous"? Barney wrote the letter over and over in his head and fantasized mailing it. Should he sign it Marilyn Chambers? She might think it a joke. He could sign the name of her best friend. That was no joke. But that would be cruel and Barney wanted never to be cruel. Reeney had not been cruel. She'd been pathetic . . . in bed with a cabana boy, a gardener, whatever he was, a long-haired, sunburned twenty-two-year-old. Not that Reeney didn't have every right to play around. Blame her? Judge her? Never. Since the sex between them was scarcely enough to keep the hormones flowing in a parakeet, Barney must have somehow subliminally assumed Reeney had lovers. But in broad daylight . . . with Candy maybe yards away on the beach . . . in their very own bed. He was shattered. On a sudden whim he'd taken the afternoon off and driven out early to Amagansett. There was no answer when he called, twice, to see if there was anything Reeney wanted from the city.

There was no car outside to signal a warning. Just two

bicycles. Barney was annoyed because the sliding screen door was off the track again and there were flies licking up spilled sugar in the kitchen. He also noticed big water spots on the bleached wooden floors where it had rained in. "Reeney."

There was no answer. Barney loved that house almost as much as if it were a second child. He had sanded those floors himself, not only to save money, but because it pleased him to see his touch on the sander stripping the floors to this pure bleached beauty. He took care of that house as if he were making love to it, a notion he could not possibly have explained to anyone, certainly not to Reeney, a woman who did not see dust ever or mold till it had almost strangled the refrigerator, or ants about to walk off with the sugar bowl. Such blindness was bliss in a way, he supposed. But not being blind himself, her indifference drove him wild. Barney kicked the laundry basket out of the way and pushed the bedroom door open with his canvas duffel. Swollen by the dampness, the door stuck. And then flew open.

Reeney sat up in bed wide-eyed, the sheet pulled to her chin.

"I tried to call but—" Barney suddenly realized there was someone in bed next to her. A form. Big. Feet sticking out at the foot of the bed. Good feet. Young feet. Incredibly, even in his shock, he could see they were remarkable feet. The scene seemed strangely familiar, as if he'd seen it in a movie.

"Tommy. Take that pillow off your head," Reeney said, dignity restored by her own anger.

Barney stomped out of the house, surprised to feel himself swept with relief as well as rage. He drove down to the beach, with an afterimage of those feet as if a flashbulb had gone off, blinding him, engraving the image forever.

The beach was sparsely populated, a weekday-afternoon beach, mamas and kids and au pair girls. Just a few yards down from the parking area was a dazzling woman, breasts tumbling out of an untied bikini top, very tan and shiny with oil. Beside her sat a naked baby in a floppy white sun hat under an umbrella, sucking the sand from its fingers.

Barney had a vivid image of himself as a baby on a sunny beach, all bundled up, stockings on his arms—he'd had some kind of skin rash, the stockings were to keep him from scratching. Struggling against the wrap, whatever it was. He wasn't sure if he actually remembered the anger or remembered only the infant's face lost in wrinkles of rage in an old photograph in Mama's scrapbook. How did that flaxen-curled child come to be born into that tribe of hairy brunettes? For a time he had pretended to be adopted. He imagined himself a Nordic prince abandoned in a garbage can near the Brooklyn Museum and discovered by Joseph Kincaid strolling to his first Fine Shoe Emporium. But of course, Mama was not a hairy brunette. Mama, except for light-brown hair, looked like Betty Grable. And Barney's blue eyes were Grandpa's eyes, everyone said, and he had dimples just like Dad. Barney thought he remembered kicking and screaming to be free of all that confining garb. Poor Mama. Didn't know any better. Betty Grable didn't have to worry about money or cranky babies or rashes. Mama wore that upswept hairdo and posed beside the squalling brat looking over her shoulder in a great imitation of Grable's famous pinup pose. Even today at sixty-five she was still being cute, blonder now, and wore stockings with seams on the same spectacular legs. Hubba hubba.

Someone had switched on the overhead television. Barney hunted for the remote control.

"As far as you know, Daddy, is there anything in the law that says you can't keep a horse on East Ninety-third Street?" Barney had the feeling Candy had been prattling away about horses for several minutes. In fact Candy had been astonishingly cool, acting as if nothing were wrong. She had brought him a bar of soap in the shape of Snoopy and a rose in a Perrier bottle—"I thought of that myself"—and she'd moved right in, grabbing Barney's hand and not letting go, to show Reeney who came first now. Barney loved Candy. She was small and thin and tough, a bossy little miniature of Reeney without the rasping demand in her voice. Her poise was astonishing and every once in a while she tossed off some precocious insight that made Barney dizzy with fatherly pride. Well, of course he spoiled Candy, but why not? That's what money was for. That's what divorced daddies were supposed to do. "Daddy, ignoring the horse question will not make it go away," teased Candy. She didn't seem at all concerned about his heart. Perhaps Reeney hadn't told her anything. Perhaps she had (wisely) minimized the seriousness.

"It's not unusual," said Reeney. "Little girls fall in love with horses. I don't think it's necessary to examine all the psychological implications because in this case, Candy seems willing to settle for a dog."

"As long as it's a substantial dog," said Candy. "I'm small for my age and I would look good with a substantial dog. A St. Bernard would be perfect."

Barney groaned. "Just what we need weekends in Amagansett. A large dog that shits large turds, and guess who cleans up. Candy, darling, you'd look even more substantial with a Siamese cat."

"How did we go from a horse to a Siamese cat?" cried Candy.

"Why don't you discuss the question of pets at some later date, when Daddy is stronger," said Dad looking up from *Newsweek*. The shock of his speaking chastened everyone. At that moment, thank God, the phone rang. It was Lindsay, Lindsay with the grace and intelligence to phone from the lobby. What do they do to gentiles when small that makes them so polite? Barney wondered. How did parents drill into their brains the subversive concept that the world

was not automatically their toy? Nobody promised them
waters would part and rains let up and Harvard awaited.
They did not surge out into the world hotly competitive,
knowing they were the chosen people but . . . how ironic . . .
in fact, they were.

"You must go now," Barney said. "I mustn't get over-
tired the first day."

"We're dismissed," said Mama.

"I'm scheduled for tests," Barney improvised lamely.

"He doesn't want us to intrude on his shiksa cheerleader," said Mama.

"Barney is entitled to his hobbies, Mother," said Reeney,
gathering up coats and hats, sending dried apricots flying
across the bed. "Don't tax your aging heart, dear," she
said.

Mama lingered after Dad had given Barney a hug and
Candy had kissed him four times and torn herself away.
"Maybe now," said Mama, patting the surviving apricots so
he wouldn't forget they were close by. "Now, with this heart
of yours. Maybe now you're going to come to your senses.
Reeney is not such a monster."

Barney closed his eyes. "Mama, darling, we've been
through all that before." It was true. There had been good
times with Reeney.

"Life is not like fairy tales. There is no perfection. So, I
gather this shiksa thinks you're Prince Charming. Of course
she does. She should be so lucky to get a fabulous rich
doctor like you. Do you wonder why Candy is so thin? Her
heart is broken, Barney. Just like yours. You and Reeney
had a beautiful family . . . a regular life. An American
dream. Listen to what your heart is saying."

"My heart is saying I need to cut down on cholesterol.
That's all, Mama, honest."

"Tell me please, what was wrong. I'm coming, Joseph,"
she called. "So a man wants to hop into bed with some tramp
here and there. So. So go. Oral sex. What is this oral sex? It's
just people talking dirty. This thing with shiksas, Barney.
Tell me please. I have an open mind. Tell me seriously,

Barney, aside from sex, could you ever have a real friendship with a gentile? I mean, do you think it's possible?"

"I have a fever, Ma."

"So now I'm giving fevers. All right. He's hot. Hot stuff. This isn't the world they promised me."

Lindsay stood at the door behind the day nurse.

"Hello there," said Mama. "So nice to see you. I'm gone. I'm gone. Goodbye."

Barney suffered through the twenty-ninth blood-pressure check of the day as Lindsay busied herself admiring the jungle of flowers. She turned as his tormenter retreated. Lindsay's smile was like the sun, truly dazzling. Barney felt so happy to see her, in love with her perfect teeth, the delicate laugh lines, that unbelievable neck, her graceful endless neck. Ah Lindsay, his delicious, elegant, serene ladylike Wasp. What man could resist that nose, one-third less of it than most ordinary mortals? Equally appealing was a sense of distance, dignity . . . reserve. There was not a haimish bone in her spare athletic body. There was always a hesitancy, a cloak of . . . you wouldn't exactly call it indifference, but integrity was perhaps too vague. The triumph was to break through it. Think of that. Measure the undeniable joy of pleasing a sensuous voluptuary against the exhilarating triumph of transforming a snow princess into a flushed, quivering wanton.

"Mama doesn't mean to be so rude, darling," Barney apologized. "It's just she doesn't know what to do about you."

Lindsay kissed his left temple. He caught a cloud of her dazzling mixed scents—peppermint blurred with Ivory soap. "She wants desperately for me not to exist. I *do* understand, darling."

Yes. Mama did not want to meet Lindsay. "Spare me your parade of tramps," she had said. Mama wanted to believe Lindsay was just one of a nameless, faceless, futureless army bouncing in and out of Barney's bachelor pad. A game he'd soon tire of. That this remission to adolescence was just a stage through which Barney must pass before coming back to his senses, to Reeney, to the cocoon on East Ninety-third Street.

But Barney had met Lindsay a month after the separation. She'd nursed him back to strength and in the front of his brain was the awareness that surely one day he would marry her. Probably. Did that sound like a wobbly sense of commitment? There is no question that last summer's wild passion for Debra had thrown all assumptions into question. But time seemed to have frozen Debra into a more sensible perspective. She was fun to play with. And the truth was simple. Lindsay was the woman of Barney's dreams. He had often fantasized himself married to a quietly handsome Anglo-Saxon woman with two perfect blond children, living somewhere secluded, suburban and prudently zoned in Connecticut or even Westchester. The dream assumed intelligence and sweetness. Lindsay had these, plus energy and ambition. Starved for direction, she had plowed through continuing education courses at Connecticut College in the years before and after her own divorce and was still pursuing a degree, though already working part time for a small publishing house that exploited her eagerness as if she were an untried twenty-one-year-old just out of college. The two perfect blond children were, alas, three, imperfect only in that they breathed and needed attention and one was a slightly insecure eight-year-old boy, fathered and starved for affection by an allegedly heartless blond bastard squash-playing orthopedic man trained at Yale General. Why was blond so important to Barney, who fathered brunettes? Genetic, probably, like hemophilia, carried on the Y chromosome of Jewish males, the passion for blond monkeys. Clearly, Philip Roth did not invent this complaint.

Lindsay's hair was, to be brutally honest, not as blonde as the Wasp of Barney's dream. He had Eva Marie Saint visions. Lindsay was a born blonde, with pale-blonde skin and fine golden down, but her hair had darkened—she wore it sun streaked, by a hairdresser he supposed. Still she did have that nose, a delicate, insouciant two-thirds of the normal American upturned nose, and enough chin to make up the difference, a pert heart-shaped face, wildly changeable green eyes, green flecked with gold. No, they were not blue. Barney accepted that flaw. He would never father blue-eyed blondes, although actually, the fact was he didn't intend to father anyone from now on. One child of his and Lindsay's three were more than enough.

But he had made a commitment to Lindsay—even if he'd not yet found the discipline to be monogamous—and it was not as if his folks were living on the far edge of Outer Mongolia. They were clearly in residence in Manhattan and he saw them once a week, usually with Candy along to keep the conversation comfortable. He could understand if Lindsay felt hurt not having met them. That's why he had decided less than ten days ago to fly boldly into the fire— with a family dinner. "They'll be civilized," he had promised. "And Candy loves you." Which was only half-a-truth. Candy for some reason considered Lindsay the least competition among Barney's weekend companions. Lindsay's reserve had lulled her too.

*M*ama had not been gracious. "Why don't you order the sweet and sour pork," she said to Lindsay, her first sentence since their tense handshake.

"The dried shredded beef with rice noodles is usually good here," Lindsay said to Mama. Her proprietary tone was like a red flag.

"How about the ham with dates?" said Mama. Her face was crooked the way it got whenever she forced that smile. And her voice was unnaturally low with the telltale British affectation.

"I'm sorry. What did you say?" Lindsay asked.

"For God's sake, Mama, gentiles are not *required* by their religion to eat pork."

"Barney." Lindsay was shocked.

"Are we going to have a fight now?" Candy wanted to know. "If so I might throw up although I haven't thrown up for years."

"You haven't thrown up since you were five," said Barney.

"I'm having the wonton soup and I'm not sharing it with anyone," said Candy. "Fight if you must. I probably won't throw up."

"Does anyone like egg foo yong?" Mama asked in a voice so sweet it could bring on a diabetic coma.

"Nobody likes egg foo yong, Grandma," said Candy.

"One egg foo yong," said Barney. "You order what you want, Mama. Whatever you don't eat is fine."

"I don't want egg foo yong, Barney," said Mama. "I have it all the time. I'm happy to order something everybody likes."

"As long as they leave out the MSG," Barney's father interjected. It was the first time he'd spoken all evening.

"I'm with you, Mr. Kincaid," said Lindsay, deliriously happy to agree with anything.

"I hate shrimp," said Candy.

"Never mind what you hate, Candy, tell the waiter what you like."

"You know what I like, Daddy," said Candy, grabbing Barney's hand and kissing the fingers.

"Don't be a baby, Candy. And don't kiss my fingers during dinner."

"I can kiss your hand in the movie?" asked Candy.

"Where did we get this dialogue?" cried Barney. "For whom are we showing off? Yes, waiter, we're ready to order. Two wonton soups. Five egg rolls."

"Lamb with scallions."

"Without the scallions," said Candy.

"Lamb without scallions. Dried shredded beef." Barney was sweating. "Egg foo yong. War shu opp for me."

"We're sharing or we're not sharing?" asked Candy.

"We're sharing whenever possible. And two orders of barbequed ribs," said Barney.

"Extra well done," said Mama.

"And no MSG," Dad repeated.

"And no sugar," said Candy.

"And no cornstarch," his mother added.

"Cornstarch too," cried Barney. "That's a new one."

"And no scallions," said Candy.

Lindsay looked as if she were about to be sick or scream. Her eyes were all gold and very wide. "Tea," she whispered.

"Oh, they always bring tea," said Mama.

"Lindsay, I think what we need is a drink," said Barney.

"Make it a scorpion so I can have the gardenia," cried Candy.

"Just tea," said Lindsay firmly.

Candy was sitting on Barney's lap again. She pretended she was sort of half leaning against him, but the truth was she had a hard time sharing Barney and she was always creeping in and over and under, grabbing his hand or his neck or his chin. "Candy darling, please. My left knee is not what it used to be."

"Nothing is, Daddy," she said.

*L*indsay set her attaché case on the windowsill to drip dry. The snow was starting to melt and her boots, serious snow-trooper boots, squished full of water. "I better dump the slush," she said, biting her lower lip. "I told them at the office I was going to the library and then to lunch with an author—someone they'd love to woo from Simon and Schuster. I knew her at Chapin." She grinned. "I'm a terrible liar."

Of course. That was what Barney loved. She did not

approve of lying and when she lied she would frown,
reflexive disapproval of the shameful act. Oh how he loved
her. She was so good for him. Good to him. They shared the
same values, the same goals, the same cultural urges, the
same preference for restraint, the same embarrassment with
excess. (Except one, alas. Sexual excess depressed her and
endlessly engaged Barney.)

He often wished she had a bit more style. At the same
time he was fond of her stylelessness. That was a style in
itself, after all. Whatever Lindsay wore, she made it look like
a shirtwaist. No matter if it cost three hundred dollars or
fifty dollars or carried an Yves St. Laurent label. On her it
looked like a shirtwaist. He loved the barrette in her hair. He
imagined she had worn that exact same fake tortoise-shell
barrette at Chapin. He pictured her as a girl scout in the
forest—lithe and uniformed like her daughter Fawn—
rubbing two sticks together, getting fire in an instant,
rescuing wounded birds, tossing captured trout back into
mountain streams to live again, all the wholesome outdoor
things gentile girls do.

In a way it was astonishing how comfortable they could
feel together, how their priorities and philosophies meshed,
considering they'd grown up in such contrasting cultures.
Frustrated Ruth Mann Kincaid frittering away brains (Dad
had told Barney how he'd won the smartest girl at Erasmus
Hall) and energy on charity bazaars, canasta, and envy,
nursing her lifelong Betty Grable look-alike contest, obsessed with life's promises broken, Barney her great white
hope for status and revenge. Joseph, the melancholy martyr,
had quit college so his young brothers could become lawyers
and slumlords (and one, a compulsive gambler), moonlighting after a ten-hour day selling furniture on time,
parking cars and hacking, finally striking a modest success
with his Fine Shoe Emporium, meanwhile Lindsay's Mumsey
and Dad courted summers in Tuxedo Park on vacation
from prep schools. Contrast Brooklyn and his tribe's
hungry ethnic howl with generations of Wall Street law
firms, Fisher's Island, two centuries of Social Register

belonging, and the mild bemusement of the upper crust when Ethel and Dixon Gardiner went off at the age of sixty to join the Peace Corps in Guatemala.

And yet Lindsay and he had much in common. Two only children, both bookish and gangly, each absorbed in an imaginary playmate, growing up feeling cheated (and secretly blessed) by only-childness, obedient, defenders of the virtues of their time: family, community, country, success. And though both had gone through wrenching, disillusioning domestic upheavals to brave new autonomy, they still both believed in the same institutions, even though, yes . . . all the rules had changed. Through Lindsay, Barney felt he shared a direct line to Plymouth Rock.

Lindsay was peeling crumpled aluminum foil from a shriveled banana bread she'd baked for Barney. If prunes and dried apricots symbolized the Jewish mother's obsessive mothering, somehow banana bread could be perceived as serenely gentile, thought Barney. Fawn, her eleven-year-old, had sent a crocheted potholder for his kitchen—perhaps the ninth she'd done for him. This one was black and brown.

"Somber," said Barney. "Funereal. Do you think she knows something they haven't told me?"

"Fawn thinks these are masculine colors," said Lindsay.

"I thought little girls were growing up liberated from all that sexist stuff," said Barney.

"Fawn spent her formative years with a very unliberated mother and a classic chauvinist father. Anyway, I believe the last potholder she made for you was yellow on yellow."

"Yellow because she said I seemed sad and yellow was a cheerful color they use a lot of in mental hospitals was how she put it." Barney squeezed her hand. "Fawn is terrific, darling. So thoughtful, a lot like you."

She smiled. "I brought you this book," she said. "I can do a little editing while you read. Is there room for me next to you now that the monitor is unhooked and you're a free man?"

"Oh, lots of room," said Barney. She was clumsy and boney and had a way of rocking the bed. But he admired her professional dedication. He had discovered that he preferred women of accomplishment. And he was proud of Lindsay trudging back to school against her husband's opposition, practically blackmailing a cousin in publishing for this job. Why couldn't Reeney do it too?

"I have no career, no work to fall back on, because this sexist pig wouldn't permit it," Reeney had told her lawyer. Permit it. Permit what? Reeney had been a mediocre dancer with a nonexistent career, damned grateful to be rescued by marriage from inevitable failure. It was true, Barney admitted, he'd thought it important for a mother to stay home raising kids. And Reeney had believed that too. Barney had saved this lazy, extravagant creature from having to confront drudgery and the reality of her minimal talent. Now she had grand delusions of what might have been. Liberated, she sat on her ass complaining he didn't give her enough money, a parasite. And if he got the contract to take over New Grace Hospital's ER, she'd take thirty-three percent of that too. As the advantages of a professionally run ER became more apparent on the East Coast, Barney's corporation could supervise and staff dozens of ERs. He could become a goddamn millionaire and she'd get her vengeful cut of everything. She would never remarry, the mean bitch. She couldn't afford the luxury.

Barney studied the end flap of *The Love Bond,* a new weapon in Lindsay's campaign to convince him that passion could survive marriage . . . that "caring," as she put it, "was the ultimate aphrodisiac." Barney longed to believe that. But he was still hooked on intermediate aphrodisiacs. He wanted strangers in the night, anonymous bodies in steamy hideouts. He wanted threesomes and swinging, Plato's Retreat and heart-shaped asses and two or three pussies lined up in a row aching to be filled. It was only a question of time, he was sure, before he got all that out of his system, and then he would marry this tall, slim, dowdy, truly beautiful woman.

Lindsay nuzzled against him, one bare leg thrown across his lap, and he touched the silken skin inside her knee. It was intimate and unexciting. Staring at his book, Barney came up with a thought that startled him. If a powerful genie were to appear at this moment and promise him an attractive new woman every day for the rest of his life, Barney had the uncomfortable feeling he could happily sign his soul away.

"Sleeping, Barney?"

"Henderson Turner. Why are you holding my hand?"

"Aw c'mon, Barney. You know that reflex. See a wrist, take a pulse." Henderson pressed his stethoscope against Barney's chest.

"Jesus, Hen. You too. I feel like public property."

"You are. This is a teaching hospital, my friend. I'm sending three music majors up to hear your heart. You can give them a little lecture so they'll know what they're hearing."

"E. Power Biggs plays Bach."

"Stravinsky with a little wheeze."

"That bad." Barney put his own stethoscope on to listen. "Don't frighten me like that. What's exciting downstairs? I see Djarta missed a hairline fracture this morning. That was a tricky one."

"Hey, you've not been sneaking in to the office disguised as a doctor, Barney," Henderson scolded.

"I have my spies. I see we got osteomyelitis in the sternum we fractured doing closed chest massage on that bronchial asthma patient, Mrs. Minna Jervis."

"Yeah. You should write that one up for the journal, Barney. Damnedest thing. Osteomyelitis in a closed fracture site. They're giving her cloxacillin. That will clear it up. What's all this stuff? You're not writing your memoirs?"

Barney had drifted to sleep sifting through charts of patients treated by Dr. Gunderson, his roster of sudden deaths and similar cases handled by other men on the staff. "It's my Gunderson documentation," he said. "I'm afraid this hospital is staffed by a bunch of ostriches—I'm not sure if they're digging their heads in the sand because they're stupid or scared to take on one of their own. I find this whole Gunderson case incredibly disturbing."

"I was waiting to speak to you about that," Henderson said, pulling up a chair. "You've got a lot of the attendings bristling, kid. Fusco, Laurent, Jennings, they are telling everyone you're a full-time rabble-rouser and a Bolshevik."

"You see what fuddy-duddies we're dealing with," said Barney. "The worst they can come up with is Bolshevik. That's how far behind the times they are." He laughed. "No one wants to see a colleague discredited. I understand that. Especially an old guy with no place else to go. But Henderson, this old guy is killing people. I realize we aren't supposed to go around complaining about mediocrity among our associates, but total incompetence, for God's sake."

Henderson sighed. "I'm sure you're onto something, Barney. It's not like you to exaggerate a foul-up. I'm just worried about your . . . health. It's a strain trying to function in a hostile atmosphere. And some of these guys are hysterical. They're saying you have a grudge against Gunderson, that you're a perpetual troublemaker. I'd hate it if anything bollixed our bid for the New Grace ER . . . with my brood I really need the money."

Barney knew Henderson was right. He was going out on a limb pursuing the Gunderson case. But no one else seemed to care. He was proud of his image as a trouble-maker. Damn it, someone had to make waves. He'd never dreamed the medical staff would just sit there determined to ignore what seemed so obvious—just because the man had been hanging on at Goodman for twenty years, just because disciplining one man for incompetence made them all more vulnerable. Damn it, Barney had better things to do with his time. Especially now. With his complaining heart and his life in upheaval, why should he buck the system? Waste precious days and wind up antagonizing everyone. Except that he had to. Gunderson was dangerous, a fool or a madman or simply incompetent. His colleagues would have to see that.

"I've come too far to stop, Hen," said Barney. "The evidence against him is too damning. What kind of man calls himself a doctor and tolerates repeated malpractice?"

"Oh God," Henderson groaned. "That word."

"Let's say I'll think about it carefully," Barney tried to soothe him. "I'd never do anything to jeopardize the New Grace contract. That I promise. I'm getting out of here tomorrow. I told Foley I'd rest a few days at home and then Lindsay and I are going to spend a weekend in Bucks County." He had booked a room overlooking the river at the Black Bass Inn, not far from the town where Mama remembered Margaret grew up. Barney was exhausted. "I'll think about it, Hen. Shove this stuff in the drawer for now. So, my friend, who gets to write up the osteomyelitis in a closed fracture?"

"Well, nobody I know in orthopedics can even spell," said Henderson. "You're the writer, kid."

*N*ighttime was dark and hushed, every sound exaggerated. Barney had dozed too much during the day. Now he lay awake hearing the occasional car pass in the melting snow below. Coughs echoed. A tray dropped. Someone cursed. He should have taken the sleeping pill Foley ordered. Defying doctor's orders was a patient's way of feeling less helpless, less controlled. Knowing patient psychology apparently was no insurance against succumbing to it, Barney realized. The nurse had almost gone bananas when he refused his sleeping pill, till the wise old superior came in and drummed him out of the corps of obedient patients for whom call lights would be instantly answered and alcohol massages generously given. It was true about hospital nighttime. You lay awake all night monitoring your aches and listening to the asthmatic murmurs of your unfaithful heart. Worrying about probate and estate taxes. Worrying that Reeney's extravagance would exhaust his estate before Ivy League college tuition was due, and about all the psychoanalyst's bills it would take to patch Candy's bruised psyche. Maybe that's why little girls needed horses. Maybe a horse was a kind of prophylactic therapy for potential Electra conflicts. Like fluoride for cavities. Barney did not believe in psychoanalysis. But everyone else did. Debra spent hours discussing him with her analyst, at one dollar a minute. "I'm not sure I'm worth it," Barney had pointed out, edgy yet fascinated at this constant secondhand scrutiny. "My analyst says of course you have heart problems," Debra reported. "Your heart is overworked trying to love so many women at one time." Hooked up to his heart's monitor, feeling a fragile victim in the jaws of fate, Barney was not amused by such simplistic observations. Freed from the monitor he felt stronger already.

Funny, even Lindsay believed in psychotherapy. Between Debra's therapist and Lindsay's, Barney was surely one of the most analyzed-by-proxy guys in town. Lindsay was one of the few Wasps Barney knew with a shrink. Liberation does weird things to women, he thought. Makes them slightly Jewish. Barney fell asleep pondering this extraordinary alchemy.

The door opened. He jerked awake. The door closed. The nurse tiptoed towards him.

"Put this under your tongue, Dr. Kincaid."

"It's not morning already."

"Hmmm. Hmmm. Hmmm." She swayed against the bed. Barney got a whiff of her powerful perfume.

"Nurse. That is not a thermometer. This is a finger." Barney was fully awake now. Good God. It was Debra.

"Be quiet, Dr. Kincaid. You have a fever. You're very hot. I'm the night nurse. Miss Lovelace."

Barney laughed. And groaned. "Debra, you nut, where

did you get that uniform?" She was wearing the shortest nurse's uniform he'd ever seen. And somehow she'd managed to walk through the corridors with lacy white garters and stockings and lots of bare skin in between without inciting a riot. He groaned again wondering how he was going to get her out of here.

"Oh, the patient is taking a turn for the worse. His pulse is racing. Oh he is hot and flushed all over." She stroked his chest and arms. "Oh poor patient. Nurse Lovelace doesn't need a thermometer to know this is a dangerous fever. It could be tropical in nature. And there is only one cure. I'll have to ask you to stop pulling on the covers, Dr. Kincaid." She tugged the bedsheet out of his hand and folded them down.

"Debra, you've got to get out of here."

"This could hurt a little, Dr. Kincaid. Try to be brave. I'm just going to cool you off with my mouth. Oh look at this. A dangerous swelling between your legs. No wonder you're so hot. . . ."

Her makeup was incredible. She was so wonderfully sleazy, pouting and posing, teasing, creating a tempo and frenzy for an electric explosion. Boy, she sure knew how to get to him. "You're a slut, Miss Lovelace," he whispered, when he could speak again.

"Yes. I'm a slut," she said, licking her lips. "Yum. Yum."

Barney lay there willing his heart to calm down again, slowing his pulse, mind over matter. "You've got to get out of here, darling, without being seen. It's the garter belt that's obscene. Leave it here, Debra. Please darling. Don't you have a coat. Fast, sweetheart. It's getting light outside."

She giggled. He could smell her musky scent long after she'd tripped down the hall.

"*H*ave I told you about Margaret, our maid Margaret when I was growing up?"

Lindsay looked up from her manuscript, round owl-eye spectacles sliding down that wonderfully abbreviated nose. She'd been miles away, scratching emphatically in the margins of her manuscript, carrying on a muttered dialogue with her absent author. What is it now? her face seemed to say.

Lindsay had been delighted to escape with Barney to Bucks County this first slow, recuperative weekend. It had taken much juggling of children and visitation rights, trade-offs with the inflexible jock orthopedic man, her ex, and the reminder that there would be manuscripts to read and a difficult nutrition book to finish editing. But Barney had homework too and a pile of new novels to choose from. It was a clear, crisp, sunny winter day, perfect for a drive. The roads were clean except for a few icy patches. With luck and a few leads from Mama he hoped he could find Margaret.

Once past the stinks of industrial New Jersey, Barney relaxed. The conversation had an easy intimacy that delighted him. In the corner of his eye Lindsay was a fuzzy peach glow, the peach of her sweater. Lindsay, cheerful and wise, full of the power of positive thinking reinforced by a Friday session with her therapist. "Be the Barney you like best," she was saying. "Indulge Candy if it makes you feel better. But let the guilt feeling go. She has more of your attention now than before you left Reeney and the quality of your time together is infinitely better."

She put her hand on top of his resting on the handbrake and squeezed. Barney felt too good to tell her the guilt came with the chromosomes. He decided to get her interpretation on the Gunderson uproar. "Their threats just make me more determined," said Barney. "And I'm sure when the chief gets back from vacation, he'll back me up."

"Perhaps you could let it go for the moment and wait till the chief returns," Lindsay said, stretching her long legs and arching her neck. "Could we stop for a stretch . . . not coffee . . . just a stretch."

He pulled onto the shoulder. She unfolded a bit clumsily and stood beside the car, stomping her boots in the snow, doing an abbreviated runners' warm-up in her fuzzy shetland turtleneck. She ducked inside again, cheeks glowing. "Wow. Is it cold."

Barney sat there. "I know Hal Wechsler will back me up. He's chief of medicine, tough, good, my kind. I can't let up now, Lindsay. A little boy died, eight years old, Lindsay, and a woman a few years younger than your own mother. And a man with five kids. Because Gunderson practices obsolete medicine."

"You said that committee review cleared him."

"That was sloppiness. Or stupidity. Or chickenhearted-ness at worst," said Barney, surprised she didn't see there was really no choice.

"I love the kind of doctor you are," she said, taking his hand and holding it to her icy cheek. "I'm just thinking you need to avoid collecting enemies, especially when you're going after the New Grace Hospital contract. Talk spreads. If you're right about Gunderson, it's a disaster for Goodman Memorial and if you're wrong, it's a scandal for Goodman and a disaster for you. Can't you just fix it so someone in charge has to approve all his orders? That way he can't make mistakes."

Barney was annoyed. She was right about the danger of seeming to be a troublemaker. But she was wrong. He couldn't drop it. He was surprised to find that pressed, her idealism—the idealism he had admired as if it defined her—quickly faded. How could she have misled him so? And now next morning he was annoyed she wouldn't taste blueberry waffles, insisting on yoghurt and tea. She was incurably rigid. Weekends were not a time for self-denial. She'd leaped out of bed so fast there'd been no chance for morning love. Barney wanted to talk. Barney wanted to touch. He felt her forced smile and eagerness to get back to her quack nutritionist. As always her indifference excited him.

He had an image of grabbing her foot and having her step on his hand with a shiny black spike heel. He thought about throwing back her skirt, ripping her panties and burying his head between her legs.

"Not now, Barney," she said. Christ, could she read his mind? "We said we'd work till afternoon and then go for a walk."

"You just go on reading, darling, while I make love to you. Can you do that, Lindsay love? Can you do that?" Barney knew damn well, Lindsay could do that. There were times he felt she responded only by making a conscious decision to respond and she only decided to respond as frequently as she did because her analyst said she must not ignore the message of her clitoris. Lindsay was only tentatively, belatedly, getting acquainted with her sweet neglected little clitoris. She was as respectful and cautious as she would be toying with dynamite. Barney's mouth was full of cotton. Lindsay's nice proper little girl panties.

"Cotton is healthier," she defended them. Once she had come to bed in lacy, black, bikini, baby-doll pajamas, but he noticed how strangely she moved in nylon—trying bravely, he guessed, not to create a hotbed for bacteria to multiply overnight.

"That hurts, Barney," she said. She wiggled away from his tongue, tugging at the hand that was pulling her cotton crotch to one side. His insistence, her resistance . . . it was a game that excited both of them, Barney believed. "Oh damn." She sighed. "All right, Barney. If you can't wait. Here, stop . . . one minute, stop. I'll take them off."

"No. No, Lindsay. Let me." Lindsay turned her head away, raising her ass with the ease of an Olympic acrobat. Gentle, humbly, worshipfully, Barney rolled her pristine cotton panties over the sharp boney edge of her pelvis. What a stubborn cunt she could be. He loved it. She was actually resting the manuscript on his head while he sucked her pussy. She sat there, long muscled thighs tapering to boney little-boy knees, casually open for his mouth. Even the triangle of her thighs was insolent, flaunting the bland Ivory scent of her pussy. Barney's chin scraped on the rough tweed of her armchair. He tugged her ass forward, feeling her heat. Despite herself, she was open and wet. Lindsay didn't like Barney to look at her pussy. "You make me feel like anatomy," she complained. Behind her manuscript she could pretend he was not here at all. Indeed, she was humming.

Barney marveled again at the exquisite flower between Lindsay's legs. Between those runner-squash-player-twenty-laps-a-day legs was a sweet puckered pink bud, lips like the crumpled petals of an iris—pale pink, bright pink now. Tongue she would tolerate. A flicking, darting tongue was best. Nothing too forceful. Nothing direct. Fingers drove her crazy. Her clitoris was hidden. Very unassuming. Like her nose. Nomadic too. It seemed to move around a lot.

"Barney. Barney, I can't concentrate when you do that."

Barney ignored her, making love to her iris mouth.

"All right, Barney." She dropped the manuscript, slid toward him slightly, pulled her feet up tight and presented her cunt to him open and free of musty old tweed. Barney felt triumphant. He rubbed his face in her, his nose, his tongue. She moaned, just a little. Barney pulled her to the floor, tugged her free of her T-shirt, touched the high hard little breasts with hot red aureoles, nipples like doorbells. She would not let him kiss her uptown mouth when his lips were salty from her downtown mouth. She was trying to scramble away.

"Come to bed, Barney."

She clutched the corner of the four-poster, trying to climb into bed and pull him up with her.

"No. I want you down here, Lindsay."

He felt her struggle. Lindsay was strong. It was like

fighting a young boy. He knew the floor was too dirty for Lindsay. The germs of all the feet that had paced these floors would haunt her. She longed to be capable of sexual spontaneity, but it was an effort. Baxter's Tuesday and Saturday morning predictability had created grinding boredom in her marriage, she had confided. Now she was torn. Barney could see it, reading the struggle on her flushed pretty face. "Sit on me, Lindsay," he said. It was a compromise, the floor instead of the bed, her favorite position, let Barney roll in the dust and the germs. She weighed her response. Then she closed her eyes and crouched over him—offering her pussy. That was Lindsay. Would never just slide down on his cock—never just put it inside all on her own. Wanted to be entered. Hot as she was at that moment, she was still waiting politely to be entered . . . unreformable embryo feminist. Still waiting for the cock to force its way home. Riding him, knees pressed close, her face hidden next to his ear, rubbing her clitoris, bone against bone, her favorite way of reaching that crest. That she would let herself come at all was a real triumph, worthy of a joint Nobel Prize in science to her shrink and to Barney. All those years waiting for some man to find the right button—hiding the button.

"Let me see you, Lindsay." He lifted her up, pushed her back on his cock, her face red and glistening, her chest in fiery red patches, eyes closed, cheeks streaked with tears. She covered her eyes with the back of her hand like a child. Barney could feel his cock getting harder. He had all of her mons and the front ridge of her pubic bone in the palm of his hand pressing gently.

"Too much, Barney," she moaned. She started bouncing on him, a crazy rhythm, leading him on, and on, bouncing and feinting like the tough, punch-crazy fighter she was, till she got him locked in her hug again, poised for her shuddering come.

"Aha," he cried. And let himself go. When Barney opened his eyes Lindsay was lying collapsed between his legs waiting for him to bring her a wet washcloth. He patted her stickiness with the cooling cloth. She grabbed the cloth and scrambled to the bathroom.

"I love you, Barney . . ."

"I hear a but."

"But . . . you do demand attention. I suppose it's the only-child dynamic." She sighed. "You want it when you want it and when you don't want it—then you need space. I understand that, I need space myself. Motherhood is a great cure for the only-child syndrome," she said ruefully. She stood there in her shrunken T-shirt, a lovely expanse of nakedness. "I never thought I'd come to be so comfortable in my body," she said. "I am getting better, aren't I?"

"Hmmm . . ." He kissed her, as she surrendered the bathroom. Barney showered and shaved, seeing himself in the mirror for the first time since the hospital. Thinner, he thought. Or did he imagine it? The bones of his face seemed sharper. He looked like a thug. It was a good face for the times he thought. Longer hair helped. In high school he had always looked skinned, like a Marine recruit. The curls that had once made him crazy with embarrassment softened everything. Mama had loved his curls. When he was a baby people on the street often took him for a girl. "You don't want him to be a sissy," Margaret had scolded his mother.

"Gibbsville, or Gibbstown, was where Margaret's people lived," Mama seemed to remember.

Lindsay had pulled on a fluffy, blue shetland sweater. His. She was poking the fire, getting a very respectable blaze out of last night's half-charred logs. She had a way with fires that put him to shame. From the back she could have been a boy, with her close-shorn haircut. The heart-shaped ass was the only giveaway.

"I'm going for a ride, darling," said Barney. "Shall I ask them to send up some tea?"

"My space respects your space," said Lindsay. "You're such a thoughtful only child, darling. Ask if they have real tea."

*B*arney was pleased to see how so many of these small Pennsylvania towns seemed frozen in time. Except for the rude invasion of the obligatory Golden Arches and the Pizza Huts rimming tacky shopping centers on the outskirts, Gibbstown seemed to have existed unchanged for thirty years. What kind of people are content to live and die in such forlorn hamlets? What did they do? They bowled and saw first-run movies. There was a drive-in closed for the winter and VFW hall. Yes, it was Gibbstown. He remembered it now from the postmark on the birthday cards Margaret sent after she'd been fired by Mama when she confessed that her brother was in a TB sanitarium. Mama, convinced without real medical evidence, that it was Margaret who'd exposed her Barney to TB, didn't wait for blood tests or X-rays, wasn't calmed down by the fact that the spot in his lung was healed, calcified. Margaret was fired. Gone one day when Barney came home from school. He'd found her farewell note that night tucked into a nudist magazine under his pillow. Margaret knew most of his secrets and all of his hiding places, even though he kept moving the pinups—into the cedar chest, between the mattress and the spring, inside a footlocker, camouflaged with his baseball-card collection. Mama had threatened to go through Barney's room with a giant vacuum. She wanted all the collections weeded out, discarded, the comics and children's books given away. Dad said a boy's room should be a sanctuary. Only Margaret was permitted in to vacuum and change the sheets. That was one of Mama's few defeats. She pretended to be nice about it, but you just knew she seethed at the outrageousness of being overruled. "Of course, you're right, Joseph," she said, "a boy of twelve is almost a man, a man is entitled to privacy."

Barney's mother was not a martyr. She was very proud of that. "I will not be the typical Jewish mother," she would announce. "I will not make sacrifices, you can bet on that. I want an emerald-cut diamond, but if it takes from my son's college savings, so you can cut down a carat or two." Dirt was Public Enemy Number One. You could perform surgery on her kitchen floor. Anything Barney did seemed to create an unforgivable mess. Sex was probably the ultimate mess, Barney had decided one night trying to scrub some come off the blanket. Usually he was so careful. Barney was sure she'd not speak to Dad for a week if Dad got any come on the sheet. Dad wouldn't dare. She wouldn't want it anywhere near her, either. Maybe she would make him put it in a Mason jar. She put everything in Mason jars. Labeled. Dated. She put blotters under the milk bottles in the icebox to soak up the condensation. Given such strict obedience training, Barney had secretly lost respect for Reeney throughout eighteen years of marriage because she did not know enough to keep things in Mason jars. Crackers got stale. Flour got infested with weevils. Ants got into the sugar. "If flour was supposed to go in a jar, they wouldn't sell it in bags," Reeney said.

If you loved me, you'd keep your staples in jars, Barney thought. But he didn't say it. He didn't want to seem as anal compulsive as it would probably sound. Barney could live reasonably at ease in Reeney's disorder. Still, he would have preferred a floor where a man could perform surgery.

There were half a dozen teenagers stamping in the cold at the Gibbstown bus stop. Two boys poked each other and doubled over with laughter. Sheehan. There were five listings for Sheehan in the directory. Wendell Sheehan. Margaret's brother. He had been a boxer in the Navy. He'd given Barney a Japanese bullet. Barney had found it when he moved out of Ninety-third Street, tucked into an old stud box with an ROTC medal and Grandpa's fake ruby cufflinks and a silver locket he'd bought for Barbara Bloome, his high school steady. She'd thrown it back at him for taking

someone else to a Broadway matinee. Now there was a
memory . . . an image that still made him hot—humping
Barbie Bloome in the elevator. Suddenly Barney was not
sure he wanted to make the phone call. Perhaps Margaret
had forgotten that part of her life. She'd been strange. He
realized that years later. As a child he never expected
consistency from an adult. In her room at night she was
teasing and difficult. Downstairs she was his ally against . . .
them. Everyone. A buffer against his parents' smothering,
from the teasing of his nosy relatives and the bullies down
the block. Sometimes she would get her boyfriend, Garland,
to take Barney along to a movie. He used to wonder if she let
Garland go all the way. As a kid he tried to imagine how it
would work. Garland was a misshapen monster—thick
barrel chest, short legs, thick neck. Would his cock go with
his legs or his neck? Barney worried a lot in those days about
whether things were going to fit. Life must be hell for a
woman. All those tiny holes. All those big things going in
and out. Baby's heads, giant cocks. He worried that no one
else he knew was quite as obsessed about sex, and hoped
there was a cure.

Barney sat down at a counter in the News Shop. The
homemade soup had a lot of turnips and potatoes and flecks
of something, celery seed, maybe, proving once again that
"homemade" only meant it wasn't Campbell's. An astonishingly beautiful young girl was gobbling something
from a cellophane pack. She had a baby riding in the canvas
sling tied around her torso. Barney tried to imagine what
would become of that baby growing up in Gibbstown. It was
dirty and happy, gurgling and sucking on a salty chip.
Babies used to be so fragile. They napped all day and were
protected from drafts. Everything they touched was ster-
ilized and disinfected. They were wrapped in zip-up wool
buntings and sat outside in the buggy on the porch to air.
Even Reeney, modern mother that she was, had treated the
infant Candy like fine china.

Barney had been a disappointing baby, or so his mother
had once confided. "I wanted a cuddly little doll like my

cousin Molly's baby and look what I got," she said. "A stiff, crying boy. So independent. I picked you up and you always pulled away."

"It's an exaggeration, Ruth," said Dad. "Once he pulled away—" He shook his head. "What a memory this woman has. She can give you a list of every disappointment, every mistake you ever made, every insult."

"Joseph," Mama often used to taunt, "for a year and a half I was a Queen in Woodmere till the bankruptcy came. And we had to move back to Brooklyn like thieves in the night."

Barney would watch the anger flash across his father's face. Then quickly it was hidden behind Jimmy Cannon and the *New York Post*. Barney had always thought of himself as that beautiful, curly, blond baby, cuddly and adored, every adventure captured in Mama's photo album. Why would an infant pull away? Barney tried to remember. Everything he remembered came from home movies and the sepia photos fading in the big leather-bound album. Barney's birth certificate: Baby Cohen. That was before Dad went to court and became officially Kincaid. Baby? "We couldn't agree about your name. Daddy wanted to name you for his father. I wanted a son named for my brother who died, Michael."

It was one of Joseph Cohen Kincaid's few victories. The second son would be Michael, they agreed, but there was no second son. Often Barney heard his mother confiding how she had longed for another child, a sweet little girl, "but there was never enough money. We gave up all our dreams so Barney could be a doctor," she said. Barney's eyes brimmed with tears the first time he heard that. All that sacrifice . . . he felt touched and loved till one day he heard her mouth that theme and suddenly he went into a rage. How dare they? What a terrible burden. How much would he pay for that sacrifice? He vowed he would never hang burdens like that on Candy.

Lindsay in therapy, scratching deep for memories of her childhood, begged Barney to share memories too. He studied the sepia photographs again, remembering, dis-remembering. He would dredge up some loving, warm, childhood moment and recite it for Lindsay, and even as he spoke the terror would come lashing back. And he'd find himself wallowing in a psychic swamp. No way could he ever obliterate memory of the morning he'd awakened to find his room full of balloons and strings of lollypops and paper flowers and stuffed animals. There was a green mouse with pink ears and a rubber duck that was to share his bathtub for years. At first he was probably startled, three years old, perhaps even scared, all that stuff crowding in. But Mama came in laughing like sunshine. She had stuck a birthday candle in the middle of a peach—another trick to get him to eat fruit. She'd gotten her hair cut the day before and she looked so different. She had decided to make Barney's curls more like her own. And she rolled his hair around her finger and tied it with bows. There was company for brunch—aunts and uncles, neighbors, some kids wrecking toys. Mama gave him a bubble bath and lifted him in her arms and they stood in front of the mirror. "We're twins," she cried, laughing and kissing him. Then she tied a little blue ribbon around his cock and sent him running out into the garden.

He was so happy.

He was laughing and dancing and whirling around. Everyone was laughing.

Dad shouted. Mama started to cry. Dad shook her. And grabbed Barney. And she tried to get Barney away from him. Barney was screaming. Well, what the hell. All kinds have some little trauma. So Barney grew up with a serious aversion to little boys who look like Shirley Temple. No loss. It's good to know where your neurosis originates.

Does he still walk around with a blue silk ribbon on his dick?

Only on his birthdays. Ha. Just kidding.

*T*here was something musty and authentic about dime stores in small towns. They looked time-locked with the same housedresses and thread and haircombs and cotton socks they'd been selling since Depression days. The Gibbstown five and dime had mittens in the window and ski caps and Christmas tree ornaments, though it was early February. There was a mannequin that had to be World War I vintage wearing a flannel nightshirt. Inside there was Halloween candy, reduced to half price. As a child Barney had been forbidden to eat such garbage, of course. Halloween night, Mama would dump Barney's trick-or-treat sacks out on the kitchen table, throwing away apples (someone could hide a needle or razor blade inside), and confiscating dime-store candy—anything unwrapped, even chocolates. Candy bars she didn't recognize went too. The famous name brands she hid, doling them out one at a time for Saturday matinees at the movies. Basically about the only item she really approved was money. Sneaking the forbidden was an instant outlet for rebellion. Once he hid behind the bushes making himself sick with that sweet orange and brown and yellow stuff, sugar in the shape of pumpkins, candy corn, chocolate babies. Mama was right. It was awful. He felt sorry for kids with mothers who didn't seem to mind them eating junk. But there were too many restrictions. "It's like living with the Gestapo," he'd screamed in a tantrum.

"She can't help loving you so much," Dad had said. "She only wants perfection. There's no way she can accept anything less." It was years before Barney could bite into an apple without thinking, just for a flash, about hidden needles and razor blades.

This was a wonderful dime store. "Sundries and Notions" was lettered on the window. There were still old-fashioned change pipes overhead and a pressed-tin ceiling. The counter had lotions and perfumes no one he knew used anymore. Evening in Paris. Glycerine and rosewater. Barney's heart skipped. He recognized that jar: the black label with calla lilies and a parrot. Margaret's night cream. He unscrewed the lid. That smell. Imagine, after all these years, the scent could still make his cock hard.

"Excuse me, sir, but you can't open packages unless you're buying. You'll have to pay for that. I'm sorry." The old lady smiled, rather ruefully. "Silly. The health department, you know."

Barney gave her a dollar and a handful of pennies. He shoved the package into his pocket feeling the same sense of erotic promise he felt when he picked up *Penthouse* and a little of the same embarrassment he remembered while wandering through a sex shop on Second Avenue.

A tinny old voice answered the phone. "You be looking for my son-in-law Wendell off with my daughter to Reading this morning. Well, of course I know Wendell's sister, Margaret, married to one of the Jamieson boys. You take the old highway back side of town, turn right at the Sunoco . . . three miles to a fork. Take the left."

Barney felt strangely nervous. No one he knew would stop by without phoning first. Marvin had gone to his high school's twentieth reunion and said it was depressing—to see how badly his friends had aged. "But it was warm and loving, too," said Marvin. "Everyone happy to see everyone else. A certain innocence preserved." Surely he'd gone more than three miles down this road.

"Antiques" the sign said. He could ask the way and maybe find a small gift for Lindsay. Barney was not always comfortable in antique stores. Clutter confused him. Lack of clutter usually meant highway robbery. But in between junk and serious antiques was a chance to explore the handtools of the past and quaint treasures mixed with the kind of Early American furniture he had always wanted to own. Reeney had found the look "too primitive."

There was a woman at a workbench out back. She

turned with a radiant smile. "Want to look a bit?" she asked. She was small and wore rolled-up jeans.

"I was thinking maybe a locket or a small pin." He wanted to say "inexpensive" but that was a hard word to say. "Something old but it doesn't need to be . . . important."

The woman had thin gold rings on every finger. "Does your friend like garnets?" She set a tray on the counter. "This isn't gold but it's old and it looks quite precious with the tiny seed pearls."

The pin had a familiar look. Some woman in his life, he closed his eyes for a second straining to make the connection . . . someone had worn earrings like this. But Lindsay was tall and sturdy. The pin was so delicate.

"And the blue thing on the chain?" he asked.

"Enamel and eighteen-carat gold. Two hundred sixty-five dollars." She bit her lip. "Ridiculous price but there's a real demand for enamel."

"The garnet and seed pearls then," he said. "It's old-fashioned," he said.

"She'll love it," the woman crooned, pleased at the speed of his decision. She knew Margaret Jamieson too, or at least, her pies. "Yes, she makes wonderful pies. My husband is a fool for her shoofly pie," she said. "But I recommend the apple."

*F*irst came the sign, brushed free of snow. "Pies," it read, "Homemade Bread. Magical Muffins." Then the house, roof piled high with snow, the front door blocked by a giant drift, plastic sheeting stretched across the windows. Wouldn't it be wonderful if someone invented a solar-gathering Saran Wrap, thought Barney. What he really wanted to see was a staple gun that would make perfect sutures, programmed to dissolve without leaving a scar. He'd spent months tinkering with that concept. He tapped at the door. "What is a magical muffin?" he asked, holding his breath, feeling foolish and strangely eager. She turned. Barney was surprised to see the same face, puffier and lined, of course. Her hair was dark, darker than he remembered, full of plastic curlers. The mouth thin, the same slash of lipstick. She turned off the sound on the television.

"The magic is something is hidden inside. The bran has got raisins and candied pineapple and the corn has bits of bacon and green pepper. My kids think it's magic. But most folks come for the pies. That's what counts. I got sour cherry left and apple." She had a thin blue vein in a jagged line across one temple. And the dark hollowed eyes he remembered. She felt him staring.

"Margaret. It's Barney."

"Oh good gosh. I don't believe it." She studied him for a moment and then threw open her arms.

How tiny she was, wiry and strong. Memories came flooding back. He saw himself, Barney the beanpole. Barney the sadsack. Nearsighted and overprotected after six months in bed with mononucleosis. He stuttered (briefly, thank God) and never learned to hit the ball. Voracious devourer of autobiographies first, and then the classics. Alone in his room. The great masturbator. The phantom lover in Margaret's bedroom. He had long ago learned to suppress all those images of his scrawny awkward self. "How tiny you are, Margaret. I can see the top of your head."

She touched the rollers in her hair. "Oh what must I look like?" She ran out of the room. He heard doors slamming, drawers banging. He followed. She was rummaging on the floor of her closet, tossing shoes into the room. She turned, startled to see him standing there.

"Well, now I know it's Barney." She giggled.

He looked around half expecting to see the blue chenille bathrobe, to smell that scent—the almonds and vanilla. She stepped into backless bedroom slippers, pulled the curlers out and smoothed spitcurls in each corner of her forehead. He could see the gray at the roots.

"I was just wondering if I would have recognized you. On the street, passing, I mean. It's twenty-five years at least. You surely did grow up a good-looking man."

"Thirty years," he said. "But you haven't changed at all." The lie just came flowing out. And suddenly he wasn't sure what he wanted.

"Ma." The kitchen door slammed. Margaret slipped by him. There was a little girl standing at the open icebox, a cupcake stuffed into her face, a tangle of shoulder-length hair. "Milk, ma."

"Gena. Say hello to Barney Kincaid. Gena is my youngest. A wild one. A real tomboy. Oh, Gena, is that chocolate on your chin, or blood?"

"I hope it's blood," said Gena. "Cause it isn't mine, it's the kid I almost killed for sassing me."

"Say hello to Mr. Kincaid, Gena. I used to take care of him when he was younger even than you. Yes. I bet it's Dr. Kincaid. Of course. Doctor. I should have known your ma would get her way. Here, Gena. Here's a sack of muffins for the gang. Wear your leggings, Gena. Gena." The little girl was a flash of color careening out the door. "Your ma should have been president. She was a dynamo," said Margaret, setting coffee on to warm. "Your ma coulda won the war three years faster than President Roosevelt she'd a been president."

"But I always wanted to be a doctor," said Barney. "That was Dad's dream, too. Mama just wanted me to make money . . . to be better than everyone else's son. Perfection," he grinned. "That's all."

"She used to introduce you as my son the doctor when you were six years old," said Margaret. "You wanted to be a writer. You wrote a novel when you were ten. I remember it. About a haunted house."

"And Dad has it bound in a red leather cover. I remember that."

"Well, yes, that's true. Oops. The coffee is boiling. I must like boiled coffee. I do that a lot. It's real good to see you, Barney. You must be married. And kids . . . you must have kids too. Do you remember how you and me used to bake cookies together?"

"Yes. I remember. Toll House cookies. I have a fabulous daughter, Candy . . . Candace. She's twelve. And my wife and I are separated."

"Oh dear. That must be awful. Divorce is tough . . . for everyone actually. Boy, I bet your ma will be giving you a hard time about now."

"She's not one to suffer in silence," said Barney. "But tell me about you. The famous pie maker."

"Well, my husband Andy is a mason. I got two married daughters. This one you just met was an afterthought. A real tomboy. Spoiled like you were . . . except she's tough."

"I was a freak," said Barney.

"Don't say that. You were sickly, not as fragile as your ma made out. And all those women fussing over you—your ma. Your Aunt Eva favoring you over her own boy. And your Aunt Cristal. She was lonely too, no kids of her own . . . always hanging around."

"We acted out Broadway shows together. And we even wrote one." The lyrics came tumbling into his head. "I could have been Stephen Sondheim."

"Dr. Kildare is not half bad," she said.

"Do you still use the same beauty cream, Margaret?"

"What cream is that?"

"The cream on your face at night."

"Oh." She flushed. "Barney. I just use whatever I get from the Avon lady. My thousands of fans love me anyway."

"You remember?"

She stared at her hands. There was an angry burn across one wrist. "I think we shouldn't talk about that . . . one hundred years ago, for goodness' sake."

"I need to know what that was about. I never could tell what you were thinking, Margaret. I realize it's long ago, we're two different people. But I have a feeling the answer is important."

"Maybe it was just a kid copping a feel."

"Is that what it was?" Barney imagined the room filling with the scent of almonds and vanilla. "Still, for me it was endlessly thrilling. Exciting. Fiercely exciting."

She got up and stood with her back to him, fussing with her baked goods. "For me too, Barney. I pretended you were my grown-up lover . . . and sometimes that you would grow up overnight and get me out of there. I was always terrified we'd get caught."

"But it was so innocent."

"It's okay to love a twelve-year-old boy but it's a pretty serious sin to lead him astray," she said. "Hey, you can stay for dinner and meet my Andy."

Barney shook his head. "I have a friend waiting for me at the Black Bass Inn. This is supposed to be a romantic weekend but she had homework and I wanted to find you."

"Well, you'll take one of my pies anyway. Cherry was your favorite. You know, I still have that pencil box you made for me with the seashells pasted on. You sure did turn out to be a great-looking man. Dr. Kildare. Finally got some flesh on those bones. Hey, you're not crying."

She handed him a paper towel and hugged him. He pressed his face into her breasts. Then he stood up and kissed her cheek, the skin soft, fragile, loose as old silk. He touched her cheek. "That Avon stuff really works, Margaret. When you left, Margaret, you just disappeared. I was sorry you didn't say goodbye."

"That was your ma, kid. She said it was better for you that way. I felt like a leper passing along TB to you, if I did. I figured I did. She said that was the only explanation. Some tough lady, that woman. Looks so sweet and tiny and cute. A killer. Squeezed all the juice out of your dad. But boy, she met her match in you, I bet."

For a moment Barney felt dizzy. The cortisone maybe. Or the stretch back to the present, he imagined. He reached into his pocket and pulled out the garnet brooch wrapped in tissue. "I brought you a little gift," he said.

"Oh my." She tore away the paper. "Oh my. It's so beautiful. The little pearls. And rubies."

"Garnets."

"It's a real antique, isn't it? Oh, Barney. I love it." She pinned it at her neck. "I have some earrings that almost match. You must have remembered."

Driving home he uncovered the jar of night cream and let the air fill with her scent. Weighing everything, Barney would have to say he'd survived a happy childhood. Of course if you feel like a freak most of the time, it's not easy to be convinced you're really a prince.

*O*nly a real fanatic would be jogging along the highway on a wintry day in this subarctic cold. Barney swerved wide just to play it safe. Good God. It was Lindsay looking like the Michelin man in her yellow down jacket.

"I got a little nervous when you didn't come back," she said. "So I'm running it off." She scarcely huffed at all.

"I've just had a truly extraordinary experience. I must tell you, darling. Hop in."

"I want to do another mile. You could join me."

"An icy road in ten-degree weather is not the moment for me to start jogging, darling. I promise I'll get into condition and run with you this spring."

Lindsay was chastened. "Darling, I forgot your poor heart. Well, I've come this far. I'm not stopping now." She loped off.

Even before his attack Lindsay had been determined to get Barney running. Once Barney had been a runner. As a born athlete, Lindsay couldn't understand how a man could run for six months, win a prize, and then simply give it up, quit, no regrets. The truth was Barney had wanted a high school letter sweater. In the fall of his junior year at Kingsbridge High, he had realized that girls went for guys with letter sweaters. He was not exactly well coordinated. At least he suspected that was his curse. He was too light for football—thank God, that spared him from certain death. He was too clumsy for serious basketball, a weak swimmer, and he was damned if he would risk precious limbs or sanity at boxing or wrestling. That left track. The 100-yard dash was out of the question, but, he figured with training and conditioning, practice, lots of protein . . . the power of positive thinking . . . maybe he could compete in distance running. What a glorious year that had been. Mama was beside herself with pride and anguish. "My son the runner." Till she saw him getting thinner and thinner. Whippet-sleek. "Barney, you're like a stick. You're doing yourself permanent damage. Hamburger for breakfast. Such craziness. A pound of carrots every afternoon."

She was right about the carrots. He woke up one morning with bright orange palms and it took the puzzled pediatrician several days to figure out it was carotene poisoning—too much vitamin A. Barney went into the annals of medicine. He also led the Knightsbridge track team to victory in boroughwide competition. He got his letter, bought a purple cardigan to sew it on. Tossed his running shoes into the dark hole of Calcutta in the farthest reaches of his closet. And never ran again. He was correct about teenage girls and their weakness for high school jocks. Girls who'd never noticed his existence before seemed to discover a romantic figure inside the purple cardigan with the big K in relief. He took Jill Massacio to a Saturday matinee of *Oklahoma!* Jill was a cheerleader, a Chiclette—the very elite, not-so-secret society of the most popular girls in school and she only went with BMOC and jocks. Barney was stunned when she led him into the empty physics lab late one afternoon after a dance competition meeting and let him French-kiss her. Her tongue never stopped, darting into his mouth, encircling his tongue, poking into all the corners of his teeth. It was the longest kiss in his life, perhaps the longest kiss in history, meant perhaps to help her pretend she didn't quite notice how she had unhooked her bra and wiggled out of her panties and that he was actually, yes, incredibly, yes, inside her, pumping away, close to explosion, just as she touched the Van de Graff generator, creating a shock that seared through his cock at the very moment he came, and melted his spine.

They stood there fused for what felt like three weeks but might have been three minutes.

That was the first time Barney realized that nice girls did it too. That was the only possible conclusion unless he were going to redefine his meaning of "nice." He wondered whether Jill Massacio was a stickler for details when she went to confession.

*L*indsay understood the letter-sweater fixation, even the motivation. But she couldn't understand a champion athlete retiring at his prime, even when Barney recited "To an Athlete Dying Young."

"By all the rules of gravity and aging, you should be in terrible shape," Lindsay said. "Forty-two-year-old hearts need exercise," she'd warned, even before the pericarditis. She'd bought him everything a man would need to run the goddamn marathon—warm-up suit, satin shorts with a red stripe, headband to keep the sweat out of his eyes, sixty-five-dollar running shoes slightly more colorful than the Italian flag. Sex, the Emergency Room, and Goodman Memorial's senile elevators (he could never tolerate the wait, took the stairs two at a time) were his only exercise, true, but he was lean and hard, trimmer than her ex, Baxter, who ran five miles each morning. Barney's energy on the disco floor was legendary, till now, that is. He'd have to sit down with Foley and get the straight prognosis.

He showered and dressed and sat reading the new Updike, savoring the luxury of solitude. Even in the same room he and Lindsay were able to step into mutual cocoons of privacy, she at her Yoga, her body lithe and elastic, calming down from the run. No other woman he'd ever met had such a healthy respect for privacy. He approved of the way she disappeared into the bathroom, closing the door. He didn't need to see women plucking their eyebrows and blotting out blemishes. He was happiest appreciating the final glow and sheen without sharing the cosmetic gardening women did. And he himself loved to luxuriate in a steamy bubble bath or concentrate on a close shave without fear of invasion. Lindsay would never dream of bursting into the bathroom to pop down on the toilet seat like Debra, chattering cheerfully over the sound of her pee.

Yet inherent in the serenity of their domesticity was an ogre. Boredom. How tame this is, Barney thought, as Lindsay slipped into school-girl loafers. On Reeney that dress would look like three hundred dollars. On Lindsay it looked like she'd forgotten to remove the hanger. Of course, Reeney was a querulous kvetch.

"Why are your beautiful brown eyes so sad tonight?" said Lindsay, snapping the barrette in place.

"Not sad," said Barney. "Just thoughtful. This sweater is too bright for this jacket. I'm going to change to the beige one."

"I never dreamed I would fall in love with a man who would take longer to dress for dinner than me," she mused.

"*N*ow, tell." Lindsay sipped Dubonnet on the rocks. "What made you look for her? She recognized you right away?"

"I don't think she did. Till I said, it's me . . . then she saw it, of course."

"Imagine. Thirty years. What an adventurous thing to do. I'd love to do the same thing. Look up my high school sweetheart. Maybe go to bed with the boy I was engaged to before I met Baxter."

"Lindsay."

"Are you shocked?"

"I didn't think you were interested in sex without emotional content."

"That one had oodles of emotional content at the time." She sighed. "What a prude I was. But it can be dangerous, I think, bursting back into someone's life. By now your maid and you are two whole other people beyond the country girl who cleaned for your folks and the twelve-year-old boy with the dirty magazines."

Lindsay was not too sympathetic to the dirty magazines. She still wasn't sure it was healthy to masturbate, and that a forty-two-year-old pillar of the medical community had a subscription to *Penthouse* embarrassed her.

"Well, of course, it is three decades. But isn't it that much more meaningful to find the feeling still there?" Barney felt a remarkable afternoon was somehow becoming diminished by his inability to explain. He ordered a second martini. He almost never drank more than one. "But the country girl is still there inside her, feisty and strong. And the little boy is still in me. I'm very much in touch with that sex-crazed adolescent."

"Sex-crazed?" Barney watched Lindsay chewing her salad with her incisors, a childish habit that had once delighted him. "Isn't sex-crazed a little strong . . . I mean, for a twelve-year-old?" Her fingers pressed along the edge of the table and she drew back, almost imperceptibly, bracing herself for whatever madness he was about to confide.

"Except for secret fantasies about women in nudist magazines, Margaret was my first great erotic moment."

She held her mouth in a small O like a guppy.

"At night I would go into her room and she would let

me touch her breasts. Nothing else. Just that. It's one of the most erotic memories of my life."

Lindsay's face blurred into a smile. "I guess that is a very sweet memory." She pressed her hand against his cheek. "You were so precocious." She dropped her eyes. "But now you're forty-two."

Barney busied himself scraping the singed almonds from his trout. Monogamy was a sorry subject. Twice Barney had tried to be faithful to Lindsay. Monogamy, they agreed, could be organic, natural, automatic, as it was for her. Or it could be a conscious commitment, as it must be for him. Given true love, monogamy would inevitably follow, Barney reasoned. He longed desperately to master it. He was distrustful of second-class emotions. But till now, monogamy had been like being locked in a dark, airless closet. In panic he would batter his way out. Twice they had separated. Once, forever. That hadn't worked either.

For now Lindsay and her shrink were giving him time to find himself. Lindsay had come to look upon his sexual compulsiveness as a kind of addiction. She would probably have preferred an alcoholic. There was, alas, no Insatiable Womanizers Anonymous, no Fuck Enders. She loved him. She would wait.

What was love? Barney gazed at this strong, clean, striking woman, remembering the mad heat of the first time he'd tugged at those white cotton panties, the feel of her skin, the intensity as he first entered her. Where had that gone? Why didn't it last? Her cool indifference was still a guaranteed turn-on. But nothing else was the same.

*L*indsay liked to be home when Baxter dropped off the children . . . "To guide them back to reality," she said. Barney piled her stuff at the curb for her doorman. He was tired from the drive, itchy to get home, confront the mail and organize a schedule for to-morrow, his first day back in the Emergency Room. A half day, actually. He'd promised Foley to make a gradual reentry.

From his lobby a Lolita in yellow ski goggles threw herself into the elevator, whipping a long scraggly scarf behind her just as the doors closed. "Near suicide," she trilled. Barbie Bloome, thought Barney. Would he ever see a juicy nymphet in an elevator and not remember Barbie with her ice-cream-cone tits, remember rubbing against her while the elevator went up and down and up again? Did teenagers still go in for rubbing? Barney wondered. Or did they just pop the pill and plop into bed without a pang?

Barney unpacked, threw laundry into the hamper and slit open a bill. The goddamn lawyer wanted eight hundred and fifty dollars. That's what it was costing since he and Reeney discovered they couldn't discuss money without a referee. Barney felt a surge of rage. Enough to kill a healthy man, he thought. He stuffed the mail into his briefcase. Maybe it was silly, but he'd tackle the bills within dashing distance of a cardiac rescue team, he decided. Now, where had he put that notice about his high school reunion. Barney pulled the mimeographed invitation out of a drawer. He poured himself a tall glass of orange juice and studied it.

"You can go home again, Kingsbridge Class of '55," it said. "The living know Brooklyn, too." He scanned the alumni list for familiar names. Jill Massacio Hammond. Cheerleader, jock collector, terror of the physics lab. How had she grown? What did the brave Mr. Hammond do? What does become of high school cheerleaders who can't keep their panties on? And Linda Menker, the class pig. That's what the guys called her. Of course, Fifties locker-room talk had about as much credibility as the *National Enquirer*. He never believed half of what the guys said. He hated to think the fall of Linda Menker might be his fault. One summer night at the beach, he'd lured her away from a bunch of guys, wild animals, looking for a gang bang, he guessed, only too falling-over-drunk to pull it off, and then, against his own resolution, had taken her himself. Not coercion exactly but rather heavy persuasion that left both of them angry and Linda in tears. "Help us locate our missing classmates," was printed in a box at the bottom: Linda Menker's name was among the missing.

The phone rang.

"The Devil in Miss Jones is back at Westworld," Debra announced gaily. "Let me take you for your birthday."

"It's not my birthday," said Barney. He looked at his watch. He did have a junk taste for porno movies. It had been a furtive, secret passion—worrying that he would stumble out of *Hot Cookies* or *Dominatrix Without Mercy* and bump into a colleague or even a Bloomingdale's-bound Reeney. Happily Debra shared his taste for sleaze, and she certainly enjoyed "instant replay" of her favorite scenes in his bed an hour after. But tonight he wanted to get to bed early, guard his energy for work tomorrow.

"I didn't get you a present for Valentine's Day, darling," Debra persisted. *"The Devil in Miss Jones.* You loved that movie. Remember, *Screw* magazine, your favorite consumer guide, rated it 'one hundred percent on the Peter Meter.'" She giggled nervously.

"I'm tired, darling. Tomorrow is my first day back at work."

"Let me just come and keep you company then," she said.

"That's sweet, Debra, but—" Barney wasn't sure how to say no without hurting her. "I just got in from the weekend."

"We'll just hug and kiss."

He laughed. "We never just hug and kiss. Darling, I need a little turnaround time."

"Oh. That." She sounded hurt. "Of course. You were with her."

Barney felt his resistance melting. Sex was his favorite tranquilizer and Debra wanted desperately to please him. "If you don't mind missing the movie," he said. "Come." He poured a splash of rum into his orange juice, slipped Donna Summers into the tape deck, and took a shower.

"O f course I remember Margaret," Debra said, sipping her rum. "I remember the first time you told me. How vivid the memory was. The blue chenille bathrobe. Her night cream. Yes. Barney is a naughty little boy." She laughed, clearly relieved and happy to find him available on the one level where she felt totally secure, relaxed against the sofa pillows in baby-doll pajamas, a wisp of see-through and lace.

She disappeared into the bathroom. The tyranny of the diaphragm. He lay in bed with his risen cock, watching it— letting his mind wander in sexual fantasy not to lose the edge of excitement. Debra stood in the bedroom door. Her face was strangely shiny in the moonlight. He could smell it. Margaret's night cream, almonds and vanilla. She had wrapped herself in Barney's blue bathrobe. He started to laugh.

"Are you playing with yourself, little boy?" Her voice was stern and strange. "Don't try to hide your dirty magazines from Margaret, naughty boy." Barney felt his blood pounding. He had the strange sense of being a voyeur of his own seduction. She piled the pillows against the headboard of his bed and sat there, yawned, stretched. "You want to touch, don't you? Dirty little boy."

"Naughty." She slapped his hands away, pulling the robe off her shoulders, taking a breast in each hand. Barney passed his thumb over each nipple, feeling them harden. "I didn't say you could do that." Her voice caught. She spoke through clenched teeth as her own excitement mounted. "Stop that. I'll lock you out of the room." Barney reached between her legs. She gasped and twisted, fought his hand, caught up in the game. "Stop that, you dirty little boy. I don't have any desire to touch your nasty . . . thing." She was cradling his cock in both hands as she said it.

"Please, Margaret," he said. "Pretty please."

She tugged the robe closed.

Barney grabbed the robe and ripped it apart and rubbed his cock in her wetness.

"No."

He covered her mouth with his mouth and thrust into her. Everything merged, blurred, exploded, Debra, Margaret, Barney now, Barney then, the Goddess Diana with her archer's bow, all tied up in pale blue ribbon.

"What are those ridiculous thingamabobs, pray tell, Dr. Kincaid?" Nurse Atkins was his welcome back. Barney had yet to shed his overcoat and already the day was beginning badly. He'd forgotten to pick up his laundry. The only clean shirt in the drawer had a frayed collar. Reeney would have confiscated it for rags months ago. The bathroom fixture was on the fritz and he hadn't had time to find the super to fix it. His socks didn't match and now here was Nurse Atkins. He could not stand Nurse Atkins. She was one of those querulous old biddies who figured they owned the place just because they thought they were smarter than eighty-five percent of the doctors and had been there forever. But Emergency was two nurses short that day, it seemed, and she was the only senior available to rotate, Mallory explained. "You survived," was the Fudgesicle's greeting, though her eyes seemed warmer than the indifference of her tone.

Nurse Atkins had been virtually running Goodman Memorial's emergency service when the Kincaid-Turner team took over the ER. There was never a doctor strong enough, or sure enough, perhaps, to stand up to her. The dullards and weaklings who moonlighted in the Emergency Room had been content to bumble along benignly under her direction. To make a dent in the rigidly antiquated system,

Barney had insisted she be moved out. Now here she was questioning his reforms, his colored clip system, thing-amabobs, indeed.

A patient shuffled into the office carrying a cup of urine. "Is this for you, doctor?" she asked Mike Steffans as he tried to duck out the door.

"I don't drink during office hours," Mike responded, moving the woman down the corridor to the nearest aide.

Mrs. Atkins shook her head. "It seems to me you doctors have gotten sassier than ever since they started showing *MASH* on television."

"These little thingamabobs are foolproof organization, Mrs. Atkins," Barney began. "Things have changed a little since you left us but I know you'll be pleased." No harm in being positive. That was how the behaviorists said you should be with children and it worked in hospitals, where almost everyone reverted to childhood, Barney had found. "The red clip on the chart means the patient is waiting to be seen. Blue means the patient is in X-ray. Yellow means waiting for lab work. If the marker points this way it means 'waiting.' This way stands for 'finished.' This way is the signal for 'stat.' There is no way we can lose a patient with this system. When we first got here there used to be patients sitting out there lost behind a partition sometimes for days."

Steffans picked up a chart. "What have you got for me, Mallory? What about the auto accident?"

"Two bumped heads," Mallory said, chalking the new arrivals into the blackboard lineup and tagging their charts. "No loss of consciousness. They're alert now."

Barney was really proud of his system. He could tell at a glance what was happening, and the staff could tackle the load efficiently without sifting endlessly through charts and lab orders written in chicken scratches. In a year or so there would be a computer that might be more foolproof. Maybe. "See, Mrs. Atkins. Nobody strays or gets stolen anymore."

"What's wrong with the lab this morning?" Mallory grumbled. "I know the blood in Three-G has been drawn because she's got a hole in her arm. But Four-B and six have been waiting forty-five minutes."

"I have a clavicular fracture in a one-year-old," Dr. Djarta said, poking her head in the doorway. "Do we have any kind of clavicle strap for an infant, Anne?" Mallory led her down the hall to the supply closet. Barney stared after them—seeing female asses where he'd only seen uniforms till now. He'd never heard anyone call the Fudgesicle Anne before. He caught himself.

Barney had started the day comparing the ER reports with his own readings of last night's X-rays. "Dr. Liss missed a hairline fracture in this man's finger. Somebody, Mrs. Atkins, will you get the man to come in for a splint."

"Radiology just called that one down, Dr. Kincaid," she said proudly. "The new chief starts *his* day at eight-thirty."

"This is not a contest," Barney growled. But the truth was he did thrive on competition. He could get a headstart on the new radiology chief by getting Turner to check out the X-rays before he went home at four A.M. If Barney were ten years younger, he might even come in at eight. If he were still married, he definitely would.

There was an infant squalling behind the curtain of 2G. Barney examined the baby's mangled little finger, the tip hanging on by a thin shred of flesh. The kid screamed louder. The mother trembled.

"He put his finger in the movie projector," his mother said.

"That's a brave young man," said Barney. "We'll just sew that back on, mother, and he'll be as good as new." Injecting the lidocaine set off a major howl. Even so, there was shouting above the din.

"A drunk with a dog bite," Mrs. Atkins reported. "Won't let anyone near him." She had blood on her skirt and shoes. "I called Security."

"I'm here, Atkins," he said, annoyed. "First you call me."

"He slapped an aide, doctor."

The aide was standing in a corner. The guard had thrown on a yellow slicker to protect his uniform from the flying blood. He had strapped the big burly howler down on the examining table and was calling for reinforcements on his walky-talky. "He split that leather strap, doc," said the guard. A second guard raced up and they wrestled him down again.

"Slam my head," the man shouted. "Slam my head again. I've been in Vietnam. I can take it."

"Big Vietnam vet," said the guard. "Have you seen the American flag flying over this hospital?"

"What's the problem here?" asked Barney.

"How you got me fucking taped up you old mother-fucker." The man dropped his head to the table and stopped struggling. "Sew it up. Sew it up."

"The doctor won't sew if it isn't clean." Mrs. Atkins took his hand. He pulled it away. Blood spattered the walls.

"You're losing a lot of blood," Mrs. Atkins said.

"That doesn't mean a thing. See your friends' faces blown away. A little blood doesn't scare me."

"I'm the doctor," said Barney. "Even more important than sewing the wound in a dog bite is cleaning it out."

The man looked at him. "Hey. I know you. Yeah. This is the doctor. I remember you from before. You're all right, Doc. Right on."

That was easier than Barney had expected. The drunk had just needed to see a doctor's face. He suspected Atkins had somehow exacerbated the man's drunken rage. "Okay, Atkins. We'll inject some anesthetic. Clean it up. And then call me."

Barney went back to the child with its anesthetized finger. Mallory had wrapped the boy in a papoose board to keep him from wiggling. Mike Steffans stepped into the cubicle. "Want to take a break now? I'm going to the cafeteria for lunch."

"I can't take that my first day back," Barney said. "Stick around. I'm treating to pizza. But first, I'm going to sew this fingertip on. Where's Dr. Djarta? Want to watch this, doctor? I have to use very fine sutures because it's such a tiny finger with such delicate skin. We let mother stand by because she is very brave, right Mom?" The mother whim-pered and nodded. The baby sniffled but seemed otherwise oblivious. "What do you think of my needlework, kiddo? In six months this boy won't know he almost lost his fingertip."

"Emergency doctor," said Mike Steffans. "The pizza has arrived."

The Fudgesicle took in the crowd. "I'll be in the War Room," she said, retreating. "We need someone up front to make it look like this is a functioning Emergency Room."

"Thank heaven for Anne," said Rabbi Tarnapol, arriving just at that moment. "I trailed that distinctive perfume of rancid olive oil and forbidden sausage through the parking lot. Is there enough for a starving rabbi to share?"

Everyone converged on the back room. Barney took a sip of sweet raspberry soda. "Why is even bad pizza so fundamentally pleasing?" he asked.

"There's something wicked about it," Mike Steffans offered.

"Exactly. It was something your mother would never let you eat."

"*Your* mother maybe, Barney. My mother hardly ever gave us anything else. Spaghetti out of a can. Pizza. Hotdogs. I could sue for nutritional malpractice."

Something was troubling Barney. He wolfed his pizza down. "Which do you think does the most psychological damage?" he asked. "Child neglect? Child abuse? Or child deification?"

Tarnapol made a face. "This is beginning to sound like a panel discussion at a Hadassah meeting."

Barney realized what was making him feel uneasy. He took a last sip of raspberry soda and winced at the sweetness. "Come along with me, Dr. Djarta." He waved to Tarnapol. "I think I'll take that fingertip off and resuture it. I'm not happy with the way I put it on. It looks a little crooked. If the mother asks what's going on, I'll say we always do a full dress rehearsal."

"*D*octor. Dr. Kincaid. Barney." For a moment Barney couldn't remember where he was. The room was pitch black. And that was the Fudgesicle standing in the doorway. He had worked longer than he should have and then, suddenly exhausted, had decided to nap in the room set aside for interns to grab an hour or two of sleep on their thirty-six-hour shifts. He had a crick in his neck from the lumpy pillow, a cheap polyester number that had long ago separated into three stale-smelling lumps.

"Dr. Turner's car is stalled in a snowbank somewhere on the Saw Mill River Parkway and we're suddenly busy. Do you want to join the rumble?" She came toward him. "Will coffee help?" She handed him a mug. "Are you all right, Dr. Kincaid?"

He'd been so deep asleep, dreaming, pursued in the dream, running. He lay there for a minute stunned, coming awake, waiting for his heart to stop racing. "Just waking up," he said. "Damn it, Mallory. This heart thing is a drag. Whenever it jumps or skips or speeds up, I sit here like a . . . cowering fool. It's like living with an undependable Siamese twin."

She placed her fingertips on his wrist. "Normal for a weary, hard-working man rudely awakened from a deep sleep," she said, not letting go. "C'mon Barney. We've got a little boy who swallowed a frog. A toy frog," she added hastily. She was gone. Barney. The word sounded almost foreign coming out of her mouth.

Billy Williams, three years old, temperature 103. Barney looked up from the chart. He was always drawn to children. A doctor must not get caught up in pain or despair, but he had always felt a special empathy for children. Their pain was such a terrifying mystery, a betrayal. Billy Williams sat on the edge of the examining table leaning forward, short of breath but not coughing. His mother had thrown a man's stiff plaid hunting jacket over her nightgown and rushed him to Emergency in a taxi. She was shivering and scared.

Even before she spoke the thought process had begun in Barney's head. Was it croup? Billy was the right age for croup or epiglottitis. That usually meant respiratory stridor, a mean rasping sound. The kid was silent. Barney had a reputation for lightning-fast diagnoses. It began with an uncanny memory. As a kid he had assumed everyone had the same kind of fact bank and instant recall. He remembered conversations from long ago. He could figure out in his head what day of the week a particular date fell on. He remembered his weight at every birthday and his blood pressure at every checkup. He remembered smells. And colors, although he didn't always know the name to communicate the hue he knew in his head. He had discovered the world of color as an eleven-year-old convalescing from mononucleosis, ripping pages out of Mama's magazines and making collages. He fashioned bizarre puppets on string from photographs he clipped out of *Vogue*. Barney didn't need a full-dress psychoanalysis to figure out he was lucky to escape Mama's clutches, obsessed by women instead of obsessed with wanting to be a woman.

Barney couldn't remember when he first became aware of a bell that went off in his head, that caught his attention just as he might be about to let something important slide by unnoticed. The trick was to hear the bell in the chaos of the Emergency Room, he would tell his students. He'd had the bell in grade school, warning him to check again before handing in a term paper or an exam. Barney believed anyone could sharpen and refine the memory reflex, the way body builders work on muscles. Ironically, it was the seeming miracles colleagues remembered, he observed. The hunches that missed or were slightly off were quickly forgotten, especially when the patient survived, as most of them did.

"Billy was a little dynamo all day," Mrs. Williams was saying. "But he woke up in the middle of the night. He was kinda dribbling like and trying hard to catch his breath." She hesitated. "I do remember he was playing with a little wooden frog. So small. I know I shouldna let him have it. I can't seem to find it. He tells me he swallowed the frog."

"Swallowed a wooden frog," Barney repeated. "Is that true, Billy?" He tapped the boy's chest and listened to his lungs. Why would he have a fever unless it was a coincidence, Barney thought, or worse, perforation of the esophagus?

Billy nodded.

"You're sure you swallowed the frog?" Barney asked. "Don't be scared. It's okay. Nobody will be angry at Billy. Anyone can swallow a frog. Tell us and we'll get the frog back for you."

"Yes." Billy nodded. "Frog in Billy's tummy."

"Come, Mother, we'll go see if the X-ray machine can find us a frog." Barney picked up the boy, still bothered by something.

Mallory grabbed his arm just as the cardiac alarm went off. A paramedic ambulance team on the street somewhere, feeding an EKG reading into the hospital by radio, needed supervision. "Dr. Steffans is with the gunshot wound. Can you handle it?"

"Take Billy Williams to X-ray," Barney instructed her. "We're looking for an ingested toy frog." He lay the boy down on a roll-away table and raced down the hall toward the radio room. From thirty feet away he heard that terrible sound behind him. The unearthly rasping sound of respiratory stridor. Barney wheeled around and ran back. He shoved the mother aside. The boy lay there struggling to breathe. Barney pulled a 14-gauge Intracath out of his pocket. He made a small curve in the needle and pierced the boy's cricothyroid membrane. The mother screamed. "Get an ambu bag," he snapped, "and get the mother out of here." Barney started breathing into the cath tube. When Mallory returned, he pulled an endotrachial tube adapter from his pocket and fitted it onto the catheter. "That's better," he said calmly, putting the bag in Mallory's hand. "Call the ENT resident," he said, "since we now know it's epiglottitis, we can forget about frogs." He ran down the hall to the radio room.

"I gave her lidocaine," the paramedic reported when Barney radioed to the ambulance. "You better make it look good on the chart because this poor lady wasn't waiting for your okay."

Barney was scanning the EKG fast. "Textbook perfect, Liza my friend," he said. He felt his own heart pounding, only this time it felt good, more of a hallelujah chorus than a requiem.

Mallory stuck her head in the door. "Not bad, Superman," she said. "And when did you start carrying that handy little adaptor in your pocket?"

Barney felt ten feet tall. "Neater than a scalpel, isn't it?" he said.

"*D*o you remember Linda Menker?" Barney was feeling so exhilarated by the last hour in the ER that he'd lingered for a sandwich in the coffee shop with Dick Rogin, Goodman's house psychiatrist. Dick had graduated from Kingsbridge High School two years before Barney. But even then Linda Menker was a legend.

"Linda the pig?"

"The class reunion committee is asking if anyone knows the whereabouts of Linda Menker," said Barney, weighing the heartburn of chili versus the boredom of tomato soup.

"I wouldn't have gone near my twenty-fifth high school reunion if they'd hired me to do Rorschach tests on the entire crowd," said Dick. "Hey. Wait. Now that would be a project worth pursuing."

"I'm not sure Linda was really the nymphomaniac the guys made her out to be," said Barney. "If even half their boasts were true, they were a team of budding Rubirosas. If a girl's sweater was too tight, we were convinced she was an easy lay . . . right?"

"Nothing about women was ever easy for me," said Dick. "You order, Barney. I'm fasting. Give me another Tab, Edith," he ordered. "With this fast you've got to get down liquids."

"What happens to a girl like Linda Menker, real or imagined nymphomaniac, whatever that is . . . overamply endowed girl in too-tight sweaters?"

"Oh no, Barney. You and Linda? You too? I remember Howie what's-his-name took her out. Figured how else could he get laid. I heard she once took on the entire football team."

"Basketball. Actually, it was maybe three guys," said Barney. "They forced her. And the rest just stood there pulling their dicks, too chicken to join in. She went crazy her senior year. I actually did take her to a movie once or twice before then. You know, Dick, she was really sweet, and very funny. She used to wear Max Factor pancake makeup, something dark called 'Suntan,' because she read that was Elizabeth Taylor's beauty secret."

"We were a bunch of louts," said Dick. "I guess you got them with compassion even then, Barney. Well, today Linda Menker is a Westchester housewife, mother of five. Or a Baptist missionary in Peru. Maybe she's a long-haul truck driver. Women these days." He shrugged. "Go to your twenty-fifth reunion and you'll see. All those lithe little girls grown into forty-year-old Jewish mothers . . . and Wall Street lawyers. It's awesome."

"I'd like to find Linda Menker now. Why wait till June? I think it would be interesting to look up women from the past. Remember Barbara Bloome . . . Barbie, my girlfriend in high school. Pixie haircut . . . she looked a lot like Audrey Hepburn. She married some merchandising mogul and lives in an upper-crust ghetto near San Francisco."

"Would you just kind of butt in to someone's life?"

"If you think of it as butting in? I think I'd be touched and pleased if she were to call me. Is it all right if I eat dessert, Dick. I don't want to torture you."

"I'll dull the pain with another Tab. You've been through a crisis, Barney. It's made you nostalgic for the past. Go ahead and see Barbie. Find Linda Menker. You don't have to hire a detective. Get your reporter friend at the *Post* to check around for you. You're a single man, friend. Have an adventure." He lifted his glass. "Do you think marital status has anything to do with preferred sexual position?"

"Is that a riddle?"

"Is the single man more likely to make love in the male-superior position than a married man?"

"Jeanette likes to be on top?"

"Always. Since she discovered her clitoris."

Barney was amused to play the sexual scholar to Dick's exaggerated Sad Sack. "A lot of women need to be on top these days. What I do, Dick, is try to show them there are other ways."

"I pay a high price for the serenity in my life," Dick brooded. "I'd be a real washout playing around. It's so fucking complicated. You meet a girl in a bar. She doesn't even know your name. You have sex. Twenty minutes later, she's talking about a house together in the Hamptons. It's in their genes: settling in. You know Barney, I can remember every woman I've ever fucked. Not that there's so many. Do you remember them all?"

Barney nodded. "You know how your life supposedly flashes before your eyes just as you're going under—that's all I seem to be thinking about these past few days."

"Yeah. With you it would take a computer to keep track. Me, I was never greedy. You know what I remember? I remember their teeth. All the different teeth. Crazy?"

"I remember their cunts," said Barney.

"Well of course."

"Vividly, I remember all the different tastes and how they all feel different. You know, the ones that grab you.

The tight little ones, sticky but tight."

"And the mean arid ones," Dick prompted.

"And the ones that are so sloppy you don't know where you are."

"Yeech. What I remember is the tunafish," said Dick.

Barney wasn't sure he'd heard correctly.

"They all make tunafish differently. I remember it so well from my bachelor days. There is always a point somewhere on a Saturday afternoon where they would offer to make tunafish for lunch. No two women make tunafish the same way. Some of them use chopped onion. Some of them use too much mayonnaise. Mustard. No mustard. The pseudointellectuals use capers. Pickle relish. Apples and walnuts."

"Apples and walnuts?" Barney repeated. "That's one I have yet to fall in love with. Since you haven't been a bachelor for a while, you'll be interested to learn they do it with bean sprouts now. And water chestnuts. And once I dated a woman who did it with fresh raw tuna. It was wonderful but I realized she cared much more about the tuna than she cared about me."

Dick laughed. He ordered a Tab to go. "Keep me informed," he said. "If Linda Menker is running for Congress, I want to know."

Dick might become a confidant, Barney thought. A man needed a male friend. He realized he hadn't had a serious personal moment with a man in years. Not since Marvin's death. He missed Marvin and the wild flights of fantasy that ultimately led to moments of intimacy and, sometimes, stark revelation. That kind of intimacy with another man was rare. Was it possible, he wondered, at the age of forty-two to find a friend? Only recently he had noticed how few friends had survived his separation from Reeney. Were all *their* friends really Reeney's? He'd been so caught up juggling the complex demands of his life—changing specialties at thirty-two, going back to school for certification, setting up Goodman Memorial's ER, teaching, discreet philandering. He'd never noticed till now that, except for Marvin, his close confidants had always been women. Women were lucky. Spilling their guts didn't seem to frighten them. They never held back for fear of seeming silly, weak or vulnerable. Amazing how comfortable they were able to be with a measure of vulnerability that would paralyze Barney. Women tell each other everything. Unlike locker-room bullshit . . . with women it's the real truth. Barney had been shocked when he first discovered women he'd slept with shared secrets—what he said, the special qualities of his cock, size, shape, morning behavior. Women shouldn't need psychotherapy when they have each other, comforting and encouraging, sympathetic, endlessly wise. Everything Barney knew about women, he had learned from women. Lying in bed after making love . . . how they loved to talk. As if the orgasm of one mouth touched off the orgasm of the other. Most of what he knew about men and a lot of what he knew about himself Barney had learned from women. No wonder women were so frightening. A man really needed women. And they knew it. They knew too much. Perhaps the women in his life would tell him something he needed to know. Something he'd been told and forgotten. Anyway, it would be great to see Barbie. And Audrey. Even sex-crazed Caroline. He'd been too tough on Caroline, cutting her off so abruptly after all those wild times. He missed her zaniness.

He would make a list. He would call his friend Carl at the *Post* tomorrow.

*T*he Emergency Room was an island of tranquillity. Barney looked at his watch as he slipped on his overcoat. Not a soul in the waiting room. Not even Joe di Renzo, the actor who practically lived in the Emergency waiting area, shuffling around in bedroom slippers, peeling an orange, memorizing scripts for parts he never got. One morning Barney had realized di Renzo had actually moved into residence.

"If you don't mind, I'll just kind of hang out here," di Renzo had said. "With a heart like mine you never know when a second attack will hit. I want to be right here if it comes." Di Renzo spent so much time in the cafeteria with his briefcase that a lot of the students thought he was the administrator.

"Where's di Renzo?" Barney asked Nurse Mallory. "Intensive care? Old heart finally go?"

"He's moved into our supply closet," said Mallory. "The super read him the riot act and said he had to go home."

Barney groaned. "You must be kidding. He's living in our supply closet? With his sardine sandwiches and his rotting bedroom slippers."

"It was Dr. Turner's solution," she said. "I myself am nauseated by this invasion." She smiled. She actually smiled. "Do you have a minute before you go?" She led him to a window in the deserted waiting room. He was shocked to see a tendril of dark hair loose from her tight bun. She seemed slightly flushed. "For now, just between us . . ." she was saying. "About Dr. Gunderson, I understand you are gathering information. For an investigation. You probably realize that most of your associates are not at all happy about this. The medical staff is quick to look the other way, protect themselves . . . afraid to see what's really going on. There was a nurse. Do you remember Frieda Thompson? She covered for Gunderson once when a patient died. Maybe she even believed his story. They were . . . romantically involved, I believe. That could be a rumor. Or exaggeration. I don't know. She's left the hospital but the nursing files might give you a lead on where she is. She shouldn't be impossible to find."

Barney took the Fudgesicle's hand. "I want to thank you." She started, pulled her hand away, quickly busying herself with the stray tendrils, hairpins, her cap.

"I admire what you're doing. I like the kind of doctor

you are," she said. Then she darted away. "I'm coming," she called out. To no one. To the air.

"*T*ake a cross-table lateral of the cervical spine before you move that head, Dr. Djarta," Barney instructed, taking a quick check of the ER lineup before running upstairs, fifteen minutes late to a department-head meeting. "And please come up with a topic and choose a date to lecture our paramedics."

The room fell silent as he walked in. "What have I done now?" said Barney.

Carl Guenther, the hand man, the East Coast's foremost hand surgeon, as he liked to be billed, was glowering.

"We are privileged to have the East Coast's most brilliant hand surgeon on our staff, Dr. Kincaid," Enoch Whitaker, the administrator's fussbudget assistant began. "You have that room downstairs in Emergency all set up for hand traumas, a hand specialist on call, and a resident trained by Dr. Guenther. I can readily understand why Dr. Guenther is disturbed. When we get a hand injury, he should get that case."

Barney saw Gunderson in the rear of the room leaning back, exaggerated in his nonchalance, whispering into the ear of his crony, the cretinously benign Evans, chief of Ob-Gyn. Gunderson smiled at Barney. An evil smile.

Barney knew his impatience with inefficiency and error made him seem like a troublemaker to his lazier colleagues. He was proud of being a pain in the ass. "We gave Dr. Guenther a doozy last week, I'm told," said Barney. "The guy that got his hand mangled in the diaper-folding machine."

"I thought everyone used paper diapers these days," Dick Rogin observed. "Imagine opening a bundle of diapers and having a finger or two fall in your lap."

"It's the last two cases Carl is protesting," Whitaker interrupted with a small, disgusting snort.

"Oh hell," said Barney. "Why can't you discuss these things with me, Carl, instead of calling a congressional investigation. Dr. Turner repaired two minor thumb lacerations. Kindergarten stuff. And if you're referring to this morning, that was not even a finger . . . it was a tiny tip with viable circulation. I wasn't going to make a big deal out of it. The mother was hysterical already."

"You sabotage me Barney because it's your service and I'm the one element you're not in charge of," Guenther interrupted. His face was red, making the scar on his cheek even crueler. Guenther enjoyed having people suppose it was a university dueling scar. Barney went around telling everyone Guenther had fallen on a skate key.

"You made us wait too long on that amputated hand two weeks ago. The Matthews boy," Barney snapped back.

"You see Enoch. It is retaliation. The hand will work," Guenther exploded.

"Not well enough. Not perfectly. Not as well as it might have."

Whitaker snorted again. "Either you two work this out or I'm appointing the chief of surgery to arbitrate. Agreed? All right. Dr. Kincaid, you have some documentation you were preparing."

Gunderson sat up straight and stared out the window. "I'll have that at our next meeting," Barney said. "I've been out with a virus for several days."

Whitaker's chin went down into his neck making ripples on jowl. "Oh yes. That. Good to have you back with us, Dr. Kincaid. Have you had a chance to check us out on our chickenburgers? I understand the dietician has even decided to offer them at breakfast."

"Is that what those singed sawdust pancakes are?" said Dick Rogin. "I hated to ask."

"You cholesterol counters wanted better protein. You've got it," said Whitaker. "We're making our own fish sticks, too. No additives, I'm told. No artificial anything."

The doctors stood up. Evans slapped Gunderson on the back.

"Our holy grail," Rogin was saying, giving Barney a thumbs-up sign. "The chickenburger. A point for your team."

"Don't forget our celebrity auction," Whitaker called after them. "Dr. Peachtree has donated a facelift."

"Maybe Guenther will donate a hand job," muttered Barney.

"No, no," moaned Rogin. "Not Guenther. Bo Derek. Please make it Bo Derek."

Barney was trying to catch up with Hal Wechsler, the medical chief, when Gunderson stepped up, blocking the door. Evans loomed behind.

"Why don't you lay off, Barney," Evans said. "You're stirring up a lot of nasty feelings. Over what? Over a difference of opinion. We all make decisions that later prove . . . uh . . . unfortunate."

"I would bet even the brilliant Dr. Kincaid has made his share of mistakes. Oh yes." Gunderson was still smiling.

"Risks. Emergency medicine is rife with risk, Gunderson. Just deciding which patients must be treated first is a decision with inherent risk. Often we have two or three options for treatment. We choose. But I hope we do not make the one totally misguided choice . . . the fatal choice."

Gunderson's smile deepened. "You're a stiff, Kincaid. That's why nobody likes you—always second-guessing, always butting in. I'm not the only one who can't stand your smugness . . . that holier-than-thou attitude. You have more enemies in this hospital than you imagine, my friend."

"Listen to Emile," said Evans. "Don't ask for trouble. You're opening a Pandora's box."

Barney had been annoyed. Now he had to bite his lip to keep from smiling. "I bow to your expertise," he said. "Excuse me. I'm late." He brushed by. Wechsler was standing at the elevator. "Do you have a minute," he began. "It's about the Gunderson matter. You were away skiing when that—"

"I've heard the rumblings," said Wechsler. "I'll walk

with you. Gunderson is an asshole. I've been trying to get him off the staff for fifteen years. He doesn't know what he's doing half the time. Make that most of the time. For a while we had him on suspension. He couldn't leave orders without someone co-signing. But Barney, I've only been back two days and all I hear are complaints about you. How you have a secret grudge against Gunderson."

Barney was surprised Wechsler would even listen to such garbage. "A grudge. What bullshit. I don't even know the man personally. We're talking about total incompetence now, Hal. Three patients died, maybe more. You admit you think he belongs in a zoo."

"I agree he's incompetent. But I've been here a long time now and I've done my stint beating my head against brick walls. Your efforts will be futile. They won't listen. They'll find excuses for Gunderson. At the most he'll get a slap on the wrist. And you will have made an enemy of everyone in the hospital."

"But Hal, a critique from you has real meaning, extra impact."

"Forget it, Barney. Let it go."

Barney was shocked that Wechsler, a man he had idolized, was refusing to back his stand. He stood there. Medicine was not a popularity contest. He couldn't accept Wechsler had a point. He stormed off. But a seed of doubt had been planted. He could wind up scorned, with a legion of enemies, while Gunderson escaped with mild censure.

Barney needed to calm down. He decided to work on his outline for an emergency-medicine text. He was debating whether it should be organized traditionally or alphabetically by symptom. He'd been squirreling away material for more than a year.

There was a strange smell in the supply closet. Joe di Renzo had his feet on Barney's secret desk. The toe of one sock molded in a way that invoked thoughts of leprosy. There was a tiny telly in one corner, a basket of groceries, donuts, salami. The place smelled like a third-rate delicatessen. Joe had a stethoscope at rest around his neck. He was reading *Variety*.

"Give me that stethoscope," Barney cried. "Get your stuff out of here. Joe, this is ridiculous. You can't live in the hospital. You've got to go home."

"It's my stethoscope," said di Renzo. "I bought it. And I'm not in the way here. I'm basically unobtrusive. You're driving me to the men's room."

"You're going to live in the men's room?"

"Just till I feel stronger."

Barney groaned. Every piece of gauze or fabric-wrapped kit coming out of the supply closet would smell like salami.

"This is it, Joe. I'm driving you home myself. Unless you want to deal with Security."

He helped di Renzo pack up his things. He was wheezing a little as he slid into the car. Barney watched the man take his own pulse. He sighed. Barney knew. Once a man's heart complained, you would never trust it.

"What exactly are you looking for, Barney? Tell me, I could help." Anxiety made Mama's voice high and British. She was less than overjoyed to have Barney burrowing in her basement storage bin. Actually, it was astonishing to think that his grade-school garbage and college souvenirs were still here. God, she was meticulous.

"If everything is marked and dated and arranged chronologically, how can I go wrong, Mama?" Barney protested.

"Chronological, I didn't promise," she said, reluctantly withdrawing.

"This has got to be it," he said, shifting four or five cardboard cartons to get at the big blue Tiffany box labeled "Barney II." "Barney I" proved to be his old footlocker from camp. Amazing how her obsession for neatness and order did not contraindicate the preservation of clutter. But here it all was: school essays and report cards, blue books, a tin Popeye bank that ate spinach when you deposited a coin, baseball trading cards, oh no . . . even baby clothes ("I threw them away long ago," she had lied when Reeney asked. They were poor then and Reeney had thought it would be cute to dress Candy in Barney's layette). There were Hardy Boys books saved for the boy he and Reeney never had, cereal-box-top decoders, a lamp he'd glued and stained in wood-working. Ribbons from camp: a third in archery, a second for knocking them dead on Indian Legends Night. At twelve already a legend, never an athlete. In a box all by its own he found wrapped in crinkled white tissue . . . his baby shoes. "By the time we could afford to get them dipped in copper like all the cousins', Barney's feet were already size thirteen and I felt silly," Mama had once apologized. Letters. Among them a copy of his application to Harvard.

"Harvard is important to me, not merely as a center for the ultimate in excellence, the academic fount where I can immerse myself in history and the fine arts before the inevitable scientific focus of medicine, but also as a symbol. From childhood I have made Harvard my goal. I am an only child. I am the only hope my parents have. My life is their dream."

For an instant Barney's stomach ached. He could feel again the anxiety of the eighteen-year-old Barney, applying to Yale and Princeton and even Michigan but not able to imagine being rejected by Harvard. He set the letters in a pile with Mama's photo album and the college stuff, a purple Capezio, his track shoes, prom photos, a lipstick-stained white glove, embroidered panties ("Wednesday's Child is Full of Woe"), some vintage *Playboys*, a knotted hanky. Inside, Barbie Bloome's silver braces, the orthodontist's masterwork. Barney felt a feverish rush, remembering the vision of Barbie licking his cock . . . trying to suck the tip without massacring his eager, painfully yearning dick with the barbed wire.

How pitifully he'd begged to go all the way.

"I love you too much," she would say.

*M*ama was in the kitchen upstairs. "You couldn't take it all, I suppose," she said. "A little space down there wouldn't hurt."

"Throw out whatever you like that's left," he said.

"Fat chance." She smiled a mock grin. "I should have worked for the Smithsonian I'm such a good keeper."

"Are you still in touch with Barbie Bloome's mother from the old days?" asked Barney.

Oh yes. Mama kept in touch. Sarah Bloome was always boasting about her son-in-law's triumphs in the import-export business. "Dime-store stuff from Hong Kong and Taiwan you didn't know you needed till you buy it and then you're sure you didn't need it." They lived in Sausalito. Mama would try to remember the married name. Of course she would telephone Sarah. "You're not staying for dinner," Mama announced with her uncanny power of divination. He had not even looked at his watch. She sighed; clearly it was a mortal wound.

"It's not even six o'clock, Mama. I never said anything about dinner. I want to make a quick stop uptown. And Lindsay is expecting me."

"Oh. That one." A nail had just been driven into her coffin. She was so hurt she managed to walk him to the door without remembering the cooked prunes always set aside for him in the refrigerator.

The first time in forty-two years, thought Barney. She'd forgotten his prunes. He felt wonderful.

Window-shopping the wine store without finding anything he was tempted to buy made Barney realize that he wasn't all that anxious to go home. He felt vaguely annoyed, disoriented. Lindsay had been camping out in his apartment for three days now. And nights. Lindsay in serene residence, bringing comfort and terror into Barney's bachelor existence. She had parked her kids with her mother-in-law and moved in to study for final exams. "I feel so serious and confident studying here," she said, "as if your brilliance might be contagious."

Barney had almost forgotten how unsettling it could be to surrender one's bathroom to female invasion—his only bathroom. Wet pantyhose, moisturizers, protein goo for the hair, a razor with a blade that looked like it had been in use since 1962. Bottles opened, uncapped. Strange implements scattered, rusty. Somewhere between Mama with her blotters under milk bottles and scrofulous razors was the perfect woman. Still, the refrigerator looked as if human beings inhabited the apartment for the first time ever. There was a clean sponge on the sink. He hadn't realized how much a man needed a clean sponge. His socks had been washed, as if by magic, and rolled into pairs, matching pairs. Scary how happy that made him feel. The luxury of being able to reach for a pair of socks and know they'd always be there was almost sufficient reason to take a mate. No cleaning woman had ever shown such enterprise.

The house was still. There was a vase of tulips drooping in graceful arcs and the smell of her pine-scented perfume and peppermint, but Lindsay was out. A note said she would be back with dinner at eight.

Barney hid the salvage from Mama's cellar under the sleeping bag in his front closet and collapsed on the bed with the photo album. How constricted most people are in snapshots, Barney thought. Stiff, formal, self-conscious. Especially gangling Barney himself crossing his eyes, tugging on a ridiculous bow tie. Or on the beach, striking a macho pose, arms folded across scrawny bare chest, all ribs and bony hunched shoulders. Pathetic ninety-seven-pound weakling growing four inches in less than a year. Adorable dimpled Barney at six with Cousin Heidi on a pony. Barney's dad with his arms around them both. Margaret, her hand and half her face, cutting a birthday cake. Eleven candles. Birthday balloons, a toothless little girl eating a hotdog and this time his mother's hand blocking out Margaret's face. At his first formal. Barbie Bloome with her hair piled high and a gardenia on her wrist, clearly annoyed. He'd been smashed silly on rye stolen from his folks' liquor cabinet. Barbie and Barney again, at a college dance. He was annoyed then, having counted on the mythic aura of Harvard to weaken her defenses against seduction. "But you're the one I'm serious about," she had wailed.

Months later he discovered she had fucked half the men in his house—everyone almost but Barney, even Bones Grossman, who was skeletal and stupid, too. "I love you too much," she moaned, locking her legs, open always to his mouth, closed to his throbbing cock, immune to philosophical treatises on sexual hypocrisy. "Hypocrisy is all I've got," she cried. They had been "lavaliered" for God's sake. That was probably a strategic mistake. She was holding out for the long walk. Marriage. Actually, Barney had assumed they would marry, too. Till Reeney came along. And Amy. The siren shiksa call. Here was Aunt Cristal, hugging Barney. Barney puffing on his pipe pretending to ignore her. And Reeney looking at Barney worshipfully. Mama hanging onto the other arm never going to let go. Oh they were honest photos all right. But there was scarcely a significant moment captured in the book. Except for the wedding pictures with Barney's sickly grin as the sentence was pronounced. The damning realization of . . . no exit. Amy gone . . . sacrificed for this dread limbo.

Why did we never use the camera to capture the moments of breakthrough. The look on Reeney's face the first time Barney came in her mouth. Aunt Cristal kneeling at his feet, naked and laughing, her big plump breasts jiggling wildly. Amy in the bathtub squealing at the intensity of the windup rubber duck unwinding against her clitoris. Lindsay crying as he begged her to come. Her tears. Their faces as . . . finally . . . shockingly . . . awesomely . . . she came. Coming. That was the moment Barney loved. That was the face Barney loved. So one day he had pulled his camera from the dresser, seconds after a spectacular coming. And captured that face. Debra's face. Standing directly over her on the bed in an inn north of San Francisco. The triumphant smile, pale hair fanning across the pillow. That was the beginning of Barney's secret carousel.

Barney made himself a short drink and took out the carousel of slides he kept hidden in the farthest corner of the closet. He glanced at the clock. Not yet seven-fifteen. He switched off the light. Debra draped over the arm of a chair, ass up, begging him not to shoot. Click. Debra again. That afternoon in the yellow hotel room. Mouth contorted, tears streaking her face, streaked blonde hair in a tangle on the pillow. Caroline photographed in orgasm, the obsessed photographer's heart still pounding from his own climax, reaching for the camera to watch her bringing herself over the edge again and again. Click. Caroline again on the bedroom wall in a classic *Penthouse* pink shot. She loved the camera. But then so many women did. And women loved to be photographed naked. Women who worried about exposing too much cleavage at dinner. Women who could not be persuaded to go topless on a deserted beach. For some reason most women could be persuaded to pose naked. Click. Even puritanical Lindsay. Yes, even Lindsay, trusting him . . . caught in the shower with the soap in her hand between her legs, a beatific smile on her face. Click. Barney grinned as one of his favorites flashed on the bedroom wall. A background of sun-browned skin, deliciously indented by a sublime old-fashioned navel with four bright coral geranium petals enmeshed in the ferny tendrils of Debra's sweet blonde bush. Click.

Barney stared at the blank square of light on his wall. It was almost seven-forty. He had to get away. He tucked the carousel back into its darkest corner, put on his warmest tweed jacket, and took the service elevator to the lobby. For months he had been carrying an ad clipped out of *Screw*. He knew just where to go.

What Barney wanted was sex, straight sex, hot sex, no conversation . . . no games, no obligations, no complications. A whore. *Screw* recommended Caesar's Palace. That sounded too big, too flashy. He might run into someone he knew. This was a small apartment, discreet, with a mirrored pool room and waterbeds, the ad said. There were three women lounging around when he walked in. None resembled the wholesomely sexy Cybill Shepherd-lookalike in the *Screw* ad. Barney quickly eliminated the big gum-chewing blonde in the baby-doll pajamas and an eager brunette with a fatal resemblance to Reeney. That left a pretty beige girl reading a comic—Hispanic, he supposed, with flawless skin, doe eyes and . . . alas. Someone should have instructed her never to smile. That's me, thought Barney. So quick to focus on the flaws. Such an excess of gums. Her breasts were too tiny but he loved the way her ass flared and the bottom of her buttocks peeked out of a kind of satin leotard. She wobbled on her platform mules like a little girl in her mother's high heels. Barney said no to a lemon-scented bubble bath. And wasn't sure he was relaxed enough to survive a halfhearted massage. Then he realized what he wanted. He wanted to make this pretty automaton react. To him.

She was humming sort of tunelessly, moving in a little jiggle step, wobbling till she stumbled. He grabbed her arm. She pulled it away, shocked, perhaps offended, by his touch. He followed her into a room, smaller than he expected—just a massage table and a mirror but no waterbed in sight, only a mattress.

"You can take off your clothes," she said.

"Will you take off yours?"

"You first." Barney closed his eyes for a moment and pretended she was playing coy. Of course, he had to strip first, to prove he wasn't a cop. He'd been to prostitutes before during his marriage, after a porn flick when it was sex he wanted and no strings and definitely no recriminations.

"It's twenty-five for the massage," she said. "And twenty-five extra for a hand job. Fifty for French. Seventy-five for sex. I don't do Greek." She stood there for a moment. Then she put out her hand. He gave her a hundred dollars. "Make yourself comfortable," she said, leaving the room. Like a nurse, thought Barney, draping his clothes on a wooden hanger.

In a moment she was back.

"I'm Barney,' he said.

"You're what?" she said, looking a bit anxious.

"My name is Barney."

"Oh yeah." She skimmeyed out of the leotard, revealing little doorknob nipples. Didn't remove her black net g-string. She was humming again.

"Your name is—"

"Maria."

"You have a nice voice, Maria. Are you a singer? Or an actress?" She was cuter than he'd realized. If only she weren't so vacant. He lay face down on the table.

"Nah." She kneaded his neck and shoulders with minimal commitment.

"A model?"

"Do I have to be something?"

Maybe she was more sensitive than he'd thought. Yes, Barney would have liked her to be a Ph.D. in sociology working on a thesis. "Well, I don't know why not," he said. "You have a lot of style."

"You think?"

She was taking a sincere and sensual interest in the muscles of his ass and thighs. He felt himself getting hard.

"You can turn around now."

If she noticed his hard-on she gave no indication. He

could see the flesh of her vulva through the mesh of her g-
string. He touched it. He pulled her toward him, between
his legs. She suffered his kiss. He was nuzzling her neck,
biting her lip, kissing, making love to her, always with the
nagging knowledge that she would probably prefer to
dispense with the crap and just get him out as quickly as
possible. He rubbed his palm across her pubic bone. Rubbed
the clitoris with his index finger. She looked at him wide-
eyed. Then she moaned. She threw her head back, bit her
lip. "Put it in," she cried. "Put it in." She was hot. Real or
phony, he wouldn't know.

He slid off the table, lifted her from behind, arranged
her face down on the mattress, and slid into her from
behind. She was very wet. That thrilled him. He was getting
to her, Barney thought. She thrust her ass out to him,
banging into him. Her head thrashing. Grinding against
him. Speeding up the pace. Making him come. Barney
arched and shuddered, trembling. She was silent beneath
him for three or four seconds. Then she sighed and pushed
him back, sliding out from under. She walked away with a
striped towel trailing between her legs, sandals slipping, her
clothes in her hand.

Barney noticed a hand-lettered sign on the door. "We
take Master Charge and Visa." He wondered what kind of
customer used credit cards in a massage parlor. He felt
exhilarated, full of energy, pleased. She'd been wet, really
wet.

"Hey wait, Bobby," she called after him as he left. She
kissed his cheek. "Hurry back."

Barney smiled. He was hopeless all right. Trying to
move a mindless little whore. Probably she'd faked it. Then
again, maybe not. It was snowing, big wet flakes. He
wrapped his scarf around his neck . . . long, soft, cashmere,
a present from Debra. He admired himself in a store
window walking up Broadway. Everyone he passed was
bundled up against the cold. Barney thought he looked
rather British in his tweed jacket with just a scarf to keep off
the snow.

*L*indsay had been studying. She jumped up when Barney's key turned in the lock. "I was so worried," she said. "I brought dinner. There was no note. I thought you'd call. The hospital said you left hours ago."

"I should have called," he said, taking so long in the closet you might have thought he was hanging the Mona Lisa instead of merely a scarf. He shook out his jacket. "I went for a walk." He hugged her, loving her smell, rubbing his nose into the soft layers of her hair. The table was set. "You didn't eat."

"Well, of course not. It's just stuff I picked up at the deli." She seemed tentative, as if she wanted to ask a question but didn't exactly wish to know the answer. Or perhaps he imagined it.

He pretended to eat. He hated cheap coldcuts. He was a delicatessen snob. Nothing but kosher salami and really serious rye bread was worth getting heartburn over. That was an ethnic conceit, he supposed. Perhaps being Jewish was more physiological than he would like to concede. They finished two pints of Häagen-Dazs rum raisin. Afterward they sat at opposite ends of the sofa, she with a text and a notebook, he, with the *New England Journal*, unread, their legs stretched out on the pillows, enmeshed. Barney thought he ought to say something. He wanted to be honest. Love should be open, not the rotten hypocrisy he'd shared with Reeney. Barney felt a drink might help. He was not really a drinker. He examined his urge for a minute, then got up and mixed rum with a big slug of orange juice. That way he could justify the alcohol at least partially with the vitamin C. Lindsay did not want a drink. No, not even a sip.

"I'm still studying."

He stared at her face. The intelligent forehead. Her

thick wing brows. The perfect cheekbones and adored nose. She liked to study in a man's shirt. He had given her four or five of his striped oxford-cloth shirts from Brooks Brothers, frayed at the collar, so she could get rid of Baxter's castaways, rip them up for rags or something. She was braless in his shirt. He touched her breast in passing. She shivered. He would have expected that to be sexually exciting. He did not want to speculate why it was not.

"Kant," she said. "Can't. Can't, Kant. Kant can't." She smiled at him. He finally got it.

"Kant," he said, smiling, patting her foot. He hesitated and then found himself speaking. "I did something tonight, Lindsay. Something terrible. Well, in one sense, not terrible. In that sense it was meaningless . . . for me, meaningless. For you . . . I hadn't done anything like it in months. But I had to. I think in a sense I had no choice. I'm surviving, you know. In that sense, it wasn't meaningless, it was—"

"Barney. You're making Kant seem simple."

"I went to a place. A massage parlor."

She looked confused. "Massage?"

"A massage parlor. I wanted sex."

"But Barney, darling. I'm here. We've had sex every night. It's been wonderful. I've been so happy."

"Yes. I don't know why, Lindsay dearest. I don't know. Maybe that's why. We're feeling very cozy, aren't we? Is that why? Maybe I need to pay for it. I needed a stranger. I needed something hot and impersonal. That's crazy. Oh shit. I needed to do it."

"And afterwards you were sorry?"

"Yes. No. Afterwards I felt great. I felt free."

She looked stunned.

"Of course I was sorry."

Her eyes were brimming but she made no sound. She was the worst crier he'd ever met. She was constipated with her tears. He wished she'd weep and wail like all the rest.

He felt sad, too. For her. Because he was impossible. A rat. For himself. Because he did love her, and he couldn't stop wanting that intensity—the heat of that kind of sex.

"I'm hopeless," he said. "I'm no good, Lindsay. I don't know what monogamy is all about. I don't feel it. I've never felt it. I love you but there was no way that could stop me. I have to be honest. You want me to be honest, don't you?"

She was silent. He imagined her sitting there, porous, reabsorbing her tears, measuring her love for him perhaps. She'd been so patient and resourceful for more than a year, nursing him over the hazards of separation. Her devotion and his sense that they would ultimately marry had given structure and direction to a year of panic fucking and unbearable loneliness. Knowing she was waiting for him to heal had cut the frenzy.

"You're sorry?" she asked. "You want me to forgive you?" She looked at him. "You want me to accept that uncontrollable part of you." She sighed. "I do forgive you." They both knew that was the most she could handle.

Barney felt pleased. Indeed, he was feeling horny again. Amazing, he thought. Then again, not amazing at all.

*H*e would miss the morning session of the Emergency Medicine Conference in San Francisco, but Barney wasn't scheduled to deliver his paper on "Traumatic Rupture of the Aorta" until the next day. And Candy's home-room teacher had requested a family conference. In a highly civilized gesture, Reeney asked if Barney felt the two of them could face the music together.

"There's no reason for you to take a cab," Barney told Reeney, equally civilized, pleased by the relaxation of hostilities. The anger of women, it struck him, was the world's most virulent pollution. "I'll drive by and pick you up."

When Barney pulled up on Ninety-third Street she was chatting with the mailman, wearing the dimpled smile Barney hadn't seen for months. She saved that smile for doormen and gas station attendants, for her tennis teacher, and that unfortunate oaf with the beach feet imprinted forever now in Barney's memory bank. Oh yes, Reeney could be a charmer. Barney had forgotten that Reeney was beautiful. Away from her he remembered only the anger. From the car her beauty took him by surprise. How he had delighted in her athletic grace. She was tall, not as tall as Lindsay, but tall in spike heels and gleaming black boots. And thin, a gym addict. The narrow black coat she wore accentuated her slenderness. She had muscles in her legs like a long distance bicycle rider—hard but long and smooth. And astonishingly full breasts for a slender woman. Barney didn't like her new hairdo. She wore it in weird uneven wisps that made her chin seem more prominent. He felt better. He had almost begun to see Reeney as a stranger and wondered how a sensible man could leave such a magnificent woman. The chin helped. And the sharp whine that came into her voice. It was liquid honey for the mailman, rasp of chalk on a blackboard for Barney.

For ten blocks the topic was the usual—money. Not enough money. Never enough. They had just managed to maintain a suitable life-style on Barney's full income. Now she was struggling to stay afloat on half. She looked damn stylish for a drowning woman.

"More than half, Reeney."

"My name is Renee," she said. "Renee. Nobody seems to remember. I always hated Reeney. It's so tacky. I've always hated it. Strangers pick it up from you."

"Well damn it, Reeney—Renee. You could have said something sometime in the last twenty years. I would have been happy to call you whatever you liked. Reeney, it's kind of affectionate. That's what your Dad called you. Reeney-Beeney-Teeney . . . what was that nonsense he used to do?"

"A family thing. My family hates me. I don't really like Renee all that much either. Some kind of affectation is what it is."

"Change it. For your new life," Barney said brightly.

"Oh you. You're full of changes," she snapped. "It's a

little late for profound changes, my friend. If you think it's a cinch for a woman of forty with a teenage daughter in private school in this town—"

"I pay for the school, Reeney . . . darling. I'll always pay for the schools. And the camps. Now you know that." She had a way of staring into space whenever he scored a point. "Darling. If you were going to change your name, what name would you choose?"

She smiled and tossed her head in a gesture that had once made him weak with lust. A thousand years ago. "I love the name Quentin."

"I could see you as Evelyn."

"How about Gwen."

"Gweneth."

"That's a stupid name."

"Lucretia?"

"Borgia, I suppose. This is a stupid conversation. I see you as Bruce."

He laughed.

"Wilfred."

He laughed again. "How about Dennis? Irwin?"

"Morris," she said. "Irving."

"Not bad, kid." He smiled. He had once been terrified of this woman. Once? For a long, long time. His fear had tricked him into marrying her. He had come out of the bathroom that night in the Hotel Pierre suite still licking the toothpaste from his teeth and seen Reeney in a filmy milkmaid bridal nightgown that fanned out on the bed, a touch she'd probably picked up from some deflowering scene in a Loretta Young epic. In a lightning flash he'd become riddled with dread. Just at that instant he'd known it was a mistake. He could not remember why he had decided to marry her. Everything blurred. He had staggered, pretending to be drunk. Years later he understood. He had married Reeney because she wasn't going to sleep with him anymore if he didn't. She said he'd led her on. He was halfway through medical school and it wasn't easy to find someone else bedable fast, and especially it wasn't easy to

connect when she was always hanging around, making plans
. . . being a good sport when he fell asleep in the middle of
dinner. Everyone in both families seemed to think it was all
settled and a fine match.

He was terrified of her anger. Before he had ever
consciously made a decision, there he was, married, coming
out of the Hotel Pierre bathroom, drunk but not drunk
enough. He felt sick at the thought of touching her. She sat
there posing, dimpled, waiting. He wanted to run. All those
years of being a good boy, dutiful Barney, seething, angry,
dutiful Barney. He stumbled. She caught his hand and
pulled him down. She kissed his ear. He touched her breast.
He tried to see it as a breast—the magnificent full round
breast that it was in a strictly anatomical context, the
delicious sensitive blue-white breast that had driven him wild
all these months—separated and apart now from its unfortunate attachment to Reeney, this woman for whom his
passion was already totally defunct.

He thought about perky girl-next-door breasts in
Playboy. He closed his eyes and dove under a tangle of white
silk looking for the pretty pink rosebud pussy he'd imagined, for the nudist Goddess Diana. But all he found was the
faint familiar musk of Reeney. At that moment she reached
to switch off the light. She crossed her legs and he felt a
sense of resistance. "Oh yeah," he thought. The perverse
bitch. Holding him off. The Princess Cunt. He would show
her.

*B*arney followed Reeney to
the conference office, a corner of the Dalton library. How
disgusting that Reeney would go after teenage meat—a
cabana boy, what an ugly cliché. It was humiliating. In their
own bed, too. That was the ultimate insult. In two decades of

playing around Barney would never have committed such a breach of taste. He could not forgive her. Clutching what he had to admit later was a highly exaggerated sense of outrage, he had moved out of the house, found the furnished sublet, more money than he wanted to pay but big enough so Candy could stay overnight. He was deaf to the pleas that he forgive, and frightened, too. He was free. He was alone.

Ms. Gilligan, a very white young black woman with big blue eyes was leafing through a pile of papers. Candy's schoolwork was excellent. "She's only average in math and yet surprisingly good in science," Ms. Gilligan (she emphasized the Mzzz) observed.

Candy was working on a class project at home involving bacteria and milk.

"It stinks," Reeney reported. "So I guess it must be working."

Barney must have tuned out. He came back focused on Ms. Gilligan's high round rump as she bent over the desk. She turned to look at him.

"Ms. Gilligan says Candy is upset because you love her little brother more than you love her," whispered Reeney. "Candy is an only child," Reeney said.

"Well, yes, I know that from the records," Ms. Gilligan said. "But I put that together with the closet game—"

"They're playing doctor in the closet," Reeney updated. "Barney aren't you listening? Sex. I always thought we were terrific about sex. Honest, modern, relaxed."

"What could be more honest than playing doctor in the closet?" said Barney. "I did. What about you, Ree—darling? I bet even Ms. Gilligan—"

"What do they do in the closet, I hate to ask?" Reeney interrupted.

"Not they. Not everyone," Ms. Gilligan corrected. "Candy and some of the boys."

"Oh God," groaned Reeney. "Candy and the boys."

"It's nothing serious," Ms. Gilligan interjected. "They just look. I don't think they are actually touching. One of the boys was very upset. He came to me."

Barney remembered the tree house and Cousin Woody playing doctor with Heidi. Barney watching, nervous and fascinated. Heidi, flattered to enter the sacred treehouse, lured by the rare chance to play with the big boys. Woody holding out a Milky Way, getting Heidi to take off her panties. "See this, Barney. It opens up and the baby comes popping out." Heidi sulking. Woody with his flashlight. Heidi screaming. "It's just a game, stupid," yelled Woody, trying to keep her from smashing the treehouse, wrestling her down the branches. "Give her back her panties, Barney. Shut up, stupid. Come, we'll buy you some comic books."

"Kids play doctor, Reeney," said Barney. "It's not a tragedy. But this little-brother thing—"

"We appreciate your sensitivity, Ms. Gilligan," Reeney was saying. "We will talk to Candy. I'll talk to Candy. Her father will—"

"I'll talk to Candy, too," said Barney. It was not that he wasn't genuinely concerned. He had dreaded that his leaving might have some devastating effect on Candy. But sex in the closet? The genes do tell, don't they? What did he want for Candy sexually? Just posing the question made him uneasy. She was so young. And so damned precocious. Joy. Yes, what he wished for her was . . . joy. But he realized more and more now that his own joy depended on an element of the forbidden.

He dropped Reeney at Bendel's. "I'm just returning something," she said defensively, the impoverished divorcée, not a Bendel's package in sight. He let her get away with it and, since he had two hours till plane time, drove to the hospital.

There was Dylan Tarnapol with a glorious woman, tucking her into a shiny red Porsche. Barney waved. He'd never seen Tarnapol looking happy, stoned yes, but always melancholy. Barney strolled over. "Are you living beyond your means or is the religion business picking up?" he asked. The beauty in the front seat looked up. It was the Fudgesicle. She was laughing. She had bright red earmuffs on and she was laughing.

"A barter deal with my brother-in-law, the cardboard-

box magnate. I'm giving his Hare Krishna kid a complete
education in Judaism and Hebrew in time to be bar
mitzvahed this spring. Hey, Anne, we're late." He stepped
on the gas.

For some reason Barney was annoyed. A Porsche was a
ridiculous extravagance. And why would he drive a car that
was fire-engine red? So Rabbi Dylan Tarnapol with his
Puerto Rican moustache had his Errol Flynn moments. So
what. Barney must be nursing some sort of anger. He felt
low again, and his throat ached. He was so logy and dull he
managed to leave his attaché case in the War Room, only
noticing he'd left it behind when he was a mile away from
the hospital. He had to run like an idiot from the long-term
parking lot at Kennedy to catch his flight.

*B*arney unzipped his plane
case, threw shirts and underwear into a drawer, hung the
suit to unwrinkle and took out a small leather address and
date book. Chances were slim he could entice Barbie Bloome
out for dinner. Perhaps he should wander around downstairs, find some friend, colleagues from Yale Medical
School or New Haven Hospital or a favorite student to
exchange gossip with. He tried to remember taking his pills
on the plane, decided he hadn't, and swallowed them now.

Barney strolled through the exhibits set up in the
Golden Gate Ballroom. The Emergency Medicine College
had asked everyone delivering papers to prepare charts and
exhibits. His was simple, almost inconspicuous. And as usual
the space was hogged by the drug touts and gadgeteers.
Disposable was the theme of the decade—everything from
disposable syringes, of course, and gloves, disposable lum-
bar-puncture trays (perhaps that made sense) to disposable
suture sets and suture-removal sets. He hated them. Sutures

that melted had some legitimacy, but he wouldn't be surprised if they came up with casts that could be programmed
to self-destruct. A chocolate tongue depressor would be cute
for kids. Or a lemon-drop speculum for that matter. What
would really be gratifying would be a disposable chart for
hypochondriacs that would melt as you wrote down the
imaginary symptoms. Or better, a hypochondriac that would
self-destruct the third time she cried wolf.

"Barney, Barney. Come say hello." He recognized Hilary Sontag signaling from a small snack bar. Hilary was a
baby-faced Oriental, latest wife of Carter Sontag, the un-
rivaled marvel of Barney's graduating class at Yale Medical.
An architect, an engineer, a lawyer, and now a doctor of
emergency medicine at the advanced age of forty-three,
Carter collected Jaguars and wives as well as degrees. Hilary
was his third, half Japanese. He specialized in Asian women
and even they weren't submissive enough to suit Carter.
Hilary was still in the glow stage, the only smiler in a coven
of what had to be medical wives. He would recognize them
anywhere, restless, bored and angry, always a full-blown
martyr or two. First wives were particularly adept at martyr-
dom. Good doctors did not reluctantly sacrifice family life
because medicine demanded it. A lot of mediocre men
wilfully wallowed in their work to avoid intimacy at home
without necessarily recognizing the fact. And the etched
anger on aging female faces reflected their disappointment.

"Carter was asking for you," said Hilary. "He got the
local physicians' Wine and Food Society to order a Chinese
banquet for us somewhere. Hmm, I can't remember. Can
you and Reeney join us? Is she here?"

"So Carter is still playing around with the foie gras
crowd," said Barney. "And how is his cholesterol?"

"Low as an adolescent boy's. Honest," said Hilary. "He's
a madman. He runs five miles every morning and eats
safflower oil and wheat germ for breakfast. It's my cholesterol I'm worrying about."

Barney was explaining about Reeney and their breakup
when he caught a flash of flaxen hair and turned to see

Audrey staring at him from three aisles away. She reached up and fluffed the pale-blonde straight-across bangs—a gesture out of the past he would have recognized from a helicopter circling over the Himalayas. He took the Sontags' room number and walked toward Audrey with apprehension and excitement.

She wore white. She always wore white. The nurses couldn't wait to shed their obligatory white after work. But Audrey as an intern never wore anything else, pleated wool skirts, a white shetland pullover. He remembered a fuzzy sweater that shed on him that midnight he had first teased her into going for a hamburger after the last-night shift.

"I don't eat before I go to bed," she had said.

Her skin was pale, blue-white, perfect, clean-scrubbed, her body round, fuller than the times seemed to demand, but shapely, deliciously proportioned.

"Remember who writes the recommendations," he had said, a mock threat.

She was not a tease. In a hospital climate of nonstop sexual play, she was a cultural anomaly, astonishingly serious, so serious that at times she seemed slow. Working with her as a senior resident, Barney found it took some pressure situations before he realized how brilliant she was.

"I didn't realize diplomacy at late supper with senior staff was an area to be judged," she had said.

Barney had discovered that being married was scarcely a damper on a man's seductive powers. There were few single women on the New Haven Hospital staff he couldn't have and a fair quota of wives yearning to be led astray. But Audrey was immune. When she finally succumbed, finally said yes—no, she never said yes, simply said "Oh God, what am I doing?" Sitting in a tangle of her clothes in the rusting and ragged old Dodge he drove in those days, her hands on either side of his head as he kissed and licked and pinched and bit her breasts, one hand pressing the soft full mound where it divided and grew wet as she let herself go so far, no farther. "No, not a motel," she whispered as he pulled up to the infamous Seven Year Itch Motor Inn. "It's a waste of money." What man could resist such a woman? They drove to her apartment, a big room under the dormers of an old clapboard farmhouse. And made love with a hungry intensity that took Barney by surprise. Audrey remained scrupulously passive. She never made an overture. That was her morality. Not to pursue a married man. But when he called, she was there.

When he actually left Reeney that first time almost thirteen years ago, stowing most of his fraying shirts and good tweed jackets in the Dodge, he didn't tell Audrey (not really sure that he'd left, not wanting to provoke some half-assed ethical resistance). "How is it you haven't been home for two days?" she said one morning, whispering as he lay there, not wanting to respond yet to the alarm, so happy to lie there enveloped in her softness.

He had planned to say Reeney was visiting her family. But then, turning to look at her, her eyes closed, her forehead wide and bare of sleep-tousled bangs, his fingers reaching for her pussy instinctively now, without thinking, without even desire, every morning knowing he would be turned on in minutes by her instant response: "I'm leaving her. I've left."

She moaned.

"Jezebel," he said.

"I don't think that's funny," she said, pushing his hand away. That made him hotter.

*A*udrey was demonstrating the computer storage system she had adapted to hold a patient's permanent lifetime hospital records. "No one ever again will send a heart patient home alone assuming he lives in an elevator building and has him keel over walking up five flights," she said. "Everything goes on file. Allergies, surgeries, congenital abnormalities, sibling history, living arrangements, drug history."

"Ideally, every hospital in America would feed into the storage bank," said the computer technician, demonstrating her system. "Till then, the patient gets a readout from the member hospital, which he keeps, and a microchip to carry with him . . . in case of emergency or accident."

Audrey looked untouched by the years, more beautiful, still clean-scrubbed, except for something she did to her eyelashes that made her eyes even bluer. "Of course we put most of that stuff in the chart and then nobody looks at the chart," Barney protested. "Then somebody gives the neosynephrine eye drops to the patient, forgetting he happens to be taking medication for glaucoma."

"You punch the prescription into the computer and the computer says, 'Forget it, chum, the patient has glaucoma.'"

"And where is the computer?" asked Barney. "At the nursing station. Under the pillow. Bedside. In the glove compartment. I like the concept but—"

"But. But. But. This is the famous Barney Kincaid, emergency chief of Goodman Hospital," Audrey introduced him to the computer technician. "He was the man who put together the symptom-diagnosis cross-reference microfilm concept. I was so happy knowing you're here, Barney," she said. "I read your paper on that mysthenia gravis diagnosis and that beautiful stuff on cosmic inspiration. I love that. It's you. Braving the mystery. Well, braving some mysteries." She said it ruefully. "He had all his students listening for extrasensory bells. The mysteries of the universe. . . . They're much less scary than the mysteries of one's own feelings, of course." Audrey touched his hair. "Barney, you look wonderful. The times really agree with you. Where did these wonderful curls come from?"

Barney stared at her. He hadn't seen this woman since his days as a resident at New Haven Hospital. How could she crawl into his head like that as if it hadn't been thirteen years since their last intimacy. She spoke as if she still knew him. As if he could not possibly have changed. Didn't she realize he was a different Barney then, a hyperphrenetic miracle worker, an animal, functioning on animal energy, moving instinctively without thought or analysis, knowing he must get out of his life with Reeney, out of a stultifying deadened marriage, behaving as if it were inevitable he would go, trapping himself again and again. How clever of Reeney to come down with mysterious fevers, fevers to rival his fever for Audrey. How clever to check into New Haven Hospital's third floor, looking flushed and beautiful, breasts big and swollen, tumbling out of black lace nightgown. How clever of her to agree, slightly incoherent from the fever, yes, Barney needed to be free, yes of course, she understood . . . the old give-him-a-long-leash gambit. Yes, she would wait. She would get a job and share the expenses so he could have his own place. How could he resist? Her hands stroking his face, the nipples bright rose through the spider webs of lace—Barney's deadly black widow. Yes, it was insane. The woman who hadn't turned him on for six years was suddenly irresistible—hotter than a *Playboy* centerfold. Poor spineless creep. He fucked her. Couldn't resist his own wife. And naturally she got pregnant. Every year in beds all over America trillions of sperms lose their way and this hapless sperm just manages to bump into a black widow egg.

Audrey refused to talk to him. She moved through the hospital—out of his service, thank God, and running herself ragged in surgery—pale as a ghost, subdued. In her weariness she got distracted and forgot to check the fluid balance of an ER patient en route to surgery, who just happened to be the administrator's father-in-law. Severely dehydrated, the man went into shock. A nurse discovered him just as Barney came on duty. In an instant Audrey got a second IV flowing as Barney put in a central venous line. The old man came out of it and Barney lied, saying he had meant to order fluids. The chief of medicine wasn't convinced. He knew damn well it wasn't like Barney to forget. But it was even less like Barney to lie. Audrey was not dismissed. Barney was reprimanded. The patient lived to die of a heart attack at a bingo game. He would always be remembered as the sport who wouldn't let the paramedics carry him away till he'd filled his bingo card.

Still, Audrey had not spoken. Instead, she wrote:

> I want to speak to you and behave like a healthy person who isn't suffering. But I can't. Not now, not yet. Thank you forever for saving me. I know you would not have done what you have done for any sentimental reason. I have to believe that you saved me because you consider my career worth saving. I respect how much you have given me, this extraordinary gift of your honor, especially as I have felt how difficult it is for you to give emotionally. If we speak now I will fall apart. I pull myself together every morning so I can survive the day because all I want is to finish here and be a good doctor and get on with my life.

"I hear great things about you," said Barney. "This record system is getting a lot of attention, of course. But your work with paramedics is great. Our dazzled mentor, Ken Stern, tells me you're his most brilliant disciple."

"After you, of course," she said.

"Of course."

"I loathe false humility," she said with a smile.

"And you're running three ERs or is it four?"

"Our corporation. My husband. He came out of Ken's program, too. He was at Yale. After us. You do look wonderful."

"Reeney and I have separated," he said. They had strolled into the lobby. In one corner a jazz trio was playing rather astounding improvisation. No one seemed to notice. "Isn't that something? After all these years."

She flushed. "Yes, I heard. I'm sorry, Barney. I hoped you were happy. Or content, at least. You hated hurting your folks. I think I knew you would never leave Reeney . . .

even before she got pregnant, because you thought it would devastate them. You used to say, 'My mother will kill me.'"

"No."

"Oh yes. 'My mother will kill me because I didn't drink orange juice this morning.' 'My mother would die if she knew I was wearing an unironed shirt, or worse . . . no underpants.'"

Barney laughed. He guessed he did have, still had, taunting dialogues with Mama. "You'd have a fit, Mama, if you could see me going down on this hot little shiksa pussy." But he had gone without underpants in laundry emergencies and started the day from time to time with a Heineken's instead of orange juice and finally left Reeney and there was Mama, struggling along on her celebrated Betty Grable gams, healthier at sixty-five than most women of forty-five. So she hadn't perished for the disobedience of her beloved princeling. What the hell did that mean? Should he stop trying to kill his mother? It was too oedipal to delve into. Imagine, living the Jewish joke for forty-two years and not even being amused by the punchline.

"Oh, here he is." There was something odd about the tall, slightly gangly man Audrey was hailing. "Barney, I want you to meet my husband. Boyd Dickstein." Odd, indeed. Dickstein was an inch or two taller and thinner, but he could have been Barney's younger brother. It was not just a slight resemblance. There was the same curling light-brown hair, the same slightly too-broad nose and blunt cheekbones. His ears stuck out a little. Barney was relieved about that. And the moustache made him feel safer. Dickstein had a bushy little moustache.

"You see," said Audrey. "You two do look alike. Ken Stern thought it was spooky." She hugged Dickstein's arm. He looked younger than she.

"You're really a legend at Yale, you know," he said. "And Audrey says you saved her life any number of times. She's a legend herself, now," he added proudly. "And a great teacher, too."

Barney wondered what she'd told him. In a funny way,

lying to save her was a greater intimacy than their affair. If she had betrayed that confidence, he wouldn't want to know.

They asked Barney to join them for dinner. He begged off.

"She's great, isn't she," Dickstein marveled. "Except for this congenital weakness she seems to have for Jewish-American princes from Brooklyn."

Barney decided to take that as a compliment. Back in his room he flipped through the guide to San Francisco nightlife. He knew he should be exhausted but he felt up, warmed by Audrey's knowing affection. How sweet she was and clever . . . to find her own Barney clone. He liked that. Now what did he want? He flipped through the entertainment come-ons and knew. He wanted junk food and sleaze. He wondered if the sex shows of San Francisco were real or faked? Only one way to find out.

*B*arney had delivered his paper on aortic trauma at the morning session. Then he wandered into the coffee shop, bored with all the doctor talk. Halfway through his grilled-cheese sandwich he knew he was going to call Barbara Bloome, now Mrs. Peter Battler, according to the note he'd jotted on a prescription form. His heart was pounding. From the booth he watched a woman testing lipsticks on her wrist. She was wearing bikini panties, a little too tight. And she could feel him watching, he knew, because she suddenly tugged at her skirt, trying to smooth down a bulge of hip.

"Mrs. Battler?" He recognized the voice, only a shade deeper perhaps. "Barbara Bloome?"

"Who's this?" she said.

"Barney. Barney Kincaid."

"Barney," she repeated.

"You remember," he said. She sounded so cold.

"What should I remember?"

Very testy she was. No way she would have forgotten. "Well, a long time ago, we were pinned. You wore my track sweater. I was the tall, thin—"

"The moths got it."

"What?"

"The moths ate your sweater. Yes, I remember, Barney. I promised myself I would erase the memory. But I remember. We were engaged."

Engaged? Surely he would have remembered that. "Not formally engaged," he began. "I remember we talked—"

"Are you selling something? Jesuz. There's a giant bug crawling around here."

"I was hoping to see you, Barbara. I'm in San Francisco at a medical meeting but I could rent a car and drive out to Sausalito."

"Nelson," she screamed to someone at her end. "There's a giant bug crawling around the telephone. Come take it away."

"Lunch, Barbara," he said. "I could skip the afternoon sessions."

"I bet you're a gynecologist," she said. "Or maybe a proctologist. You were quite an ass man. No, your mother wouldn't go for proctology."

"Hey, why are you so hostile? This is Barney. An old friend, a long lost love. I'm calling because you were always terrific and I want to say hello and catch up with the woman you are today."

"You weren't so terrific, Barney Cohen. So why don't you crawl back into the woodwork. Oh dear, did I say that? That doesn't sound like me."

"Barbara. I loved you. You loved me. We were children. I was really a child . . . silly, scared, insecure. You can't still be angry after all these years."

She sighed. "That would be neurotic," she said. "To be that angry after so many years. Okay. I'm curious. I'm an adventuress. I'll meet you at the Taco Rose Drive-in in

Sausalito at two o'clock. I'm curious to see if it's true a man gets the face he deserves."

Barney laughed. "I'll be the one that looks like Robert Redford."

"That will be a remarkable metamorphosis," she said. "You'll know me. Everything's the same. It's all just fallen a little. If you're a little late, don't bother coming. I've got a kid who gets chauffeured to obedience class this afternoon."

Barney weighed forgetting the whole idea. Barbara could be a pain in the ass as a seventeen-year-old. And she sounded like a postgraduate pain in the ass today. But what the hell. He was here, a bridge-span away. How could he resist? You can't get hurt if you don't really care. He was only curious, after all. It was late. The people at Avis did not try noticeably harder. Barney got lost coming off the bridge. He was twenty-five minutes late pulling into the Taco Rose. There was a convergence of motorcycles and a battered Porsche, no one over twenty in sight. He pulled in anyway and ordered a burrito because it came with sour cream and that made him feel less alien. The waitress wore overalls, cropped with a manicure scissors to reveal an inch of ass, breasts almost totally exposed. Barney knew he did not look anything like a California person. They were all uncoiled a notch or three. Everything was open. Their collars. Their windows. Even their wristwatches were looser. Barney felt uncomfortably tight and overdressed for eating burritos in a parked car. A Mercedes 450SL pulled up beside his orange Pinto. A Mercedes the green of old money. She sat there staring straight ahead at the Taco Rose price list, shades propped on top of a tangle of tawny hair—very California. He would not have recognized her anywhere. She had blossomed from pert little rabbit to golden goddess.

"Barbara?"

"It isn't Henry Kissinger, my friend." She turned to look at him. "You can't go home again. I won't say you haven't changed. I guess I could have guessed you'd put on a few pounds eventually."

He gave up on the burrito. A man can't defend himself

in verbal warfare with sour cream on his chin. "And you—" He smiled. "You look smashing."

"I got a little of everything they were selling," she said. "New nose. Caps. A good haircut. Aggravation. Tennis lessons. Dermabrasion. A laparoscopy. I'm in better shape than I've ever been. You were just going to say that."

She was not the same Barbara at all. Barney was fascinated by the change. "Is the Mercedes your permanent armor or are we going somewhere we can talk?" He thought he saw her jawline soften slightly. "My car or yours?"

"Anything less than a BMW would be conspicuous in my neighborhood," she said. "Okay. Get in."

Barney was excited sitting just inches from this woman. He loved feeling the strangeness and the nagging familiarity.

"What's up, Doc?" He touched her hand. "Don't. Touch. Me."

"What's an obedience class?"

She pulled out into traffic. "Oh that. The kid's on parole for selling coke to his gym teacher. I asked his father to be responsible for delivering him today so I'd have this time free. Barney, what do you want from me? Why are you here?"

Barney didn't really know. Chasing after your past was a strange occupation, fascinating but dangerous. Still, finding Margaret had been a curiously warm and positive experience. Imagining Barbie Bloome at his wake had reminded him of a time he'd been confused enough to run from unresolved confrontations. Had he come to seduce petulant little Barbie Bloome the dry-hump queen? "I thought we'd always be friends," he said, rather lamely.

"Men in midlife crisis do strange things," Barbara observed. "For goodness' sakes . . . we haven't spoken in twenty-two years."

"Less than that. I saw you during intermission at the theater. It was *Two for the Seesaw*, don't you remember?"

"We didn't speak. You spoke. I sneered."

He had forgotten. "Was I that bad?"

She pulled into a parking lot at the edge of a shopping mall, angled between a Citroën-Maserati and a custom Caddy, kelly green. "This is a nifty shopping center," she announced in the voice of a tour guide. "Don't touch me, Barney." He had only turned toward her. "I decided to see you again so I could find out how much I hate you. It infuriates me to find I still have that much feeling for you after twenty-two years. If I had a daughter of twenty who got jilted by some hotshot premed student, I'd tell her it was puppy love. That the pain would go away in no time. I dreamed my daddy would smash your head against a brick wall. I still dream of revenge."

"Well if making me feel like shit is revenge, you got it," said Barney. "I did love you," he said, feeling he must say it even though he wasn't sure what he had felt.

"You stopped loving me. You just turned it off. We were Jack and Jill. Remember? Two forlorn waifs. Remember we used to pretend we were orphans because we didn't want to believe we were actually born in such proletarian families?"

He had forgotten. The Barbara Bloome he remembered was popular, confident, teasing and fickle. He was the one that had been betrayed. After all, she had fucked everyone, everyone but Barney "because you're the one I want to marry," she had explained.

In his fantasy scenario of seeing Barbie again, the movement was static. He'd imagined a grown-up woman with a ponytail, daughters looking like the Barbie of the Fifties. Sex was not a specific, though he had toyed with the image of humping her in a supermarket and got himself off last night with that and images of fucking a sandwich of Debra and the Goddess Diana, realizing only the next morning that, in fact, the two looked uncannily alike. Now, without a word, Barbara drove the car through three flashing yellow lights and up a scraggly ravine road, turning in at the marker, "Imported Dreams." She drove silently past a big pink stucco house to a studio with a large palladium window. "My playhouse," she said.

There was a vast waterbed on a platform, soft indirect light and dimmer switches and Donna Summer wafting from somewhere. There was a pale, unfinished oil painting on an easel and canvases stacked in bins. "Mrs. Battler paints a bit," she said. She stopped before a tall platform mirror. She tossed her head. She arched her back. She stood thighs apart—like a Bond woman, Barney thought—and started to unbutton her shirt. Just like that. The surprise of it made him hard immediately. She undid an Indian belt and unzipped tight white pants. He stopped her hand and pulled her into a closet, pressing her against the wall, digging his body into her. The heat of the elevator humpings came flaring back. How she used to blow in his ear. How they would choke on each other's tongues. He almost felt the closet rising. She was getting it, too, he believed, fighting his fingers tearing at her pants just as she had then, a thousand times, maddeningly resisting. Barney was close to coming when she pushed him away and held him still.

"Show me what you've learned since the elevator," she said, leading him back into the room. She stepped out of her pants. She was wearing pale-blue underwear. It shimmered and felt like silk. He sensed that she had planned this from the beginning and he marveled again, as he often did, how sexual a woman could be when she decided to be. She lay back on the bed, not touching him, no longer kissing him, touching herself—letting him do everything to her. Eyes closed, purring now and then, provoking him by her heat and her passivity till finally he was banging away, going against the roll of the water bed to penetrate deeper as she braced herself against the frame of the mirrored wall, one corner of a pillow gripped in her teeth, refusing to give him the tiniest gift of a cry.

They lay still as the bed's rocking slowed. She seemed unmoved, calm, a bit smug even, he thought. "I was very vulnerable once," she said.

Her teeth were bright white and perfect.

"I loved kissing you with the braces," he said. "I think I actually miss them."

"Well, I say thank God I'm graduated from braces. My bite represents the masterworks of not one but two crazed orthodontists, whose wives wear mink stoles thanks to my wayward incisors."

Barney did not say that he still had abandoned wires from orthodontist one in his front closet. To tell the truth, Barney was depressed, so depressed he could not move. When he awoke forty-five minutes later he was glad to find her gone. He looked for a note. There was none. How was he supposed to get back to his car? On a chair he found his high school letter sweater. It had indeed been under siege by moths. A black man in a white jacket knocked at the screen door.

"To the Taco Rose," the man said, grinning.

Barney nodded. He rolled his old sweater into a ball and tucked it under his arm with exaggerated nonchalance. Was the Taco Rose her meat market? He felt like a sex object and he was unnerved to discover that it did not feel good.

She called just as he snapped the lock on his suitcase. "I can't leave well enough alone," she said. "I'm not the cunt I meant to be."

Barney didn't know what to say. "I'm sorry," he said.

"We never did figure out what *you* wanted," she said. "I was too busy getting mine. Which isn't like me at all, really, I'm a nice woman."

"You are—"

"You don't know," she said. "I'm married to a very bright, funny, serious man. Everything he's done, in business, I mean, we did together, which he is always quick to acknowledge on his good days and likes to forget when he's down. Anyway, I do have a good life and I only fool around a little, just sex, you know, nothing serious, and probably he does too only he's very private about it and I'm a bit brazen. I would have loved to know you as a grown-up Barney. I think I'd like you better. You always were special . . . sensitive, not like most boys your age. You could always see into my mind, finish my sentences. I remember. Today was mean. I just had to do it. I couldn't stop myself. If you have time, I'd like to pretend it didn't happen and meet again. We could talk."

Barney looked at his watch. He was catching the red eye. "We could have a drink at the airport," he said.

"Should we?" she asked.

"There really isn't a lot of time," he said.

"The important thing is I did love you," she said. "And you in your way wanted to love me. And I wasn't just being sneaky. I was trying to be smart, not going all the way with the one I hoped to marry. That's the way we were in those days."

"I remember," said Barney.

*I*t was after three P.M. when he got home. The doorman handed him a package from Florida. He recognized Mama's script from Fort Lauderdale, where after pleas of poverty and exhaustion his parents had reluctantly been persuaded to retreat from the snow. Barney slashed the mailing tape with a kitchen knife. Inside were four sacks, each weighing at least two pounds, a king's ransom of raisins, dates, figs, and prunes, with a note:

> On our anniversary. Posies, pickles, prunes and prisms are all very good words for the lips, especially prunes and prisms.
>
> Love,
> Mom and Dad.

He laughed. "Prunes and prisms," he repeated aloud, enjoying his mouth's double pucker. That dame was really something. If he were an emotionally stable adult he would eat a prune and to hell with her. But he wasn't sure he wanted to risk it. He would drop the box off tomorrow on East Ninety-third Street. Candy would not take a prune personally. She could share them with her imaginary little brother.

*B*arney was exhausted. He stayed late organizing the takeover proposal for New Grace Hospital. Professionally staffed emergency rooms were just beginning to catch on here in the East. Older doctors were suspicious, rigid, and tough to persuade. But New Grace had a dynamic young director who had worked with Ken Stern in Denver. Now he had to persuade him New Grace's ER would be better off under a local team with only one other ER contract rather than a Midwestern consortium already running a dozen shops. Barney wanted to nap before picking up Candy for dinner at Lindsay's. Automatically he switched on Channel 3. A smirking wimp was interviewing two child actors. He turned the sound off. His eyes closed. He jerked awake. There was Debra. She looked earnest and sincere—big blue eyes open wide, teeth flashing. She looked like all those wholesome, peppy, asexually Middlewestern American women that clutter the TV screen. She had a bag of potatoes in one hand. She held a potato up to the camera. Now she was tossing the bag of potatoes over her shoulder with exaggerated disdain. Barney lay there mesmerized. She reached off camera and came back with a giant nurse doll. She made another face at the camera. She stroked the doll's hair, tugging at the arm. The arm came off in her hand. She tugged at a leg. The leg came off, too. She tossed the leg over her shoulder. She picked up a cigarette lighter and set fire to the doll's other leg. It burst into flame.

Irwin Storm, Channel 3's weatherman, crashed onto the screen in a fireman's slicker and hat and sprayed the doll at Debra's feet with a fire extinguisher. There was a long shot of the two of them staring down at the charred remains. Then a closeup of the weatherman laughing. And Debra scolding him. "This is not a laughing matter," Barney was sure she was saying. He switched the set off as she wiggled her accusatory finger at him. And went off to shave. She had great spirit, that woman, Barney marveled, and spectacular legs.

*B*arney meant to buy flowers but the florist between Ninetieth and Ninety-first streets was already closed. What a foolish hour to close. Barney thought he ought to bring something. Gifts were not easy for him. Whatever he bought seemed to be wrong. Mama was allergic to wool, she announced out of nowhere when he gave her a cashmere bathrobe. He'd never seen her wear the jade he'd brought from Hong Kong. Reeney was just as difficult. He'd given up on gifts. Every woman he'd known had complained.

"Narcissists can't be bothered thinking of anyone else," he'd once snapped at Debra. (That was her analyst's latest discovery: Barney was a narcissist. Debra couldn't resist a full-blown narcissist. "Is that my fault?" he had protested. "I'm just a kink in your life pattern.")

Barney studied the drugstore display. There was a Water Pik, an electric curling iron, and a threatening platoon of vibrators. One of them was three-speed and looked like the Concorde. Everything in the window was slightly faded and layered with dust. The next shop window was full of leotards, pantyhose, garter belts, and handknit

babyclothes. All the women on the leotard packages had
bodies in a permanent S-curve. There was a stiff half-bra
with a narrow border of lace that exposed the aureoleless
breasts of a plaster mannequin. Barney was suddenly reminded of the black strapless armor Reeney had worn to
college dances, lace braced with wires and metal to pinch her
waist and push her breasts into two high soft bouncing
melons unnaturally close to her clavicle. Breasts were really
high in those days. Women had trussed themselves into very
serious suspension systems. It had taken an aeronautics
engineer like Howard Hughes to invent the ultimate suspension system for Jane Russell. What innocent days those were
. . . when tussling with Jane Russell in the hay had been
fiercely hot masturbatory material. "What do you want to be
when you grow up, little boy?" grown-ups always asked. "A
doctor," Barney would say. Who would have dreamed he'd
become a grown man secretly haunting Bloomingdale's
lingerie department endlessly fascinated with women buying
panties.

The lingerie shop was closed. There was a line at the
cashier's in the Korean food market and the carnations were
wilted anyway. The tobacco stand sold magazines, candy
bars, and ball-point pens. Stupid. Whatever he bought
would look like the last-minute desperation it was.

Candy was watching from the window already scarved
and furred for the street, perspiring in her bunny-fur
bonnet. "It isn't too late for the movies, is it?" She bit her lip.

Barney had forgotten the movie, of course. He'd promised a movie and chicken à la king crêpes, her favorite food
of the moment. She was sulky when he broke the news that it
was dinner at Lindsay's. "That's rotten," she said. "It was *our*
time together. You promised."

"It's a surprise," Barney said lamely.

"Surprises are something that makes you happy," said
Candy. She was wearing high-heeled boots, weird grown-up
boots. The streets were still messy from the last snow. "Can
you walk on those heels?" Barney asked.

"Of course," she said defiantly, wobbling along in an
odd mincing gait.

He decided to promise her the moon, a movie on Saturday and a hot fudge sundae at Serendipity on the way home. "If you keep it a secret between us so Lindsay and her kids aren't jealous."

"And maybe I can buy a small little treasure at Serendipity, too."

"We'll see." They trudged across town. He was trying to think of a casual, unthreatening approach to the psychological problems suggested by imaginary brothers and closet peepshows. Was there a way? He couldn't imagine. "Why did you tell Ms. Gilligan you had a little brother?"

"I explained that to Mommy."

"I would feel special if you would explain it to me, too."

"I wrote a novel. And in the novel . . . well, it was probably more like a short story, there was a teenage girl whose parents split and she had a little brother. And the father in my novel definitely preferred playing with the brother. But actually, you see, the little brother was really you. He looked like you in the pictures at Grandma's, I mean. And I don't know why I told her the story like it was my true life. It just came out that way."

"Whew. That is fancy, Candy," said Barney. "That is very complicated." He thought for a moment. "I am the little brother?"

"Daddy, it's just a story."

"You certainly don't feel I love Lindsay's children more than I love you? The affection I feel for them is not in the same ballpark with my love for you. You know that?"

She was silent.

He stopped and pulled her into his arms. "You know that?"

"I'm stupid," she said, sobbing. "I'm insecure. I'm just insecure. I'm only a kid, you know." He hugged her. And licked the tears.

"Those tears are salty so they can't be real," he said.

"Oh daddy."

He didn't have the courage to take on the peepshow stuff. He decided to discuss it first with Dick Rogin.

*U*sually dinner with Lindsay and her children was relaxed and easy. The food was there, neither startlingly awful nor remarkable. Just food, served without flash or pomp or an inherent demand for congratulation. The conversation was cheerful and affectionate. No temper tantrums, no competition, no innocent comments designed to maim or kill. All very gentile, Barney thought. The girls cleared. Leftovers were speedily dispatched and Lindsay went off to supervise homework. Barney would be left alone swishing the heavy oval casserole clean in Lindsay's kitchen. All those years married to Reeney, Barney had never touched a pot. But the times had raised his consciousness. Yes, even *his* Jewish-American-princely sexism had cracked. Barney had never realized how comfortable he would feel with a woman who had a life of her own. Never sensed how much rage simmered inside him at carrying Reeney, financing her career as the world's most insatiable consumer. It's true Reeney had some time ago made noises about getting a job, part time with some society publicist, but they both believed in full-time mothering. Everybody did in those days. If he was guilty of oppressing his wife, Reeney and Dr. Spock were certainly co-conspirators. By his chauvinism, Barney had almost certainly saved Reeney from humiliating failure. Barney grunted. That was a clever rationalization. But he liked to believe it.

Tonight at Lindsay's, Barney felt a strain. He shouldn't have done this to Candy. She sat between Lindsay's two willowy sylphs sipping water after each bite of tuna-macaroni casserole as if that were the only way she could keep from throwing up. Emily flirted outrageously with Barney. And Fawn watched, giggling. They were breathtakingly beautiful, both tall, reed-thin and astonishingly graceful.

Emily was fourteen going on thirty, with mahogany eyes, thick straight brows, and a heart-shaped face. Already she knew she made men weak. Even Barney got her message. She smiled at him knowingly, white cotton nightgown drooping low over nonexistent breasts, taffy-brown hair pinned high with a few curls drooping. He felt she knew everything about him and definitely did not approve. Fawn giggled a lot and bit her lower lip and was always scratching imagined itches. She thought her own pink-and-white poster prettiness was plain beside Emily's stunning beauty. Between them Candy's misery made her seem hunched and sallow, a sad sparrow.

Little Baxter (they called him Pooh) stared at Candy. "You look like a goldfish the way you do that water," he said.

"And you're a frog," Candy snapped back.

Pooh was caught midswallow and began to choke.

"Quick Daddy, do the Heimlich mover," cried Candy, leaping out of her chair. Pooh was really turning blue.

Barney hit his back. Whatever it was came flying across the table and Pooh started breathing again.

"Ohhh," cried Candy. "Why didn't you do a Heimlich mover? Debra did it on television twice last week."

Lindsay held a sobbing Pooh on her lap. She hid her head in his neck.

"Oh you're so wonderful," cooed Emily to Barney. "You moved so fast." She danced forward and kissed Barney's mouth.

"Emily, clear the table," Lindsay ordered.

"It's too bad what's happened to the nuclear family," Candy proclaimed, hiding the remains of her casserole under a leaf of lettuce. "Once they start splitting, whissshhh . . . that's the beginning of emotional devastation."

"How old did you say you are?" Lindsay asked pointedly, knowing damn well how old.

"It's not age, it's I.Q.," said Candy. "Mine is one hundred and forty-two. I read a lot and I might be an actress and a novelist."

Barney hated himself for finding Candy, ordinarily

precious and lovable, quite sullen and unrefined next to the shimmering delicacy of Lindsay's wispy Wasp beauties.

He stifled such disloyal thoughts, hugged Lindsay quickly (as her analyst had suggested when the children were around) and left much earlier than he'd planned, rushing Candy to Serendipity, where he hoped the hot fudge would be soothing and an instant shot of consumerism would prove restorative. Candy had no trouble at all finding a pair of enameled flower earrings she could not live without.

"But sweetheart, these are for pierced ears," said Barney.

"Daddy," she cried, exasperated. "I have pierced ears."

He was upset. When had that happened? Wasn't she too young for pierced ears? He couldn't remember if she'd had them pierced before or after the separation.

*B*arney went looking for Dick Rogin early the next morning. Dick's office was empty but the light was on. There was no one in the cafeteria either except for a couple of aides in the corner and Joe di Renzo, who sat surrounded by his usual shopping bags and duffels. "Hey, Joe," Barney began. "You can't still be here. I thought you promised the administrator and me you'd stay home." Joe had socks and underwear spread over the table. "What the hell are you doing?" cried Barney.

"I'm folding my laundry," di Renzo said aggressively, as if folding laundry were a requirement for his survival. "I did go home but I came back last night because I had shooting pain in my arm. This arm, Dr. Kincaid. I think I should hang around till we're sure I definitely am out of danger."

Barney, having so recently survived his own shooting pains, decided not to argue.

"Hey, Dr. Kincaid." It was Dick Rogin, being formal, calling from the cafeteria doorway.

"You coming in?" asked Barney. "We can talk."

"I don't know," said Dick. "I'm not safe. I tell myself I'll just have tea and then I sit down and order donuts. I'm afraid to come in."

"Let me get you a tea to go," said Barney. "Then we can talk in your office if you've got a few minutes." He never ceased to be amazed at how nutty Dick could be and still function as the competent psychiatrist he was. Or so Barney assumed. With psychiatry how could you really know?

Dick looked torn. "Tea? Yeah. Were you going to get a donut or a Danish for yourself? One bite might get me through the morning without a glucose fit."

Back in his office, Dick was definitely calmer. "You sit in my chair," he said. "My neck is killing me. I'll lie down. It's from lack of necking."

"What?" Barney hadn't followed that at all.

"My neck is stiff from lack of necking," said Dick. "It's symbolic of course, but the pain is real. There is no spontaneity in a marriage that is one hundred two years old. No matter what I would tell my patients about black nightgowns and new positions. You just don't get to sit in a car and neck." He popped a small wedge of donut in his mouth and chewed with a beatific expression on his face. "Eat the rest of it fast, Barney," he said. "Or flush it. Whatever you do, don't toss what's left in my wastebasket." He sighed. "I feel better." He sat up. "Are you still seeing Debra Teiger? She looks like a handful. Never mind, don't tell me. I get too many steamy confidences in my line of work. What about Linda Menker? Have you found her?"

"Not yet, but I took your suggestion and got my friend at the *Post* to trace her for me. I'm not sure it's particularly productive to be chasing after the past like this. Remember Barbie Bloome?"

"The dry-hump queen."

"I called her in San Francisco and, well, hell, Dick. It's twenty-two years. She's a stranger. I'm a totally different person than the rotten kid she knew. But she needed to get revenge on the rotten kid."

"In bed?" Dick prompted.

Barney was surprised. "Well, yes. Is that some Freudian axiom, too? There I am wondering if I dare touch this glorious golden woman and she's already decided to get me in the sack and make me feel like a piece of meat. Somehow getting even for . . . whatever. I'm not the same man. After all, your body cells change completely every seven years "

"The memory cells seem to transfer the agony," Dick noted. "You know, Barney. It's not just you. It's this hospital. The place is a sexual swamp. I get the feeling people are making out everywhere. Clerks. Candy-stripers. Students. Nurses. You heard about Ed Filmer and that cute little X-ray technician, Anita, I suppose? And Dr. Djarta went out twice last week with Ernie Cooperman in orthopedics, who, by the way, is fooling around with what's-her-name in radiology on the side. And the interns and residents are all screwing every minute they're not actually on duty and some of them do it on duty. One of the student nurses told me she was attacked in a supply closet by a certain attendant who shall remain nameless."

"Attacked? Well, that's something else—"

"She just used the word 'attacked,'" Dick corrected. "She loved it. She agreed to be attacked again the next afternoon. In the parking lot even, I saw a couple in surgical greens making out in an ambulance. Yes."

"The morgue, too," Barney egged him on. "Are they screwing each other or diddling the corpses?"

"I wouldn't be surprised. Necrophilia. You're not discounting my observations, are you?"

"Necrophilia," Barney mused. "She's not too lively in bed but at least she won't gossip. I think you may be exaggerating the reality due to your own frustration, Dick. I feel silly analyzing the analyst. But maybe you want to see sexual anarchy as a way of justifying whatever it is you are thinking . . . planning. You and Jeanette have a solid partnership, it seems to me," said Barney, wanting to be helpful. "I've never seen you two ever be anything but loving and respectful together. You know how rare that is. Endless sport sex can be very empty."

Dick groaned. "This from you. Oh Barney, I don't want to be a faithless husband, but I don't want to atrophy before my time. I'm looking at eighteen-year-old bodies all the time now. Hungrily."

"Maybe you should go off your diet," Barney advised. "It can't be good to suffer deprivation in too many areas at one time."

"Very wise advice," Rogin agreed. "If I get grossly obese, no one will go to bed with me anyway. No. I must get rid of this paunch. Obesity is too disgusting." He sat up, craning his neck. "At least I want to hold on to my options. And if I get a big fat hard-on, I don't want my stomach blocking the view so I can't even see it." He laughed. "Well, we've solved my midlife crisis. You wanted to see me?"

Barney had forgotten why he'd come. He sat there a moment. Closets. Oh yes. "This probably isn't complicated at all. My little girl, Candy, our only child. She's twelve, going to be thirteen. Seems she told her teacher I love her little brother more than I love her."

"She's an only child you said?"

"Right. We're dealing with an imaginary little brother. When I asked, she told me she'd written a story about a teenage girl whose parents get divorced and the father favors the younger brother. And she says she patterned the brother after a photograph of me. Me as a child. And then she just pretended it was her true story when she spoke to the teacher. Listen, I know Candy has been hurt by my leaving home. I suspect being an only child can't make that any easier. As a single man my life seems to be more complicated instead of simpler. The sexual round robin you seem to be seeing all around you. And then my illness put me out of touch for a while. Cortisone does weird things to your mind. I'm up and I'm down. But I try to be there for Candy when we're together. Alternate weekends and one night a week, sometimes two. Fortunately, she and Reeney are extremely close—almost like sisters. So Candy could not be more loved, or spoiled, I suppose."

"The Linda Menker thing may be more meaningful than you realize," said Dick, standing and getting into a professional posture that instantly projected authority. "It is connected. This wild search of yours. Forgive me, I don't mean wild. Barney, you've just gone through two major crises. Divorce and serious illness. Both create enormous stress. If you're scared, of course Candy has to be frightened, too. And your reaction has been to go chasing after your past. I don't say that isn't important and useful," Dick added hastily. "I believe it is. But you could almost say you are trying to get in touch with that little boy, the child you were, aren't you?"

"So if Candy takes off her panties with little boys in the closet, it's my fault?"

"Aha. The father's real problem emerges. Sex play in the closet. Give me my chair," said Dick. "She wants to know what little boys have down there. Twelve seems a little old for that. Exaggerated sexuality is a way of getting back at you, my friend. Getting you to pay attention, which in fact, you are. She can punish you because she can't have you for herself."

How is a man trapped in his adolescence supposed to handle so much emotional responsibility? Barney wondered. "Reeney is right." He sighed. "We should buy her a horse."

"A horse should do it," Dick mused, tilting back in his leather tilt-chair. "A horse is the classic sublimation for little girls. Catherine of Russia carried the horse sublimation to its ultimate expression. Women are awesome," he brooded. "I say stop feeling so guilty, Barney—ha! as if we could deny our destiny. Give up the guilt, my friend. Treat her like a daughter and not like a girlfriend."

Barney was thoughtful. It could be too late for that. Candy had been marrying him and stealing him away from Reeney since she was three. He got up to go.

Dick got up, too. "You don't want to miss that gal from the Human Sexuality Institute at Lynfield. She's lecturing here Wednesday for our residents. She's the one advocating sex for the disabled. The orderlies should help the disabled with sex and then close the door and leave the room. I hear she's got great tits."

"Sounds good to me," said Barney. "Sex for the disabled."

"If sex comes to the disabled, surely it will come to me," cried Dick.

*I*t was only a little after nine in the morning and already Barney felt tired. Henderson was off at a meeting of the city's fire and emergency medical services to draft protocols governing the responsibility of fire fighters and medical corpsmen at a fire or accident. Only a month earlier a Goodman Memorial paramedic had punched a fireman in a tugging match over a burn victim.

Barney was studying the patient lineup chalked on the board by the Fudgesicle and Nurse Gilles Coburn, when a Security cop raced into the room and grabbed his arm. "There's a woman choking in the parking lot," he cried. "Husband says she's asthmatic."

"Bring a stretcher. Mallory. An IV." Barney grabbed an instrument bag out of a startled paramedic's hand and raced outside. The woman was gasping for air, in severe bronchial spasm, her head thrashing the seat in a stationwagon so packed with gear it would have given anyone claustrophobia.

As they pulled her out of the wagon, she stopped breathing. Barney inserted an endotrachial tube and started ventilating her.

"I shouldna been so stubborn," the man with her moaned. "I was just tryin' to get to Yonkers before lunch. She's always thinkin' she's about to have an attack and most times she don't." The resident, Timothy Trees, had already got one IV going. "Move her fast," said Barney. "She's so tight we're not getting much air in." Wheeling her through the parking lot with the IVs held aloft was like a primitive dance, he thought, sweat freezing on his forehead. Barney stumbled over a crust of frozen snow. In that instant he saw her dead, saw Trees's face accusing him, heard his own voice presenting the case to the mortality committee. The husband tugged at his sleeve. Barney shoved him away. "Stand back," he snapped.

His heart was pounding. The sound of his own blood in his ears was like an angry ocean. He was afraid his chest would burst. The sound in his ears was deafening. He felt himself being pulled down, caught in a powerful undertow. He fell against the wall, caught himself, as the chorus of white-coated figures and IV lines wiggled the stretcher through the door. Everything blurred as he stood there, drenched in sweat, willing his body to behave, consciously calming the surge of his blood. He took two or three deep breaths and felt control returning. Already the woman was hooked to a respirator and the color was coming back into her face. Barney was overwhelmed by a sense of relief that was almost three-dimensional. No one had noticed his distress. They had all been focused on the patient. Barney had to sit down. He was shivering with cold. He locked himself into his supply-closet–office. If they needed something, let them knock.

He had a dozen phone messages in his hand. He could not remember picking them up. Debra. His mother. Names that were meaningless. A former student wanting to use him as a reference. A lawyer. His reporter friend at the *Post*. "Linda Menker" was the message. And a phone number. Barney smiled. He remembered Linda Menker's astonishing breasts, bigger than his hand, her cool, exquisite skin. He tilted his chair back. And then he remembered why the drowning sensation moments ago seemed so familiar. It was like the drowning of his nightmares after Amy died. The helplessness. Not being able to reach her. He gathered enough saliva in his mouth to swallow two cortisone pills. He still felt too weak to go for water. He dialed Carl at the *Post,* curious for details. Would Linda remember his—what would he call it?—gallantry, his sensitivity? Would she remember him at all? Barney recalled feeling intent at the time upon proving that not all high school jocks were animals.

"I'm hot on the track of that nurse, Lilyanne Beech," Carl reported. "That is, I've located her daughter, one of the twins, Iris, married now, Iris . . . what's that fucking name? Here it is . . . Iris Takapolis. Lives in some small town upstate, near Kingston. It's the nine-one-four area code. Maybe she'll give you her mother's number. For some reason, she was very evasive with me. But listen . . . if you don't get what you want, let me know. We have our ways."

Barney sighed. Iris Takapolis. He dared not imagine what Lilyanne's sex-mad moppets had grown into. No porn movie he'd ever seen was as hot as those hours with Lilyanne's twins often followed by intense, almost painful times being aroused again and pleasing Lilyanne.

What a hobby Barney had discovered, this stepping into the past. For a man with professional ambition, time was very precious. He would sleep less and do more, he decided. He congratulated himself on the simple brilliance of his decision.

He picked up an inter-office envelope on his desk. Inside was a note in careful printing, by someone who was obviously not much in the habit of printing.

"Vengeance is a double-edged sword," it read. "Let he who is without blemish cast the first stone."

Barney snorted. Gunderson's work, he supposed. The man had a point; Barney suspected Goodman Memorial's board would probably not be overjoyed to find their emergency chief among the stained-raincoat set at the Pussycat Cinema. He sighed. Perhaps he would have to be more discreet.

Someone was pounding at the door.

"Why is the door locked?" It was Mallory. "Are you in there, Dr. Kincaid?"

He sprang out of his chair and opened the door.

"Dr. Kincaid. Quick. Come to three-B. We have a baby with something caught in the larynx."

Barney raced around a couple of stretchers. A boney little boy was gasping for air. "I need some hands quick," Barney said. "Here Steffans. Trees. Mallory. Grab a foot. His arms. Hold him down. Mother, you wait outside, please. Jesuz, Stef. Keep him still." It was hard to hold the boy's head rigid. His eyes were wide, full of terror. With the boy's mouth forced open, Barney could reach in with the laryngoscope. "I see it," he said. "It's a plastic fork." The fork was lodged between the vocal cords. He caught one of the tines with a large hemostat and pulled. The tine broke off. The kid tore loose, struggling, kicking.

"Hold him down," Barney roared. "Hold him down." He got a second tine with the hemostat and pulled. It broke off too. The kid was starting to turn blue. "Hold him. Damn it. Hold him," Barney bellowed. The child was fighting harder. Stef braced himself against the wall. Mallory was panting, hair loose. Barney's heart was pounding. What if this prong broke? Barney's whole body was a river of sweat. Am I going to have to do a thyroidectomy? he thought. There's no time left. This isn't going to work. He reached in again. This kid is going to die, he thought. And the last tine held. The fork came loose. Barney stood there shaking, his whole body weak, knees buckling, staring at the fork. He couldn't believe it. So close. So close. Stef was holding the boy, hugging him. The kid was screaming. What a sublime sound. Barney backed out of the room.

He had played against the odds. That was not like him. He had often felt that combination of anxiety and exhilaration but never such doubt, such remorse, never so intensely.

Barney felt strange, hollow. That child . . . it had been too close. Did he think he was some kind of god, that he knew that fork was coming out of there? He should have tried once and then cut—played it safe. He was dizzy and confused. He ducked into the stairwell. He felt a sadness falling over him like a deep fog, a depression so heavy he had to sit. He collapsed on a step and began to sob. Ugly wracking sounds came out of him.

Mallory stood in the door. "Dr. Kincaid." She backed away, unwilling to invade his sorrow.

Barney grabbed her wrist. Her skin felt cool. He was hot, eyes burning with salt, cheeks stinging. "No, listen," said Barney. "It's all right. The fork didn't break. Everyone has doubts. I wasn't sure that we'd win that one." He was still crying but he felt much better. "There's always that question in your mind, you know, when you make a choice. I didn't want to cut, not when I could see the thing there and reach it. Especially a kid, you know." He wiped his eyes. She mopped his face with some gauze. "Don't go yet," he said.

"We all think of you as the steely Superdoc," said the Fudgesicle. "Crazed at times and a bit rigid but no sign of emotion. Are you all right? I'll get you some water."

"So that's me? Well, I guess that's how I like to be perceived. I didn't know I had tears in me." He grinned. "Well, it's probably the steroids I've been taking for my virus. Steroids do strange things to the brain." He wanted to think of something to say, to keep her there.

"What it is . . . " he began. "I know I'm good. I can say that, straight, you'll understand. I know I'm good. But once in a while I remember that I'm just human. I'm not God. I'm going to hurt so much if that patient dies. It is my hurt too, right?"

"Yes. That's why we have to be more than human. I suppose that's why some people see us as . . . cold."

She seemed uncomfortable talking about it.

"I'm fine now," he said. "Don't let me depress you."

"You should lie down for a while," Mallory said. "Go into the interns' room. Can you fall asleep, do you think? I'll wake you if anything serious comes in."

He had astounded himself. He couldn't remember the last time he'd cried. Barney's throat ached. It felt parched and raw. He drank nearly a quart of water, forcing himself finally to stop drinking, and lay down in the dark.

Nurse Emerson woke him. He was furious when he

realized it was after one A.M. "How could you let me sleep like that?" he said.

"Mrs. Mallory told me to let you sleep," she said, indignantly. "You must have needed it or you wouldn't still be dead to the world. I woke you only because there's a patient I know you'll want to see."

"I'm going home, Mrs. Emerson," said Barney. The night-shift nurse was a stickler for protocol, a relentless old fussbudget and worth three times her salary, a brilliant nurse. "Give him to the resident, whoever's on." He stood up, searching pockets for his pills.

"Her," said Mrs. Emerson, pointedly, with a knowing smirk. "Not him. Her. And you'll be quite annoyed if you don't see her yourself. A cute little blonde who claims she was raped at Plato's Retreat."

Barney pinched Mrs. Emerson's cheek. He felt better already. "You naughty girl. I recognize my duty," he announced, buckling his belt and tousling his curls, as he followed Mrs. Emerson to the gynecology examining room.

Her face was streaked with mascara, purple lipstick, and tears. She studied him, wary and faintly hostile. Even so the resemblance to Amy was startling. The chart said she was twenty-two but she looked younger, young enough to be Amy's daughter, Barney calculated. But he did not know Amy had a daughter, only that she'd been killed on a Georgetown street when a car drove up over the sidewalk and pinned her against a mailbox.

"Amber Sinclair?" he said. "Amber St. Clair. Hmmm. Is that your name?"

"You know Amber St. Clair?" she said. "It's amazing how few people do remember her. *Forever Amber*. My mom was madly in love with that book as a teenager. So here I am . . . a great adventuress. Getting raped at Plato's Retreat." She scowled. "Your nurse is very snotty. Didn't seem to think anyone could be raped at Plato's. Wanted to know wasn't that what I went there for? Imagine."

Barney imagined. Oh how he imagined. He had often imagined himself at Plato's, naked in the pool, wrapped in a tangle of arms and thighs and breasts in the orgy room.

"How did it happen?" Barney asked, examining her body for contusions as Mrs. Emerson fussed with the draping of sheets.

"It's so incredible," Amber went on. "Imagine anyone having to rape someone at Plato's. Everyone is there for fun. Guys are basically laid back. No one ever gets really aggressive." She let Mrs. Emerson put her feet in the stirrups. Barney pulled her rump toward him. There were some bruises, purpling fast. "This big fat brute. He pulled me into one of the private rooms in the back and tied his belt around my mouth. For a minute I thought it was a joke, you know. Then he twisted my arm till I thought it was coming out of the socket. We've gotta get him."

Her vagina was raw and flaming and there would probably be more bruises. She was so fair, almost blue-white. Barney tried to convince her she would have a hard time getting the average cop to sympathize with someone's getting raped at Plato's. He nodded at Emerson to leave.

"But that isn't fair," she said, tears running down her face. "If I get raped on the street I'm furious enough but I figure, hey, that's New York. The city is full of creeps. But Plato's should be . . . sacred. Like a church, you know. A place where you find sexual sanctuary."

Barney stared at her. She was so earnest and beautiful. And utterly indignant. "What do you do?" he asked. "For a living?" She was an actress. Of course. What else? She modeled and auditioned, worked as a waitress, and had once scored two days' work as an extra in the disco scene of *Nighthawks*. Barney kept her there talking, leaning against the wall, letting her vent her rage and move beyond it.

"Hey, you're a real neat guy," she said. "I came in here hot to commit murder. Boy, anger sure can eat you up. I can't hardly believe it but I honestly feel better. I think I don't have to cut off that creep's balls to get rid of the pain. How can I thank you?"

Barney dropped her off at a high-rise in Riverdale before heading back to the city. "You should go to Plato's and see what I mean," she said, kissing his cheek, catching him totally by surprise. "I'll take you if you like."

"Well, we'll see," said Barney, but not even for a moment did he consider not accepting the offer. It was not Amber herself that he wanted—Barney wasn't interested in the embryo of a woman. But he could use a guardian angel at Plato's.

"*E*veryone misses you," Barney began with highly uncharacteristic diplomacy. Frieda Thompson had died her gray hair bright red. She seemed a bit evasive, surprised to find him in the gloomy waiting room of a nursing home in Queens, a crummy, morbid-looking dump.

"The money here is good," she said. "And the old folks are real grateful for whatever we do." When Barney got down to the question of Gunderson, Nurse Thompson got very oily. "Oh, you doctors know more about those technical things. A good nurse is a good soldier. We follow orders. You don't expect me to recall details of every case." She smiled as if smiling hurt and looked at her watch.

Barney snapped open his attaché case, noisily, almost brutally, considering it was a Gucci case and cost a fortune. He had copies of the patient charts with him. He gave her time to glance at them, then handed her a graphologist's report. "This man, who interprets handwriting for the federal government, says these cramped letters and the misspellings here and here suggest that whoever wrote them was lying." She looked at him. She looked away.

"You don't like Dr. Gunderson," she said. "He says you're out to destroy him."

"Aha," said Barney in what he believed was solid private investigator style. "He's been in touch with you. Of course.

Look, Frieda, we're talking about patients who died. One was in your care. And now another. And I've found three more. You're a nurse. You can't want to leave that man loose. You haven't done anything . . . except in response to his threats."

She stood there, eyes averted.

"Frieda. The man is dangerous."

She looked at her watch again. She turned away. "It's more complicated than you imagine."

"Your relationship with Gunderson. I know about that."

"Even more complicated. Give me time to think," she said.

Barney snapped his case shut, rather proud of himself. He'd saved several hundred dollars by writing the graphologist report himself instead of hiring the graphologist Dick Rogin recommended. Let Frieda Thompson stew a while. She'd come through.

*B*arney was in the mood for a mindless movie. How had he guessed? That was Candy's exact mood too. She wanted to see *Dressed to Kill.* "You gotta take me, Daddy," she said, "Because Mommy absolutely refuses."

They had hamburgers after at Jackson Hole. Barney ordered a salad as he always did. "Do you know I'm eating this salad to please my mother? Why can't you eat a salad too and please yours?"

Candy smiled a superior smile. "The difference is your mother doesn't bug you about it all the time. When I grow up, I'll eat salad, too."

"If you grow up—" Barney muttered. "Your body needs leafy things."

"I'll take some leafy cheesecake."

She was so cute.

*B*arney was restless after dropping off Candy, wanting not to be alone, a depressing throwback to the first days after his separation, when he was constitutionally unable to be alone. Debra's machine answered her phone. "I've gone out to get food for my fierce Doberman pinscher, who hasn't eaten in three days," said her voice on the answering machine. Barney barked back, anonymously he hoped. He found himself actually missing Debra. She had phoned to crow that the scion of a Portuguese wine empire was courting her with reckless abandon and she'd scarcely noticed Barney's recent neglect. Lindsay was cool. Apparently he'd been neglecting her too. "You haven't called all week," she said. "You were strange and distant the last time we were together. And it's after ten. I suggest you consult the classified ads in *Screw* if you're lusting after you know what." That was Lindsay. You-know-what. Too bad Caroline had disappeared. He would enjoy a night of her unpredictable kinkiness. That made him think of Amber Sinclair. "How is Plato's on a weeknight?" he asked her.

"It can be kind of tame," she said. "And I'm sort of awfully busy at this exact moment. I'm auditioning."

"Auditioning, Amber, at ten-thirty? What are you auditioning for?" She promised to call him back.

*E*veryone seemed to know Amber at Plato's. Even so, it cost Barney a hefty fifty dollars for a membership card. He signed in, Dr. Sigmund Zhivago, and wrote a fake address. The perfume in the air was definitely chlorine. They explored the Jacuzzi. Barney's glasses, more a disguise here than an essential weapon against the first gentle onslaught of presbyopia, immediately fogged up. There were two couples on the dance floor. Fully clothed. Some couples sheathed in bath towels on beach chaises. "That's the orgy room," Amber pointed out. It was dimly lit, wall-to-wall mattresses . . . and empty. Barney was deeply disappointed. Just his luck to arrive at Plato's on an abstinence night.

"Hungry?" Amber helped herself to a bagel from an uninspired delicatessen buffet, heaping it high with egg salad. Barney looked around at the scattered couples. Everyone seemed to be waiting for someone to make the first move.

"Why is everyone dressed?" he grumbled.

"Maybe they're all voyeurs," said Amber with an indifferent little shrug. "Let's us get undressed and break the ice."

"I can be second," said Barney, "But not first. Let's dance." Amber was unbelievable on the dance floor. Uninhibited, as he might have guessed, and spacy. Sometimes she danced with him. Sometimes she danced *at* him. Sometimes she danced off into outer space, wiggling a shoulder or grinding her hip in a kind of orgiastic frenzy. That was it. She looked like she was having sex, all by herself. Beside him a beautiful black woman bounced around in a wisp of lace-edged rompers. Her partner had a towel knotted at one hip.

Amber twirled close and whispered. "There's a woman

going down on a man in that corner behind you."

Barney danced himself into focus. Action was really accelerating now. The chaises ringing the dance floor were beginning to fill with couples coyly swathed in towels. Suddenly breasts began to appear. There was a small line of couples waiting to get into the locker room.

Was he really going to take off his clothes and get into this orgy? For a minute Barney wasn't sure. It was so . . . tacky, grungy. He'd lost track of Amber. Barney glanced toward the egg salad. A few feet away several men were crowded around a chaise. Barney stood on tiptoes. Good God . . . it was Amber, playing with herself. Skirt high, fingers inside red ruffled panties. Her eyes were closed. Her head thrown back. Her bottom wiggled and bounced but what was electrifying the crowd were her keening moans, the purrs and gurgles. The gents ringside had unzipped their flies. A burly bald guy was pulling a stub of a pud. An old geezer was settled on the adjacent chaise, leaning forward for a close-up view.

"Amber," said Barney, seriously fearing the wrath of the crowd for interrupting. "Let's get undressed."

She opened her eyes, inspected her audience and smiled. "I love being watched," she said.

*T*hey stood at the entrance to the mattress room. There were a few bodies pumping away in the farthest corner. Barney felt silly with a towel knotted on one bony hip. Amber had slipped into an ounce or so of see-through g-string and ribbon with a sliver of bra. She looked like an artist's fantasy of the perfect body, luminescent and graceful, with a delicately wicked slither.

Barney's cock, swollen in anticipation, led the way to a clubby corner where it looked like there might be hope for sharing partners and exotic permutations of three and four and five. Strangely, it was not Amber Barney wanted. He found her perfection and childlike quality curiously un-erotic. It was sleaze and lust and kinkiness he craved.

Amber knelt over him and began to lick the tip of his cock, poking her tongue into its small eye. Unmoved, Barney found himself distracted by the bouncing and flailing all around them. For some reason Barney had expected the habitués of Plato's to be older, ugly and fat, and there were, to be cruelly frank, a few disgustingly obese men, but the women were mostly young. Was everyone jaded so quickly these days? Had the sexual revolution quenched that sweet jolt of sin that filled Barney with thrilling disgust as well as shuddering excitement at this very moment?

Right within the reach of his left hand was a squealing beauty with a shiny mane of black hair and big, high, perfect breasts. Why didn't she glance at him? Maybe if he got Amber keening again, that indifferent creature would throw him a beckoning glance. He kneeled between Amber's legs and entered her, sideways, holding her leg in the air—a position that let him go deep. The appropriate gasp was immediate. The brunette, dismounted from her mate, seemed to be taking in the scene. Not staring. That would clearly be bad form.

"There's a hand on my leg," Amber breathed into his ear. "What do think that means?"

The hand was attached to the handsome bearded young man who had been under Barney's brunette. "You know what that means," Barney hissed. "Do you want him?"

Amber peered into the shadows. "All right," she said. "Then you'll have a chance with his friend."

Barney vacated the premises and the bearded man began to suck on Amber's breasts. Barney reached invitingly toward the brunette. "I don't swing," she said. He sat there feeling like a leper. Amber was wiggling and moaning, her bottom rising to meet the bearded man's rhythmic thrusts. Barney noticed a languorous black woman smiling at him. He reached out to touch her ankle.

"Sorry. I'm resting," she responded.

The bearded young man was shooting his load all over Amber's breasts. She lay there collapsed, stroking the stickiness. She put one finger in her mouth and licked it. Barney recognized the gesture from countless porn films. Barney touched Amber's shoulder. She sat up on one elbow. "Well, what happened?" she asked.

"You got fucked," Barney snapped.

"I know what happened to me, Dr. Kincaid," she said. "I mean, you. Did you . . . ah . . . you know?"

"No." He was glum. "Let's get something to drink." He wrapped his towel low on his hips again. Amber stood there stark naked at the bar, ladling pineapple juice into a plastic glass with great style, as unself-consciously as if she were swathed in a floor-length gown pouring tea for the Daughters of the American Revolution. A young Adonis walked up to her.

"Where you been hiding all night, sweetie?" the guy asked. He had a rough accent, Turkish maybe or Israeli.

"It's okay," Barney hissed over his shoulder. "Take him. Maybe I'll do better on my own. I'm going to look around for a nice couple. Are you game?"

"Oh for sure. Find some groovy people. Please."

Barney got to chatting with a couple from Toronto. "Since it was our last night in New York, we flipped a coin. I voted for the Four Seasons," the man said, "and Ellie voted for Plato's. So here we are." When Barney brought up the idea of switching, Ellie perked up, but Ned stuttered a bit and said he wasn't ready for that. Barney tried a flat-out bold approach to an athletic young man and his slightly blowsy older companion.

"We're here writing an article on Plato's for *Der Spiegel*," the woman said.

Barney looked around for Amber. He imagined he could hear her distinctive gurgle and moan somewhere not far away.

"I can't believe I'm here," said the woman next to him at the bar. Barney turned and looked down. She was short, plump and very pretty, a golden-skinned Puerto Rican he guessed from her accent. "Yes," she confirmed. "Visiting from San Juan. My girlfriend dared me."

Barney invited her into the whirlpool. He put her hand on his cock. She looked around to see if anyone was watching and then gave him a frightfully efficient hand job. Barney was really hot now. He persuaded Rosita to towel off and join him in the mattress room. "I can't believe I'm really doing this," Maria Rosita giggled, her plump soft ass jiggling.

The mattress room was wall-to-wall bodies now. Barney arranged Rosita half on top of somebody's thighs. "Ouch ouch," she cried as he entered her. "That's too big. Ooofff." He found a position that turned off her protest and rocked gently. "I lub all that," she said. "I come." If she hadn't announced her coming, he never would have known. From a far corner of the room he heard Amber's squeal.

Barney deposited Rosita on a chaise, squeezed her hand, and went off to find Amber. There was a crowd blocking the corridor in the maze of private back rooms. He peeked inside. There was Amber, hanging from a leather belt, being fucked from both sides by her Adonis and someone Barney was sure he recognized from porn movies—an obscenely well-endowed blond. He decided not to say goodbye.

Walking back to his locker from the shower room, Barney felt a familiar anxiety. It was walking on that flat dark green carpet in his wet feet. He could imagine Mama's hysteria. "Sex, all right, I understand, but how can you walk where a bunch of strangers walk without bedroom slippers. And those mattresses. I hope you insisted they give you clean sheets."

Itching a little, Barney decided to take a good hot bath as soon as he got home. A jolt of prophylactic penicillin might be nice too, he thought.

*T*he internal clock that woke Barney at seven every morning failed him, and he jerked awake after eight to the sound of brakes screeching, cars smashing on the street below. He saw Amy's face as the car jumped the curb, his brakes useless. Barney screamed as she was crushed against the mailbox. How astonishing that the dream had returned. He lay there thinking about Amy, the first Wasp he'd dared. Jill Massacio didn't count, being crazed, a wanton, and Italian. He let himself imagine Amy's death as a case of mistaken identity. The phone would ring. It would be Carl, his reporter friend. He'd traced Amy to Kenya where her husband was the ambassador. No, she would be divorced, living on Central Park South. With amnesia. No not Amy, it was Linda Menker Carl had found, a housewife, apparently, in Teaneck, New Jersey. Linda's vulnerability had shaken him and whenever he encountered a woman even vaguely like her, he would retreat. He could not escape the unpleasant feeling that somehow he was responsible, although he kept telling himself no one incident could turn a sixteen-year-old girl into a nymphomaniac.

Everyone had been slobbering drunk or pretending to be on one of those humid September nights, letting booze take the blame for macho swaggering, vile puns, indiscriminate ass grabbing, and preposterous sexual braggadocio. The guys in the Big K Club, jocks mostly, wanted to go swimming. Barbie said they were a bunch of animals and, failing to persuade Barney to retreat, had gone to a double bill with a girlfriend.

Linda, voluptuous with a pudgy prettiness, was clearly scandalized but too intimidated to protest. "Best boobs at Kingsbridge High," Howie kept announcing, shooting beer spray all over the car as they lurched toward his folks' cabin at Loon Lake. "Gonna go skinny-dipping with my little chickadee," sang Howie.

Linda looked like she was being driven to Auschwitz. "How come Barbie didn't come?"

Barney smiled and winked at her.

In the tumult, shoes flying, guys belting each other with underwear and splashing and rolling on blankets, Howie had passed out. Barney, exhilarated by the sweet warmth of the night and the tick of the crickets, took Linda by the hand and strolled down the beach.

She would not skinny-dip. No. Never. Nor let him touch the "best boobs at Kingsbridge High." No. Not at first. "Howie is silly," she said. "He just loves to exaggerate." But she was a fool for e. e. cummings. "who knows if the moon's a balloon," Barney recited. Snowing her. Dazzling her the way he almost never dazzled any girl (because with her he didn't really give a damn). Playing the intellectual. He reinforced the illusion of worldly upperclassmen with liberal measures of orange juice and gin from his Thermos, till her breasts were spilling out of cotton armor and into his hands. Till finally, even though she was struggling and whimpering "no, no," she was letting him press against her virgin pussy. What a joy. What a mess. She lay there sobbing when he rolled away, clutching him as if she'd never let go.

At the very instant of disengagement, Barney was sick with regret. Caught up in concentrating on seduction he had not really weighed the act. Taking a virgin was a serious responsibility. He'd always felt that. And the truth was he didn't really care if he ever saw Linda again.

As he might have predicted, she was shattered when she realized that penetration was not linked to a lifetime con-tract. She had pursued Barney after that, with stubborn passivity, that is, hanging around, lurking outside his classes, phoning and then hanging up, looking at him from across the table, Howie's date again, with tragic moon eyes. To reassure himself that he was not a heartless prick, Barney did see her once every two or three weeks for a while. He would take her to a movie or a White Castle for burgers and root beer, anywhere it was too frenetic for sustained talk. She was boring. And once in a while they had sex because she wanted it and Barney didn't know how to say no without being cruel. Word was she fucked everybody. Her sweaters got tighter. She dressed like the bad girl in the movies and jerked guys off in rec rooms and closets. Or so Barney heard.

At first Linda had seemed touched by his interest on the phone, even a bit flirtatious. She then hung up three times in a row, sobbing. Barney went into the box he'd brought home from Mama's cellar and pulled out a purple Capezio. Linda's from that night on the beach. They'd tried to drink screwdrivers out of it. The shoe was stiff and discolored from the stains. There was a copper mug too, a Moscow Mule cup from the Cass Lake days. Boy, people did a lot of drinking in those days. In all the years since, Barney doubted if he had consumed as much hard liquor as he had in the four years of college. Women used liquor to obscure their surrender then. Barney remembered Aunt Cristal falling down drunk on Moscow Mules that night on the cottage swing at Cass Lake. Who had seduced whom? And who had kept the sexual tension hot for almost five years?

Visiting him one afternoon in the hospital, Cristal had asked Barney to call when he was fully recovered. "Even a busy doctor could give an old broken-down aunt a visit." She'd chattered away in her breathy high voice. "I'm threatening to cook dinner," she said. "The brisket you used to love." On impulse now, Barney called and agreed to come for dinner. Then he decided to drive out to Linda's anyway in daylight. With a map it shouldn't be difficult to find the address Carl had given him.

The houses of Teaneck were imposing yet huddled close. Expensive real estate, Barney supposed. The front step at the number he was looking for was a jungle of newspapers and waterlogged weeklies. No one answered his ring. He walked around to the back where an aged Ford stationwagon was parked half in, half out of the garage, one door open, the lights apparently burned out.

The kitchen door was locked but he'd once seen a cop use an American Express card to slip a lock. It was a cinch. For a minute Barney hesitated. He could be arrested for housebreaking. He could always say it was a medical emergency, he told himself.

The stink of rotting food hit his nose as he walked into the kitchen. A milk carton had tipped over on the table and the milk had dried. The trashcans overflowed and he almost tripped over a length of rock-hard French bread. Something was terribly wrong here. He took the bread with him. It would make a weapon of sorts, he thought. After all, Linda had answered the phone. She'd been here this morning.

"Linda," he called out. "It's Barney Kincaid. Linda." He stood at the stairwell. There must have been a robbery. The house had been vandalized, he decided. Clothes had been pulled out of the front closet and lay in heaps. Books were ripped apart. There was a slash of red across one painting. Paint? Blood? He sniffed. It smelled like catsup. There was a blob of mayonnaise beside an open jar on the stairway. And something sticky on the railing. He smelled it. Could it be apricot jam? From upstairs he thought he heard something. Sobbing perhaps.

"Go home, Barney. I said not to come. Go away, I'm busy."

The room was dark, the curtains drawn. But through a crack in the drapes and the light from the door, he saw her—a hulk of flesh in the middle of a giant bed. He slid on something. A pizza-to-go carton. That was the familiar scent he'd noticed at once. Pizza. There was a chicken carcass sitting on a paperbag beside her. She had a plastic carton of something in her hand. She tossed it at him. A loop or two of wet ziti fell on his shoe. "My chicken dropped. I can't reach it," she said. "Just hand me my chicken, and go home, please, go home."

"Good God, Linda. What's happened?" Barney reached for the light beside the bed.

"Don't touch the light. Give me my chicken. As long as you're here, be useful. It's nothing so serious. My chicken."

Barney pushed the chicken carcass toward her. "I think you ate it, Linda." He looked into her face for the sweet prettiness he remembered. Her hair was blonde straw at the edges, dark streaked with gray at the roots and matted with . . . mayonnaise probably.

"I am having a little eating binge," she said. "Every once in a while it happens. Hand me that chicken. Try the floor. Look under the bed," she snapped.

Barney thought she might eat his arm if he didn't. In a carton on the floor he found a small sparerib. He handed it to Linda.

"What a pleasant surprise," she said. "Isn't this disgusting? I'll have to be locked up at a fat farm for months to get over this one. The problem is, these days everyone delivers. Pizza. Chinese. Deli. Don't look at me like that, Barney. I told you not to come. You never gave a damn anyway. I had a crush on you for months before that night on the beach. You never gave a damn. For you it was just some Pavlovian reflex. That was a hundred years ago. Shall we send out for more barbeque ribs? Where's the phone. Oh God, Barney, I've lost the phone. Do you think I've eaten it?" She laughed.

For the first time Barney thought she might still be in touch with reality. That was her face, the same sweet face twenty years older, a few more dimples, a few more chins, but still winsome, sitting like a pea atop a massive body in a yellow cotton muumuu.

He had learned something from that night on the beach. He was not a professional seducer of virgins. Barney preferred seductions less riddled with guilt, seduction that was really mutual collision without awesome responsibility. Unfortunately, there was something in the nature of the female (was it estrogen or the double chromosome?) that made them see a mutual lust as a mutual commitment. "But I was fond of you, Linda. We went to movies even though I was, supposedly, sort of going steady," he said, picking chicken bones off his arm and sweeping some debris into a brown paper sack. He hadn't really been such a bad boy. Braving tearful complaints, recriminations, one poison-pen letter, a suicidal poem she actually had published in some little literary magazine that only lasted one issue. Guys laughed when Barney defended her.

"You were the only one who treated me like a person," she said. "To Howie, you remember Howie what's-his-name, he never bathed, I was just a piece of baggage with tits. You never met Winston, my husband. Winston is brilliant. He's a nice man too and our son is some kind of a math genius—"

"Let me call someone, Linda. Is your husband home? A neighbor. Give me a number to call. A girlfriend. Your sister." He breathed through his mouth to shut out the stink.

"Have a fig newton," said Linda. "'If I knew you were coming I'd have baked a cake. I've got a crush on you, sweetie pie,'" she crooned. It was a song they had danced to.

"Oh shit," said Barney. He wanted to get out of there but he couldn't leave without finding help.

She hit him with a fig newton. "Don't 'oh shit' me, kiddo. I'm the one's in trouble here. I'm the compulsive fresser whose husband isn't coming home anymore. What the hell do you have to 'oh shit' about?"

Barney stood up. "Linda, if you don't tell me who to call, I'm calling a hospital. Have you a doctor? A therapist? Where is your sister, sweetheart?" He sat down again. "Please."

"If you'll eat a fig newton, I'll tell you. I don't trust skinny people. I love them but I don't really trust them. But if you prove yourself, I'll let you save me."

He took a bite of her fig newton. It was stale.

"Linda." He stroked her arm. She was silky and firm, with the extraordinary skin you find on a young fat woman. He started leafing through the address book. "Your therapist, Linda. Is it Dr. Freidkin?"

"That's Winston's cousin, an opthalmologist."

"Dr. Garvin?"

"My gynecologist."

"Linda. This is not a game."

She gave him the therapist's number. The woman agreed to drive over if she could clear an hour. Barney waited.

"So guess who Winston's in love with," said Linda. "My Weight Watchers leader." She laughed. "That's a joke. He's not in love that I know of. He's just left. He's saving himself from this. . . ." She shrugged. "If it wasn't so funny, I'd laugh." She hiccupped.

Dr. Rezniak arrived with an ambulance. "We can't leave her here alone," she said. Barney kissed Linda's cheek and left the ambulance attendants to figure out how to get her down the stairs. On the kitchen table was a salt shaker in the shape of a pig. For some reason he stuck it in his pocket.

Lost for a few wrong turns in affluent Teaneck, Barney congratulated himself. What had begun as an idle whim, tracing the women who had loved him, was actually an adventure full of rik. Like life. Like emergency medicine. For a man who was afraid of responsibility, how remarkable that he braved it every day.

*B*arney was scheduled to lecture the interns at Downstate Medical in the late afternoon. He arrived late and lingered late, held by their questions. Several of them were intrigued by the idea of emergency medicine as a specialty. The minimal hours for good money that left you free to have a life of your own were obviously part of the lure. But one or two students seemed genuinely attracted by the challenges of diagnosis and even the religion, the need to inspire disciples with the faith in professional emergency care. There was one bright, willowy,

Midwestern girl who seemed loath to let Barney go. Was it medicine and the pressure to choose a specialty or the incipient hots? Impossible to say. She took Barney's phone number. Barney loved that, the unabashed aggressiveness of women today. But he had promised Aunt Cristal an early dinner. And Carl kept coming up with leads Barney had to pursue. This afternoon, out of nowhere, he'd thought of Sarah Washburne, Reeney's best friend, hot little maid of honor stalking the groom to the altar. I must be really flipping now, thought Barney. He'd not liked Sarah then. Why would he want to see her now? To close the book, he decided.

"*I* wasn't sure what you drink these days," said Aunt Cristal. "But I remembered you liked vodka. What shall we do with it?" Her blue-black hair was full and stiff, probably fresh from the hairdresser. She wore a black velvet hostess gown, cut low to expose her shoulders and a daring inch or two of cleavage.

"I guess nobody drinks ginger beer anymore," said Barney.

She blushed and didn't answer. "I have rye too and Cherry Heering. Your uncle loved that. I think this bottle is from before he died. Does it spoil, do you think?" She bustled around examining the bottles in the old-fashioned liquor cabinet, selecting a footed, carved-crystal goblet.

It was the first time Barney had visited since Uncle Ira's funeral. What did she do all by herself in this giant apartment with the big dark portraits of flamenco dancers and pirates, the massive furniture with its graceless machine carving? The view of the park in the fast-falling twilight never ceased to move him. The street lights made warm circles in the blue-gray snow. What had always puzzled

Barney about the summer games with Aunt Cristal was Uncle Ira. She adored him. And so did Barney. Uncle Ira had been an athlete in high school and he walked like a star. He built his tenants cheap hovels with flimsy plumbing and window boxes full of flowers and they adored him too. He treated Cristal like a precious baby—"My child bride," he called her. "I found her, a flower in a flower shop." He was twenty-two years her senior, a lusty widower with money, well, some money, it was hard to judge money in those days. A little went so far and Uncle Ira was a spender (Mama said).

Summers, the whole Cohen clan and some of their friends rented cottages in a bungalow colony on Cass Lake. The women moved upstate bag and baggage as soon as the kids got out of school and the men drove out Friday nights for noisy, frenetic communal weekends.

An only child all year, often solitary for hours, Barney loved the feeling of being part of this immense, teasing family, although at times the anarchy sent him fleeing to the woods where he kept a tent in a clearing and wrote poems. Everyone seemed so affectionate and loving. Not till the summer of his daddy's financial downfall did he begin to sense the competitiveness beneath the teasing.

Uncle Ira had the money and Uncle Ernie was the workaholic lawyer (he came out from the city by dinner Saturday if Aunt Clare was lucky). Uncle Pete spent August in Saratoga at the track. Daddy was the good-natured, self-sacrificing oldest brother who had left school so they could go to college. Mama and Aunt Clare and Aunt Eva never stopped talking about Aunt Gilda, her tragic "passing," what a fine mother, what a splendid cook, what a magnificent soprano, and they barely suffered the summer presence of the widower Ira's passion, Aunt Cristal—"She's not as scatterbrained and helpless as she pretends," Clare observed. "And what does she do all day with both Ira's kids in camp?"

Alas, Aunt Cristal, beautiful Aunt Cristal with her almond-brown eyes and tawny skin, was cursed. She was not Jewish. She was something very strange and foreign, Arme-

nian. She had not been born in America, poor dear. The
proof of the curse, Barney had believed as a young boy, was
her inability to have children.

And Cristal loved children. She was always making doll
clothes for Heidi and finding odd old-fashioned games and
riddles and if you were looking for lost cousins, chances
were they'd be found baking cookies in Cristal's kitchen.
Whiny brats and ailing cousins were sure to be dumped at
Cristal's by the Cohen coven of matriarchs, who didn't mind
at all taking advantage of the free baby-minding service.

Friday nights the men arrived exhausted by the weekend traffic and everyone went to bed early after roaring and
groaning over a disgustingly big dinner. Saturday Uncle Ira
was in charge of organizing a team to crank the homemade
ice cream. There would be fireworks or the children would
stage a pageant and sometimes the men played poker, the
women grumbling, "But you have all week in the city for
that." That Saturday there were fresh ripe peaches from a
nearby farm. The women peeled. Aunt Cristal, an apron
over her bathing suit, flushed and sweaty in the terrible heat
wave, bit into a ripe peach and the juice dribbled down her
arm. Uncle Ira leaned over and licked her elbow. Barney,
chipping away at a huge block of ice, sat transfixed. He
could not imagine his own parents playing like that. Mama
would not eat a peach without a napkin, of course. No one
would dare to lick her arm.

Barney had never told a soul, but from his window he
could see into Uncle Ira's living room. Ira and Aunt Cristal
loved to dance. He would watch them dipping low, twirling
in an exaggerated tango, stopping to hug and kiss and
wrestle on the sofa. That night Uncle Ira glided into the
living room bare-assed, wearing just his sleeveless undershirt. Aunt Cristal ran behind a chair. He went after her and
she fought him, laughing, tossing her hair wildly, punching
his shoulder, then taking him in her arms. Uncle Ira bent
over her; what he was doing Barney couldn't really see, but
he would never forget her hands with the perfect crimson
ovals clutching Uncle Ira's naked butt.

She still wore the same dark-red polish, her nails in perfect ovals, not a chip anywhere as she handed him a bottle to open. It was an old wine, a Burgundy, a label Barney always avoided on wine lists because it was invariably too expensive.

"Save this," he said. "I think this wine is really very special."

"What could be more special? Your Uncle Ira saved it for twenty years and look where he is now. You could be hit by a car on your way home, God forbid." She knocked on wood. "Do you know how many times I had to promise him I wouldn't die before him, as if . . . well, he was so much older. But I wasn't supposed to cross the street by myself . . . or eat a rotten oyster. He was strong like an ox. He was eighty-two but he worked and played like a man of sixty. So how could one little stroke kill him? Other people have their strokes and live forever."

"He was not a man who could have tolerated being incapacitated," said Barney, almost automatically. He no longer knew about things like that. Patients fought to survive when life was a cave of pain and deprivation. "Ira would have been furious surviving unable to speak, in a wheelchair."

She nodded. "He had enormous appetite, all his appetites, if you know what I mean." She looked at Barney, right in the eye.

Barney sipped his wine. He wasn't sure if it was spoiled or if great Burgundies were supposed to taste like broccoli. He sensed she was remembering. If Uncle Ira was such a lusty man why, he'd always wondered, had she let Barney make love to her? The first time she had pretended to be defenseless, disarmed by the vodka and ginger beer. But after that? Barney had never felt free to ask. What was he afraid to know? That women steam with hunger too? Even knowing all that he seemed to know today about pleasing women, their lust still surprised him, still somehow terrified.

Barney had only a few weeks between summer school and the new semester of his sophomore year. He'd talked about hitch-hiking West with Marvin. Marvin was in love with a girl who lived in Santa Fe. "With a little injection of our New York smarts, we could promote all that Navaho Indian junk into big business," Marvin enthused. "And imagine, my girl is just one of four sisters. Don't say no!"

But Mama insisted Barney give her just a week or two at the Lake, "so I can fatten you up a little and make sure you get the sleep you need." And Barney did feel exhausted, not quite at home in his body that year, a freak of a beanpole—he'd shot up three inches in his freshman year. All the aunts fussed over him. And he did gain weight. In a week, his sloppiest khakis were feeling tight. He did hundreds of push-ups and sit-ups on the beach every day with Aunt Cristal cheering him on. He was sure he could actually discern the beginning of serious bicep and pectoral definition. Long hair that needed a trim made his face seem fuller. He looked almost human with some tan. And his tomcat forays into town had yielded a few hot necking sessions in Dad's old Ford, including one that had steamed the windows so thoroughly they hadn't realized the state trooper was standing there till he rapped politely on the glass. Barney had thrown his T-shirt over Daisy's nakedness, saying a silent prayer of thanks for her passionate resistance to his pleadings. She was only sixteen, in the full torturous throes of dedication to virginity. But she was thrilled to jerk him off. Tonight she'd gleefully caught his come in a Snickers bar wrapper. Once he got over his fright at being so close to arrest, he got a snicker out of her gesture himself and couldn't bring himself to discard the wrinkled wrapper.

Nights were, needless to say, wet and hot with endless jerkings off. Everything was stained with his desperate come, the *Playboys* he still had to hide from Mama, even the bungalow wall, and the bushes where he shot off while watching Aunt Cristal lounging around in halters and shorts that did not have a hope of containing her voluptuousness. There was nothing like Aunt Cristal in *Playboy*. Now in her early thirties, she was incredibly ripe—a cross between Anna Magnani and Ava Gardner, Barney thought, with the same wild spirit both actresses projected. Nothing could get him hot faster than imagining her hands with their blood red nails clutching his own ass.

Barney collapsed on her porch in front of an electric fan one sweltering August night. She was fanning herself with a magazine. Barney wondered if he should read her his poems but he was too lazy to move.

"You're so pale," Aunt Cristal said. "You should get more sun. Look, I'm black next to you." And she pressed the length of her arm against his. Her arm was burning hot.

"Oh, that's not fair. You're dark to start with," said Barney. "I bet you're dark all over." He tugged at her halter, revealing the creamy whiteness of one breast and part of one large dark aureole.

She acted as if nothing were happening. "That's some difference, isn't it?" she said. "In the dark from a distance I could skinny-dip and anyone would think I was wearing a white bathing suit." She giggled and made herself another Moscow Mule.

He sipped his. The metal cup was icy on the edge of his teeth. "Show me," he said, tugging at her shorts.

She slapped his hand. "Silly."

"You've made a serious philosophical declaration," he said, the words slurring pleasantly. "You are required to prove it."

"You sound like Adlai Stevenson," she said, bouncing off the porch glider to switch off the outside light. She sashayed over to the farthest corner, partially hidden by a huge wheel of geranium pots, and stepped out of her shorts. She untied the halter and draped it over the rail. She stood there in her panties. Then with a shrug, she rolled them down and dropped them to the floor. Her body was full and lush and the white patches of skin were almost luminescent in the faint light coming from the house.

"You have established your theorem," Barney began.

"The intellectual speaks," she said.

"It does look exactly like a bathing suit. But what is that dark fluffy triangle there in the middle between your legs?"

She giggled. "That's a design on my bathing suit," she said, switching her hips.

"I don't believe it," said Barney. "Come closer and let me see." He was afraid if he got up, she would run. He slid off the glider and moved forward on his knees. Boy, he was really sloshed himself, he realized.

"Oh goodness," she cried. "It's Toulouse-Lautrec. Or I have a dwarf on my porch. Are you Sleepy? Happy? Grumpy? . . . I know. It's Doc."

He took two knee-lurches forward. She grabbed her panties and pulled them on. He tackled her down to the glider. He had both hands on her breasts. They were huge, with aureoles large and kind of bumpy. The nipples grew under his thumb. He leaned over to kiss her, missed, hit her chin. She pulled him closer.

"Oh dear. This is nuts. We're really crazy." She was tugging at his belt. Barney tore off his T-shirt, unbuttoned his cutoffs. His full, beet-red dick fell into her hands. "Oh dear God," she said. "Such a young boy. Such a big one. Oh what will we do?"

He kept kissing her. He wasn't sure exactly what he ought to do. Her parts were awesome.

"Am I really doing this?" she asked the ceiling. "I think I am." She stroked his arm, the inside of his thighs, his ass. "Oh my, I'd forgotten what it feels like . . . young skin. You feel like a baby," she cried.

He guessed she really was going to go all the way. He fumbled around looking for the opening. There was a lot of fleshy stuff down there in that furry underbrush. He was running into odd flippets and indentations. Giggling, Aunt Cristal took his cock in her hand and cleared the way. And then he was fucking her off the glider and onto the pillow-strewn floor, her crimson nails clutching his ass.

He had fled to the city early the next morning, not sure he could face the whole bungalow colony without provoking a major scandal. He would never be able to look Uncle Ira in the eye again. Away at school he managed to avoid family rituals and ceremonies. The summer after he intended to pretend it hadn't happened. But she seemed to be lying in wait for him late at night and he was flattered. The next summer he worked as a waiter in the Adirondacks and never got to Cass Lake. The following spring he found himself reluctantly engaged to Reeney and if Aunt Cristal seemed from time to time to eye him hungrily, he decided it was just affection.

She fussed about getting the food on the table, lighting the candles, brushing against him. Barney imagined he could feel the heat of her inside the velvet housecoat. She chattered away about the cousins, her stepchildren, their kids.

"I'm too young to be a widow," she said. "It's not that I thought Ira was going to live so long. He fooled everyone, so strong at eighty, living till eighty-two. I loved him, you know that, but the last ten years it was hard, you know, being married to such an old man. You know what I mean?"

Barney could guess.

"I need a job, I think. I got to be where I can meet people. I'm the perfect age now for some nice man. The problem is I don't have any experience, no training you know. I was working in a florist shop when I met Ira. Of course, I'm not much of a flower myself anymore."

Barney protested as she needed him to and anyway, it was true. "You could easily pass for twenty years younger," he said. "I would guess your age as maybe forty."

She smiled and tilted her head flirtatiously the way she used to. "Are you going to sit all night in your jacket?"

Barney took off his jacket and rolled up his shirtsleeves. The wine made her tipsy. She laughed and in the candlelight she was still lush, her tawny skin smooth, cheeks flushed, and almond eyes snapping.

"Shoo. Shoo," she said. "We'll have coffee in the drawing room the way they do at Buckingham Palace. And you'll have some brandy. Your Uncle Ira loved good brandy."

For some reason he could not isolate, Barney sipped the brandy she gave him. He hated brandy.

"I just want a sniff of it," she said. She set the snifter on the table and kissed him on the mouth. Her lips were soft and full. She smelled of some familiar perfume from long ago. Her mouth beneath his was slightly open. This was not what Barney wanted, not what he had expected. She shrugged her shoulder and the velvet dropped away. She put his hand on her breast. The skin felt like wrinkled silk. She reached for him. Her hand on his fly. He was slightly hard. At her touch he felt himself grow harder.

She undid his belt. "So big for a young man," she said. She bent over and took his prick in her mouth. He caressed her breast. He reached under her skirt. Her skin was so loose. Barney wanted to be there for her but he felt himself shrinking.

"I'm sorry, Cristal. I don't know what to say."

"Don't put it in a poem," she said.

He laughed. "I'm not laughing at you . . . at us. I'm laughing because I was such a pretentious kid. It's been a long time since I wrote a poem."

She pulled her gown straight and stood up. "You were an adorable kid." She hugged him. "Always so busy trying to educate me. T. S. Eliot. F. Scott Fitzgerald. I never would have read anything but Harold Robbins if you hadn't pushed me." She sighed. "I'm a little high as usual."

"You'll get a job," said Barney lamely. "I have friends that might help. I'll check around. You'll meet a man."

"An old tart like me."

Barney kissed her and fled. He was glad he was a little high too.

Using his beeper pickup, he listened to the messages on his machine: the hospital twice, Candy wondering if she could go to riding camp next summer, Mom's "It's only your mother, nothing important," and a breathless message from Amber. She had a job. An acting job. At the Fantasy Burlesque. He must come at once. A quick call got the hospital protocol dispensed with. It was too late for Candy and he didn't feel strong enough for Mama. Barney headed toward Times Square. Burlesque, whatever that meant these days, fit his mood exactly.

Barney walked into the Fantasy Burlesque on Forty-eighth off Broadway, not knowing what to expect, vaguely excited and vaguely uncomfortable. The theater smelled of stale bodies and cigarette butts and it wasn't quite dark enough for Barney. Amber had sounded manic with happiness when she called. "An acting job," she said. "Six shows a day. Big money. Oh Barney, this could be the beginning."

There was a trumpet fanfare and some clown in the glassed-in sound booth was calling her name. The curtains parted. And there she was. The spotlight was magic. She was more beautiful than he'd realized with that luminous skin and the fragile, almost aristocratic face. As if Amy had gone Hollywood. Not even a mane of wild blonde teased curls and a cloak of white feathers detracted from a certain delicacy. She stood there, tapping her foot, cool and arrogant. For a minute he believed he had found Amy again in some mystical twilight zone. Then she began wiggling and grinding to a disco beat, moving her mouth in an inane sexiness reminiscent of Marilyn Monroe parodying herself. It took her two minutes to shed her white crêpe gown. Amber writhed behind the feathers, long slender legs in white lace stockings attached to a ruffled white garter belt.

The audience was howling, taunting her to shed the feathers. Her smile was like sunshine—pure and ecstatic. She dropped her feathered cloak to the stage and arranged her ass on it. Spread her legs, touched her pussy, caressed her breasts. The more they screamed, the wilder she became. She was naked now except for her stockings, thrusting her pussy at them. She tried to prance down the runway, but she could scarcely move because of the clutch of men lining the edge of the stage waving dollar bills. She seemed so hot. Wildly turned on, in love with herself . . . her eyes shining as if transported by some fantasy miles from this sleazy scene.

That's why he couldn't believe his eyes. She was letting them lick her. A dollar a lick. Barney was so upset, he thought he would shove through the mob, tear her away. It was disgusting. He backed out the door as she settled on a chair, legs held high in a deep V. Men lined up to eat her. On her face was an expression of ecstasy he knew from Plato's.

He was damned if he would be just another wild-eyed geezer drooling at her dressing room. Who knew what went on there for how many bucks. He started down the street but he had to turn back. He couldn't just leave. A big black guy guarding the door insisted he pay to come in again.

"Amber." His voice was stern. She didn't seem to notice. She took his arm and pulled him into the dressing room. Five or six strippers were more or less naked and oblivious. She jumped up and down.

"They love me," she said. "They adore me." She threw a wad of bills on the counter. "Money means nothing to me, honestly. It's getting the audience in the palm of your hand. It's their response that counts. I'm in love with the stage."

There was no way to reach her now.

"Is this the last show?" he asked.

"I've got two more to go," she said. "Oh wow. Do you think I need a Valium?" She was jumping up and down. "A joint. I've got a joint." She inhaled. "I was hoping someone would send me roses. I'd love to celebrate later with you . . . can we?"

"I'll be asleep in forty minutes," he said. Her face fell. "Well, all right. You can wake me." He wrote his address on a prescription form. "We need to talk."

"I can wake you?" She hugged him. "Oh Dr. Kincaid, I'll be so hot by then."

"*O*h God." The ambulance was headed for the wrong hospital. Amy's blood made a trail on the street. Barney raced alongside trying to signal the driver. "I'm a doctor," he cried, jerking awake out of the dream. It was the intercom. The doorman buzzing her arrival was apologetic. "I didn't want to ring, Dr. Kincaid, at this hour, it's so late, but the la— Miss Sinclair insisted you were expecting her." Barney detected a snide tone in his voice. He had a vision of Amber in the lobby naked and shedding feathers. "Send her up," he said, suddenly hot.

Her feathers preceded her. And she wasn't actually naked. Not quite. She had changed her garter belt—it was red to match her boots. "I played with myself in the taxi," she said. "The cab driver went crazy." She knelt at his feet. It's all right now, isn't it. I feel it's all right." She untied his bathrobe, playing right into his fantasies. He remembered vaguely planning to avoid sex with Amber. She was too young and her resemblance to Amy disturbed him. He had wanted only to help her, warn her, to save her. And now he was breaking. She teased him, finger flicking, tongue darting, till he grabbed her by the curls. Her wicked, knowing laugh blotted out the Amy face. Then she took a deep breath and swallowed him. She was every wanton siren in every porn movie he'd ever seen. He pulled her up and bent her over the back of the sofa. He found her clitoris and pinched and stroked till she seemed to collapse. Then he spread the lips—trying not to think of all the night's tongues—and lost himself in a hard, angry fuck. She lay there when he finally withdrew, making little gibberish sounds. Then she picked herself up, and began bouncing about.

"I'm starved. I was too excited to eat all day. May I?" She strolled out to the kitchen and studied the refrigerator. "Hostess Twinkies. Kodak film. You must have been expecting me." She giggled. "I need an avocado. Avocados are the most sensual food in the world. I would like you to put some avocado—guess where?" She had torn off a hunk of Swiss cheese. "Is this cheese antique. Boy, are you a bachelor, Dr. Kincaid, boy, do you need help. Do you need me."

Barney sat in the dark watching her in the light of the refrigerator.

"This is a very balanced meal," she said, standing on one foot and pouring a glass of tomato juice.

Barney was really feeling the hour. "I'm going to lie down," he said. He must have fallen asleep immediately because he woke when he heard her come into the room. She had lit a candle.

"Guess what I have between my legs," she said, walking a strangely hobbled gait.

"I can't guess," he said with a groan. "I'll guess tomorrow. We have to talk tomorrow."

"It will be stale by tomorrow," she scolded.

But he was a half a second from total unconsciousness.

"Is it noon?" she asked when he woke her. "I will be born again at noon."

"I have to leave at noon," he said.

"I won't get up for anything but great sex or champagne," she said, eyes shut tight.

He returned with a split of champagne. It was flat but she was too thrilled to notice.

"I don't suppose you've got a pinch of caviar out there," she said.

Barney was already regretting that he'd let a moment of genuine human concern sink into undisciplined hedonism. How could he hope to rescue her from Sodom and Gemorrah if he was a compulsive citizen of S & G himself?

"I'm worried about you, Amber," Barney began. "What you're doing at the Fantasy Burlesque is not acting." He looked at her. He had never seen her in the morning before—in daylight. Her skin was translucent with a light sprinkle of tiny freckles across a perfect nose. Without makeup she looked very young. "How old are you?" he asked. "No lies."

"Twenty-two?" She said it with a question mark.

"Haven't you decided?"

"Well, twenty-five, actually, but I have to be careful. You age so fast. As an actress, it's best to be young and vague."

Barney felt as if he hadn't had enough sleep, which wasn't strange considering he hadn't had enough sleep. He had never expected to feel so decrepit in what ought to be his prime. At twenty a few hours of sleep had brought him bouncing back. He sat on the edge of the bed sipping coffee from the lopsided mug Candy had made in pottery class. What was he going to do about Amber? He just didn't have the heart to send her back to the dirty-raincoat crowd. Have the heart . . . my big fat heart. Barney couldn't remember whether he'd taken his cortisone that morning. He decided he hadn't. "Are you really an actress?" he asked. "Have you studied acting?" She insisted she was, that she'd been a dancer at the High School for Performing Arts and had studied at the Neighborhood Playhouse and done menial things in summer stock.

"I'm not Katharine Hepburn," she said, imitating the Hepburn voice, "but then I'm not simple street trash. Do you know how hard it is even to get into an audition?"

"Well, getting your pussy licked six days a week isn't the

way," Barney snapped. "You *must* be an actress. You sure looked like you loved it. Tell me it was just an act."

She looked at him. "I did feel that they loved me. The whistles and cheers . . . you know, they did love me." She disappeared, exploring his apartment. "Hey," she called out, "this is a cute little guest room. Oh I could be sooooo cozy here." She slithered toward him, playing the sex goddess incarnate again, not knowing how infinitely more appealing she was as her sweet daffy self. "You have piles," she said. "Piles. Piles of laundry. Piles of mail. Probably piles of unpaid bills and errands. I could be your girl Friday. Give me your errands. I can shop. I can't iron." She frowned. "I cook. A little."

"You're right," Barney agreed. "I need help." A man needed a wife, because who else remembered to buy birthday cards, Barney thought. Barney had taken Reeney's wifely services for granted. She'd balanced the checkbook, doctored the houseplants, supervised periodic house paintings, wrapped Mother's Day gifts—hardly enough to make a marriage but small graces he'd no longer sneer at.

"You wouldn't have to pay me much," Amber was saying. "Room and board and just pocket money."

"I definitely do not need a resident girl Friday," Barney protested. "My daughter sleeps on that day-bed back there, alternate weekends. I guess you could use it in an emergency but I'd rather just pay you by the hour. You keep your present place."

"I don't exactly have a place," she confided, gathering her feathers. "I camp out here and there."

Barney looked at his watch. He was late. "Well, you just keep camping out. I have a friend who's an agent. If you're serious about acting, I could call him. You'd probably be great in commercials. All right, you're my girl Friday. This is serious. Organize my closets. My refrigerator. My income-tax file. And please, take your feathers home in a shopping bag or something. Wear a sweater of mine and some jeans on your way out. I hope this isn't a mistake." He was astonished with himself for getting invoved like this. When he thought of the women who'd pleaded and connived to creep into his life by taking over the laundry. He shuddered.

Surely it was wisest to pay someone to handle the mundane details of domestic survival. They couldn't very well sue you for alimony later or punch too many guilt buttons if you canceled the arrangement.

He was halfway down the hall when he remembered he'd forgotten his cortisone. He went back and swallowed a couple of pills with the last ounce of Amber's champagne. He was actually pleased with himself.

*T*he morning at Goodman began with the leftovers of the night shift still waiting to be seen and it went on that way till midafternoon—steady pressure, nothing dramatic but no letup. Barney had a strange nagging sense of unease, as if something were wrong. He scanned the waiting room, the War Room, the aisles—fixing each area into a frame, playing that old childhood game, What's wrong with this picture? The bell in his brain was teasing him. If something was off, it was eluding him.

Barney stared into the parking lot. Tarnapol's bright-red Porsche pulled into a vacant space. The Fudgesicle burst out of the car. Tarnapol seemed to be pursuing her. She tried to pull away. She wore a long, full, gray-flannel cape and the hood fell over her face but she seemed to be crying. Tarnapol seemed to be trying to comfort her. It was that old familiar scene. How often Barney had picked it up on Manhattan street corners. A woman weeping. The man silent, or trying to reason or comfort. Lovers, he imagined, splitting. She is pregnant. He refuses to leave his wife. Always a variation of the same scenario: he has failed her. Barney turned away. He could not imagine a more unlikely mating: Mallory and Tarnapol. The Steel Amazon and the Reluctant Rabbi.

The Fudgesicle was wearing sunglasses when they met an hour later over a nasogastric tube (a young woman who had stabbed her boyfriend with a barbeque fork *after* swallowing a few dozen sleeping pills). So, he decided, she had been crying.

"I saw Frieda Thompson," he said. "I want to thank you for that lead."

"I know. You told me day before yesterday."

Barney was confused. He had no memory of the conversation. "I'm not sure she will say anything against Gunderson," he said. "She may not show up for the Ad Hoc Committee. She's scared."

"I could talk to her," Mallory offered.

He looked up at her. She looked away. What could she possibly see in Dylan Tarnapol? Out of the corner of his eye Barney saw a cockroach scuttle across the floor. "Mrs. Mallory. Get Maintenance to do something about the cockroaches. We've got a major invasion here." Barney felt drained already by midafternoon. He returned to the War Room.

The case load had thinned somewhat. An ER regular was back, Mrs. Klingenstein, but he didn't have the patience to deal with her hot flashes and swollen glands and the constipation, all of which had to do with chronic loneliness. Joe di Renzo was flat on his back again, too. Barney was exasperated. One of these days a real emergency would be delivered to the door and the nuts and drunks and hypochondriacs would be taking up every stretcher and cubicle in sight. Mallory had written on di Renzo's chart, "Shooting pains and numbness." Why hadn't she talked him out of it? Damn, now someone would have to do a full-scale work-up. He moved di Renzo's chart to the bottom of the pile.

"You picked a busy day, Joe," Barney warned him. "It could be hours before we get to you."

"That's okay, Doc. I'll wait." Di Renzo lay there, hands

folded across his stomach like a corpse. "This numbness seems to be creeping up my arm."

"You keep tabs on it," said Barney. "And yell if it gets to your heart."

He ducked into the next cubicle, looking at the chart: Richie Michaels. A two-year-old. No specific complaint. "Mother says he just isn't acting right," it said.

The child was blond, very light-skinned and unusually pale even for one so fair complected. He was unnaturally subdued. After examining him Barney came up with nothing. "The babysitter called me," Richie's mother said. "Said he wasn't acting right and stuff. She thought maybe he fell off the couch."

"Does this hurt, Richie?" said Barney, pressing his stomach. "Does this hurt?" He manipulated all his extremities. Poked and prodded. The child's temperature was normal. He had no pain. But something was wrong. Barney could feel it. He would think of something to keep the boy here a while just to watch him. "We'll do a blood count," Barney said, thinking that was a good excuse to buy some time and pulled the examining gown back on the boy's shoulders. He began to write on the chart.

"Doctor."

He wheeled on his heel and back into the cubicle. "He just fell back," Nurse Mallory said. She'd tossed her sunglasses aside. "As you walked out. There's no pulse." She pressed the cardiac alert. Barney pulled back the boy's eyelid. The pupils were dilated. "Wait outside," he instructed the mother.

Mallory had started CPR.

Barney let Steffans start the IV while he intubated the boy. "Nothing," said Mallory. "No response." Inserting a catheter he noticed a small red spot on the child's penis. What could that be? He glanced at the heart monitor. Nothing was working. He was losing this boy. Barney felt himself choking. He was sweating and he had the feeling he was going to vomit. "Mallory," he cried, as if she could come up with something. Steffans had taken over the external heart massage. Barney pushed him aside. How could he let this baby die? He had to save him. It's my fault, thought Barney. He felt the blood pounding in his own ears as he pressed and released . . . pressed and released. I can't let him die. What's wrong with this kid?

"Dr. Kincaid. It's over."

Barney looked at the listless flat beep on the monitor.

He kept on massaging. Press. Release. Press. Release.

"Barney," said Steffans sternly.

Barney stopped. The boy was dead. He touched his forearm, so smooth and white. What kind of shit am I? Barney thought. "What am I going to tell that woman?" he cried. No one said a word. What could he say? "She brought a child into this Emergency Room. Alive. And now he's dead." Mallory was wrapping the baby. She seemed to be crying. Steffans was disconnecting the tubes. I have to tell that woman the boy is dead, thought Barney.

She stood up looking at him, a slim redhead with a mass of freckles.

"I'm sorry," Barney began. "There was nothing we could do to save him. We tried everything. His heart failed. Everything."

She began to cry. The hand pressed to her mouth was stained with nicotine. The man with her became hysterical. He started to shout and punch the wall. "What did you do to him?" he howled. "He can't be dead." A guard rushed across the room. The mother tried to calm him.

"Sweetie. He's gone. Sweetie. Shhhhh."

"I sent for a minister," the nurse's aide said. She led them into a small private waiting room.

Barney was numb. He was walking toward his office when a handsome blond man in greasy overalls grabbed his arm. "My son. Where is he? Richie Michaels."

Barney was confused. "Who's the guy with your wife?" he asked.

"Her boyfriend. We're separated. How is he? Doc, please."

"I'm sorry," said Barney. "His heart suddenly failed. We

don't know why. We did everything we could to revive him but . . . we will find out what it was."

The father insisted on seeing him. Barney watched the man embrace the dead boy. Something weird was going on. Why had the boyfriend behaved so insanely? "What's this?" said the man. He held the boy's penis in his hand.

Barney looked at the spot again. Now it came to him. It was a cigarette burn. Perhaps the child had been abused, even beaten. He led the father out of the cubicle. "You leave us your number and we'll call you as soon as we have more information," he said.

"Did you see the Fudgesicle?" Steffans asked. "She raced out of here. I think she was crying. Shall I send one of the nurses after her or . . . will you?"

Barney looked in the supply closet. Then he thought of the stairwell. The door squeaked as he opened it but Mallory did not turn. Her body was heaving.

"Mrs. Mallory, is there . . . It was terrible, the boy dying . . . may I?"

"I'm all right," she said.

Barney stood there. Women want to be comforted, he knew that. But she was not like other women. He was hesitant to touch her. He put a tentative hand on her shoulder.

"Oh God," she moaned. "I can't bear it." She collapsed against him. "It's not really the boy. Maybe that's part of it. I hate to see a child die. But it's me. My life. How could he do it? I can't believe he could do it." He held her away from him. She opened her eyes and shut them quickly against the light. "This is ridiculous," she said. "I need to blow my nose." She started to cry again.

"Use my sleeve," said Barney. He set her down on the step. She huddled there. "Should I get some tissues?" Perhaps he should call Dick Rogin or even Tarnapol.

"I hate being grown up," she said. "I hate being alone. That unloving bastard."

Barney was astonished. Till he'd seen her with Dylan Tarnapol, he had perceived Anne Mallory as a piece of professional equipment. A fine precision instrument that never failed to function. Scrupulously impersonal. Professionally responsive with no intimation of feeling. That was Mallory. He'd only recently speculated that she might have a private life: her manner did not permit curiosity. But boy, when she let go, did she let go.

"I'm embarrassed," she said, blowing her nose, trying to tuck the loose wisps of hair back into her bun. "I can't believe I let myself fall apart like this." She looked at him and started to weep again.

"You don't have to say anything," said Barney. "I'm not prying, honestly. I admire, I have always admired your professionalism." Indeed, he was seeing Mallory as a woman. A soft body, full petulant mouth, long lashes now matted and spiked by tears. Seeing her hair free of that tight bun was like seeing her naked. That was not what Barney needed in a life already crowded with eager bodies. He needed her strength, her cool . . . her unemotional reflexes.

"It's such a cliché, I should be embarrassed to tell it," she said. She tossed back her hair with a hand he now realized was small and graceful, a geisha-doll hand. "There is a man."

"Yes," said Barney. "Dylan Tarnapol."

She stared at him, and laughed. "Dylan is my friend. A confidant. A pal. No, I mean the man I've been living with," she said, "a heartless, unfeeling, greedy, spoiled creature. When he was good he was so good." Her eyes filled. "Oh dear, I must be crazy to think I was going to get him to love me. I shouldn't be telling you all this."

Barney almost agreed. He longed to be able to comfort her. Alas, he was a pushover for any woman in tears. But he was loath to lose the Fudgesicle, the cool unimpassioned professional that made the Emergency Room tick like clockwork. "You can tell me anything. I'm afraid I'm practically an expert on the subject of men and betrayal . . . I've been accused of it so many times," he said.

"You say that as if you were proud of it," she observed, studying him through a veil of mist.

"No. Is that how it sounded?" He couldn't accept that. "I definitely am not proud of it. I've only just gotten accustomed to the possibility that it may be true. Do you want me to go?"

She was silent. "Well, the cliché is that I have been working like a fool for three years helping this man pay for medical school and now he's gotten himself engaged to the daughter of some filthy rich people. I think he said they gave three million to the medical school. How could they be so naive . . . falling for that snake? Of course she fell for him. In the beginning he was irresistible. I'm so smart, and I couldn't resist." She started to cry again, tears coursing down her cheeks.

"You ought to be furious," said Barney. "You seem to be angry with yourself when you ought to be in a rage about him."

She looked at him. "I know. I . . . I'll have to work on that." She stood up. "I'd better do something to my face. We have a house full of patients. At least we did." She threw back her head, pulled all the strands into a long tail and twisted it back into its tight bun. Barney could feel the armor sliding into place again. He thought about holding her. But he was distracted by a parade of cockroaches scuttling away as they stood.

"Mrs. Mallory. For God's sake, let's do something about the roaches."

"I'll get a rifle," she said.

"Excuse me," said Barney.

"Maintenance has sprayed. I'll get them to spray again."

He followed her into the chaos of the afternoon. There was so much to do. He would have to notify the police about the possibility of child abuse. There was a man sitting just outside the War Room wearing a contagion mask.

"Where have you been?" Stef asked irritably. "We've been running our asses off out here."

"TB?" Barney asked, indicating the masked man.

"Yes," said Stef, "And guess where he works? He's the short-order cook in our favorite deli."

Barney groaned. "That means we'll probably have to do tuberculin tests on the entire goddamn hospital staff?" Automatically his eyes scanned the progress board. He moved Joe di Renzo's chart to the bottom of the pile again.

"We should do a few unpleasant diagnostic procedures on that guy and scare him away," Steffans suggested.

"At some point you might just check in and make sure he isn't in cardiac arrest," Barney instructed.

"Fat chance."

Barney looked around for Mallory. He heard her voice low and firm coming from the supply closet. "You shouldn't be setting an arm with the textbook out on the table like that," she was saying. "No wonder the patient got hysterical." Barney heard the intern Jim Eastern trying to defend himself. Barney stood there torn between his sense that the conversation with Anne Mallory was unfinished and a wisdom that told him to resist temptation for the sake of the Emergency Room.

Eastern came out of the supply closet sideways, his eyes glued to the floor as if he were hoping to find a pothole to disappear in. Mallory brushed by.

Barney stopped her. "Are you all right? Would it help if we had dinner somewhere later tonight?"

She frowned. "I'm so sorry," she said. "I do have plans." But it was clear from the way she said it she was lying. Barney felt as if she'd knocked the wind out of him. He stood against the wall for a moment, catching his breath. What a killer she was, he thought. Once a Fudgesicle, always a Fudgesicle. For a minute he felt ugly, rejected.

He sat down and then everything hit him, the boy's death, the residual of fear that he was responsible, the great rush of relief sensing he was not, the discomfort of watching Mallory break down, her indifference to his concern. He knew he did not have the strength to drive one hundred miles to Kingston as he had planned.

"Get out of here, Barney," said Steffans. "You look awful. Do something to lose yourself for an hour or two and get to bed early."

"I appreciate the diagnosis." Barney heard himself, his voice curt. "Sorry. You're right. I've had it."

He decided to call Debra. "It's been longer than I can remember since I saw a porn flick," he said.

"I guess I should be happy there's at least one area in which you're true to me," she said. She had a cocktail party she couldn't miss, she said. "I promise Joe Heller, maybe Ed Doctorow, and absolutely Kurt Vonnegut," she said.

Barney knew that crowd, a nest of vipers she palled around with, mostly third-string media celebrities, always totally immersed in their own clippings and gossip. But he was a fan of Ed Doctorow and if they ate meatballs from the buffet, they could go right home after the flick and she'd dream up some delightful kinkiness to distract him. What a shallow man I am, thought Barney. How seducible.

*B*arney slipped into the room. He might have been the Invisible Man. That's how nonexistent he was for these piranhas. Three or four people had looked directly at him and then through him without dribbling a drop of guacamole. Except for a predatory tigress who eyed him hungrily as he ambled toward the bar.

"Do you belong to the bride or the groom?" the woman asked.

Barney was baffled. "Try that again," he said.

"This party. The Goldensons. They're announcing their separation. Are you his or hers?"

Barney was trying to think of a witty response when he spotted Debra spotting him. "I'm here to find out," he said, squeezing her hand and excusing himself with a mumble that he would return.

Debra stood in the middle of a particularly fierce circle. "What is love?" she was asking.

"Excuse me," said a rather flashy older woman poured into black leather cowboy chaps. She looked like she could gobble Debra whole and spit out the pit.

"Is the quiche gone already?" someone asked Barney. He moved out of what seemed to be a direct flight path to the buffet.

"I said, 'What is your definition of love?'" Debra addressed her question to the leathered woman. "I don't know you. You don't know me. I don't know anyone that well at this party except Lee Radziwill, who I once ran over with a shopping cart in the peanut butter section of a supermarket in Southampton so I feel I rather know her. I'm just conducting an opinion poll. On love."

Barney thought Debra sounded slightly smashed already. Like most people who didn't drink, when she did finally take a drink it was usually a disaster. She took Barney's hand and patted it. Love was a subject they had endlessly debated and she considered herself his mentor.

"Love is like breaking your leg," said the woman in leather.

Debra shook her head. "Could you explain that?"

"This is too serious a subject to discuss meaningfully at a cocktail party," the leathered one dismissed her.

"I'm sorry you think that," said Debra, clearly miffed. "Perhaps it's difficult for you to be serious in a vertical position. But I'm no good at small talk. So I'm stuck with big talk."

"And what is love to you?" asked a very handsome weatherbeaten man in high-heeled boots, reaching through the conversation to spear a carrot stick.

Debra pounced, ready to expound. "Love is caring for someone as much as yourself." She looked at Barney and smiled. He smiled. He recognized the line as her psychoanalyst's national anthem.

"As much as," he challenged. "Not . . . more than?"

"As much as," said Debra. "That's the point. You can't love anyone unless you love yourself. We're talking about love," said Debra, as persistent at play as she was on a news assignment. "How would you define it?" she asked a man who looked like a middle-aged Pinocchio.

He contemplated his drink. "That glorious moment before disillusion sets in." Behind him, two young women booed.

What am I doing here? thought Barney. The frivolity was so intense. He pressed his fingertips together. A few hours ago he'd touched a dead child. He imagined these people, Debra's chums, gift-wrapping the corpse. He felt himself drowning, shook his head, cleared it, reached for a drink.

"Love is David," said a tall, strong-looking woman clinging to the arm of a plump young man.

"They're engaged," said a fragilely thin woman with cat eyes. "His family owns five or six blocks in downtown Boston," she whispered. "Where it counts."

"Engaged? Do people still become engaged?" asked Pinocchio.

"Loving is feeling secure when you let someone else see you all the ways you see yourself," said the inexplicably insecure heir to downtown Boston.

"I'm always afraid something will happen," his fiancée confided.

"Oh yes," said Pinocchio. "The pogrom theory of life."

Barney was astonished at how eagerly people got caught up discussing intimate feelings with total strangers. Debra was choreographing with inspired fervor. "And what is love to you?" she asked a man dressed in prep-school crewneck and untied sneakers.

"I haven't the least idea how to answer that." He smiled an aging, schoolboy, haven't-done-my-homework grin.

"But surely you have been in love," Debra persisted.

"Oh yes." He pondered. "I got a dirty phone call a few days ago. It went on for twenty minutes. I also had an automobile accident. The windshield shattered like lace and yet not a shard or crystal fell into the car. It was a terrible day but I survived."

Barney shook his head. He signaled to Debra but she

ignored him. He was about to walk away when a deeply lined man Barney recognized as a popular novelist and a legendary womanizer began. "Love is what you think you want when you're alone. I think people who feel romantic love after the age of thirty should have their heads examined."

"Is this spinach pie?" an innocent bystander asked no one in particular. "I suspect it's escarole. With pine nuts. Or walnuts."

The novelist glared at the interruption. "I'm about to tell you something quite profound," he said. "This is it. You have to create a creature that is other than you. We are not really that different . . . men and women. So we create the difference. It's good to think that Woman comes from Mars and Man comes—"

"From Barney's Men's Shop," said a horse-faced woman.

The novelist ignored her. "One willingly suspends disbelief, as Coleridge suggested," he said. "I like what Maeterlink said in his play, *The Bluebird.* 'As for loving, let our servants do it for us.'"

Maeterlink. Good God. Barney remembered the actor di Renzo. The poor scared slob waiting patiently all day with the numbness creeping up his arm. He found a phone in a bedroom. There was a woman passed out under a big fat mink coat. Barney took her pulse. She was alive. "Stef. Whatever became of di Renzo?"

"Shit." Steff dropped the phone. Nurse Coburn came on: "He's checking, Dr. Kincaid." She held the phone. "Here he is, Dr. Kincaid."

"He was asleep," said Stef. "The creep. Says the pain is gone now. He's going to sign himself out but he insists he'll hang around in the snack bar for a while, till he feels really confident."

Barney groaned.

"Hey, by the way, preliminary autopsy on the Michaels boy. You were right. Child abuse, my ass, child torture. He died of a brain injury but there was evidence of all kinds of internal damage. I'll leave a copy on your desk."

Barney's relief was edged with anger. So there was nothing he could have done to save the boy. If he had his way, child abusers would be killed with slow torture. He went looking for Debra. "Let's get out of this zoo," he said. She took a curl of cucumber, dipped it into something green and fishy and put it into his mouth. He took the cucumber out and dropped it into an ashtray. He did not trust anonymous fishy things. "Can't you forget about love for a few minutes?"

She looked hurt, as if he had slapped her. "You of all people might really benefit from a thoughtful dissection of that feeling that seems to elude you."

"I don't look for emotional epiphany at a cocktail party," he said. "Besides, I guess I'm feeling down. We lost a little boy this afternoon. Just a baby. You feel so damned stupid. Helpless."

Her face distorted with concern. "Oh Barney love, how terrible. Oh. I'm so sorry. You must feel miserable." She hugged him. "Why are we here?"

"Well, I thought it would help to distract myself," he said. "If you let failures get to you, you won't be able to function. I need to bury myself in . . . sensation, I guess."

"Were you thinking of something really inane?" she asked, with that sweet intuitive caring that had appealed so when they met. "Wet Dreams is playing at the Pussycat Cinema."

"Wet Rainbow," he corrected.

"Exactly." She took his arm. "All I ever wanted was to be the author of your joy and the choreographer of your pleasure. I just wanted to convince you that two people like us who really care about sex will always find ways to keep it hot. Anyway, when Plato discoursed about love, the Greeks turned it into a best-selling paperback," she said.

"Tonight you are my author and my choreographer, my mistress and my slut."

"Ah," she sighed. "You sure know how to win a girl."

*D*ebra wore her morning-after-sex incandescence and a bright-pink silk robe with slits as high as an elephant's eye. Barney enjoyed the flash of thigh and a sense of himself as the source of that incandescence as she poured hot water over coffee grounds and managed to toast the bagels without burning them. Mornings were a shock for Debra. She woke slowly, dropping things and burning toast as if it were a sacred ritual of her sworn religion. But even moving through the kitchen in a semitrance, she couldn't resist the domesticity of sharing breakfast. Normally Barney loved these mornings too, the easy after-sex intimacy and emotional insights Debra came up with almost intuitively. And this morning he felt especially good, full of energy, his old self again, anxious to take advantage of a free day for an early start toward Kingston in search of Lilyanne. He debated whether to call her daughter Iris first, or just arrive and confront her. Lilyanne's twins, demonic Iris and submissive Ellen Sue, had been both uncaringly competitive and yet protective of Lilyanne.

But Debra was up to something. She seemed to be struggling to overcome her morning vulnerability. Always mornings had been safe from painful confrontations (the hour disarmed her). Evenings too were sacrosanct. She'd learned that attacking him for real or imagined neglect before bedtime too often led to sexual deprivation. So, sagely, she saved verbal attacks and recriminations for the neutral moments in midafternoon, usually over the phone. Not today. He could sense the barely contained storm ahead as she asked: "Would you like to drive up to Vermont with me next weekend? My sister-in-law has offered us her ski house. It must be heavenly up there right now."

"I can't next weekend, darling." He hated to see the hurt on her face. And the anger was worse. "Actually I won't be seeing you for a few weeks. I'm taking Candy away for her semester break."

"Not this weekend," she said.

"No, not this weekend," he conceded.

"What's her name is this weekend," she said.

Barney didn't answer. He wasn't sure what he would do this weekend. Work Saturday, he knew, and . . . everything depended on what he found today in Kingston.

"Does she know about me?" Debra's tears salted her bagel. Barney never ceased to be amazed at how she could eat her way through these tragic scenes.

"She thinks I've stopped seeing you." Lindsay had made Barney promise to give up Debra last fall.

"Why is it she doesn't know about me but I have to know about her?"

"I like to be honest," said Barney, trapping himself. "This coffee has got to be ready by now," he grumbled. "I couldn't stop seeing you. That's why I'm here."

"Well, why not be honest with her? Why am I the only one forced to suffer through your noble, self-congratulating honesty?"

Barney gulped his coffee. "I suffer too," he assured her. "I can't be honest with her unless I stop seeing you." How had he gotten into this? Lindsay was threatening to stop seeing him. Debra was impossible. He had tried so hard to keep them both happy. A man in his stage of domestic upheaval was obviously not supposed to be attached to anyone. "I'm late," he said, slipping into his coat.

"If you leave now, don't bother to call again," she stormed.

Barney was silent. Then he walked out the door.

"You fucking animal," she screamed after him.

He was shaking as he fumbled with the lock on his car door. He rammed the car through a red light, furious to be starting the day with a headache. At home he took his cortisone and a couple of Exedrin. There was no sign of

Amber but from the looks of the desk in his guest-
room–office, she'd been organizing the income-tax file. Her
trail in the kitchen was easy to track. A quart of heavenly
hash ice cream in the freezer. His film in a pile organized
sensibly by expiration date. A small jar of caviar and some
tissue-wrapped packages of cheese, everything labeled. A
giant bottle of cranberry juice. And a note.

> I opened a house charge at Zabar's. The cheese
> is for your sleepover guests. The cranberry is
> mine. It's a cure for almost anything. Try it. If
> you leave your check stubs out, I'll balance your
> checkbook.

Barney checked with his service. There were the usual
S.O.S. calls from the ER, an invitation from the administrator, Jonathan Adams, to reschedule his Gunderson case or
drop it, calls from salesmen, and one from his favorite free-
lance medical writer. And of course, the personal calls.
Candy, Reeney, Mama, somebody named Deirdre—he knew
four Deirdres. Frieda Thompson. Barney stashed the rest of
the messages in his pocket and phoned Gunderson's former
nurse. She wanted to see him. He called Kingston to
postpone his lunch date with the twin, Iris.
"Oh, was that for today?" she asked, sounding dopey or
asleep. "I'm glad you called first because I won't be here."
He got her to agree to meet him for a drink after dinner.
She really sounded vacant. Barney wondered if perhaps her
intellectual development had been arrested at thirteen, her
age the last time he'd seen her. She'd been bright enough
then to make a slave of her twin, Ellen Sue, and drive their
mother nutty.
He picked up Nurse Thompson outside the nursing
home in Queens. They drove to a diner under the Fifty-
ninth Street Bridge. She had decided to tell everything she
knew, she announced. "You have a real fan in Anne
Mallory," she said. "She persuaded me I owe it to our
profession." In Frieda's version of the story, unfortunately,

she didn't want to discuss the chart, still seemed reluctant to put Gunderson on the spot. Yes, she knew sedating the patient had been a mistake, a fatal mistake, but it was obvious she was holding back. Barney pressured her.

"You must have known more," he said. "You must have known he corrected the orders in the chart *after* the patient died. You had to know."

She sat silent. "I altered the orders," she finally said.

"You." Barney shook his head. "But why?" He was confused. He worked on her for several more minutes. She was shifty and evasive, trying to give him something but determined to protect . . . who? Barney felt really dense.

When he mentioned that he needed her to appear in person, she was ready to forget everything she'd given him so far. "You can write it down and I'll sign it if it fits what I said," she offered.

She touched his arm, "You can afford to be a hero, Dr. Kincaid, with your big practice and all your cronies egging you on. Do you have any idea what I get paid for wiping all those incontinent asses abandoned by their children to that fleabag nursing home? Where did the world get the idea nurses are paid in glory instead of money?"

"I'm sorry," said Barney. "I *do* appreciate your courage."

"Well, I suppose, in the end, he dropped me anyway, so what does it matter? You write the story down the way you want it and give me another call."

Barney decided to stop at the hospital on the way to Kingston. Maybe the Fudgesicle had some unused ammunition left to persuade Frieda Thompson.

*B*arney went directly to the administrator's office. Adams was out. Enoch Whitaker grimaced and snorted as he took Barney's message: "I'm ready for the Gunderson hearing when you are." A slight stretch of the truth, Barney conceded, but he would be ready.

Mallory was not in the ER. Barney hung up his jacket, slipped into his white coat. There was something in the pocket, a sheet of his personal stationery. Folded. He opened it up. It was a list, the names of women, names he knew at once, names he didn't remember, check marks beside some, circles around Barbie Bloome's name, around Audrey's, Linda's, Margaret's, Cristal's, the women he'd seen, addresses and phone numbers jotted in the margins. He did not remember making this list. But it was definitely his handwriting. Why couldn't he remember?

"Are you working today, doctor?" Nurse Coburn asked.

"Of course I'm working," said Barney, stuffing the list back in his pocket. He studied the board in the War Room and rifled through the charts. Then he remembered. He had to find Mallory. She was not in the cafeteria. But Dick Rogin was there, huddled with Mike Steffans. Dick was sipping his usual Tab and forking up cherry pie à la mode.

"What happened to your fast?" asked Barney.

"This is my new fast," Dick replied. "I eat fast. And mostly I eat fast food fast. That's my new secret fast. I am thinking of a diet book. *The Riverdale Fast Food Diet Book.* Does it sound like a best-seller or doesn't it? Sit down, Barney. We were discussing mothers. Since you have a mother-and-a-half, you'll be interested."

"Dick says most men marry their mothers, that is,

women like their mother," Mike said. "Women too . . . they marry men like their mothers. Right?"

"Then there are men who marry women as much *unlike* their mothers as possible," Dick went on. "Which men are evidencing the greatest attachment to their mothers?"

Barney was mesmerized, watched the coffee machine spitting out hot chocolate. "The question seems so obvious I'm going to assume the obvious is not the answer."

"Right," said Dick. "The man who *must* marry a woman totally unlike his mother keeps the mother for his real love. To make a good marriage, a man must be ready to give up his mother. So usually these marriages are doomed."

"These days all marriages seem to be doomed," said Barney. "Who's happy?"

"I'm not unhappy," Mike offered. "Oh, by the way, the autopsy on the Michaels boy. The kid probably hit an emergency room or two before ours. Didn't you speak to the city once about some kind of child-abuse alert? A clearing house for information, suspicions."

Barney sighed. "Yes, I did. The whole metropolitan area needs to be wired for medical alerts." He wiped a cockroach off Mike's sleeve. "This hospital is getting to be a zoo."

"What was that?" said Stef.

"A cockroach, damn it. They're taking over."

"Gee, I missed it," said Stef.

Barney watched him walk off. "Am I losing my mind?" he asked.

"Seeing cockroaches in New York is not considered delusional," Dick responded.

"I'm not imagining cockroaches, Dick. But I am getting caught up in this ridiculous search for the women in my past. Not just the truly important ones. Now I keep thinking of women that aren't important at all. Suddenly I feel driven . . . compelled to find them. Every one."

"Barney, you're exaggerating. A bachelor, a free man, forty years old, having a crisis of passage, go, my friend, go

in good health. When I think of your life, I'm sick with
jealousy."

"I better get to work," said Barney. Oh yes, Mallory. He
had been looking for Mallory. She was taking a history in the
cubicle next to the War Room. He stood there, admiring the
measured honey in her low, intelligent voice. He could
imagine her voice was actually two-dimensional. He could
imagine it dripping in a honey pool on the floor and spilling
out of the cubicle.

"Oh, are you working today, Dr. Kincaid?" she said,
brushing by him.

"Of course," he said. "And I want to talk to you for a
minute." He reported his progress with Frieda Thompson,
thanking her for encouraging the woman to talk, explaining
her refusal to appear. "May I ask you to talk to her again?
Her appearance will probably be crucial."

Nurse Mallory broke into a smile. "Look who's here.
Dylan." She took Tarnapol's hand. "Why are you so cold?"

"Got a minute, Barney?" The young rabbi had lost his
laid-back air. "I just need a minute with Barney, Anne."

Barney led him into a distant cubicle away from the War
Room. Dylan lit up a joint and passed it.

"You gotta be kidding, Dylan. Not here."

"I'm having a little pain. It's probably heartburn. But
you know how it is, hanging around hospitals, death can be
contagious. It's nothing. Probably a pulled muscle. A hot
flash." He grinned. He groaned. "I'm not old enough for
hot flashes."

"Lie down, Dylan," he said. "Let's listen." In minutes
Mallory had the reluctant rabbi hooked up to the EKG.
"Any numbness?" asked Barney. "Describe the pain."

"Barney, honest, it's about a one-and-a-half-kosher-
hotdogs-with-mustard-and-sauerkraut heartburn. You guys
are giving me a heart attack. I just wanted a quiet con-
sultation," Tarnapol protested. "A fast professional reas-
surance. I'm auditioning tonight for a nice little gig. A
wedding. First I marry these two gays on a snow-covered
mountain top. Hey, what are you doing with that needle?"

"Just blood," said Mallory.

"And then I play my guitar for the reception."

"Stop talking for a minute," said Barney. He studied the EKG. I don't see anything here. Looks really good, Dylan. We'll see what the blood gasses show. But anyway, if I were you I'd sign in for the night. Just to be safe."

Tarnapol groaned. "Come on, Barney. You gotta be joking. It's not just an audition. It's a hot date too."

"With a couple of queers," said Barney.

"The bride has a sister," said Tarnapol. "She tries to make up in heterosexuality what her brother lacks. And I'm the lucky guy in her life."

The blood work showed everything normal. Tarnapol was determined to leave. He was only thirty-six, a jogger, a nonsmoker (except for the grass), no family history, the cholesterol count of a Nepalese monk. "Don't check in if you don't want to" said Barney, "but let us make you comfortable here in the ER overnight." Mallory read Tarnapol a scarifying lecture on the heart's cries of wolf.

Tarnapol laughed. "You guys have cured me already. I haven't had a twinge since I sneaked a couple of Alka Seltzer. I gotta go."

Barney suddenly remembered Kingston. He grabbed his coat. "You're a big boy, Tarnapol. We are not about to get a court order to restrain you. Lay off the delicatessen for a couple of days."

"Are you leaving?" the Fudgesicle asked. "And you're letting Dylan go?"

"Sign me out."

"You do know you weren't scheduled in," she said.

He looked at her. "Of course," he said. Everyone here was nuts. "Sign me out anyway."

*B*arney cursed and snarled as he inched ahead in the five o'clock going-home crush, cutting in and out of hobbled traffic on the wounded Saw Mill River Parkway. Was it an omen? Should he cancel the Kingston odyssey? Iris had sounded flaky and distant on the phone. Certainly those decadent, guilt-sodden hours with Iris and Ellen Sue had taught him nothing about love and nothing about himself that he wanted to know. But Iris seemed to be his sole link to Lilyanne, the only lead Carl had come up with anyway.

Lilyanne was his love, Lilyanne, the great earth goddess. Lilyanne, mother of precociously wicked twins, Nurse Lilyanne making a scared first-year resident look good on her service at New Haven Hospital, making him feel horny and alive when he ought to have been comatose from fatigue and the strains of trying to deal with Reeney's demands. What a fool he had been . . . how weak and greedy to let the twins act out their vendetta on their mother by attacking him. What is revenge, after all, if you don't alert the victim? Of course the twins *had* to tell.

Barney realized he needed Lilyanne's forgiveness. He would have to see Iris to find Lilyanne. He headed north along the Hudson. At eight he was sitting at the bar of a steakhouse overlooking Kingston, New York, sipping vodka on the rocks, a lethal drink. He would stick to one.

The steakhouse was Iris's idea. "I get hungry guaranteed three times a day and I haven't tasted a steak in months. With four kids under nine, I'm lucky I get to go to the bathroom," she said on the phone.

Barney recognized her at once in the dim orange glow of the lantern at the bar entrance. At thirteen the twins had already reached six feet. They were an awesome duo with their high, budding breasts, the little squirrel cheeks, and wild frizzy black hair. And there she was. Even with the friz trimmed to just slightly longer than a man's brush cut, there was no possible doubt. She wore stenciled cowboy boots with rundown heels and towered over everyone in the room.

Barney stood up and took her arm. She looked down at him with a sneer. "Hey, hands off the merchandise, mister."

"Iris. It's Barney."

She looked at him. Her eyes were smudged with black makeup. Her kewpie-doll lips were painted bright red. "You're not Barney." She looked around the room. "You were taller and had slicked-back hair, shiny black with sideburns. And a skinny long nose that was always cold. Barney Kincaid?" She seemed genuinely perplexed. "Which one are you?" she asked.

"Dr. Barney Kincaid. You and Ellen Sue tied me up and attacked me one day. You were thirteen. I worked at the hospital and spent time with your mother. Come on now, Iris, you must remember. You used to slip little notes under the door when you thought your mother and I were asleep. It drove your mother crazy. You had those bedspreads from India. I remember they didn't match. There was a Beatles poster. You two used to do gynecological surgery on your Barbie doll. Come on now Iris."

"Oh, yes. That was Ellen Sue. She was a nut. She made us do such insane things. I thought you were the one with the sideburns." She shrugged. "I'll have a Black Russian. That's vodka and chocolate milk." She took a handful of peanuts. "Barney Kincaid. He used to take us to drive-in movies. And he'd buy two of everything at the Refreshery and take off our panties and we'd play away through both halves of a double bill. He had one of those foreign cars with the seats that go all the way down. His dad was some big-time anesthesiologist."

Barney was only a bit depressed. He grinned because he was amused by the irony, a hundred-mile case of mistaken identity. He wished he'd been cool enough to enjoy the twins with the elan of "Barney Kincaid," sn of the big-time anesthesiologist. He had never been with them for one minute when his lust and joy had not been tainted (if not fueled) with guilt. "Well, let's see. How can I establish my identity without dimming your enthusiasm," he began. "Perhaps a refill and a big sirloin steak would help." He ordered fresh drinks for them both.

She eyed him from under the weight of those smutty eyelashes. She ran one finger down the straight of his nose, felt a bicep, brushed her knee deeper into his crotch (or did he just imagine that?) as if her own personal braille would provoke the elusive memory. "Oh, wow," she said. "It's coming back now. That was Norman. Norman something. Oh yeah. Norman ended up having to go to dental school. Barney Kincaid. You were the one we had to drag kicking and screaming. You were the one that kept complaining we'd get you arrested. For child molesting." She laughed. "You old child molester you."

There was something about her mouth, that voluptuous swell of glistening red grease and her pose, knees in brown corduroy spread wide, boot heels locked behind the rung of her stool, that made her bigger than life. He had a flash image that at any moment she could drag him away again kicking and screaming. He was aware of her strength and his own growing excitement.

"I was that shy?" Barney wondered. "No one else lived in fear of the vice squad?" Barney remembered. Day blurred into night into day then and the intern was everyone's gofer and scapegoat. Exhausted and emotionally drained by the constant fear of fucking up on the ward, Barney needed a retreat. Rather than go home and get involved in some confrontation with Reeney, he would crash at Lilyanne's and nap till she got home or flop on the sofa, drifting in and out of a catatonic stupor while the twins watched *American Bandstand* or did theater.

Iris and Ellen Sue, dimpled knees and narrow thighs in denim cutoffs, endlessly wiggling their asses. They acted out *I Love Lucy*. And scenes from *Ben Casey*. "Watch," Iris commanded. "Ellen Sue will dance. If we're good enough you can send a telegram to Ed Sullivan." They did bizarre fables and depraved fairy tales. All their kings were seducers of innocent maidens who didn't speak English. All the wicked stepmothers tortured foundling virgins. Snow White was impure and so was Rose Red. Paralyzed after forty-eight hours of duty Barney was drifting off when his eyes jerked open and he saw Ellen Sue going down on Iris or Iris on Ellen Sue. He could only tell them apart close up. Iris had broken her little finger as an infant and it was crooked.

"Let's see," said Iris, sipping her sweet drink, eyes closed. "I think Ellen Sue tied your feet to the bedposts with the sash from Mommie's bathrobe. That was you? Or was that the track coach? No, that was you."

What am I doing here? Barney tried to remember. Maybe they should order dinner. He was already too smashed to drive. He had one knee pressed into her crotch too. He remembered how he had berated himself for succumbing to the twins but his resistance was low. He was prey to every virus that came along that year and a pushover to these cunning Lolitas. Those were his sexiest days. Watching Iris and Ellen Sue finger each other. Knowing that Ellen Sue would crawl between his legs. Knowing that Iris would come dripping and sticky to sit on his face. Tackling each other in corners and closets, scampering for cover when Lilyanne's car pulled into the garage. Then letting Lilyanne massage his battered bones with fingers that stretched and soothed, cured and then teased. Loving Lilyanne before finally crashing in her arms.

"They're too precocious," said Lilyanne, worried the twins were too much alone without her attention.

Barney worried too. What would become of them? They lived in the blue light of the TV, lost in a child's garden of sexual madness. Incest at thirteen. Where could they go at twenty? What was left for them at thirty?

"Well, Ellen Sue married the advance man for a rock group that lives in Saugerties, up the road. Only four months ago she ran off with some coke dealer from Texas. And guess who's got her kids? Yeah, she just dumps them on my doorstep, her two plus I got two of my own and my old man just happens to be temporarily on vacation."

"Laid off from work?"

"Gone. Disappeared. Split."

"And your mother?"

"I sure hope you're going to feed me," she said. "Besides you're going to fall on your face if you don't get something to eat." She sent the waiter for steaks. "Rare," she said. "I want mine black and blue. That shouldn't take too long," she observed. "Mom is . . ." She hesitated. "Mom is very beautiful."

Barney was drunk. He may or may not have staggered to a salad bar because suddenly he was looking down into a strange collection of leaves and seeds, beans, and bits of god-knows-what in a murk of creamy mucilage that could have been designed by a squirrel planning to build a home.

"I'll do almost anything to make money," Iris was saying. "The bills are piled up. We're down to powdered milk and day-old bread and whatever the kids can shoplift from the A & P. I have a neighbor who's real good. I left them eating lasagna she sent by."

"They must have vitamin C," said Barney, gratefully watching the waitress carve their steak. He wasn't sure he could have handled what looked like a major portion of some cow's middle.

"Yeah. Yeah," said Iris. "I need a dollar for gas to get home and a couple of dollars for orange juice." She turned the full force of her smouldering sooty gaze on Barney. The food had sobered him, reviving his aesthetic sensibility enough so that he could marvel at how sixteen years had refined her face. What had been pudgy and cute was slimmed and contoured. Her eyes blazed with passion although it might have been passion flavored with desperation.

"I have this really cute friend," Iris was saying. "Cute and really hot. And we could . . . you know. And it wouldn't be faking it at all because she's someone I fool around with anyway. She'd do it for fun," Iris went on. "Nina never gets enough sex. I need the money."

Barney felt sad, sorry for Iris; really what he felt was

sorry for Lilyanne, that Lilyanne's grandchildren had to be deprived of orange juice. "Iris. Sweet Iris," he said. "I think you've misunderstood, I mean, I need to be understood but I think I have neglected to explain. Do you understand?" He took her hand. Her hand was as big as his. Visions of amazon breasts and red slashes of mouth tumbled through his addled brain. Oh Barney. Two women in bed . . . two luscious women all to himself. Barney's constant fantasy. There was no way he could resist. So he was a pushover . . . so what. So what if pure sex were ultimately meaningless, as Lindsay kept trying to convince him. What a lark it would be to frolic with this truculent giantess and her chum. Sure it would be goddamned convenient if he could feel the commitment that came so easily to Lindsay. God knows he was trying to find that commitment. But couldn't he take one night off for a little fun? Damn right, he could.

Iris had her other hand on his crotch. "Whatya say, Norman? You gonna let me call my friend Nina?"

He wished she were more subtle, less common, not so trapped by poverty. "Who could say no?"

Iris grinned and hugged him. "Hooray!" she cried. For a minute he thought she might throw him up into the air. "The money part is not a problem?" she whispered.

"I was going to give you all the cash I had anyway," he said. "For food. You've got to feed those kids." He pulled out his wallet. One hundred and twenty dollars. It was more than he'd thought, but he was embarrassed to hold back more than twenty. "I'll need gas, too," he apologized.

"Got thirty cents for the phone?" she said. "It's a toll call." She came striding back, looking pleased. "Nina will meet us down the road at Hojo's. We can take a room there. I got all my kids in the trailer and her husband refuses to go out on a Knicks night. The louse."

Iris decided they should stop for ice cream cones. He watched her licking the mint chip drip as it dribbled down her fingers and got hot again as they lurched toward the second-story room. Nina was an inch or so shorter than Iris, thin with a sweet kind of blank face and a shiny fall of chestnut hair she kept twitching around. "She's a dancer," Iris said, hugging Nina close, burying her face in that hair. So it was not an act, thought Barney. Nina was a surrogate for Ellen Sue. He stood at the end of the bed watching them embrace. The smoulder of Iris's eyes came off on Nina's cheeks as they kissed. Nina was naked under one of those old-fashioned furry white sweaters. Iris tugged off her boots. Under her shirt she wore a black silk thing, short and lacy, very French. Barney brushed the strap from one shoulder and Nina kissed the breast that tumbled free. There was something sacred about all those breasts pressed together. He hadn't felt that moved by a religious ritual at his own bar mitzvah. They were not the little-girl buds of the teenage twins but great, full, womanly breasts. Two such breasts would have been enough for any sane man. Four were sublime excess.

Iris tugged Nina's bikini panties down slowly and threw them into a corner. Nina spread her legs and lay back exposing a flower of pink. Iris pinched it into a bud, licked her finger, and began to rub.

It was everything Barney had ever imagined it would be. Mouths everywhere. Breasts flying and colliding. His cock inexhaustible, riding first one and then the other as they kissed and stroked each other beneath him. In his masturbatory dreams Barney had fucked a mountain of women. Now he arranged his two amazons, sticky and stained with their own delicious juices, on their tummies in a sandwich—Iris on the bottom, Nina crouched over her, that fall of hair veiling Iris's face—their cheeks pressed close, their pussies lined up one on top of the other so he could move from Nina to Iris back to Nina without missing a stroke. Oh God, it was pig's heaven.

*B*arney woke alone the next morning, aching all over. He felt like a man of ninety as he crawled out of bed and tried to stand straight. He staggered to the bathroom and looked at himself in the semidarkness through a weird red haze. His face was puffy and covered with stubble. Had last night really happened or had he dreamed it?

There was no way Barney could pull himself together now. Foley was right. Drinking and cortisone definitely did not mix. He pulled the edge of the pillowcase over his eyes to shut out the daylight and went back to sleep. Waking again in mid afternoon he was still shaky, but the pain behind his eyes were gone. The weird red haze of the morning turned out to be a message in lipstick on the bathroom mirror. "Mommy, Kingston Hospital." Barney took a scalding shower and stopped for coffee and a vitamin-C fix at the Hojo counter. Amazingly, he felt restored sufficiently to feel hunger for blueberry pancakes. He told himself not to feel guilty about loving last night . . . whatever he'd done. It was important to believe what a man did for kicks was just kicks and not a reflection on his serious feelings. Because if it isn't so, thought Barney, I'm just an unfeeling shit. He was here, he reminded himself, because he needed Lilyanne's forgiveness. And maybe he was never going to find a way to rule the selfish, spoiled adolescent that lived inside his supposedly grown-up head.

At Kingston Hospital, Barney drew a blank in the personnel office. "Lilyanne Beech? Is she a volunteer? Is she a patient?"

Barney was exasperated. "She's a nurse, for God's sake. Give me that list. Lilyanne Beech. B-E-E-C-H." Barney suddenly knew. Lilyanne was a patient. Why hadn't Iris warned him? He felt a vise of anxiety constricting his walk. He hesitated outside her door, fearing what he would find. Two of the beds were empty. In the fourth bed an old woman lay snoring a rasping low death rattle. Barney drew the curtains from around Lilyanne's bed. Iris had not exaggerated. Lilyanne was beautiful, wax-white, her skin smooth, amazingly unlined. She had always had sooty lashes—Iris's exaggerated smudgings were a cosmetic homage to Mommy's natural beauty. Lilyanne's hair was very black, dyed, perfectly coiffed, possibly a wig. She wore a flowery bed jacket over her hospital gown.

When she opened her eyes he felt the certainty of her fate as if it were a blow. Lilyanne was dying. Her eyes were huge and black, the dark brown swallowed by pupil, dilated by drugs and anger. Oh God, what a pig I am, thought Barney, to come here, like this. Now. He wished he could take another shower. His heart was in his mouth. He tried to swallow it.

"Barney. You came." She tried to pull herself higher, smoothing her hair. She moved in slow motion. Her hand reached toward him as if crossing a vast distance. He reached for it.

"I'll help you up." She was thin and heavy, the heaviness of dead weight.

"Be careful. I break easily." She smiled. "Just like that. My bones are invaded by the enemy. I can feel them crumbling." She looked at him. "I like you with longer hair. Even your wrinkles are becoming. Age does good things for some men."

"I was selfish, spoiled at . . . how old . . . twenty-seven. You were so good for me, Lilyanne." She seemed happy to see him.

"Was I good? Good? Good old Lilyanne. Are you still with the same . . . I was about to say 'awful' but how would I know . . . I just listened. The same wife. Are you still rushing home, trying to look innocent?"

She seemed to gain strength and color as she talked. "I'm divorced," said Barney. "In the process of divorcing. Don't have to be innocent anymore." He kissed her wrist. The older women in his life had been his teachers, his pampering, indulgent earth mothers, the nurturers of his eager sensuality. How devastating it was to see them age, to see them die. He almost wished he had not come. He would have spared them both a searing memory.

Lilyanne was bubbling now. "Well, you won't believe this, Barney Kincaid, but I'm engaged. Can you imagine? He's a really super guy. A drug company rep from . . . oh, this is crazy." She fell back on the pillow. "I can't remember where he's from." She closed her eyes and lay motionless for a long time. Barney wondered if she'd fallen asleep. "It's so awful, Barney. You don't know."

"Yes, it must be terrible," Barney said. That's what they taught you these days about the dying . . . to let them feel their anger and pain. "You are so strong to bear it." He realized now he was not just there on this solipsistic mission. He was there because she needed him.

She whispered. "He won't make love to me anymore," she said. "George. He's afraid if he makes love to me I'll break a bone." She was sobbing. She closed her eyes again. Barney blotted her cheek with his fingertips. She lay motionless then, asleep perhaps. Her eyes blinked open. "That's all I have now. His loving me. Sex. His making love to me. Everything else is sick, hurt, ugly, you know." She sat there looking at him for some moments. Then she laughed. "You could show him how to love me, couldn't you? Oh my. Barney knows all the ways. Barney knows all ways."

'Yes," said Barney, stroking her cheeks.

She looked exhausted again. Her eyes seemed even deeper, the sockets bruised and hollow. She closed her eyes and drifted off again. Outside it was growing gray and dark as if it might snow. In the open drawer of the bedstand Barney saw her nurse badge. "Lilyanne Beech R.N." He held it in his palm.

She opened her eyes. "It doesn't hurt anymore," she said. "I won't break." Minutes passed. It felt like an hour. Her skin was hot and dry. "I promise not to break," she said. "Make love to me."

Barney kissed the inside of her palm. He took a rose from the bouquet next to her bed. Bright red, slightly unfurled, the smell was strong and sweet, intensely female. He touched the rose against her jutting clavicle. With the lightest touch he traced her temple and the socket of each eye. He drew the rose across her upper lip. "So good." She sighed.

Barney leaned over and blew on her ear and neck.

"Oh yes."

He opened her bed jacket and pulled her gown down. Pressing the edge of the rose against a breast, he watched the nipple grow. The rose enclosed the nipple.

"Yes," she said. "Please, yes." Eyes closed, she seemed to drift off again.

Barney held the rose to his own nose again and inhaled deeply. He was remembering something she had once said to him, long before the twins' hateful telltale destruction. "The way you love tells me everything," she had said, smoking the cigarette she always lit after sex, blowing the smoke across the room, one thigh thrown over his possessively.

"Oh you think so," said Barney half asleep, words slurred and wet against her breast. "What does it tell?"

"The way you make love tells me you admire yourself as a lover."

"Hey." He was alert enough to feel that as an insult.

"What is a great lover, Barney? He's a man who knows how to please women. I don't always have the sense that it's me you're pleasing specifically."

"Lilyanne. Lilyanne. Silly Lily. I do please you." He pulled her close.

"Yes, you do. You always do. But a woman must be wary of the great lovers. Is he a man who loves women? Or a man who fears women?"

Barney let himself retreat from her nonsense into a half sleep.

"Sleeping?" she had asked.

He hadn't answered.

Now he thought about her accusation, and felt a chill of truth. Then he scolded himself. How quick he was these days to convict himself of any emotional crime. Would you say that of a great poet? That a great poet is fired by his hate of words. Bullshit. Hate of blank paper maybe. Do the empire builders strive to build empires or to fill a vacant space? He rather liked the comparison. He was the Robert Moses of the bedroom. She moaned and Barney was drawn back to the hospital bedroom.

"So good, George," she said. "Loving." She smiled and a tear rolled down her temple.

Barney caught it in the rose. Then he pulled up the covers. In the parking lot he realized he still had her nursing badge in his hand. It took him a few minutes to remember where he was. Then he headed back to the New York Thruway home. How good, he felt, that he had seen her. There would be no more guilt. The hurt had been erased. In the past he had often worried that his sexual curiosity could become a disabling obsession. Now he was sure of his strength.

Driving south on the Thruway, Barney decided he wanted to be alone. The afternoon with Lilyanne had been like a tranquilizer. He felt that he'd survived a hurricane of emotion and landed safely. He wanted to hold on to that feeling. He called Lindsay to apologize and cancel dinner.

Her voice was low and icy.

"I am sorry, dearest," Barney repeated.

"You've canceled our last two dinners," she said. "Now you just don't show up."

Barney was confused. What did she mean? Now that he thought about it, he couldn't remember the last time he'd seen Lindsay. "Forget that I called to cancel," he said. "We'll go somewhere special. That new little French bistro near you. You wanted to try it."

"I've been there," she said. "Barney, you can't do this to me. What makes you think I'm free tonight?" she went on. "Perhaps when you get back from your vacation with Candy we can talk . . . decide if we want to see each other. I'm saying goodbye now," she announced flatly. And hung up. To the end, polite. Barney thought he should feel hurt, even sad, at least, or scared. Actually he was annoyed. Since when had she become so moody? Indeed, he was strangely relieved. Less tired. Free.

*T*here was a light on in his guest-room–office. He was pleased to find fresh daisies in a basket on the desk. The trailing curtains he had hemmed himself with paper clips were now neatly sewn. Everything was in meticulous order. His letters lay there in duplicate, with checks drawn to pay all the bills, ready for his signature. He sat down and wrote his name two dozen times. Looking up he saw a small collector's display case. Where had that come from? He turned on the overhead light. Christ. He wasn't sure whether to laugh or be annoyed. That Amber was really a certifiable nut. She had arranged his collection of memorabilia on the glassed-in shelves as if they were butterflies or fossils. How bizarre. There was Margaret's face cream in the black jar with the parrot and calla lilies. His letter sweater folded to show the big K and hide the moth holes. A salt shaker in the shape of a pig. Debra's white garter belt. The stained purple Capezio he and Linda had tried to drink screwdrivers from. The Snickers wrapper in its original jism-sculpted crumble. What, he wondered, had Amber made of that? There were the white cotton panties with tiny rosebuds stolen from Lindsay's suitcase (worn and left unwashed. Amber was very sensitive, thought Barney). The Moscow Mule mug from the Cass Lake days. A falsie. An old nudist magazine open to the Goddess Diana. What madness, thought Barney. He set the rose from Lilyanne's room on the shelf, with her nurse's badge. He picked up a matchbook from Eddie Condon's. Inside was Amy's mouth—her lipstick blot. Very red. It must have been the color of that era. Twenty years ago. He could almost visualize the ad. "Cherries in the Snow." The words flashed into his head. They had laughed at the name. Amy was his cherry in the snow. Still a virgin, sworn to remain so till marriage and full of rules, though gradually she had surrendered one orifice after another to his fevered pleadings. He was never sure she actually felt the passion she displayed. Her heat never melted the chill of her vow. That was what counted. He closed the matchbook and set it back in place.

He spied the New Grace Hospital file under a pile of books just as the phone rang. He'd forgotten. Tomorrow was the New Grace presentation. He was furious. He really needed to work. He willed the phone to stop ringing. It did. He pressed the bell silencer. The service could take messages. New Grace ought to be a cinch, he thought, and the contract would almost double his income. What time was it? His watch seemed to be gone. Had he left it in Kingston? Why was he so sleepy? He would lie down just for a few minutes.

He heard the screech, the smash, he felt the car lurch. He heard her scream. The windshield shattered. He was covered with blood. Barney woke and wiped the dribble from the corner of his mouth. Someone was in the apartment.

"Barney." Amber was lying on his bed. He could see her in the light from his slide projector. "I didn't want to wake you," she said. She had found the hidden carousel—Barney's erotic gallery. That was Debra's dazed just-come incandescence on the wall. Barney's heart lurched. He was caught. How dare she? He marched to the bed.

Amber giggled. "You're such a case, Barney. I love it. Come, lie with me." She was puffing on a joint, and touching herself. She was wearing red satin, some hearts sewn together—an incredible Valentine.

Barney groaned. She was a living, breathing, stoned little *Playboy* centerfold. "I knew you were a dirty old man," she was saying. "Something about you—your list of old girlfriends. Chasing around the country. Naughty. Naughty." Click. There was another of Barney's pillow shots. Lindsay. Click. Another. Caroline, the kinky Riverdale housewife. Click. Caroline on all fours snapped from behind. Amber giggled. She passed the joint to Barney. "Oh yes. So naughty." She opened her knees. "Play with me, Dr. Kincaid."

Barney settled back on the pillow and took a deep puff of grass. Oh yes, he always enjoyed seeing his hot little carousel. And Amber with her odd, almost detached, sexuality would obviously love it too. He'd never gone with a woman he could share these slides with. They were all too jealous. Amber didn't seem to know the meaning of the word. Click. There was Debra again, naked under her yellow slicker. ("My fantasy is a naked woman in a raincoat," he'd told her and a few nights later she'd taxied crosstown, as specified.) Click. There was Amber herself, sucking her thumb, naked except for her feather boa.

"Hot. Hot. Hot," Amber squealed. "Do that more." She snuggled against him. "Do that harder."

The grass was dynamite. Two puffs and he was floating. He took the projector control from her hand and ran through the whole face-on-the-pillow series again. Click. Click. Click. There was a photo of Caroline in the surf, naked, her body glistening with oil. Click. A tiny inverted nipple. Lindsay's. Amber again, licking her knee. Amber and a Eurasian beauty making love. She'd stuck that slide in there herself. Barney giggled. The grass was making him feel so light. He could hear time stretching. The machine's electric pulse was like a heartbeat in passion. He imagined his mouth was somehow attached to a tightly furled bud between Amber's legs. He imagined he could make her clitoris grow. He imagined tiny teeth inside, a powerful sucking mouth . . . his own. She arched into the air. Riding him. A thousand years now between clicks. Click. Afterwards he couldn't move. The drug had paralyzed him. He lay there locked inside her and fell asleep. The machine still clicking away on automatic pilot even as he dozed.

The phone woke him. Projected on the wall was his prize slide of four geranium blossoms tucked into the soft blonde tendrils of Debra's pussy. He pulled the plug and fumbled in darkness for the phone, trying not to crush Amber. But Amber was nowhere in the vicinity. It was morning. She must have turned on the phone and left.

"How could you forget, Barney?" It was Mama. "I had chicken and rice, your favorite. Enough for seven I had." Barney honestly could not remember promising to come for dinner. "Such a waste. They talk about the ecology. Chicken for seven and the fuel I used to cook it. That is waste," she said.

Enough for seven meant enough for twelve, easily, thought Barney. He felt the old nausea that used to sweep over him knowing she would always get her way. Had he promised both Lindsay and Mama dinner last night?

"And I went all the way uptown to get big fresh prunes from H. Roth."

"Exercise is good for you, Mama," he said.

"I don't cook for exercise."

"Oh Mama, you woke me. I could send a messenger to pick up the leftovers I can have them tonight at the hospital. What do you think?"

"The prunes too," she said. She sniffed. "A total waste has been averted, at least. But when are we going to see you, darling?"

It was late. After eleven. He'd never been this late before. He wished Amber were still here. He needed coffee or a glass of water just to sit up. He lay there thinking. Waste. Perhaps the motivating consideration of his upbringing had been ecology. Economy they called it then . . . avoidance of waste. He had comfortably assumed he was the center of the world, his own world and Mama's. His stomach, his digestive system, his clockwork bowel movements, his growth and grade-school performance, the neatness of his room. Perhaps it was not his preciousness and lovability but thrift that made all the rules. Nothing could spoil. Nothing was ever thrown away. Everything must be lined up in neat labeled packages. Perhaps that was why he found Amber's preservation of his sexual archives so amusing. A kettle of fishy thoughts I'm collecting, thought Barney. I know all the answers. And slowly I'm stumbling over at least some of the questions.

The phone rang again. He had dozed off. He must be sick. His feet felt like cement blocks. "Barney, where the hell have you been? Since when don't you leave a number with your service if you're out of beeper range? I've left a dozen messages with your service." It was Henderson Turner. Barney suddenly realized he had not seen his beeper in . . . how long? Two days. "Have you any idea what day this is . . . what day this was?"

"Henderson, I'm sleeping. I'm only a few minutes late."

"You were supposed to appear before the New Grace Hospital Board yesterday. They called the ER when you didn't show and I didn't know what to say. I tried to persuade them to hang on till I found you. But I couldn't find you. Your service had no idea where you were. They thought you must be out of town because it's been so long since you called in. I had visions of you murdered or—I don't know, paralyzed by a stroke on the bedroom floor but we got some woman there late yesterday and she said you were out of town. She didn't give you a message? Barney, I don't believe you could fuck us up like this."

"But the meeting is this afternoon," said Barney. "What

day is this?" He began to sweat. Already he knew.

"Thursday, pal. Are you telling me you simply misplaced a day? God, I'm so upset I'm not even stuttering." Hen started to stutter.

Mallory came on the phone. "I guess you know about Dylan," she said.

"What about Dylan?" Oh God. Even as he asked, Barney knew.

"He's dead."

"The chest X-ray was normal, Mrs. Mallory. The enzymes were normal. He was definitely not short of breath. You saw that yourself." He caught himself. Funny sad Dylan. "It was his heart." In his mind he went over the case.

"Yes. It wasn't like you, Dr. Kincaid, not to admit him."

"But I did tell him to stay. Stay overnight. I begged him to play it safe. What was I supposed to do, Mallory? Bully him. Nothing in that work-up justified getting out a shotgun. He had no history. No cholesterol problem. For God's sake, get off my back. He was only thirty-six, for God's sake." Barney started to cry.

"I'm sorry, Barney." Mallory's voice broke and then she became very composed. "Dr. Turner wants to speak."

Hen took the phone again. "I'm not condemning you on Tarnapol. You went by the book. It was a freak. But because he was a staff man, there will probably be a review. Your fuck-up with New Grace is being taken as a sign of total irresponsibility. Damn it. Barney, we were so close. We had it. I know we had it. This is going to cost us a lot of money. Plus our reputations, our credibility. I don't know what you're up to, pal, but I really needed that money."

Barney was stunned. How could it have happened? Tarnapol had nothing, a little deli-heartburn. A jogger, with no family history. Thirty-six years old. Barney's heart was pounding, about to break his eardrums. Where did that extra day go? What a nightmare. "I must be very sick, Hen," he said. "I don't know. Oh that poor sad guy, Tarnapol. I've got to think for a few minutes. Did I miss something, Hen? The chart. You have the chart. Look at the chart. Tell me.

What a fuck-up. Oh God, Hen, forgive me. I have to figure out what happened. Look, let's try to calm down. I'll think of something to save us at New Grace. I have to wake up. I'll be in."

Barney lay there soaked in sweat. Was he a killer too? How dare he accuse Gunderson of murder? Okay, yes, there was a difference. Barney had gone by the rules, releasing Dylan. Not a single indicator said "Hold him . . . hold him against his will." Yet he knew that Barney Kincaid in full control, in focus, would have tied the bastard down to keep him there, fuck the indicators. He felt drenched in panic. He could not salvage New Grace. He knew it. He would never forgive himself for Dylan Tarnapol.

Barney turned off his phone. Cautiously, slowly, not to snap a tendon or cramp a muscle, he got out of bed. He stood there, dizzy at first. Still high perhaps from the grass he had smoked. Somehow he'd lost a whole day in that Kingston motel room. Barney had better see Dr. Foley. Maybe he was actually sicker than anyone had told him. Poor Tarnapol. All he'd wanted was to be a rock singer.

As the small twenty-seat Otter took off from St. Martin for St. Barthélemy, Barney studied Candy's face. How impassive she was. Imagine being jaded already at twelve. Of course he and Reeney had taken her everywhere on all the vacations that were designed to distract the two of them from the dissonance of their marriage. Candy caught his stare and smiled coquettishly, then went back to reading *Cosmopolitan,* oblivious to the sea-green sweep below. Barney wondered if Reeney permitted Candy to read *Cosmopolitan.* A quick glance at the titles on the cover and his paternal blood ran cold. Thirteen seemed too young to be exposed to "Clever You Works on a More

Beautiful Bosom" and "Sexy Bachelors Tell You How to Turn Men On." On the other hand, the kid could learn a little forebearance if she bothered to read "Winning the War with Your Boyfriend's Children."

Barney was feeling better than he had in weeks. The belated, much postponed visit to Foley had solved the mystery of Barney's frenzy and fatigue. He had been overdosing on cortisone, losing track of how many pills he'd taken, popping a few whenever he felt crummy, enough to provoke all sorts of delusions.

Foley was livid. "I suppose you were drinking too."

"A glass of wine, maybe two," Barney defended, embarrassed.

"If you're going to doctor yourself, I'm off your case."

Just tracing the source of his problem made Barney feel calmer. But the climate in the ER was still chilly, Henderson Turner bitter. In fact, the whole ER team seemed wary of Barney even though the ICU Mortality Committee had cleared him of all fault in Dylan Tarnapol's death. Barney's only neglect was legal. Not getting Dylan to sign an AMA, official proof he'd left "against medical advice." Only Anne Mallory, his toughest judge and Dylan's confidante, showed any compassion for Barney's pain. Because he definitely blamed himself. His peers had recognized that he was technically innocent. He would never convince his conscience. His toughest no-nonsense self had been out to lunch that afternoon and he knew it.

Foley had insisted he take a week or two off as he reduced the dosage gradually. Turner was tough too. He wanted Barney fit or not at all. And since Barney was already scheduled off for a week during Candy's Easter break, he agreed. He couldn't disappoint Candy. But he did manage to persuade her to settle for St. Barts instead of Paris. It would be more restful for him, he pointed out, and she could practice her French there too.

For him, it had to be St. Barts because the investigative tentacles of Carl, his friend at the *Post*, had traced Caroline Rao, his deliciously crazed Bronx housewife, to the tiny island, settled by Huguenots from Brittany who had inter-married, Barney read, and still wore native costumes with starched white headdresses. That part thrilled Candy. Not to mention the lure of duty-free shopping.

Candy had not been caught in any coeducational closet activity lately. But she was not any happier with the upheaval fate had introduced into her life. For her ballet-class recital a few days earlier, she had decided that Barney and Reeney should sit together flanked by both grandparents in a fantasy of old-fashioned family togetherness. She did not want Lindsay. Definitely not Debra. Candy had always pretended Debra didn't exist, once going so far as to step on her toe rather than acknowledge there was a woman standing next to Barney on line at the movie. Lindsay was an enemy to torture. Candy alternated feigned sweetness with sulk. Reeney's new suitor, Irwin the peddler ("He's not a peddler, he owns more than one hundred outdoor food stands," Reeney protested), was definitely not to be toler-ated.

Candy announced a hunger strike on the issue, which lasted twelve minutes because Barney was seeing a patient and it took that long to get him to the phone plus ten seconds for his acquiescence. Candy's stand made Barney realize that both women had somehow been lost in the wake of his preoccupation with the past. Was he making a serious mistake, risking the loss of a serene Wasp life with Lindsay . . . or even the fierce devotion of Debra for . . . what? What was he doing anyway?

*T*he plane made a sudden jerky drop coming in for a landing on the abbreviated dirt strip at an angle that brought squeals and gasps from everyone. Barney was pleased to see Candy jolted from blasé boredom, even if it took fear to animate her face. Candy reached for Barney's hand and Barney was struck with instant remorse. What kind of a father was he? Dragging a thirteen-year-old daughter to some unknown little island so he could park her at the beach and run off to pick up the tangled lines of Caroline Rao's flight from the Bronx. Would he slush off by dogsled to the North Pole if Jill Massacio turned up there selling Kool-Aid to the Eskimoes? He'd always been curious about Alaska. Why not the North Pole? Still, St. Barts was an odd retreat for someone like Caroline, thought Barney. What sort of kinkiness could thrive on such a tiny island? Or had Caroline mellowed?

"You don't have to love me. All I want is sex.' With that line, he was hooked. She had sounded like a hit-and-run philanderer's dream. Caroline was Barney's first experience with serious (well, really, playful) kinkiness. In an amateur, that was. Odd, wasn't it, how he got caught up from time to time with women whose taste for the bizarre matched his own, how his appetite inspired them to new heights of decadence—make that lows—till finally, of course, he had to leave them. Fleeing just in the nick of time, sanity barely intact. He was a doctor, after all, a married man, a father . . . Mama's crazed, naughty little boy.

Caroline was a Goodman Memorial candy-striper, one of the volunteers who ran the gift shop and staffed the library. She came into Emergency one afternoon complaining of pain in the lower abdomen. Wouldn't see anyone but Barney. Took him by surprise. Women weren't often that aggressive eight years ago. She had pleated the paper examining gown and draped it low over her breasts. He'd written that off as nervousness. She was perspiring and moaned as he palpated her abdomen. He asked about the pain. How long? What kind? She answered in a whisper. Embarrassment, he supposed. He bent to hear. She flicked her tongue in his ear and bit the lobe. "I feel empty," she said, taking his hand and putting it between her legs.

He looked at her chart. "Mrs. Rao," he said sternly. But he did not remove his hand.

"You don't have to love me," she said, the memorable lure. "All I want is sex."

Beware of the kinky-housewife con. That line should be a dead giveaway. They all want love. Still, to her credit, she had a unique appetite for "just sex." She wanted it neat. No conversation. In the beginning, anyway. She wanted him to fuck her on the examining table. "I have been imagining it ever since I sold you a copy of *Money* two weeks ago," she said.

He used to meet her after work in a Yonkers motel. Once she grabbed him from a janitor's supply closet. She tried to talk him into braving the morgue. She went down on him in the back pew of a porn theater and tried it again in a small Polish church. Barney, laughing and anxious, refused. One afternoon she greeted him at the motel dressed as a belly dancer. Brought her own taped music and did a pretty hot imitation. Once she brought a friend, Mimi, but that was a mistake because Mimi had a hard time coming and Barney devoted so much energy trying to get her there, Caroline was sulky and mean and wouldn't speak to either of them for days.

Just sex? What a miscalculation. When Caroline heard he'd left Reeney, she announced she was leaving her husband too. Barney was appalled. For one thing he could have been killed. Her goddamn husband was a butcher and a Sicilian. Either way he could have been killed. How could Barney confide that it was the danger she created that he loved and her wild unpredictability that made it last? That he was a hopeless snob. The Bronx speech patterns and flashy stretch pants and Frederick's of Hollywood outfits that were so perfect in a Yonkers motel did not mesh with

Barney's fantasy of high Waspdom in Connecticut.

"I'll never marry again," he said. Then realized she intended to move right in anyway. "And I need to be alone, need to get myself together, need to prove that I *can* live alone." Barney realized he had to stop seeing her. He heard she'd left the Sicilian butcher anyway. The crazy thing was that Barney had really missed Caroline, missed her zaniness, her intense, almost cyclonic sexuality, her sweet affection.

St. Barts proved to be idyllic, a green island with every kind of surf and water, ranging from jade green to the deepest blue. There was no sense of poverty, no rumble of discontent or impending revolution, no high-rise hotels, no jazzy nightclubs, no need ever to dress up, just a single town square with a few tax-free shops, a bakery that turned out long thin French bread, a couple of bars where sailors and beach bums mingled with the scatterings of tourists and the nomadic rich from medium-sized yachts. The cardiologist Foley would definitely approve. Except for the presence of Caroline Rao there seemed to be little in the way of decadence to tax a healing heart. Not even a movie theater. Barney hoped the need to make their own entertainment would provide some real closeness for Candy and himself. He'd felt her anxieties, her blatant attempts to possess him and dispossess all paramours, but he longed for real spoken communication. He also hoped the hotel would yield other kids her age to relieve a need for full-time togetherness. But Candy had already rejected the polite overtures of a little French girl. "She's just a baby," she said.

All that first afternoon she never left his side. She wouldn't even swim unless he swam too. The only time she seemed happy was when they went shopping. Barney hated himself for giving in to her avarice so easily. They made the rounds of all the stores and Candy settled on Revelations, where she had to have a pair of sandals with chunky cork platforms. They made her six inches taller. "I'm tall as Mommy," she cried, measuring herself against Barney, practically eye-to-eye, a highly creepy condition, he noted.

"You would never wear sandals like that at home," Barney said.

"Why not?" cried Candy.

"You would?" He looked at her. She looked away. That goddamn lower lip was creeping into a sulk again.

"They're only seven dollars," she said.

Barney sighed. "All right."

"What do you think, Daddy?" Candy flexed her ankle. "I love the green ones passionately but red goes with everything."

What a familiar dilemma. Barney could close his eyes and hear any woman in his life uttering that line. He could imagine Eve herself—"I feel like eating this peach, Adam, but then I've never actually tasted an apple." Barney studied Candy's extended foot. The shoe seemed clumsy, almost grotesque, at the end of that skinny, scarred leg with a moon-shaped scab on the knee. "I think . . . red," he said. "Pay and let's get at least an hour in the sun, honey." He handed her francs and walked out to the street.

A wave of anger gnawed at him. This was not how he had planned to spend the best decade of his life—listening, constantly alert to the beat of an aging heart, trying to make up to Candy for leaving her mother, trying to double his income overnight to support two households, reenacting his adolescence to prove . . . to prove what? The timing was wrong. At forty a man should finally be settling in, comfortable in his identity and accomplishment. Having mastered a trade, at forty he should be gathering force for a creative accomplishment, his legacy to his profession. Home in this timetable was stable, long ago established, mellowing now, cozy and comfortably warm, with a beautiful devoted wife and a garden. A vegetable garden. Barney thought of the half acre behind the house in Amagansett, a jungle of weeds now, and up for sale. The Ninety-third Street house, where tomatoes had shot up on spindly stalks in the soot. He had walked out leaving everything. Just removing his clothes and camera equipment, books and a few records had been a wrenching, draining exercise. He took exactly eleven records—eleven out of some four hundred and they'd fought over every one.

"You have everything," he shouted at Reeney. "Twenty years of accumulated crap. Keep it. I leave it to you. Even my Christmas gifts I'm leaving." He would not take pictures off the wall and leave nail holes. He would not strip his child's home of the artifacts she'd grown up with.

"*The Decline and Fall of the Entire World* is my favorite Cole Porter and it's out of print," Reeney protested.

"Tough shit," said Barney. "I can't believe you're carrying on about a record."

She was crying. "It was just sex, Barney. I swear it. You know it. A dumb little lifeguard. You don't have to leave."

"I don't want to hear about it," said Barney. "Take your goddamn Cole Porter." He slammed the record down on the table. A ceramic candlestick broke. The record did not. He left it lying there. Hardly anyone realized how disorienting it was to be the man in a divorce, the one who leaves everyone, everything, behind.

*B*arney deposited Candy at the supermarché to pick up snacks and explore French *Cosmo* and comic books. They agreed to meet in half an hour at the Select for guava juice on the rocks before lunch. Barney knew exactly where he was going. The tiny island Real Estate and Travel Agency was tucked onto the balcony of a small flower shop. Caroline looked up from her perch, put on rose-colored glasses to be sure.

"Dr. Love." She stood up, towering above him on the balcony, a halo of sun from behind framing her hair. He liked that. Saint Caroline. She had a face like a cherub and rounded limbs, slightly tanned, and, as he came closer, new laugh lines around her deep-brown eyes. Saint Caroline possessed by wry demons. Mischief was like a drug for her. He remembered the time at a movie she persuaded him to stick his cock into a box of popcorn so that she could stroke his buttery rod whenever she reached for a few kernels. Married, he wielded a measure of control over Caroline. She respected his need for secrecy. But once he was single she became obsessed with new demands. She was half out of her dress and it took brute force to keep her from leaping into the pool at the Four Seasons one evening .

She seemed pleased to see him. Her rage over the breakup was past, he thought with great relief. After Barney's farewell, she had sent him a bunch of bananas gift-wrapped in a box with a note: "Stick this up your ass." Inside there was a tarantula. It looked like a tarantula. It was big and black and furry. He trapped it in a jar and fed it a lettuce leaf till he had time to take it to the Natural History Museum, where a polite and amused curator insisted it was a harmless spider.

Now they sat, watching for Candy, in the tiny port bar sipping daiquiris. She spoke French rather well with an occasional Bronx inflection. "I owe you all this," she said. "Indirectly." She'd left her husband anyway, fallen in love with a mechanic who quit his job to sail in the islands. He took charters and appeared in port now and then. An ideal arrangement for her because she'd fallen for a local politician, married of course, but . . . ah, the danger, the intrigue. She thrived on it. Barney found it difficult to imagine an island so small and incestuous that it could contain her hunger. Perhaps she'd grown more discreet with the change of territory. She shrugged. "I wouldn't say so."

Candy's eyes telegraphed daggers as she teetered toward them. "Aren't we late for lunch?" she began. Barney was embarrassed by her rudeness but he felt guilty too.

"This is Candy, my number-one girl," he introduced her. She perched on his knee and ordered a guava. "Mrs. Rao is going to show me houses. She's the real estate magnate here."

"Daddy, are you crazy?" asked Candy. "We have a house. Two houses. What about Amagansett?"

"Candy has a tennis lesson at four," said Barney.

Candy rolled her eyes in pained exasperation. Caroline stood up. "Don't miss the market on the pier," she told Candy. "And there's a little place down the road toward St. Gustave where they sell dolls in the costumes of Brittany."

Candy sneered. "I'm no longer interested in dolls. I understand the natives are morons because they marry their cousins."

Caroline laughed and ambled off, her bottom bouncing in tight white pants.

"You're a lech, aren't you, Daddy?" said Candy.

Caroline came for Barney at four-thirty. They drove in her yellow convertible beetle around the island. The blacktop ended on a steep climb and they lurched upward over the unpaved ruts. She pulled her skirt up, showing most of her thighs. "Hot today," she said. "That funny feeling, doctor, is right here." She put his hand under her skirt. She was not wearing panties.

"Aha, that's my girl," he said. "The girl of my dreams." He rubbed his finger lightly the way she liked.

"Do you remember the last time?" she asked. He was silent. "Scared ya, I bet. Of course, it scared you." She shook her head and smiled at him, screeching over a hairpin turn. "Dr. Love. Wanted to try everything. Wanted to discover himself. Didn't like what he found."

"I want you to tie me up," she had said. She liked to be

bound, teased, tickled, diddled, eaten, fucked, to come again and again.

"It's too much work," Barney had protested.

She'd handed him an old necktie, some clothesline, a sash from his bathrobe, a belt. "I'll be so hot, you'll love it. C'mon. You haven't tied me up for so long. Scare me," she said. "Hurt me."

All right, he decided. Don't be so lazy, he told himself. He loved watching her go crazy, loved being the one. He had always known she responded to force and pain. The idea of hurting her repelled him. He hated hurting anyone. Yet the way he'd tied her this time, with her ass up in the air, had got him really hot. He slapped her bottom lightly. He slapped it again. He squeezed her breasts hard. She cried out. He felt himself getting hotter.

"You dumb bitch," he said. "You stupid cunt." He slapped her again. He spread her pussy roughly, shoved fingers inside, twisted till she moaned and pulled away. He slapped her bottom so his hand would glance off her clit.

"Stop it," she said. "You're scaring me."

"Shut up." He rubbed and dug into her, probed, pinched, slapping her at random, hard. She screamed and pulled at her bindings trying to protect her pussy from direct attack.

"Please stop. You're hurting me. Stop. Who are you?"

"Bitch." He slapped her with incredible force. Her ass was bright red. He felt his heart pounding, a tide in his ears, the heat searing. He shoved his cock deep into her throat. "I'll show you who I am." Her face was streaked with tears. He fucked her mouth till she started to gag. He sat back. Her eyes were wild, terrified. She stared at him as if he were a stranger. Then she wiggled her butt, a playful twitch of invitation. And he slapped her again. Twice. Then he rubbed her asshole with pussy juice and thrust his cock in halfway. With his fingers inside her pussy he could feel his cock. She was in a frenzy.

"Oh yes. Yes," she cried. "I love it. I know you." She screamed as if in exhilaration or rage. She laughed when he came and collapsed on top of her. They both lay there not speaking. There was a terrible taste in Barney's mouth and a deep ache in his throat. He felt like he might throw up if he moved even an inch. He did not like the creature he'd seen. He had done exactly what she wanted him to do. And he was scared because he had enjoyed it too much. Once you'd unleashed such a monster how would you ever get him to go away, Barney wondered. He had never seen her again.

Caroline turned the car into a narrow drive almost hidden with vines and parked in front of a white stucco house framed with mahogany. "Are you serious about renting?" she asked. "Or is this just another game?"

"I never thought about actually taking a house," Barney said, wondering if he was inventing all this or was possibly serious, "but I do love St. Barts. Sharing a house with a friend, someone with children, might make sense."

The door was unlocked. "You get a constant breeze in this room when the shutters are open," she said, unfolding doors that opened the living room to a terrace overlooking deep blue water in a cove below. Everything was white— walls, sofa, chairs, wicker, a padded, leather-topped bar. There was a collection of colored sea glass in jars. "Modern kitchen," said Caroline. "Gas stove, good refrigerator, small freezer. The maid comes with the house. One bedroom off the garage. You'll find a nice little colony of transplanted New Yorkers here."

"You do this very well," said Barney, watching her move through the room delivering her sales patter.

She sat down in the farthest corner of the angled sofa. "I ran into an interesting woman who knows you. Nancy Kragen. She said her husband—"

"Was my best friend Marvin. Nancy is here?" Barney was astonished. He'd lost touch after Marvin's funeral. He was remembering. Nancy and Amy had lived in the same house at Wellesley.

"She's living with, I forget his name, I think he was an engineer, he's an island dropout now. And they're building a house on the side of a cliff, themselves, with just a couple of handymen to help. I can take you to see them."

Barney slid toward her and took her hand. Caroline stood up. "There's a small bedroom down here," she said, "with a shower, but upstairs . . ." She led the way outside. Even the steps were mahogany. A bright-red hibiscus brushed her hair. He followed her into the master bedroom, a great bare expanse of white. The bed was tented with blue-and-white-striped cotton and a fall of mosquito netting.

Caroline stood at the shutter struggling with a latch. Barney watched her, feeling a surge of nostalgia for her bottom. The shutter gave way and he came to stand beside her on the tiled balcony. A parade of ants was marching into the tunnel of a hibiscus.

Barney put his hand on her ass. He felt her stiffen. He pulled up her skirt. "Sweet, lovable ass," he said, caressing her.

"What do you want from me now, Barney? It isn't friendly drifting in and out of a gal's life, leaving her to feel like a second-rate reject." She had her head on her arms, her elbows folded on the railing, her ass pointed coolly, calmly, expectantly . . . how the hell could he know for sure?

"Come to bed," he said.

"I'm not moving," she said. "I'm not contributing to this . . . act. You're on your own."

Barney ran his finger along the damp edge of her vulva, separated the lips and pressed against her clitoris. He wet his fingers, tasting her delicate musk. He played with her gently at first, building the intensity the way she liked it. She arched her back. "Shall I tell you about the rainfall?" she asked. "Pollen is nonexistent on St. Barts—if I recall, you do suffer some from hay fever. There's a gardener too."

Barney opened his pants, and dipped his cock into her. She arched her back against him, taking him in, thrusting up.

"The population. I want to say about the population—"

Barney held her hip with one hand, the front of her twat with the other, rubbing his thumb. She cried out and caught herself midcry as two little boys walked by on a path below. One boy waved. Caroline gasped and waved back, pressing her hand over his, increasing the pressure and squeezing his cock with every thrust. She shuddered. As the boys disappeared down the incline she cried out. He felt her coming and grabbed her ass, framing it, holding it rigid, fucking her faster till he blacked out. He lay on top of her, both of them grasping the wooden ledge. For a swift second, he saw stars, then a blur and then the sea.

"There's a gorgeous view from the back bedroom too," she said when she could find her voice again. He felt her legs trembling, her insides still contracting. "You always love it most when I don't really want it," she said. "What a game."

"Was that a game?" Barney asked. "Wasn't I playing to please you too? Don't you love to be . . . seized, invaded? I can play any game you like."

"Except house," she said.

He started to wipe his cock with her skirt, caught himself, looked around. "I think those things are sometimes a question of timing." He found the bathroom and helped himself to a towel. He went back to the balcony and patted her dry, rearranged her skirt and pulled her into a hug.

"Have you ever in your life had really hot sex with a woman you loved?"

"I felt the most extraordinary tenderness for you just then," Barney responded, thinking he had. He truly had felt a great wave of affection.

"It was probably tenderness for my rear end," she said.

He didn't say anything. He had, it was true, always been moved by the sweet heart shape and deep dimples of Caroline's ass. He couldn't insult her by saying she wasn't Wasp enough to be the woman in his life. He couldn't even reveal his own pitiful snobbery in that unalterable fact. He kissed her neck. "I never told you how fond I am of you," he said. "How important it was to me having you in my life."

She stood up. "What do we do to men that makes them think the world revolves around them?" She turned, looking at him directly through those rose-colored glasses.

"You always said it was just sex that you wanted. I'm not such a wonderful person. I couldn't resist."

"You're not such a wonderful person," she agreed, smiling. "But I *did* love you."

"It felt like games."

"To me it felt like love."

"What does that mean, Caroline, please, everyone says love. Love. Loved."

"Feelings, Barney," she said wearily. "I'm not the literary type. I'm no good with words. What it means is feelings of attachment, tenderness like you said . . . letting yourself want someone, knowing that means they can hurt you if they don't care. I bet no woman has a chance to leave you, Dr. Love. You're too fast."

"And today?" He was concerned. He did not want to hurt her again. "What was today?"

"Oh, today was just a game. I still love to fool around. Just like you, my dear. I can't resist either."

"Just sex?"

"Just sex."

"We're so naughty," she said smiling. He helped her pull the shutters back in place and they drove toward town. Love, he was thinking, has something to do with not needing resistance.

Caroline had gotten word to Nancy Kragen via a plumber. There were no phone lines yet on the cliffside building site where she and her guy camped out in a tent. They were all invited to dinner. Barney parked his rented jeep as instructed and they began a treacherous descent down a steep pebble-strewn path with thorns and spiked weeds tearing at their ankles.

"I think there *are* snakes," said Candy, who had been assured several times there were none.

"There are no snakes on this island, I promise," said Caroline. "No one is more afraid of snakes than me. There are no snakes on St. Barts."

Barney was glad he had persuaded Candy to amputate the cork wedgies from her feet (she wore them every waking moment) and wear sneakers. He looked better himself with some color and the puffiness gone from his face.

"Do we really have to go?" Candy had asked.

"Darling," said Barney, exasperated. "This is an adventure."

"I'm too old for adventures," she said. "And too young. I'm at that difficult in-between age," she informed Caroline, as she fought the vine whiplash. "I can't understand how people can exist without movies," Candy was saying. "An entire island without a movie theater. The natives ought to revolt. I would. Oh Daddy.' She licked the blood from a cut. "I suppose we'll be covered with bugs."

"There it is," said Caroline.

"Oh dear," said Candy as what looked like a gypsy encampment (if you were romantic) or a garbage dump (if you were Barney) came into view. It definitely smelled. Candy took it all in and turned to Barney. She rolled her eyes. "Watch out for the shit, Daddy," she said sweetly, stepping over a pile of turds.

"Barney." It was Nancy, tanned, some gray in her hair, but otherwise slim and if possible, looking younger than ever. She gave him a hug. There was a long silence. He felt her start to cry and then catch herself. "Oh my. You look so good," she said. "And these are the best piña coladas you'll ever taste, okay?" She handed Barney a paper cup. "And Candy. A grown-up woman, my goodness. How astonishing."

"I'm taller than you when I wear my wedgies," said Candy.

"I bet," Nancy agreed. "Come, I want you to meet Gabe. My older boys are living with their grandparents and going to school in Rye, but the baby is here, not a baby anymore, Eliza."

Barney found it strange to see Nancy in another existence, looking happier than ever, totally at home on the side of a mountain. Disorder always made Barney anxious. Now he smelled something vaguely unpleasant and decided it was the proximity of goat. He doubted he'd ever be comfortable with goat cheese again and had no patience at all with the part of himself that was so fastidious.

"Where are the crudités, Gabe?" Nancy called as an enormous man abandoned the barbeque. Gabe Fosburgh looked down at everyone from an awesome height, six and a half feet at least, Barney guessed. He had a large, handsome head and a shock of white hair. He passed an aluminum pot with unpeeled carrots and raw string beans. Eliza was shy and hid behind him.

"I think I'll just have a baby banana," said Candy, helping herself to the least speckled banana from a bunch that rested against a wheelbarrow.

"You have a magnificent view," said Barney. "Aren't you lucky, Eliza." He took her hand. She'd been an infant when Marvin killed himself. Now she must be seven or eight. "You have a beach and that wonderful surf just below your bedroom window."

"The windows aren't in yet," said Candy. "Oh Daddy, I'm being eaten alive." She slapped her ankle.

"Gabe, find the Off," instructed Nancy.

"I know exactly where it is," said Gabe, digging in a cardboard box at the base of a tree where clothes hung from branches on hangers. "Good heavens. This is wonderful," he cried. "I found the corkscrew," he said, moving a plastic basin full of dirty dishes. "We've been shoving corks into bottles all week. Here," he said. "Before the light disappears. Let me show you what we're building."

The dark seemed to race across the hill as the sun disappeared behind a cliff. The last crimson streak turned the water below rose. "Everytime I see it, I could cry," said Caroline. "We have the most astonishing sunsets here."

Barney did envy Gabe and Nancy all that beauty. The spectacular setting, the dream realized of building your own house by hand, the serenity of their affection, but on a purely practical level he couldn't help wondering what kind of miracle Gabe had in mind for cutting a drive into his mountainside. A funicular might be the only solution.

Gabe unrolled the house plans and looked at Nancy proudly. "We're doing all the tile and brick and some carpentry ourselves. Even Eliza will help when we paint. Right, Eliza? I have a local mason to get me started and I'll use the plumber and probably an electrician."

Nancy lit a kerosene lamp. A lot of the clutter had disappeared into the shadows and Barney relaxed. Still, he wondered how they washed dishes. He tried not to think about typhoid. Nancy brushed pieces of chicken with a feather dipped into some marinade. He was glad he didn't have to know where the feather had been plucked from nor how many marinades it had known. Candy was helping herself to a tall glass of piña colada and he was about to protest till it occurred to him the alcohol would counteract the germs as well as the pouts.

"We'll never find the path back in the dark, Daddy," she whispered.

She was right. The moonless night was pitch-black. "They'll have flashlights," Barney reassured her. He watched Caroline flirting with Gabe. There was an easiness between them, the playful touching of lovers. Nancy was watching them too, not at all tense, Barney observed, but relaxed too, pleased almost. Perhaps the three of them? Barney stopped himself. Not everyone in the Western Hemisphere was as sexually obsessed as he.

Gabe was unzipping the entrance to a large geodesic-dome tent. "It's the best tent you can buy anyw'.ere," he said proudly. "We sleep here till the house is ready. And Eliza has her own little pup tent right next door."

"Dinner's ready," Nancy called.

The chicken was slightly raw. Barney poured himself a fresh drink. He prayed that Candy would not do her usual critique of the cooking. Happily, she was still chewing prudently on the same raw string bean. He poured her a big slug of piña colada. Nancy pulled up a wooden crate and sat beside him. Barney studied her face, trying to imagine how the years might have touched Amy if she were alive.

"Did you ever see Amy again . . . before the accident?" he asked. "I heard she married some uptight political prig?"

"Oh yes, an archconservative," Nancy agreed. "But not a prig. He was warm, actually boyish, with a wry kind of humor. She did have a wild crush on you, Barney. Talked about you a blue streak. I think she was afraid. Afraid to make a commitment to anyone then. Afraid you'd give in to that pushy bitch from Bennington . . . that's how she saw Reeney." Nancy shrugged. "Well, she is a pushy bitch, though I actually like Reeney. But Amy and I were like soul sisters. How many years ago? She was a year behind me at Wellesley. Two little shiksas from the Middle West in love with a couple of horny New York Jews." She looked up. "Oh my. Here comes the moon. Do you believe it?"

A giant orange ball rose low over the water, lighting up the night. Everyone was silent, almost reverent.

"*T*he moon is wearing an earring," Amy had said, pulling on Barney's ear, kissing it.

"That's Saturn," Barney told her.

He and Amy had made love in all the ways Barney knew, except the ultimate. Phallic penetration was strictly forbidden. Fingers were permitted. Fingers were heavenly, she said. He knew. A banana was messy but nice. Barney did wonder about the morality of a religious position that condoned a banana and not a sincere young penis. They wept too. Except for an occasional banana, sex wasn't funny in those days. In the intense, deprived, furtive years of his twenties, sex was serious. Falling in love with Amy gave Barney his one hope of escaping from Reeney before the gate slammed shut forever with a formal engagement notice in the Sunday *Times*. The pressure was on. Even Mama was pushing now. Probably she perceived Reeney as a daughter-in-law she could manipulate. "We'll be like sisters together," she said, and the two of them were off discussing color schemes for bathrooms.

Amy was a Baptist, whatever that was. Barney had taken a course called Comparative Religions and he knew something about the fundamentalist position, but Amy's allusions to down-home Baptism confused him. He had images of white robes and Billy Graham and underwater submersion, country-church suppers and cake sales, holy rollers, healing by laying on of hands. Her father had been a missionary among the heathens briefly. In New Jersey. Barney knew she no longer went to church. They had spent too many Sunday mornings rubbing against each other, dedicating hours to oral carnality before breakfast. Amy had never known anyone Jewish before. She found him as exotic as an aborigine. "I can't imagine what my daddy would say if I came home married to an infidel and a foreigner—a New York Jew. They consider me practically a lost soul already."

"You could show them who's boss," Barney offered.

She looked at him thoughtfully. "I don't think that's one of my crucials," she said. "I would never hurt anyone I loved unless it was truly crucial."

Barney thought that sounded quite Baptist. Lord knew it wasn't Jewish. He hurt everyone constantly and he had no idea anymore (if ever) what was crucial. Yes, he had asked Amy to marry him. That Reeney, her friends, and his own mother seemed to think he had already made a firm commitment to Reeney meant nothing. All vows would be miraculously revoked if only Amy said yes.

"I'm not going to marry till I'm thirty," Amy had said. "All those panicked little sheep wiggling their fingers to show off diamond chips. It's pathetic. I'm going to accomplish something first. Know who I am. I have this terrific opportunity in Washington and I can't say no. We can be together on weekends. You could do your residency in Washington when you finish medical school. It's not so long."

"It's forever," Barney protested. "And are you going to be a virgin when you're thirty?" Barney teased, pressing his palm against her pussy, still hot and swollen from an afternoon of rubbing and sucking.

She moaned. "I probably won't last that long."

Barney pouted. "That makes me feel great. I thought all our struggles were to save it for your husband." He cupped two tiny breasts and lifted the veil of fine blonde hair that had fallen over her cheek. "I thought maybe your husband would be me."

"What about Reeney? Aren't you engaged to Reeney? Are you talking about love or a 'Help Wanted, Female' position you need filled? How can you be in love with me if you're about to marry Reeney? Do you think marriage is just some sort of advanced degree? Like a Ph.D. Good for advancement in your career."

"Amy, darling. I thought I loved Reeney. If I hadn't

met you I suppose I would think I loved Reeney. All these years, it seems, I led her on. Yes, I thought we could make a good life."

Nothing he said moved Amy an inch.

Barney had planned that last weekend together as if he were Romeo and Amy would poison herself in the next act. Calculated and solemn, it was one last attempt to get her to stay. To live with him if she wasn't ready to marry. Reeney was trousseau shopping with Mama and her mother like a couple of acquisitive harpies, but who the hell cared. He'd fix that later.

Johnny Coltrane was at Eddie Condon's. Barney took a room at the Dixie Hotel because he knew musicians stayed there. The hotel was shabbier than he had expected. He was so nervous he forgot to ask for a room with a bath. The toilet was down the hall, a stained sink in the room. The bed sagged and they rolled toward the middle, laughing. There was an old-fashioned radio that picked up two stations, one of them playing jazz. And from the window, they could see a corner of Times Square.

"Please don't put so much pressure on me," Amy begged, as it became clear he wanted now, this once, to go all the way. "I won't be able to enjoy what we have if you're going to spend the whole time coaxing me."

They played in bed all afternoon. Listened to jazz at Condon's till two A.M. Barney abandoned all hope of coming inside her and got caught up in all the ways they'd discovered to drive each other wild, coming and getting hard again almost instantly. Watching her thrash against the mattress, straining, hanging on to the metal bed frame.

The wakeup call came at seven A.M. But she was already awake, standing at the sink in a prim white cotton slip, brushing her teeth. He would never forget the serious cavity-prevention swish and slurp of Amy brushing her teeth. She put on a suit, tailored gray wool, stiff and unflattering, and pinned her hair into a little knot. She pulled on short white cotton gloves, and then took them off to kiss him goodbye. He had hidden his eyes in pain.

She lifted his arm and kissed his eyes, licked each cheekbone and left to catch her train for Washington, where she was working as an intern for some congressman. He never saw her again. She wrote twice, once a tight little note after his engagement notice appeared in the *Times,* once to say she'd seen his name in an article on emergency medicine in the *Washington Post.* There was a story in the Washington paper—someone clipped and mailed it to him—when a car went out of control in Georgetown crushing her against a mailbox.

"I guess she thought you'd come after her," Nancy said.

"I have to go to the bathroom, Daddy," said Candy. "You don't suppose there's a ladies' room, do you?"

Nancy grabbed a roll of toilet paper and led Candy into the shadows.

Barney sat there wanting to speak about Marvin but he hesitated to intrude on Nancy's happiness. Eliza, of course, had never really known him. Even if she remembered, amphetamines had made a cartoon of the real Marvin at the end. Marvin had started painting again a year or two before giving up forever. He was still on speed, bone-thin and exasperatingly paranoid but he was painting again after two years of staring at blank canvases. The new paintings were huge, crowding the apartment—he could no longer afford the loft studio downtown and dope too. How many times had Barney promised to come see Marvin's new work? And he'd only finally come when it was all over. The canvases were unlike anything Marvin had done, Marvin the fierce abstract expressionist was painting women, nudes bigger than life, street girls, junkies. There was some evocation of Gauguin in them, very subtle. Barney observed, visiting

Nancy in painful penitence after the funeral.

"I see what you mean now that you speak of it," said Nancy. "I don't know if it was intentional. Marvin never spoke of it." Poor Nancy. She confessed both loathing his last paintings and loving them. All day while she worked as a clerk for the city, Marvin and his street girls lay on her sofa, she said, bathed in her scented bubbles, foraged in the refrigerator, posed in her mirror, stretched in her bed. "I'm not saying he was sleeping with them, too," she said. "Marvin didn't have the patience for sex anymore. He was too jumpy. Never slept till he dropped."

"I could kill myself for not coming," said Barney, for the hundredth time. "He just didn't sound any different. No hint at how bedeviled—"

"Marvin was always bedeviled." She smiled. "That's what I fell for. His tragic irony. His wit. He was handsome then too. And a great dancer."

"I'd forgotten that."

"So had we. We never danced anymore at the end. He loved you, Barney I think he felt you were his child and his father too. That as long as you were there, they wouldn't come and take him away. Only they did, didn't they?"

"You were Daddy's best friend." Barney hadn't noticed Eliza moving onto Candy's hassock. "I have his sketchbook."

"Would you like to show it to me?" Barney asked Eliza. "Is it here? The sketchbook?"

She ran to her pup tent and returned with a small spiral notebook, a ruled stenographer's notebook. She shifted toward the light and opened it. There were addresses and phone numbers scrawled on the pages and lists, names, his own, doodles and street sketches, a woman in a phone booth, obviously angry, a trio of amputees playing musical instruments, one-third of a man selling pencils, an old vagrant bundled against the cold, a creature wrapped in newspapers sleeping in a doorway, an arm shooting a needle into another arm, a hero sandwich with a worm smiling through a hole in the cheese. The last written page had Barney's number at the hospital, a post office box number, some street numbers, the word blue repeated in various scripts. The next page had been torn out. "Mommy kept the page," said Eliza. "It was a letter to her."

"You're lucky to have this," said Barney. "The drawings are good. The words . . . in his actual handwriting." He didn't know what else to say. He wanted to say something positive. "He was amazingly creative."

"I know," she said. "I'll probably be an artist too. I have notebooks too. I drew you and your daughter." She opened a large sketchbook. She'd caught Barney looking for a place to sit and Candy clinging to his elbow. Not bad at all.

"Hey, that's terrific," said Nancy, returning with Candy trailing.

"I almost sat on a lizard," Candy announced. "But I missed. For some reason a lizard is not nearly as disgusting as a snake. You draw beautifully," she said, gazing into Eliza's sketchbook. "That's us, isn't it, Daddy." She giggled. "I love him so much I can't seem ever to let go. Oh, Monsieur Fosburgh, do you think we could see the inside of your tent?"

"Show her around, Eliza," Gabe called. "What a bright little girl, Barney," he said. "She adores you." He had one arm around Caroline. With the other, he drew Nancy close and began to lead them in a solemn twirling dance.

"Come look, Daddy," Candy cried. "The sky is like a poem. You could fold it up and keep it in your pocket forever."

Candy is astonishing, thought Barney. He crouched inside the tent. Through the mosquito netting and a plastic skylight they could see a million stars, the deflated moon, smaller now and pale yellow.

Amazing, thought Barney, how many people were unmoved by beauty. He'd always found extraordinary joy in beauty, patterns in the sand, the calligraphy of a burned-out barn, the sun's translucence captured in a flower. How impatient Reeney had always been when he stopped, mesmerized for a moment by a field in fog or a rag caught in a fence barb against snow. Once she had turned away from a mystical sky over the Lake of Annecy and complained: "Oh God, where are the people? I don't need so much beauty." He was proud to discover Candy had *his* eye.

Barney left the girls chattering in the tent. Gabe found a disco station on his portable radio. He and Nancy were shimmying crazily with Caroline banging a tambourine. Barney was drifting and a little boozy. Marvin had tried to kill himself half a dozen times. How many times could you rescue a man so determined to stop living? In his twenties Marvin had sold everything he painted. When his work became too accessible, no one wanted it. Amphetamines were just another suicide route. His last show had brought the money and the approval he'd longed for. "I know my work is great this time," he had said. And then he checked out anyway. Out the window. What an ironic moment to make an exit.

"Aren't we adaptable" Nancy said, as she hugged everyone. "From fighting the cockroaches on Avenue C to fighting the sandflies in St. Barts."

Now that it was time to go, Candy could not bear to leave. She was weeping as she hugged Eliza farewell. She took the flashlight Gabe handed her and made beacons in the sky. "It's dueling flashlights," she cried, crossing Barney's beam. Then she bounded down the path. "Lizards. Get out of my way."

When Barney dropped Caroline off, he could feel Candy's tension slip away. "I was hoping she wasn't sleeping over," she admitted, sliding close, not an easy move in a jeep with a gearshift. "What do you think, Daddy, are the chances you and Mom could get together again? My friend Laura and her whole family do family therapy so they can learn to stand each other."

"Did you hear what you said, darling? Being able to stand each other isn't enough. You, or your Mom and I are not good for each other. You hated it when the missiles started to fly."

"I was an oversensitive kid then," said Candy. "Everyone fights. I admit I thought a separation would be good and everyone would spoil me to pieces to make up for their guilt."

"What do you know about guilt, for God's sake, Candy?"

"Guilt. It's ethnic," she said. "Daddy, I'm twelve years old. I read *Portnoy's Complaint*, Daddy, in case you've forgotten. I even know about the Electra complex."

"Oh yeah." Barney put his hand on her cheek. "Silly girl. I'll never love anyone the way I love you." That was true. Loving Candy was like breathing. Loving her infused him with tenderness.

"Why don't I feel it?" she asked.

"You have to just . . . know it," said Barney, wondering if he would ever feel it with the same certainty for anyone else. Wondering if at times he hadn't been there and not trusted it. Too bad science couldn't measure love. Too bad it didn't show up on X-rays. My my, Dr. Kincaid. That looks like a small hematoma but it could be love. Barney pulled Candy into his arms.

"I suppose if I brought you another pair of wedgies—
the green ones—you might feel something."

"Oh Daddy."

*T*he phone call interrupted
dinner next night. Candy had been sneaking sips of his piña
colada and getting funnier with every sip. Now she was
making up imaginary backgrounds for every guest in the
dining room, whispering sexual innuendoes based on really
clever analyses of each one's dress. Barney was delighting in
her wit, feeling very close to her, pleasantly conspiratorial.
She was the same sort of snob he was. He grumbled all the
way to the front desk at the disturbance.

It was Anne Mallory. "I've been debating whether to call
or not," she said. "I know you really need this rest, but Dr.
Evans is talking to some of the staff, most of the attendings,
about your . . . ah . . . rash behavior is what I overheard.
He's hinting Dylan's death involved a misjudgment. He's
saying your, ah, promiscuity has amounted to sexual harassment of hospital personnel and reflects on the whole staff.
Obviously, the Gunderson case must have something to do
with this. If he can discredit you, he will—" She paused. "It's
snowing here," she said.

"The ocean here is warm as bathwater," he said.

"Di Renzo has a new symptom."

"Do I have to hear it?"

"Swollen breasts."

"Order a pregnancy test."

"Dr. Steffans let him spend the weekend in the waiting
room. Di Renzo planted watercress seeds in our philo-
dendron. Why am I telling you this?"

"Because I need some good news. You were wonderful
to let me know, Anne. You were—" He fumbled for

something. "Wonderful." He knew he'd better get home immediately.

*F*ortunately, Candy was bored by the limited shopping and simplicity of St. Barts, bored even at pretending to be Barney's wife. She didn't protest when he cut the vacation short by three days, especially when he promised her Paris for Easter vacation. She refused the green wedgies. "I don't know why," she said. "I do love them. But red goes with everything." She bought a small leather-bound book with blank pages. "My diary," she said. She wrote in it on the plane, shielding the page with her hand so he couldn't see. "It's rather private." At lunch she refused wine even though it wasn't offered. "I think I'd better stop drinking for a few years." She smiled. At the house she kissed him. "I never really knew you before now," she said. They hugged. Barney felt a wave of tenderness more powerful than any he remembered feeling before.

He meant to drive right to the hospital, to investigate Evans's campaign against him to shake the ER up, to get it tightly organized again. But it was almost nine o'clock. The flight had exhausted him. The morning was a much better time to start. At home he found a pair of white lace stockings and satin panties on his pillow with a copy of *Playboy* open to a photograph of a woman being molested on the hood of a Jaguar. The woman looked very much like Amber. "I'm up for a commercial. If anyone calls tell them I'm on location in New Jersey making a movie. (It's true. Hooray.) Back soon. If you're playing with yourself, think of me."

In a pile of bills (all paid, checks left for his signature) he found another memo from Carl. Jill Massacio Hammond lived just a few blocks away. Beth Killarney was a missionary, possibly in Cleveland. He was still "pursuing." Sarah Washburne, Reeney's treacherous maid-of-honor, was divorced again and living at the Dakota. Barney wondered if it was too late to call her. He felt queasy again, hot and sweaty. He took his temperature: 100.6. Dr. Foley's calls were being taken by an associate. Fuck that. Barney took some cortisone and two aspirins and fell asleep.

Debra was speaking. He had awakened with the phone in his hand. He recognized her Consumer Affairs reporter voice, very firm, lots of inflection, hints of righteous indignation. "Please don't call again," she began (although he could not remember now the last time he had). "We're giving up on you."

"Is that the Channel 5 'we'?" he asked. "Or the psychoanalytical, your therapist and you 'we'?"

She ignored that. "I'm donating two tickets to a porn film in your name for your Celebrity Auction," she said. "I'm sorry, Barney. I'm not as tough as I sound. I really did love you. But you . . . you come on like the Prince of the World but you don't even fool yourself. You're not secure enough to marry a Jew. You're not even secure enough to marry a really sexual woman. And boy, am I glad I figured this out now. I leave you to your wispy Wasp. Boredom is safe, Barney. So are massage parlors. No commitments there."

"You're too good for me, Debra," Barney said, furious but wanting to end this with grace.

"Thanks a lot," she said. "That's what they all say as they walk out the door. That's what my husband said. 'You're too good for me Debra-loveums, Goodbye.' I say, 'Put it on a billboard.'" She hung up.

And at that moment, Barney began to miss her.

*T*he ringing phone woke him again.

"I can't believe I finally found you." It was Mama. "Is it possible you could come home and not call immediately?"

"Have I been away?" he said, being really stupid, half asleep, caught off guard, feeling twelve years old again.

"What is this? The sixty-four-thousand-dollar question? Of course you've been away. Your father could have had a stroke and been buried and no one would have been able to find you. You don't return my calls. I only know from Reeney—"

"I was the house physician at a cheerleaders, convention," said Barney. "And I'm exhausted so I went to bed."

"What?"

"Mama, darling, please may I call back when I'm awake?"

"Oh dear . . . oh my, I'm sorry. I woke you. Oh dear."

He fell asleep again.

Saturday was obviously not a day to set records straight or defuse subversion. The hospital was unusually quiet. There was no one in the administrator's office except some flunky routing emergency calls. Dick Rogin had taken the weekend off. No chance to pick up feedback from him. The great-god-with-clay-feet, chief of medicine Hal Wechsler, was off. No sign of Gunderson, though he did see Evans scurrying to the labor room and exchanged glares. He'd hoped to find Anne Mallory but she'd worked all night and wasn't due back till Monday morning.

Henderson Turner was working on a chart when he came into the War Room. "Nice surprise," Turner said, squeezing Barney's shoulder in what was an amazingly warm welcome for the undemonstrative Hen. "We're one man short and I was just deciding who to call but here you are. Back early?"

"The chanting of cannibals hoping to toss me into their soup pot reached me in St. Barts," said Barney, scanning the lineup on the board. "Things are quiet in here."

"Lots of mysterious tummyaches." Turner was filling in a chart. "The Administration's office had Enoch Whitaker nosing around down here last week. I was very straight about Tarnapol. You made a textbook decision. He said, 'Rumor has it Dr. Kincaid is . . .' What did he say? ' . . . invariably intuitive beyond textbook decisions.' 'Yes,' I said. 'Often he is. Not every time.' About women. I said it was none of his goddamned business, you were a single man and in the hospital, as far as I know, you're a eunuch. You are a eunuch, I hope."

Barney was thoughtful. He wished now he had been less greedy.

"You're not a eunuch." Hen groaned.

"I'm trying to remember if anything I've ever done could be defined as sexual harassment. I never made a pass at old Atkins. Would that count? Anyway, I'm back, Hen. I'll clear up this Evans stuff Monday. There's no salvaging the New Grace thing, but you and I should sit down and map strategy to recruit Blythe General or even Putnam Presbyterian. I hear they have real problems in their ER. And we're going to get this place in shape again. My health problem seems to have demoralized everyone."

"Well, you're back," said Hen. "Let's get some discipline here."

"Don't slouch over the charts, Trees," Barney snapped at the resident.

"Excuse me?" Trees looked up.

"Posture, man. You're going to get dowager's hump if you slump like that over the charts."

"It was a joke," said Hen, "but he's serious."

"Patients feel better if you give them a powerful presence," said Barney, squaring his shoulders. "That was a nice pickup on that ruptured spleen, Trees," he said, rifling through charts, then setting off on his rounds. Barney sutured every gaping wound in sight, directed traffic to X-ray, found an easily missed finger fracture Dr. Djarta had missed, patted heads, removed coffee grounds from the ear of a baby boy who had dumped a garbage can over his head, tucked one of the hospital's chronic drunks under a blanket to sleep it off in a secluded corner, and was surprised by a call from Lindsay.

"Maybe I'm psychic," she said, sounding happy to find Barney there. "I had a feeling I might find you. I just finished reading this sappy novel with an implausible happy ending and—I realize, darling, a lot of our problems have to do with your pericarditis and maybe, also, our meeting too soon after your divorce. But I can't just give up. We really are good together. It's rare, believe me, to find a man that enjoys women, a man who talks. Most men don't talk to you, Barney. They talk at you . . . so I love your mind, darling. We should see each other. If you think so, I mean. Forget about marriage. Forget about commitment. Let's just have one good time, dinner, cozy and uncomplicated."

Barney heard everything she said and it all made sense. He knew it was too soon though. He didn't have the patience to appreciate Lindsay just now. He had too much unfinished business: the Gunderson case, the threats from Evans, the list. He'd really like to put a circle around each name on that list. It was like a research project where you collect all possible causes and effects and proceed to rule them out or measure their impact till you knew the answer. He was on the verge of knowing the answer. But there was no way to explain any of that to Lindsay. With her logical un-Byzantine brain, she thought she knew everything. But he was tired of hurting people.

"Tonight?" he said. "Latish."

"How wonderful," she said. "Come for dinner. I'll feed the children early and give them extra TV privileges."

From the phone Barney was watching an emphysema patient getting unhooked from the oxygen. An aide wheeled him into the waiting room. The man had been rushed in suffering severe respiratory distress, practically blue. Now he lit up a cigarette. Barney was livid. How could anyone be so stupid? He grabbed the cigarette from the man's hand. "A Camel, for God's sake," he said. "How dare you come in here, you schmuck, with your goddamn Camels and ask us to waste our time saving your life." He crushed the pack and threw it to the floor.

The man's wife stood there bristling. She handed her husband a cigarette from her own pack. "It calms him," she said.

"It kills him." Barney held his face an inch from hers. She stank of alcohol. "And if you don't stop drinking, you won't be around to collect his insurance."

Henderson Turner took Barney's arm. "Excuse me," he said, and led him into the supply room. Barney took a deep breath. He was shaking.

"Jesus. I really got carried away. Thank you, Hen, for dragging me out of there. Hey, you're angry. What the hell are you pissed off about? The guy has no right smoking. He'll be dead in six months."

"The man should not be smoking, Barney. Is that reason to loathe him? Sometimes I have the feeling you don't like sick people."

"I hate self-destructiveness. I hate sickness. Sickness is our enemy," he cried. "Maybe that's a bit dramatic," he added hastily. "The body is too vulnerable. My body is too vulnerable."

Turner seemed embarrassed. "I know you're still on medication, Barney. I know Foley has adjusted it, but I am worried about you. Where's your old cool? Where's your presence, kid? You've been running all morning, take a nap. I'll send someone for you if business picks up."

*G*illes Coburn shook Barney awake. "You didn't answer your beeper," she said. "We've got a full house downstairs. Dr. Turner is overdue to go home. Mike Steffans has one of the new residents near panic. Oh my, when I think what I could have done with my life if I'd been rich and beautiful. I have a degree in nutrition, Dr. Kincaid. I could have invented something like protein supplements or wheat-germ shampoo instead of working my butt off for ungrateful—" She turned the bedside light on. "Are you really awake now? I've got to run back. We've got a bad accident. A three-car collision. The ambulances are on their way in."

There were bodies everywhere. All the usual stomach pains and head colds milled about in horror and confusion as the ER crew and a handful of residents from trauma sorted out the crash victims.

A policeman carried in a severed hand in a plastic baggie on ice.

"Does anyone know who this belongs to?" he asked.

Barney grabbed an IV and got it going on a man with multiple skull fractures. One pupil was widely dilated. The side of his face and scalp hung loose in a flap. Barney sent a blood sample for type and cross-match and ordered four units of blood just as the man vomited. Blood hit his pants and shoes. "Make that eight units," he told the intern. "Did you get Dr. Guenther, Gilles?" he asked. "He'll have a picnic with that hand."

Seconds before the sound became audible, Barney sensed that another ambulance was nearing. He was inserting an endotracheal tube in a teenage girl with the side of her head crushed. Often a difficult job, this intubation was a cinch once he suctioned the blood and bone splinters out of her throat, because the jaw was so shattered that it pulled away from her face. Amazingly, her blood pressure held steady. A surgeon took over as they wheeled her upstairs and Barney stood for a moment hearing the tumult. He had shut it off as he assessed who was critical, who could be salvaged? There was a woman screaming. Probably a relative. The young woman the paramedics wheeled in looked peaceful and happy, her little rosebud mouth in a beatific smile.

"What did she take?" he asked the cop.

"Valium was all she had, they say," he responded. "There was an empty aspirin bottle, too."

Barney was furious that a self-indulgent sleeping beauty was rolling into his ER in the midst of real carnage. "Get an Ewald tube," he said.

"Not ipecac?" one of the residents asked.

"You heard me," he snapped. A tear-stained young woman was lassoing him with beseeching eyes.

"I know you're so busy," she said. "My friend—"

"Back in three-G. The patient is acting crazy," said Coburn. "Drunk, I guess. Got a bump on his head. I asked his friends to stay with him while we get our accident victims dispatched."

"Stay with your friend," said Barney to the young woman. "We'll get there."

He lost track of time as he waded through the turmoil. All his skills, all his training, came into play under pressure like this. Barney felt like Superman. The less-wounded relatives were the hardest to handle. Finally the last of the seriously hurt were on the way to the operating room or otherwise dispatched. The teary, wraithlike Lorelei was still waiting.

Her friend, Daniel Sallamagundy, age twenty-six according to the chart, was singing.

"All you need is love . . . da da dadda da." A handsome, ruddy young man with a bump on his head. His eyes were bloodshot.

"Grass?" asked Barney.

Lorelei tilted her head. "I don't know. Sometimes he smokes. Did he smoke? I can't remember." She sounded a little spaced out herself.

"He drank a lot of beer," said a tough-looking kid in an old World War II flying jacket.

All the neurological signs were normal. "What day is it?" Barney asked Sallamagundy.

"Funday," he said with a pleased grin.

"What year is it?"

"You can't fool me," said the young man, rubbing his head. "Oh, that hurts."

His pupils were equal in size. "Grab my hands and pull," said Barney. "Who's president, Dan?"

"He not much on politics," said his friend in the pilot's jacket.

Sallamagundy was asleep when the X-rays came back, showing no fracture. The alcohol level was 110.

"He's drunk. He banged his head. Take him home," said Barney, "and let him sleep it off."

"He didn't really drink all that much," said the Lorelei.

"He'll sleep it off," said Barney.

*H*e was sitting in front of the fire with Lindsay when his new beeper went off. In fact, he'd fallen asleep. She woke him. "Call the hospital," she said.

Henderson Turner was obviously upset. Between the stutters Barney got the news. Sallamagundy had been brought in comatose. "We've got him on manitol. The neurosurgeon is on the way in," Hen said.

"All the neurological signs were okay when I saw him," said Barney, feeling icy and scared. "He was drunk. I sent him home to sleep it off, four or five hours ago."

"Coburn says he was confused."

"Hen, he was silly drunk. He stank with beer. Okay. The witchcraft wasn't working tonight."

"I'm sorry, Barney."

"I can't stand your sympathy," Barney snapped. And hung up. So what if his friends had insisted he didn't drink that much. Friends always say that. Dope . . . they could have been lying about drugs too. There were no neurological signs. But you had to go with your instinct—when all the facts say it's nothing, there was that inner warning system, the sixth sense that said . . wait. Barney groaned. To pick up those extrasensory messages a man had to be listening. He had to be all there. Had he lost it? Sallamagundy could die.

He sat staring at the flames for a long time, seeing the images of animals in the flames, entranced by the fantasy that a mutant animal could spring out of the fireplace.

"Is there anything I can do, darling?" Lindsay asked. "I feel so helpless when I don't know what's troubling you."

"You are helpless," Barney snapped, then realized what he'd said. "I mean, I am helpless . . . hopeless. I mean I don't need any help just now. If you could help, honestly, I would let you." He saw her stiffen. Nothing he said seemed to come out right anymore. "I'm leaving medicine," he said. "I'm quitting Goodman. I have a contract for a book . . . a book of photographs . . . "

"Barney. Are you drunk?" She stood up. "I don't understand you at all anymore. What book? You can't possibly leave medicine. You're a brilliant doctor. Nobody makes money on a book of photographs. Not money to live on. You must be kidding. You're a brilliant doctor of emergency medicine."

He stared into the flames. There was a giant warthog leaping about in the fireplace. It knocked against the screen.

"Barney, are you listening? Do you hear me?"

Barney decided to leave before the warthog attacked. He put on his coat. "I don't think an exterminator can handle this," he said. "It's a pretty big animal." He shoved the coffee table against the firescreen. "If he gets out, call the police. Or the SPCA. I hope you aren't going to be anti-Semitic about this," he said, as she turned her head away.

Amber was curled up asleep on the convertible sofa in his office. In the faint rose-tinged light from her twenty-five watt, "eternal flame" bulb—"I hate walking into the dark," she had explained—he could see she'd been crying. Without makeup her resemblance to Amy was haunting, disturbing to Barney all over again. What could he do about Amy? She was an uncircled name on his list. The dreams were robbing him of his sleep. Amber started and woke.

"Oh, what a mess," she cried. "I'm so glad you're here. What a disaster zone I live in. Why did I ever have to meet you?" She started to sob.

Barney felt a familiar pain and remorse. It seemed to him those were precisely the words of Amy.

"Why did I ever have to meet you? I need to do something in my life before I marry. I don't want to be a cipher. I can't even tell my dad I'm in love with a Jew. Where I come from they still think Jews wear horns."

"I'm not much of a Jew," Barney had protested. "It's nothing to me. I'm probably as anti-Semitic as your father."

"That's disgusting, too," Amy had said. "Why did I ever have to meet you? A Jew *and* a bigot. I'm so confused."

*B*arney pulled Amber onto his lap, quilt and all, and rocked her. "Sweet baby. Sweetness. What happened?"

"I'm confused," she said. "I'm a slut."

"A lovely slut," he said.

"I'm not joking," she sobbed. "I got a really good part in a serious movie, I mean a big-budget movie, not a big part but two small scenes and some dialogue. That's where I was. In New Jersey. I guess partly I got the role because the money man's nephew and I—you know, you know—and then the producer wanted a little fuckee-suckee too and he was kinda cute and I probably would have anyway. That's the money man, the uncle. And he told me he was definitely backing De Niro's next movie." And she started to sob again. "I hate myself."

Barney rocked her close. "Sweet baby."

"So then it turned out that Sweet Baby was supposed to be agreeable and available for sex with everyone, anyone, his two friends anyway. And when I was the tiniest bit indignant, he said, 'Forget it, go home.' So I serviced three guys in a motel. Only I got crazy when they started shooting videotapes of me and this other poor slut doing a scene with somebody's cousin. I mean, they were calling in cousins, Barney. Oh damn, it's your fault. I never minded playing around if the money was good till you made me feel like a piece of meat. Damn you."

"Oh Amber." Barney could feel her pain. She had tried so hard to be a person. It was *his* fault. He'd made her hate her hustling life, promised her a big payoff for dignity and self-respect. In a way Amber was his responsibility. Fuck Lindsay's shrink. And Debra's shrink, too—the whole cabal of shrinks. He was not afraid of responsibility. Hey yes, as a matter of fact, he felt proud. His heart ached in a warming way. Something between heartburn and tenderness, he thought.

"You did the right thing to quit," he said, hugging her.

"How do you know I quit?" she muttered, blowing her nose on his shirt sleeve.

"You quit?"

"I quit."

"Come, let's go to bed," he said.

"I'm a fool," she said. "But I still don't see what's the difference between prostituting your talent for a thousand a day or getting a thousand a night for the use of your body?"

"You were getting a thousand a night?" asked Barney.

"No. I was getting scale."

"Not much better than a dollar a lick."

"What if I don't have any talent?"

"I think you have talent," said Barney. "And if you don't, you're beautiful enough that you could make it anyway." He tucked her in and lay beside her still dressed, now totally drained.

She reached for his belt buckle. He took her hand. "I need to sleep," he said. "I can't afford to get sick again. I'm in the middle of everything." She wrapped an arm around him and fitted her knees into the backs of his. He fell asleep. In his dream the car skidded over the curb and he tried to scream but it was too late. She lay there, crushed and torn, still breathing, her voice a gurgle, only it wasn't Amy in a pool of blood, it was Barney himself. He forced his eyes open to get out of the dream. He lay there, his heart pounding. Carefully he got out of bed, not to wake Amber, and went into the office. He took the list from his pocket, the names and addresses of all his women, and tore it up. Now he would be free. Now he would be sane again. Now he could get back to the serious business of his life. Pleased with himself, he reached for the *New England Journal of Medicine* from a pile too long neglected. And promptly fell asleep.

Waking, Barney felt strangely depressed. He showered, shaved and felt worse. He was sure he had a fever again. He didn't need a thermometer to know, he thought, swallowing a cortisone, aspirin and a handful of vitamins. There was a great ache in his throat as :f someone had died. He hadn't realized how much he wanted that list. He dumped the wastebasket onto his desk and salvaged the pieces, patching it with Scotch tape. And tiptoed out of the apartment without waking Amber. He wasn't due at the hospital till two and he'd made a date for breakfast with a rather wary, somewhat reluctant Jill Massacio.

*B*arney passed an old woman pushing a supermarket car west on Eighty-third Street. She wore plastic bags tied over bedroom slippers and cabaret makeup—whiteface, eyes outlined in blue and green pencil—and pulled a child's red wagon behind her piled high with bulging garbage bags. She seemed to be coping well, Barney thought, as she sidled up to a garbage can and began to inspect the contents.

Watching from the stoop of her brownstone was Jill Massacio. He recognized her at once, even though she'd grown thin, almost wiry and curiously dry. Her long straight hair whipped in the wind and she had a child's knit cap pulled low over her ears.

"Where's a good place for breakfast?" Barney asked, feeling a sharp ache in his throat. Whatever he had was getting worse. His eyes blurred.

"You can come with me if you like," she said, not smiling, not offering a hand or a cheek. Grit and sand from Riverside Park blew into their faces as she led him toward the water. She pulled her hat lower. "You're a doctor now. Yes. I hope you're not part of the medical conspiracy. But I suppose you are." She stood in a small round cement plaza and took out a brown paper sack. "It's bread for the rats," she said. "Nobody feeds the rats. Everyone feeds the pigeons—and pigeons are flying rats, you know." Barney stepped back, expecting to see a parade of rats streaming by for breakfast. She tossed a crust. He imagined he heard the sound of tiny claws scratching. He took a few steps backward and bumped into a post.

Barney wondered why he was here. He was losing his voice. He felt hot. He had scarcely known Jill then. He could not relate to her now in this strange creature with the almost flat affect. He had been determined to trace Jill Massacio, to complete the list. To finish the task. To circle every name. Was it neatness that ran his life now? What a ridiculous thought. Would he insist Carl find Daisy from Cass Lake? Was he going to Cleveland in pursuit of Beth Killarney? He knew he must make a decision to end it. He felt like a drunk, out of control. He giggled.

"It's not funny at all," said Jill and he realized she'd been speaking. "I threw him out. He was a child with all his women but even worse, the football. I was a perfectly normal woman till they expanded the National League football season and made it run into the baseball season and doubled the number of basketball teams. The telly was going all the time. This is not a joke."

She was not a jokester. It was impossible to imagine this tense stick creature being hot in a physics lab. He wondered how best to retreat. "Can I buy you coffee?" he asked. "There's a nice place for espresso on Columbus."

"I'm a vegetarian, you know."

"Oh yes."

"My two kids went with him because they were hungry." She shrugged. "I said it was their funeral. Kids. What do they know? Sneaking Big Macs on the sly. Their teeth rotting from the crap, the sweets, you know. I wouldn't feed a rat Wonder Bread I don't care how they fortify it."

"Yes," said Barney.

"This, you see here, is five-grain bread I buy at the health-food store. I need a committee. A foundation." Barney gave her five dollars for the Rat Health Patrol Foundation and fled.

*B*arney knew in the chill of his misbehaving heart that it was a mistake to see Sarah Washburne. He knew he should find Dr. Foley. Maybe he'd had a relapse of some sort. Sarah had been none too friendly on the phone. But he'd put her name on a list and Carl had traced her through two marriages and two divorces and the Dakota was only a few blocks away. There was no point in stopping now. He felt himself hurtling in a kind of intense momentum of purpose and wasn't sure anything could really stop him.

The guard in the Dakota office sent him to the elevator in the far right corner. It crept up slowly, so slowly he was sure it had stalled. He was about to sound the alarm when it stopped on seven. She let him in herself, presented her cheek to be grazed by his as if she were afraid of catching a cold and stood back, her slim body lost in the many folds of a butterflylike kimono.

"You're beautiful," she said.

"You're beautiful too," he said automatically, the hypocrisy of etiquette drummed into the civilized middle class prompting the reflex. But she looked pretty good, better with her astonishing dark Afro curls than she had when she spent hours trying to iron out the kinks. A lot of plain women seemed to have learned how to make the most of whatever they had these days. She was cute. What she had, he remembered, were great legs, perfect legs. He caught a flash of thigh as she moved into the living room, which was painted black, with lots of leather and shiny wood cubes, white pillows, a painting—all white, white on white, actually, and a big bowl of bright-red poppies. He leaned over to smell them. He felt himself growing excited. What a sexy bitch she was.

"They're silk," she said. "I fell in love with a fabulous

man who turned out to be gay so I let him redo my apartment." She sat down. "He was a decorator," she added hastily. "I wasn't suggesting all fags have natural taste. You do look wonderful," she said. "I heard about you and Reeney. Too bad. I'm only surprised you two stuck it out that long. Some people have a real appetite for denial. Or pain. Or whatever it is. I'm supposed to be a therapist, I should make up my mind. You do look wonderful."

"A therapist?" asked Barney. "When did that happen?"

"Well, maybe I should say a social worker. Can I get you a drink? How old are you? Forty-two, forty-three?" She poured two glasses of white wine.

"Forty-two," said Barney.

"Do you think you'll marry again?"

Barney was amused by her directness. "Oh, I probably will."

"Do you have an age range in the women you seem to prefer? Someone your own age? Someone in her thirties . . . twenties? If I remember correctly, you're a sucker for well-bred Wasps, right? Dowdy or flashy?"

"Sarah, you're embarrassing me," said Barney.

"I hate to waste a great single man," said Sarah. "I have dozens of women friends you might find attractive. Do you mind a woman who smokes? How do you feel about drugs? Grass? Cocaine? Do you like to dance? You never were an athlete but I remember . . . you love the outdoors. I have this friend, Melissa, adorable, about thirty, I'd say . . . she's in fantastic shape, a real exercise addict, two children, a bushel of alimony . . . stuck somewhere in a big house in Sneedon's Landing. That's the outdoors, isn't it?" She reached for a macadamia nut in a black lacquer bowl and pushed them toward Barney. "Wait. Oh, wait. Pamela. Pamela would flip for you. She's in the middle of a trial separation. But if you two got on, she could make it permanent. She has a little job doing something arty at Sotheby's. Fine arts at Smith and three kids doesn't exactly equip you for much. Tall, lots of hair, Norma Kamali clothes . . . kooky but terrific."

Barney laughed. "Are you trying to get rid of me? I came here to see you." She was either playing hard to get or totally disinterested. Either way, he was amused.

"Well, of course," she said, crossing one leg over the other and letting the butterfly wings open to reveal a great stretch of thigh, still incredible. "I'm Second Chance, the adult mating service. You must have read the profile on me in *New York* magazine. But these are my friends I've mentioned so far—Melissa and Pam. Not clients. I'm giving you two or three freebies for old time's sake. After all, I was the maid of honor at your wedding." She smiled and dropped her eyes.

"You remember?" said Barney.

"Well, of course. Reeney insisted we wear those disgusting milkmaid dresses that made everyone look fat so she would look positively sylphlike. Well, I suppose you're only a bride once . . . what am I saying? Me, the power behind Second Chance. You're only a first bride once, is what I mean."

"I was embarrassed that I was too drunk to do you justice that night," said Barney. "I felt you deserved hours of slow, loving attention before . . . hmmm. If I remember correctly I think I fell asleep in the middle. Though I did feel I made up for that the next morning."

"I don't know what you're talking about," she said. "Are you confused?"

Barney was annoyed. She was being vacant and obtuse, reaching for a small notebook, staring at it with her eyes open wide. "Our time together," he said. "The night you came into my room. You don't remember?" He was dumbfounded. "Making love that night before the wedding?"

"We made love?" She laughed. "Barney, Reeney was my best friend. You can't be serious. I am sure I would remember if anything so dramatic happened. You are serious." She put her chin on her hand. Thinking.

Barney got up. "It's not important."

"Well it must be important. I'm thinking," she said.

"Stop thinking."

She stood up. "Shall I call Pamela? Would you like to

meet Melissa? Delia Norris is a likely possibility too, Barney. Not a beauty but nice looking, very clever, she runs an agency representing commercial artists. Is forty-three too old for you, do you think?" She hugged him. "It's okay. I'm not upset. Oh Barney, you're going to have such a wonderful life. The world is made for forty-year-old men these days. You own this town." She shivered. "I think Pamela first."

He was looking for his coat. The front closet looked like a zoo. Full of fat fluffy furs. He was sure he saw a live fox. He grabbed his coat.

"Give me your number," she said. "I'll call Pamela right now."

In the elevator—creeping downward inch by inch—Barney felt himself choking, unable to swallow. He took his own pulse. It was just a little fast. The list in his pocket was going to destroy him. He started to run home but he couldn't catch his breath. He hailed a taxi.

Barney looked at the meter. Fifteen dollars and forty cents. What the hell? "Driver," he snapped. "Stop this cab."

"You wanted Goodman Memorial," the driver said. "Is something wrong Mister. We're almost there. If you're sick, I can take you to a hospital that's nearer."

Barney slumped into the seat. He didn't remember asking to go anywhere. He didn't remember getting into this cab. Well, it was a wise move however he'd done it. He'd get an X-ray, have the lab do cultures, see Foley if he could find the elusive bastard.

"You look like hell, Barney," Turner greeted him.

"Thanks a lot," Barney said, hanging his coat and watching in stupification as it fell to the floor. "I think I'm having a relapse."

"Let me call Foley," Hen said, reaching for the phone.

"He keeps a robot at that number. I never find him," Barney snarled. "I'll go down there myself. Never mind calling. Where is my God damned coat? Is that my coat? Yes, that's my coat. Where the hell is my scarf." He stumbled and stepped on his scarf. "God damn it, Hen, get this place cleaned up. There's a cockroach in my sleeve." He stalked out the door, shaking his arm, slapping his sleeve, trying to dislodge the roach.

There was a gypsy cab parked outside the Emergency entrance. "Take me home," Barney said. The cabby sat there. "Are you deaf?" Barney cried.

The cabby turned. "I need the address," he said.

For half a minute Barney could not remember his own address. He looked inside his glove. When he was a kid Mama always sewed a name and address label inside his glove. Then he remembered.

"Take it easy, Buddy," said the driver. "Don't give yourself a heart attack."

Barney laughed.

*H*e looked for a note from Amber. Nothing. Just a plate of brownies with a small card attached. "Straight brownies. No hash." It was six o'clock. He lay down on the sofa and in seconds was asleep. He dreamed he was dissecting a frog in the high school lab. Only it wasn't a frog. It was Amy. Blood was pouring from her mouth.

"What can I do?" cried Barney, trying to wipe the blood away, thinking, I'm going to flunk biology if anyone finds out.

"It's too late," said Amy. Her lips moved again but there was no sound only a bubble and more blood. He felt the wetness on his hand. And woke. His hand was wet from his tears. He lay there too heavy to move. He knew it was time to take a pill but he couldn't find the strength to sit up. He tried to remember loving Amy. He certainly had loved Amy but what he remembered was wanting her, the exquisite agony of sexual frustration, the anxiety of knowing he would lose her, wondering what she saw in him, wondering why, if she loved him, she was so stubborn, remembering her lewd and pure.

"You're here. Is it okay to wake you?" Amber burst through the door, bouncing into the room, manic and happy. "I'm so happy you're here. I've got a commercial. A serious, upright, capitalistic, non-X-rated commercial. Your friend set it up and I got it. We're going on location to Utah. Utah, do you believe it? They're planning to wrap a mountain in toilet paper to prove how strong and absorbent it is."

She crouched down and tilted her head, fixing him eye to eye. "You don't look too good, Dr. Strangelove. What have you been up to? Have you been naughty again? Chasing all over the country after women, bringing home lacy garter belts. Oh my. Boy, you sure get a lot of phone calls from women. Deirdre and Debbie and Libby. Mariliese. Your mother. Do you know all these women or are you running an ad in the *Village Voice* personals column? Poor baby." She stroked his head.

"I know four Deirdres."

"I took her number."

"I don't want to speak to any of them."

"I'll tell her you went to Utah to wrap up a mountain in toilet paper. What are you up to, Doc? You're acting pretty weird. Actually, you've always been weird but lately you don't seem to be enjoying it." She snuggled close. "You've been so busy reforming me, we haven't paid any attention to you."

"Even Svengali needs a backrub once in a while," Barney said.

"Svengali?"

"I'm on a roller coaster and I can't seem to get off," Barney moaned.

"Turn over, Svengali. I'll give you a backrub."

He didn't move. "I meant that metaphorically."

"Oh." She didn't quite get it. "If you don't want to explain . . ."

He lay there trying to recapture the parade of women

he'd seen in the last few months. What an effort it was to concentrate. He imagined his brain growing rusty. Margaret . . . now that had been a wonderful experience. Barbie Bloome was, at first, a painful revelation but in the end, quite warming. And Audrey. How happy she'd been to see him, how proud, with her Barney–look-alike husband in tow. He began trying to tell his story to Amber. "It was just a whim, in the beginning. Looking up our old maid from the time when I was twelve. Seeing high school sweethearts twenty years later. You lose touch with the people who meant so much," he said. He was rambling. "Do you see what I mean?"

"Hmmm."

"Everyone of them knew a different me. Barney at twelve, Barney at twenty, Barney the poet, Barney the cheating husband. I got so caught up in it. I have this list. I found it in my pocket. All the women in my life. I'm a prisoner now of my list."

"Throw it away."

"I tried. It's not that easy. I have these terrible dreams. About the woman who was killed, Amy, the woman you remind me of. The dreams are getting worse." Amy. How eery it was . . . Amber in her Amy face, wearing a child's undershirt. He touched her nipples, doorbells accentuated by thin white cotton. What an era to be alive in. Women walked around half naked, in love with their own bodies. He thought of Amy in her prim white cotton underslip, the stern stitched cotton bra, the little white gloves girls used to wear.

"I think I could let the list go if I could talk to Amy," he said.

"I have a friend who knows a fabulous psychic," Amber was saying. "Hey, wait. I'm not saying that smart-ass. Some people really believe in the occult."

"You could be Amy," Barney said, surprised to hear the words coming out of his mouth.

"Barney, that's sick."

Barney lay there thinking. Why hadn't it come to him

before? If he could somehow get himself back to that time with Amy, he would be released from whatever had come to possess him. He would be free. His brain would be clear. He could function normally again, get back his bell, his computer-memory, all the synapses clicking. "Yes, you could just act as if you were Amy, sweetheart, just for a few hours," Barney said. "Maybe it sounds nuts. Maybe it is nuts. Do it for me, sweetness. Then everything will be all right again. I have this feeling—"

"It's not fair. I want you to love me for myself. Not by proxy. You only love me because I remind you of her."

Barney felt weak and warm. "Amber, whatever it means, love, I do love you but I can't love you like that. I'm twice your age. I'm old enough to be your father."

"But incest is really hot stuff, Barney."

"Amber, please. Even the Marquis de Sade must have had his limits. Incest is mine."

"All right. All right. Forget incest. Tell me what you want me to do. I am an actress, after all—"

"Bring me that bottle of pills. Please. And a drink. You'll need an old-fashioned cotton slip and one of those old-time bras. You'll find what you need in a thrift shop, I bet." Barney described that last weekend with Amy, the afternoon at the Dixie Hotel, the jazz at Eddie Condon's, the tears, the gray flannel suit, the swoosh of her toothbrush.

"Did you love her?" Amber wanted to know.

Barney thought. "I don't know. I'm not sure I know what that means. To love her." He sipped an inch of vodka.

"You love me," said Amber, hugging him. "I know it."

"And I love Candy," Barney added.

"Shit. Don't spoil this moment," she said.

*T*he Dixie Hotel had been re-
dubbed the Carter. That shook Barney a bit but he decided
to ignore the outrage. He was waiting in the lobby when she
waltzed in. What a delicious moment, thought Barney,
enjoying himself for the first time in days. If Amber had
walked into the Carter Hotel in some lamé gym shorts and
rhinestone pasties, no one would have batted an eye. Not in
Times Square. But in her gray flannel and white cotton
gloves, she sure turned heads. One half of Barney's brain
was moved by her incredible resemblance to Amy. The other
half of his consciousness found it difficult to keep from
breaking up as he signed the register, "D. H. Lawrence and
wife," as he had, with his unrelenting flare for cliché, twenty
years earlier.

Behind the desk, a burnt-sienna young black solemnly
accepted Barney's cash in advance without a smile. "This, I
judge, will be the legendary Frieda, Mr. Lawrence," he said,
handing Barney a key, nodding at Amber.

"Pretty serious literary stuff for Times Square," Barney
retorted.

"Just working my way through NYU," the young man
said.

Amber sashayed toward the elevator with a swing that
would have shocked Amy Collins in the innocence of the
Sixties. She was wearing her usual fuck-me shoes with skinny
spike heels and a strap around the ankle, doubly erotic with
tailored gray flannel. Barney had neglected to specify low-
heeled loafers with pennies in the instep. Barney shook his
head trying to get into the past.

"Not so much ass," he whispered. "A little more
straight-arrow, dignified but graceful."

The room was cleaner than he remembered, but Barney

was sure he heard the scuttle of roaches as they entered. From the window he could see the black-painted window of a massage parlor. "Fun Fun Fun" the lettering said. There was no longer a solitary sink in the room. Instead there was a bathroom, new but already crumbling in the tradition of contemporary schlock.

Amber looked at him as if awaiting direction. Then she sat down in a lounge chair and crossed her ankles primly. She smiled wistfully. The bright-red goo on her lips—something close to Cherries in the Snow, he guessed—was already smudged.

"Do that again," said Barney, catching her open smile and wiping the lipstick off her teeth. Amy always had lipstick on her teeth. He had a dim fleeting memory of all those lipstick-smeared faces, the girls he had kissed. How wise they were, all those little girls, smart and superior, pretending to be silly and vulnerable to keep an adolescent male aching.

He reached inside Amy's jacket. She was wearing a round-necked blouse and a circle pin. He grinned. Good girl. Did her homework well. He recognized the authenticity of the bra by its stiff stitched concentric circles. Obligatory in that period. He closed his eyes and let his fingers trace the concentric circles closing in on the bull's eye. She took a deep breath. She sighed. "Bar . . . neeee." He unbuttoned her jacket, kneeling in front of her, and put a hand inside one cup of the bra, capturing a breast. It was as clumsy and difficult as he remembered. The strap dropped off one shoulder. He reached behind struggling to unhook the catch with one hand, feeling her inert body, not exactly resisting but not at all helpful. Familiar passivity. Delicious. Twenty years of undressing women had not made the unlatching of this catch any easier. It took two hands then. It took two hands now. And there was still something unbearably exciting about cotton bondage falling away. She seemed to feel it too and began to writhe and purr, starting to unzip her skirt. Barney caught her hand. He wanted to go through the barriers slowly, savoring each surrender—stockings, garter belt, panties, skirt crushed around her waist.

"So much stuff," she moaned. He stopped her mouth, pulled her up, stood her in front of the mirror and covered her eyes with her hand as Amy had covered hers. He put his hand inside her panties, squeezing the furry softness beneath the flat of her pubic bone. She made a low sound and dropped in his hold. He silenced her again and she snapped at his finger with her teeth, annoyed, but said nothing. He picked her up and carried her to the bed.

"I'm so hot, Barney."

He stopped her mouth again. She let herself go limp, lay there collapsed, rigid, biting her lip. He closed his eyes and tasted the taste of Amy. He tried to immerse himself in that taste, to still the images, to hone in on the moment, to recapture the hope and sadness, the lust of that day, to hear her voice, to feel again his pain, the joy of playing, the frustration at her stubbornness, maybe to collide with a feeling of love. What irony. You see, Mama, I am not the prince of the Western World. The predatory blonde shiksas who prowl the street in search of Jewish princes are not scheming to steal your tarnished golden boy. Feeling it, the rage, the frustration, the mockery, the hunger, the lust, what did it feel like? Love. A distinct feeling from that afternoon burst into his mind. Intense thirst. They had ordered beer. He could taste again the grainy cold rush of that first swallow with the flavor of Amy still on his lips.

He opened his eyes. For a few minutes he could not remember where he was, why Amber was here, her mouth on his soft cock, licking her lips.

Then the alarm went off. She got up and stood at the sink. From the bedroom he could see her and hear those grim, serious toothbrushing gurgles. When she came back into the room, she was encased again in stiff gray flannel, her hair in a tight knot. She kissed him, her lips stained from the red grease but her face scrubbed clean, looking more like Amy than ever. He closed his eyes. Oh Amy. No one really cared about Barney. Women wanted a husband puppet, a puppet son, performing as they commanded. A puppet to give them money, life insurance, small unfeeling clones called children, multiple orgasms. An escort always properly dressed, a chauffeur and consort, pension plans, a puppet to be the doctor they couldn't be, a puppet to give meaning to their meaninglessness. And what would a man get in return? Love. A word so undefinable you'd never even find it in a crossword puzzle. "But I love you," they'd say as if they'd just given you the world. Better to explain the difference between blue and green to a blind man. Barney still wasn't getting it.

He opened his eyes. Amber was peeling off the flannel. She was naked underneath. She brought his hand to her pussy. He felt the heat and wet. She straddled him, rubbing herself with his cock till she was dripping and sat down on it, crying "Aha!" An explorer's "Aha!" Recognition that everything was just as she suspected it would be. Except that it was not. Barney's cock had shriveled. She sat there, eyes wide, astonished and then her mouth went into a pout. For a moment Barney felt panic, almost terror. A fear that was terribly familiar. She would yell, strike out, punish him. He would vanish. And then it was gone, the fear.

"It's all right," he said. "Sweet Amber. Nothing to do with you, Sweetheart. So tired," he crooned. "So tired." He was numb. He was grateful for that numbness because he knew when he let the fog go he would be as only as he'd ever been. Only. I mean lonely, he corrected. And he smiled, amused by the mind's teasing ways. His fingers moved over her skin. Baby skin. He felt bewitched and very tender.

*T*ime got lost. When he woke up, he wasn't sure how many hours—or days—later. But he was at home in his own bed. He woke in a fit of free-floating anxiety. The beeper and the phone had gone off simultaneously.

It was Nurse Mallory. "I'm afraid it's bad news," she said. "The Hubbard boy, Jimmy Hubbard. That wasn't appendicitis. Dr. Turner wants to talk to you. I'll put him on."

"Jimmy Hubbard," said Barney, hearing his own voice through a tunnel. "Did I see him?"

"Eleven years old, abdominal pain and fever, yes I'm afraid you did. Here's Dr. Turner."

"Barney. We're in a mess, my friend. The front office wants to know what happened."

"What was it, if it wasn't appendicitis?" Barney knew he was in the shit again but for some reason he felt almost calm, as if it were a dream.

"They aren't sure."

"Surgery doesn't operate on our word alone, Hen, for God's sake." Some knife-happy surgeon had gotten them into this, damn it.

"But it turns out this is the third kid from that same building with the same symptoms that we sent up with possible appendicitis."

"Well, why the hell didn't they get it? Clinically, he had appendicitis. We don't look at the address of every patient we see. We won't take the blame. Forget it."

"That's just it, Barney. We *should* have caught it. Three kids about the same age from the same apartment building."

"I'm on my way, Hen." Wasn't he entitled to a day off? Barney turned over and went back to sleep.

*T*he phone rang. He turned it off and dug into the pillows. He was freezing. He felt for the covers with his eyes closed, not wanting to come fully awake. Above him he felt icy metal. His hand hit the side of the wall. It was icy cold . . . metal. He sat up and hit his hand. The ceiling was only inches away. Metal too. Something was on his toe. Oh God. A string and a tag. He was in a drawer at the morgue. He could hear the voices of aides, the sliding of bodies into boxes around him, a clatter of stretcher wheels, bells.

It was the door. Pounding at the door. The door buzzer. In the gray half-light he found a robe.

How astonishing. The Fudgesicle stood there with a doorman. "What's wrong?" Barney asked. "Why are you here?"

"You didn't answer your phone, Dr. Kincaid," said Mallory.

"She told me she was from the hospital, Doc," said the doorman, "and you weren't answering your phone or the beeper. When you didn't come to the door, boy, we was worried. I was about to go down for the key."

"That's good," said Barney. "You did fine."

"Let me in," said Mallory.

Barney stepped to one side. She looked so official in her uniform, stepping through a maze of stuff lying on the living-room floor. She did not take off her coat.

"Are you awake, Dr. Kincaid? Did you take something? A sleeping pill? Or drugs? You look like a plague victim." She picked up sweaters, scarves, his coat, a garter belt, dropped everything on the chair. Barney watched her from his mooring, braced against the wall.

"I think I have a cold," he said. "Or perhaps the flu."

She led him to the sofa. "I'll make you some tea. Have you eaten anything today? Can you eat?"

"Wheatena," said Barney.

"You ate it or you want some?"

"I'll eat it if you fix it."

She picked up the phone. "Dr. Turner, please," she said. "The hospital is in real trouble right now," she said to Barney. "And we're on the spot." Then into the mouthpiece, "Dr. Kincaid is sick, Dr. Turner. He doesn't seem to remember even speaking to you this morning. You should come by as soon as you're free. The public relations office should clear everything with you. Dr. Kincaid is in no condition to—I'll stay here," she said.

"I don't know where to start," said Mallory. "Tea. Cereal. Where is your stethoscope? Get back in bed? Shall I get a blanket?"

"I like watching you," said Barney, "and I'm cold. I'll take my pulse myself."

She put on water. "You don't seem to have Wheatena."

"Oh no." Barney shook his head trying to clear it. "I guess not. I haven't had Wheatena since I was a little boy. Maybe a blanket. The bedroom is—"

She was already gone and back, wrapping his feet in the quilt, arranging bed pillows behind his head. "Stethoscope?"

"You can do it with your ear," he said.

"Dr. Kincaid." She was annoyed. "Are you crazy?"

"Aren't we all?" he said. The kettle began to shrill.

"Oh shut up," she said, grabbing the kettle and pouring hot water into a cup. He sat up a little, sipping the tea slowly when she returned with a stethoscope.

The metal was icy cold on his chest. She warmed it in her hand. And listened. "How many of these do you take a day?" she asked, holding up the vial of cortisone.

"Whatever it says. Read the label. I'd like something sweet. You're mean." He fell asleep again.

*T*urner stood there with Foley. "He really should come in for an EKG," Foley was saying. "This is half-assed and unprofessional. But, all right, I know the whole story. I cut down the dosage before he left on vacation. . . . Barney, wake up. Barney. Why are you still taking four a day?"

"I had a fever. I felt weak. Sweating a lot. I could never get ahold of you, Foley. I figured I was having a relapse."

Foley was furious. "You idiot. Steroids are not aspirin and you of all people damn well know it. My other patients have no problem reaching me."

"Looked like flu to me," said Hen. "Everyone in the hospital has had the flu this winter. It's my fault," said Hen. "He's been acting odd. Half the time, he's a zombie. Half the time, he's a genius. I was too caught up in my work and my own personal problems to talk to him seriously. I assumed he was seeing you regularly, Foley."

"Doctors are the worst patients," snapped Foley. "We'll have to taper him down again, gradually. But I want you to get him to the hospital for an EKG and a good work-up as soon as the fever is gone."

"I'll stay here for a while," Mallory was saying as Barney felt himself drifting off again.

S he woke him, her hand on his hand. He was in bed again. She had a tray. "Have something," she said. "I sent out for Wheatena. Toast. Jam. I'll have something with you."

He pulled himself up, groggy but for some reason cheerful.

"I bet you'd feel better if you brushed your teeth."

He was naked. She handed him a robe. He wondered if she had put him to bed herself. She looked softer and more human with her uniform unbuttoned and her hair just slightly disheveled. She was barefoot too. My goodness.

"Wheatena," he said. "What a great surprise. I wonder if I'll still hate it."

"Hate it? But that's what you asked for."

"I know. But it isn't anything I ever liked. It was just what my mother gave me on cold winter mornings that made me strong. Made me know that she loved me. Like mustard plaster for a cold and a cod liver oil, you know. If it's awful, it's got to be good for you." He tasted. "Not so bad," he said. "I bet it would be better with salt and pepper and melted cheese."

"My mother did malted milkshakes with a raw egg when I was sick, but they were wonderful," she said.

"That's interesting. Perhaps that's why you never came to associate love with pain."

"Excuse me," she said, looking hurt.

Barney had forgotten her lover's betrayal. "Oh, I'm sorry. I was just being flip. I think *MASH* has had that effect on us all. Except you," he added hastily. "You're always totally straight."

"Do you want to hear about the investigation?"

Barney must have looked as blank as he felt.

"The false appendicitis cases."

Barney groaned. "I hoped that was a dream. I'd managed to forget all that. I guess that must be why you're here. We don't usually do housecalls in Emergency, do we?"

"I shall assume your rudeness is a symptom of fever, Dr. Kincaid." She stood up. "But if you get too unpleasant, I can call the hospital and get a visiting nurse here for the night." She left the room. "I'm not sure what I'm doing here anyway," she said as she disappeared into the kitchen.

Barney wrapped the quilt around himself and followed her. "I think the Wheatena is working" he said. "I feel human again. You don't seem like a Fudgesicle. You're so cool. Forbidding." She looked hurt. "It was a compliment," he said hastily.

"I think not," she said. She had made a sandwich for herself and coffee. They sat at the breakfast table, Barney in his cocoon of quilt, feeling better just being in an upright position. "I have found it's dangerous to let your personal life get mixed into your work . . . and I need to buttress my feelings . . . otherwise it would be impossible to bear the suffering we see. You do the same. I guess I don't have much of a sense of humor. That's the difference maybe."

"No sense of humor?" said Barney. "Are you sure? That sounds awful. Terminal."

"No sense of humor," she said. "No irony. No wit. No dirty jokes. No limericks or lightbulb stories. I *am* serious."

"Inside you don't ever giggle at yourself a little?"

She smiled.

"Ah," said Barney. "There's some hope. All right. Tell me about the mixup. I think I remember the Noonan boy, lots of freckles and red hair that looked like he got it cut with a bowl. But it seems like months ago."

"They all had pain in the lower right quadrant. Some fever. The Noonan boy was Monday," said Mallory. "The other two boys came in a few hours apart on Tuesday. One of the nurses heard the two mothers chatting outside the ICU. When she realized the two families lived in the same apartment house—some rundown slum tenement with peeling paint and rat holes, she suspected that could be the key. That's when we ordered the blood tested for lead poisoning."

"Yes. Florence Nightingale rides again. I'm just teasing," Barney added hastily. "I am forever grateful to the sanity and observational powers of nurses. I am."

"Usually you're the one that catches these things," said Mallory. "You did the work-up on two of them. A fourth child was scheduled for surgery yesterday."

"I guess we're lucky we only went for the appendix and not a kidney." Gloom descended on Barney. It was as bad as he suspected. His thinking process was on the fritz. Shot. "I'm thinking I will leave medicine," he said. "My brain isn't working right anymore. You need that instinct, the confidence . . . I don't know what to call it . . . the famous bell I used to tell the interns about. It's gone. And I probably wasn't meant to be a doctor anyway. My mother decided that for me when I was born. I was programmed into it."

"Oh, Barney." She touched his shoulder. "Don't say that. You're so rare among doctors, caring and fast and brilliant. I believe the cortisone has affected your personality. In a few weeks, you'll see . . . you'll be back to normal. In the meantime, Dr. Turner worked with the Administration on a statement for the press. The incident is being reasonably well handled."

"Oh no. The press."

"Yes. The newspapers and TV too. Don't think about it now. Get your strength back first."

"I think I need a quick shot of Wheatena. I'm sick again." Barney hoped she was right. It was certainly possible steroids had fucked up his head. He would have to see.

Anne Mallory stood up. "Why don't you read a while and then sleep. Perhaps you'll feel well enough to come in tomorrow for that EKG. You should."

Barney stood up too, trailing and tripping over the end of the quilt. "Don't go yet. I might have a relapse. Stay. Take off that uniform and put on one of my robes. You must feel weary still in the same clothes. Take a shower maybe." He put his hand on her shoulder.

"Dr. Kincaid. You can't be feeling that well. If so, I absolutely must go. One minute you're in despair. The next, you're a sexual predator."

"I'm recovering only from the ears up," he said. "Please stay. I'm not as dangerous as you may have heard. No one could be as dangerous as rumor has me."

"I will take a shower," she said.

Barney settled back into bed, pulling the sheets taut, turning a couple of hospital corners, finding a pajama top in the drawer. He had dozed off again when she came into the room wearing his striped cotton kimono.

"Isn't your hair tired too?" he said, teasingly. "Doesn't your hair need to relax a little?"

"Dr. Kincaid, promise me you're not misinterpreting my staying. My hair feels sufficiently relaxed."

"I'm hungry again. No more Wheatena please. Please find something wonderful for both of us."

She trudged back to the kitchen. "French toast," she called out. "An omelette with jam." He heard cupboards slamming. "Canned foie gras on English muffin. Fruit and cream."

"That sounds wonderful," he said.

She brought sour cream mysteriously sweetened, with sliced bananas and canned pineapple to dip into it. And dried apricots. She dipped one into the sauce and put it into his mouth.

"Splendid." He dipped an apricot into sauce for her. She took it out of his fingers and put it into her mouth. "Were you always so serious? As a nymphet . . . as a child. Were you valedictorian of your class? The oldest child? Too many early responsibilities?"

"Dr. Kincaid. I am as wanton and silly and lazy and playful as anyone you know. I just have a certain professional manner that I never . . . *try* never to deviate from."

"Silly. Playful. Be silly. Call me Barney. Tickle my toes." She frowned. "I'm sorry. How have you been, Mrs. Mallory? Since your . . . unhappy time. I don't believe I know anything about Mr. Mallory. How long were you married?"

"Thirteen years. Ten glorious years and three terrible coming-apart years. We kept separating and coming back together again. Neither of us had the courage to end it. I think we were both afraid we couldn't survive apart."

"Where is he now? Do you see him? It sounds like you're still in love with him." Barney knew he was jealous but he wasn't sure if he was jealous of the man or of such intense feeling.

"I love him, of course. I can't imagine not loving him but I wouldn't say I'm in love with him. That's something else . . . 'in love with.' That's two people in emotional collision. And we're not like that anymore. I see him once in a while. In a way it's still painful but we can talk on the phone a lot and we do."

"And that creep? The leech you were putting through medical school who eloped with the heiress?"

Her eyes were suddenly shiny.

"Please don't cry," Barney begged.

"I'm afraid I did love him," she said. "I wasn't going to let it happen. I was going to be tough and smart but somehow, well, you know, feelings get out of hand. I did love him."

"I *don't* know," said Barney glumly. "It sounds like something that happens on Mars. For me falling in love is that incredible rush you get the first few hours or days when you can't keep your hands off each other and after that it's downhill . . . after that the feeling inevitably diminishes."

She looked at him as if she were seeing him for the first time. "I'm sorry," she said, as if he had died. "That sounds so lonely. I know what you mean about falling in love. That amazing madness. But afterward is when it gets better, more intense. I wonder if we should be talking like this."

"What's wrong?"

"It feels so intimate."

"Yes," said Barney.

"I'm trying hard not to be intimate."

"That's crazy. You shouldn't try not to be anything that takes such concentrated effort. Be what you are."

She sat up straight and hugged her arms around herself. "Dr. Kincaid, you know very well we are not permitted to be whatever we are . . . I don't have that luxury. I cannot be a baby. I cannot be a waif. I cannot be a cutie pie or a seductress. I have to be responsible. I have to be serious. There is no one to take care of me anymore but myself." Her voice broke. "Oh dear. I don't want to cry anymore."

"Come here," said Barney, wanting to hold her.

"No. I have to stay where I am," she said.

"Are you so alone?" he asked. She was silent for several minutes.

She came, she told him finally, from a family of doctors. A father, a brother, two uncles, three cousins, all doctors. She herself had postponed medical school to put the adored, adoring husband through medical school, through a neurology residency and then two years of emergency medicine training midway through which he'd discovered he couldn't claim a single accomplishment as his own. "I have to get away from you if I'm ever going to know I can make it on my own," he said (straight from the shrink, of course; they had "his" and "hers" therapists). In the next few years she had saved enough and applied to medical school herself when the earnest and boyish charmer (her late betrayer) came along and she'd invested the next four years and most of her cash in him. "He was so full of energy, ambition, sweetness, incredible affection. I loved his going back to school at thirty. With both of us working so hard, I guess it was easy to ignore hints of the ultimate treachery . . . his indifference to my needs, lateness, unexplained disappearances, long silences, explosions of rage. We were both under exceptional work pressure. I was almost relieved when he was accepted to work out of town. Now I think it's too late for me. You know, few medical schools consider anyone over thirty. I'm close to a masters in psychology now. I can't bring myself to write off med school but I will."

"It is a long haul. You'd be almost forty by the time you completed a residency."

"Decrepit."

"In your prime as a woman," said Barney, "but fifteen years behind your classmates."

"Oh my," she said. "What chivalry. You are a man of vision." It was a flirtatiousness she'd never exposed before. In a minute, though, she dropped it. "I could become a general practitioner. A prospect I rather like."

Barney was moved by her courage, especially now that he'd glimpsed the fragility underneath that steel armor. But even more he felt the lush softness of her presence, edges blurred in the dim light. She stroked her own arm as if she were caressing a lover. He longed to feel that full sultry lower lip, to be inside her mouth.

"We could help you get an education loan," he heard himself saying. "You'd be a natural for emergency medicine. If you were willing to commit yourself to us perhaps the corporation could advance you loans against salary."

"For several years?"

"It is a long time," Barney agreed. "We'd have to bind you to some kind of permanent servitude."

"You're probably still delirious from drug poisoning," she said. "We'll discuss this again when you're more yourself."

"Myself doesn't take emotional risks," Barney warned.

"You'd better get me now when I'm vulnerable. Who knows if I'll ever be so soft-headed again." She sat curled in the armchair, his new ten-speed bicycle like a high-tech monster behind her, the light from the floor spot making spidery tracings on the ceiling. He felt himself starting to doze off again, shook himself awake.

"Come closer, Anne. You're so far away."

"I should go," she said.

"No. I feel dizzy," Barney lied. "My pulse is pounding."

"You're making it up."

"Just sit closer. It's not safe to leave me alone. Here, lie down on the pillow. You can lie on top of the covers. Then you'll be safe."

"Safe from what?"

"Safe from your subliminal desire to get under the covers."

She laughed. "I never really appreciated your legendary charms. Till now, I mean. I can see how that sly touch of self-mockery and boyishness must melt resistance."

"It doesn't seem to be melting you," said Barney drowsily, eyelids drooping again.

"I don't think anything can melt me now," she was saying. "I don't know how long it will be before I trust myself with a man again. I've been a dud picking them lately. And I do want to talk to you about your offer soon. So please, for that reason, and all the other reasons that you know, we must keep a professional distance."

"You're right," said Barney. "Come be a nurse, Mrs. Mallory. My sheets are wrinkled and full of crumbs. You ought to give me an alcohol rub to help me sleep."

"You're half asleep already," she said. "And I'm exhausted. This is my second tour of duty today."

"Just the neck and shoulders," he said. "My neck is so tense."

"Alcohol?"

"There's baby oil right here next to the bed."

"Oh oh. This is beginning to sound like a letter to the editor in *Penthouse*."

"Oh oh yourself. What do you know about letters to the editor in *Penthouse?*"

"Turn over," she said. Her hands felt cool stroking the oil into his neck and across the scapulae. She pressed hard into the neck muscles. The pain of the pressure felt wonderful.

"Hmmm," he sang. "So good. Do my hands."

"Are you a baby? Your voice just then sounded like a little boy."

"No, I'm a man," he said, using his normal voice. "And I want to touch you."

She stepped back. "Barney, this isn't going to happen, I promise you. Listen to me, it isn't going to happen."

"All right," he said, burrowing his head into the pillow. "You can just sleep here beside me. I'm making lots of room. Nothing will happen. I'm half asleep already."

She sighed. "All right." She pulled the covers taut and tucked them in. "I'll lie here till you fall asleep and then I'll stretch out in the other room." She lay down carefully, almost formally.

He reached out and pulled a hair pin. "Your hair."

She began to search for the pins. Her hair fell in a dark curtain over her face. She tossed her head back and he fell in love with the perfect curve of her forehead. And her hands, graceful and delicate, almost Victorian. She lay down again. "Don't touch me, Dr. Kincaid. Just sleep."

"I won't mind if you touch me," he said.

She lay there silent for a long time. Then she turned toward him and curved her arm around his waist. "Sleep."

Barney was afraid to move, to draw a deep breath even, for fear she would take her arm away. He kept seeing her naked, feeling her naked against him, till finally he fell asleep.

A shaft of light crossing the bed woke him. He lay there watching her sleep. Her mouth had fallen open and she looked almost dumb. He rather liked that. Barney could see the lace edging of her bra where the robe had come apart. How like her to sleep in underwear, he thought, The Iron Maiden. Carefully he moved just the tips of his fingers across her shoulder. Her skin was hot. He touched the swell of her breast where it fell downward out of the bra. She took his hand away. The blood flooded into his cock. He took all of her breast in his hand, feeling the nipple grow hard inside the silken fabric. Her hands pushed him away. He kissed her neck, her ear, her lips. He felt her lips soften under his. Her eyes were closed. He kissed the inside of her elbow and the inside of her palm. He reached down for one foot, watching her face, waiting for a protest. He kissed the inside of her knee. She caught her breath. "No," she said.

Barney reached up and twisted her bra into a narrow band, releasing her breasts. He held one of them as if it were breakable, full of wonder because it was her breast and he was holding it in his hand. He began to suck and bite and squeeze. With his knee he pushed her legs apart and pressed up against her pussy. "Please don't," she cried.

He opened her lips with his fingers and touched her teeth and kissed the inside of her mouth. She began to move under him, lifting her hips and pressing down on his knee— rubbing herself on his knee. She held both his arms, then pressed her hands against his chest, his ribs, his waist, his hips, his ass, as if learning him, looking for nerves and message centers. Her hands were so strong. He felt protected, possessed, mesmerized by the ferocity of her response. Then he knelt between her legs and watched her stretch herself long, arms in the air, crooning . . . little intakes of breath leading to a silent scream as he entered her. At first he held himself aloof, unwilling to miss a second of her heat as he moved inside her, riding an incredible power high as he watched, trying to read her, the joy, the pain, submission. And then he was gone, lost in the bombardment of sensation, all thought, even awareness, obliterated.

He felt himself reluctantly returning and became aware that she was sobbing. He was holding her tight, pressing her bottom against him, wanting to stay inside her, her hair a veil over his eyes, against his mouth like nighttime.

"Something is wrong," he said.

"No." She tried to catch her breath. "I've just been alone too long. I was afraid we would be like this. I didn't want to find out. Didn't want to know anything . . . about you."

He tried to make sense of it.

"What they say . . . about you. Didn't want to be just another body in the lineup."

He took the palm of his hand and curved it lightly over the fur of her pubic bone.

She arched and groaned.

He moved the cup of his palm lower. She arched again and pressed into it. "You know everything." She opened her legs wide, arching up and giving herself to him, to his fingers. The animal sounds in her throat, the grimace in her face, were like sheet music for his fingers as he made her come again and again till her unbridled frenzy made his cock hard. And he came into her gentle but fast like the wind.

They might have dozed off. At least Barney knew he had. She was silent, face hidden again under hair.

"It could be a dream," she said.

"That's possible. I could be dreaming too."

"I feel totally invaded. Possessed. Mutilated by you. I better not get up because I know I have no will anyway."

"You're unbelievable," he said. "So violent. Responsive."

"I'm really very difficult."

"Not for me."
"For me."
"We'll see."
"Will we?"
"Yes."

"Oh dear." She opened her eyes wide. "I feel something hard against my leg."

Before, they had come together like hunters, each challenging the other, killers stalking, fierce for the kill. Now they made love.

"I submit that Sean McMurtagh died seven days before his eighth birthday while under the care of Dr. Emile Gunderson because he was given a lethal dosage of Valium." Barney could feel the anxiety and hostility in the room, and somehow he was able to feed on it, growing stronger, angrier. He was ready for them. He was sure he would persuade them. Indeed, he almost relished their doubt and indifference, loving the challenge.

Through the window he could see fresh green buds on tree branches. Today, in fact, felt like spring in the air. A month had passed since Wheatena had pulled him back from the brink of chemical madness. "Since Wheatena." That was his code phrase, sure to provoke a smile from Anne Mallory, who tried hard not to smile too much these days. "I think I'm more effective in the ER when I smile less," she insisted.

The last of the grim, gray, icy sludge had finally melted. Barney felt human again, full of energy, happy to be almost weaned from the debilitating cortisone, in tight control of the Emergency Room, preparing a presentation for Hasting Hospital, where Anne's cousin happened to be married to a powerful board member who believed an emergency room needed professional staffing. Perhaps it was impossible to measure Barney's diagnostic keenness, his speed. The fact was he felt confident again. The staff had stopped eyeing him as if waiting for a freak-out, and the students looked to him with an expectation of brilliance at the very least.

Barney was practically living out of his car these days, spending most nights in Anne's Riverdale apartment, with its almost pastoral view of the Hudson, a jungle of hanging plants, all of them impressively healthy, and the almost constant scent of cinnamon. "From time to time I suffer fits of baking," Anne had explained.

She seemed to be full of surprises, perhaps because he had perceived her with such a myopic view. Her rigid reserve masked real intelligence, uncanny intuition, a cynical irony (the romantic's usual armor) and terrible vulnerability. She could be silly, withdrawn, selfish and, most astonishing of all . . . lazy. Meticulous at work, she could be oblivious to serious disorder at home although she had the grace to feel guilty about it. Barney found that hopeful. In the kitchen she was disorganized and creative. Her closets were chaos but her cupboards were military-neat ("I have my priorities," she said). In bed she was inexhaustible, endlessly responsive, yet both shy and demanding, even truculent—a combination that inflamed Barney. She did not trust him. She did not trust that their love was anything special or could possibly last. She belittled it because, he knew, she was too vulnerable for now to believe it. And she did not try to please him. Pleased when he was happy . . . delighted when anything she did amused or gave him pleasure, she had a way of pleasing herself first. The Jewish prince in Barney was not used to such easy indifference, but for some reason he found it comfortable.

Blissed out on sex, burning in the intensity of new lust, Barney was surprised to find the ground did not move, he did not feel panic, he did not feel compelled to exaggerate her qualities. Her flaws failed to enrage or repel him. Barney had always dreamed one day he would find everything he wanted in one woman. Now that hope seemed silly, childish.

Eva Marie Saint blondeness and blue eyes were highly superficial requirements after all, he would think, one hand wrapped in the chestnut silk of Anne's hair, fascinated by the changing flecks of color in her golden eyes.

"Were you ever a cheerleader?" he asked.

"A what? You must be kidding."

"I seem to have a weakness for cheerleaders."

"Never."

"Didn't even try out for the cheerleading team? Not even once? Never played the part in a high school play? Never had a lead in *Good News?*"

"Barney."

"Okay."

"I was president of the Biology Club."

"They didn't have a cheerleading squad. The Biology Club."

"Right. They did not."

"I guess we haven't got much of a future," he said, with mock glumness.

"Guess not."

"We have a beautiful present," he said, drawing her into his arms.

"Rah rah. Sis boom bah."

"We'll see," said Barney.

*O*nce a week Barney did a laundry-cleaner-pickup trip to Manhattan and spent an evening with his folks or with Candy, whose built-in seismograph of Daddy's emotions had her skirting Anne like a picador.

"At least she has no children to compete with," Barney offered.

"She's probably very fertile," Candy retorted.

Barney felt inadequate for the role of divorced daddy. Where was the sensible parental balance a mature man commanded? "I could marry you, darling, and adopt Anne Mallory as my daughter," he said one evening, exasperated that Candy had decided Anne's presence at dinner would curdle her hot fudge sundae.

Now Candy stared at him, her lower lip moving into full pout position.

"I get what you're saying," she began warily. "You don't need an I.Q. of one-forty-two these days to understand adult life. You only have to watch the soaps. You wouldn't actually be thinking of marrying anyone, would you?" She asked it in a whisper (so the fates wouldn't hear).

"They say married men are healthier than bachelors," Barney improvised.

"Daddy."

"I might be that rash . . . someday. Nothing is imminent."

"An incurable lech like you?"

Barney was annoyed. "That's not cute at all," he said.

"I'm sorry. It was just a joke. Anyway, you wouldn't marry anyone we know now necessarily, would you? It could be someone we haven't met yet, yes? I think Mrs. Mallory looks a lot like Mommy, don't you?"

Barney groaned. "Boy, you sure know how to spoil a guy's fun."

"What did I say?" she cried.

*T*he first Saturday he'd spent apart from Anne, Barney lay in bed with the *New England Journal,* wanting to call her, knowing he would be upset if she did not answer. Best not to call. He picked up a postcard from Amber in Los Angeles. "Dear Dr. Strangelove," Amber wrote. "I'm a movie star. Lead role in a very classy X thriller: *Teenage Flesh Peddlers*. You'll love it. I get $1,000 a day, no strings (you know what I mean), but I've got a crush on the director so we do it anyway. Love you. Amber." On the front was a photograph by David Hamilton of a glorious pre-pubescent who might have been Amber at twelve. She was beautiful, of course, but presexual for Barney. He felt light-years away from whatever he had found in Amber. It was Anne Mallory's extraordinary womanliness that excited him more than anything.

Barney picked up the new issue of *Penthouse*. Cindy was the centerfold, a Rabelaisian image in half-laced corselette and white stockings . . . rosy and white with freckles and a mop of carrot curls. Barney found himself as unmoved as if he were looking at a springer spaniel. This could be love, he thought.

"Sean McMurtagh," Barney repeated. "I was reviewing several mortalities I'd been assigned. It was a shock to discover the McMurtagh boy's case among them. I was the one who saw him first in the Emergency Room. Status Asthmaticus. He didn't seem to respond to treatment on our service, so we alerted the family's physician, Emile Gunderson." Gunderson did not blink. There he sat, Barney noted. The chutzpah king. His arms folded across his chest, big shaved bald head gleaming, dapper as always with a red silk pocket-hanky flapping, eyes riveted on Barney. Gunderson's chum, Evans, the Ob-Gyn wimp, drummed his fingers on the arm of his chair. Barney would gladly have killed him for the arrogant disdain of his rat-a-tat-tat.

The hospital administrator, Jonathan Adams, hybrid aristocrat, Episcopal-Jew with all his seventh generation

American credentials, exuded charm and noblesse oblige
from every pore, nodding away. Now, those were blue eyes,
Western prairie sky blue, and what a nose. It took at least
seven generations to produce such an Episcopalian nose,
thought Barney. Adams's anal-compulsive right-hand man,
Enoch Whitaker, was practically hyperventilating. Except
for good old loyal Dick Rogin (a six-pack of Tab at his elbow
like a supply of hand grenades) not one of Goodman
Memorial's department chiefs had the guts to look Barney in
the eye. Barney was furious too because Frieda Thompson
had not yet arrived, after swearing to Anne she would
definitely appear.

Hal Wechsler, the genial chief of medicine, interrupted:
"Would you reiterate for us, Dr. Kincaid, how you came to
discover the case you are questioning?" Jack Jessul, the
pediatrics chief, yawned. George Stinton from Orthopedics
stretched and scratched. The neurology chief seemed to be
doodling on a prescription pad.

"I was reviewing several mortalities I'd been assigned to
look at," Barney repeated. "The McMurtagh case had
already been reviewed, by Dr. Riverton, and apparently
cleared. It was an accident that it appeared in my pile of
cases to review. I read it because of my personal interest in
the boy's case. Reading the chart, I was troubled by a sense
of familiarity. It recalled a case I remembered vaguely.
Another Gunderson patient, Marina Blackmann, a fifty-
three-year-old woman, also asthmatic. She had become
agitated on the ward, anxious, difficult to handle in the
evening. The nurse had phoned Gunderson who ordered
sedation. A few hours later the patient was dead. Clear-out
negligence. I went back to the files and found two other
Gunderson cases, two other patients, one asthmatic, one
chronic emphysema—dead after sedation. Patients clearly
suffering oxygen deprivation . . . the deaths somehow explained away. You have the charts in front of you. You have
my summary."

"All right, gentlemen and madam." Jonathan Adams
made a courtly bow to Eleanor Futterman, chief of surgery,

who suffered his archsexism with benign tolerance and a gentle smile. "You've had time to read the material. We'll entertain questions."

"The McMurtagh case was reviewed by a very able surgeon," said Gunderson's crony, Evans. "Why is it that only Dr. Kincaid"—he pronounced it *Kin-cay-yid,* accent on the *yid*—"seems to have a problem with the procedures of Dr. Gunderson, a thirty-year veteran in practice as a board-certified internist?"

"He is not board-certified," corrected Barney. "He's in family practice."

"Excuse me," hissed Evans.

"It may be that I am one of the few doctors around here who take the time routinely to review a mortality starting from page one of the patient's chart," Barney said. "It is, granted, a time-consuming practice but I am addicted to it."

"I'm afraid Dr. Kincaid is right," Hal Wechsler agreed. "Too many of us are content to skip right to the physician's summary at the end of the chart."

"And too many of us have abdicated critical review," Barney went on, noticing that he had won Eleanor Futterman's attention. She was one of the minority who never sloughed off a review. "The man on this staff I most respect as a doctor—respected"—Barney glanced for a moment at Wechsler—"refuses to support me today on the grounds that criticism only creates enemies and the most that results from a hearing like this is a slap on the wrist for the offender. Well, I'm not afraid to make enemies." Barney smiled ruefully. "I guess most of you know me that well by now. My oath is more important to me than lunch at your country club. You read these reports and remove Emile Gunderson from Goodman Memorial's staff or know what pitiful cowards you are."

The room dissolved into chaos. A bunch of stuck pigs squealing protest. "Please, please." Jonathan Adams stood up. "Dr. Kincaid can be overly dramatic, my friends. Let's just stick to the issues here. Let's proceed with the questions."

"I also treated the patient Marina Blackmann," Evans began. "A rather nervous woman."

Gunderson interrupted. "An hysterical patient, I assure you." He looked to Dick Rogin for confirmation.

Rogin shrugged. "I pass. A fifty-three-year-old woman is not by definition necessarily an hysteric though some therapists might contest that notion."

Futterman glared at him. "You were not in the hospital when you ordered the sedative for Mrs. Blackmann," she addressed Gunderson. "Would you say the description of her condition at the time the nurse called you at home is accurate as summarized in this report by Dr. Kincaid? Nervous, upset, thrashing around, agitated?"

"Yes. Yes. These are words taken out of the chart. Yes, so it was exactly. Exactly so the nurse reported. Mrs. Blackmann was demanding to see me. Agitated, anxious, driving the staff crazy with her carryings-on. I told the nurse to give her a shot of Valium, five milligrams."

"It says here you ordered ten milligrams of Valium, i.m."

"Ah yes. Of course. Blackmann was your typical menopausal hysteric. Chronic complainer. She once called me at home after midnight, I think it was. And in the office, constantly."

"So you ordered ten milligrams of Valium?" Futterman asked, scarcely able to conceal her disbelief.

"It says here ten. So it was ten."

"You ordered a sedative for an asthmatic who was agitated?"

"You didn't ask the resident to do blood gases?" Wechsler asked.

"Why would I want blood gases?" Gunderson snapped, throwing his shoulders back, clearly offended. "The woman was carrying on. With a little sedation to calm her down, she would sleep. The medication would have time to work."

"Surely you realize that agitation is a symptom of hypoxia?" said Wechsler. "What you may have had was not an hysterical woman but an asthmatic struggling to breathe."

"Anxiety," said Gunderson. "Anxiety we must calm."

"You saw Sean McMurtagh yourself, the little boy. He was on aminophylline."

"Yes. Yes, of course. I saw him on rounds. He was cranky and difficult. I understood his mother had gone downstairs to get some dinner and he woke up not finding her there. Naturally he was agitated. I wrote that order myself. I gave the injection myself. The nurse ran off to powder her nose. When I stopped by again, he was fine."

"In fact when Dr. Gunderson stopped by again, he merely looked in the room. The boy was already dead," said Barney. How stupid he'd been, not to send someone for Frieda.

"He was sleeping."

"Is that when you decided five milligrams of Valium was too high a dosage for a seven-year-old asthmatic and so, bringing the chart up to date the next day, you decided you'd ordered a smaller dosage?" said Barney.

"What is this lie?"

"The chart says two milligrams."

"The chart is wrong. I gave the injection. It was five milligrams. I remembered quite well. That stubborn nurse. She changed it." The room was still, as if everyone had stopped breathing.

Gunderson exploded. "This is a trick. This patient. The chronic emphysema case . . . Carlo Figueraz. The whole family was hysterical. I should have ordered them all out the door. Out the door. Such carryings-on. But, no, Emile Gunderson has compassion for people not knowing how to behave. We were trained to use sedatives to fight anxiety and hysteria in asthmatics, in cases precisely like this."

The door opened. A clerk from the administrator's office stuck her head in. "I have a Mrs. Frieda Thompson outside," she said. "Is she supposed to be here?" Barney could not suppress his grin.

Gunderson rocked back on his heels, hands thrust deep into his pockets, the fabric beginning to rip from the tension. "You don't need to listen to nurses. I follow the textbook. My patients worship me. I always have time for people. In my practice I am practically a psychiatrist. I listen always to their problems. Seven days a week I'm on call."

"I asked Mrs. Thompson to come," said Barney. "She was the nurse on duty the day the McMurtagh boy . . . fell asleep so peacefully."

"I don't think we need her just yet," said Wechsler. "Ask her to wait, Mrs. Kelling." He dropped his head into his hand and sighed. Barney felt sick, too. Relieved as he watched the staff's growing horror while Gunderson hung himself before their eyes, still he felt nausea too.

"Dr. Gunderson." Wechsler's voice was steely. "Twenty years ago the textbooks advised sedation and many asthmatics died struggling for oxygen. Today we know that agitation is a symptom of oxygen deprivation. We do blood gases suspecting the medication may be inadequate so that we can correct the dosage. The patient is fighting . . . struggling to breathe. You cannot sedate a patient fighting for air unless you want to kill him."

"Hal. I loved that little boy," said Gunderson. "Five milligrams of Valium is almost nothing. So we were taught . . . so it was."

"We can hear Mrs. Thompson now," Wechsler said.

Barney went to the door and took Frieda's hand. He pulled up a chair next to his. "Mrs. Thompson. You know most of us, of course, Dr. Wechsler, the chiefs, Mr. Adams . . . especially you know Emile Gunderson. Tell us, in your own words, what happened the night Sean McMurtagh died. Dr. Gunderson says it was you who changed the chart."

She was startled. "What is there left for me to say?" she began. "Dr. Gunderson is not only stupid. He is arrogant as well. I refused to give the Valium injection. The boy was agitated, yes, but I suspected he might not be getting enough oxygen. Gunderson was, needless to say, not interested in medical observations from a nurse. The nurse . . . ha! What do we know. But I felt sorry for him . . . I was fond of him, yes, like a fool I changed the chart, made the dosage smaller, to save him, yes. And he was furious. He lost his temper. Called me terrible names. You see, he thinks he is a brilliant doctor. He thinks he was right."

Adams interrupted. "Shouldn't we begin from the beginning?" Mrs. Thompson's story was scarcely necessary at that point. Still, the staff heard her out. The unspoken indictment seemed obvious to Barney. Not one of the doctors reviewing Gunderson's mortalities had protested. Did peer review have any meaning? Did Barney have to ask that question or would Wechsler?

"Thank you for your courage, Mrs. Thompson," said Wechsler.

"Thank you for coming," Barney whispered, as he escorted her to the door.

"I think you can go now, Emile," Wechsler said. "Yes, Mr. Adams . . . we need to talk privately now. To discuss proper procedure."

Gunderson stood there, leaning back with his characteristic swagger, face splotched, posture undaunted. "Surely I will have some say, too."

No one spoke.

Dr. Evans took Gunderson's arm. "Perhaps we should have a short recess for coffee, what do you say, Hal . . . Mr. Adams?"

Adams stood up. "Excellent. Gentlemen. Take half an hour. Everyone will want to check messages, your service, whatever."

*B*arney knew it would still be a fight to get them to make Gunderson resign. Most of them were spineless. They'd vote to censure him, require a second signature on all his orders, avoid a stink. He cut through the parking lot, breaking a small branch from the plane tree that dropped over the fence next to the gate. He touched the tight green bud with his finger. Put it to his nose trying to smell spring. Barney walked in through the Emergency entrance. Anne had her arm around a mother toting a wailing infant. She ignored Barney, looking a little to the left of his eyes as she always had—her rigid defense against the possibility that the tiniest gesture of friendliness would lead to some uncontrollable avalanche of feeling.

In the War Room, the lineup was minimal, nothing blatantly thrilling, no life-or-death emergencies. Barney glanced at the charts.

"Oh no. Not that hypochondriac di Renzo again. That turkey. What's his complaint this time? 'Bleeding down below.' That's a new one," Barney noted.

"I've moved his chart back three times already," Stef said. "If nothing important comes along, I'll be stuck doing a work-up on him after all. I had hoped to stick the night shift with him."

"Better you than me," said Barney, looking at his watch. He was due back in the conference room in ten minutes. He studied the charts of patients admitted that morning, feeling a faint sense of unease. Bleeding down below. The words triggered a . . . something. A flash, a bell. "That's a strange symptom for di Renzo," he said, jumping up. He raced to the farthest cubicle. "Mallory," he cried. Di Renzo was unconscious. There was blood all over his gown.

In seconds Barney and Stef had three IVs feeding into di Renzo. "He definitely was not bleeding when he came in here," said Anne. "I asked. He told me he had a bit of a problem last night . . . this morning. I figured, you know. He needs a little attention." She was checking his blood pressure. "It's getting up there."

"The blood pressure has stabilized," said Stef. "Well, I guess that will teach him a lesson. Not to cry wolf."

"Never mind teaching him a lesson," said Barney. "This teaches us a lesson. Even the turkeys are going to have their terminal event. We were lucky this time he didn't shove off there on the table. When I think how many times I've ignored him myself."

Barney's fingers brushed against the Fudgesicle's wrist. She pulled her hand away as if she'd been burned. Barney grinned. He felt wonderful. It was even fun saving di Renzo. In fact, it was especially fun saving di Renzo. So what if it was Mama's grand plan that he would be a doctor. So what if she'd chosen his life for him months before he was born. He was pretty damn good at it. He'd made his life his own. He'd show her, Barney thought. He would marry a shiksa. He'd never eat another prune.